OFF THE DARK LEDGE

Off the Dark Ledge

ANGIE GALLION

Beech House Books

Off the Dark Ledge
Copyright © 2018 Angie Gallion
All Rights Reserved

This book or any portion thereof may not be reproduced without the express written permission of the publisher, except for the use of brief quotations in a book review and certain other noncommercial uses permitted by copyright law.

This is a work of fiction. Names, characters, places, and incidents either are products of the author's imagination or are used fictitiously. Any resemblance to actual events or locales or persons, living or dead, is entirely coincidental.

First Edition 2018 Published by thewordverve inc.
Second Edition 2021
Published in the USA by Beech House Books

eBook ISBN: 978-1-954309-09-8
Paperback ISBN: 978-1-954309-08-1
Library of Congress Control Number: 2018901777

Off the Dark Ledge
Cover Design, Interior Design, and eBook Formatting
by A.L. Lovell
www.angiegallion.com
Cover image by StockSnap

Dedication

For all of you who
who fight your demons
on your own terms.

For my brother, Terry,
the true Leon Freak.

Special Thanks

StockSnap for the use of their original photograph for the cover of this book. Their work was made available to me through their participation at Pixabay.com, a photo/art sharing site. Pixabay has amazing collections from very talented people all around the world.

My friend, Sabrina Malan, who spent several hours one day talking to me about DID (Disassciative Identity Disorder), which provided me the understanding I needed to write this book and to effectively portray the main character.

Richard Carroll for his assistance in police-procedural details and, in general, for his positive and enthusiastic response to my writing.

Janet Fix, my first editor, and champion not only of my writing but of all my creative potential.

My husband, Jeff, for his neverending patience and support with my writing process.

1

PART ONE
Summer:
Nearly Thirty Years Ago

Baby

He's leaving me! I jolt up inside the cage just as his face disappears through the window. No. No. No. He can't leave me. I scramble out, my legs are weak and wobbly from the hours or days we've spent in lock-up. She's gonna be so mad!

I scramble to get to the box he has pushed up under the window, banging my shin against the corner. I bite my lip to stay quiet. He's leaving me!

I pull up, and I see him running across the yard. I want to call out, but then she may hear, and we'd both be in trouble. So I don't.

I pull up and push my shoulders out through the open window. I'm falling, and I hit the ground with a thud. All the air whooshes out of me, and I gasp like a fish out of water. When I can breathe again, I get up and start to run across the back yard, tucking tight into myself so I am small, and if Mama or Dr. Curtis look out, they maybe won't see me. Dr. Curtis lives in the house next door, and I'm even more scared that he will see me. He doesn't like me; he only likes Slim. We were in the cage because of something Slim did to Dr. Curtis, but he wouldn't tell me what. He is a long way ahead of me, not looking back. His long legs stretch out in front of him and behind him, and he is barely touching the ground. He is almost to the trees. Then I will lose him. Fear rises, and I stumble but keep running.

I want to call out, but I don't because she might hear me, and then we would be in trouble—because we are outside and we're not supposed to be outside during the day. I pump my legs as fast as I can, trying to find flight the way he does. I have to catch him, but my legs feel weak, and I can't run as fast as he can.

He is passing into the trees, eaten by the shadows. I can't see him anymore, and I don't know what to do. I am scared to go into the woods alone, and how will I know which way he has gone? Should I go back to the trailer and get back into my cage? She's gonna be so mad! Dr. Curtis will kick us out if he knows we've been outsid. He's only letting us stay because Mama promised we'd stay out of sight. Dr. Curtis doesn't like children, Mama says. That why she's training Slim to be a man.

I stop just at the edge of the trees, looking into the dark shadows. My feet prance... Where is he?

I call out in a loud whisper, "Slim!" He used to have another name, but we haven't used it in so long that I don't remember what it was. It's just like everybody calls me Baby, but I think my name is really Shiloh. Slim doesn't answer, and I spin in a circle, glancing back at the trailer, seeing the window high up on the side. There is no way I could get back up and through it. My legs buckle at the thought of going to the front door and interrupting Mama. A man is in the house, and Mama doesn't like it when the men see us—it's one of the rules. Only Dr. Curtis can know we are here. I sprawl on the ground, trying to flatten myself, so I will only look like a pile of dirt if she looks out and sees me.

I sob, but no tears flood past my crusty lashes.

I am going to die.

Hands lift me around my waist, and I ball myself inward, expecting the smack that I know is coming. She has seen.

It's Slim. He hasn't left me; he has come back for me. I spring up and wrap my legs around his waist, like a monkey. I bury my face in his neck.

We are out of the yard and into the shadows of the trees. I know because all the warmth is gone. He carries me, stepping through bushes. The brambles scrape against my bare legs and make them bleed.

He stops when we are well into the shadow. "You have to walk." He pushes against my hips, and I release my hold on him and slide down the length of his body, careful not to touch the long painful-looking welt going down his arm, until I am on my own feet. "You shouldn't have come. You're gonna slow me down, and then we'll get caught."

He turns and walks away from me, and I don't say anything, just run to keep up with him. I don't want him to leave me behind here; then the wolves would eat me. Mama says there are bears out here, too... and tigers. Panic rises, and I glance at the trees around me, looking for glowing eyes. I scrape my bare foot against a rock and hop on the other one, unwilling to stop. I run. Keeping my eyes on his back, I climb over a fallen tree that he only had to step over.

We finally stop, when Slim thinks we have gone far enough that they won't find us. He drops to his knees and cups his hand in the stream, drinking the water in great gulps.

I do the same, squatting beside him. It is only then that I know how thirsty I am, how empty my stomach is. I drink, and when I feel my stomach stretching against the water, I splash some on my face, washing away the crust from my lashes.

"Where are we going?"

"I don't know," he says, finally looking at me squatting beside him. "I wish you hadn't come."

I shrug my shoulders and look away from him. I am used to never doing the right thing.

Dirt and blood crust my feet. An angry red scratch weeps a thin stream.

We are on the move again, and I have to keep up or he will leave me behind. He is angry, and I'm scared, because sometimes when he is angry, he hits me. Sometimes he does other stuff, even if he says it's training.

But I won't go back. She will be so lonely without us. Guilt climbs from my ankles to my chest, and my heart squeezes. I gulp, and his head ratchets around, scanning the woods, but then he jerks forward again, saying something under his breath. He is very angry.

I run behind him keeping my mouth quiet, because, otherwise, he'll stop and push me down and run on without me, and then the wolves or bears or tigers will eat me. We run, and we run.

My stomach is churning, angry as the water sloshes. It rumbles, and when I can't run anymore, I stop, putting my hands on my knees, bending over, trying to catch my breath. All the water I drank comes rushing from my mouth, splattering on the leaves and dirt.

A chill runs through my body, and my legs feel heavy. I'm afraid I won't be able to lift them again. It's cold, but only because we're not inside anymore and I don't have my blanket. I forgot my blanket. What am I gonna do without my blanket?

When I look up, I can't see him; he is gone.

"Come on!" I hear him hissing ahead of me. "I'll kill you if you get me caught," he says, mumbling under his breath, and I stumble forward, my arms outstretched in the dark.

I finally find him at in a ditch between the woods and the empty road. "We made it," I whisper.

My brother nods, and I can tell he is trying to figure out what we should do next.

Lights flare in the distance, and we watch as a lone car travels toward us and then past. I'm happy to be squatting beside him, not to be moving. I am so tired from the run through the woods.

We wait, our breath slowing, becoming lighter and less strained.

Another car comes from the other direction, and we watch it pass.

"What are we going to do?" I whisper.

"We're going to catch one of those cars and make them take us away."

I nod.

Minutes pass before we see another car, and when it gets close enough, Slim stands up from the ditch and starts waving his arms.

My heart jolts in my chest as the car slows.

"No!" I call because the light is bright in his eyes. He cannot see the car.

He glances back to me. The car comes to a stop and the passenger-side door opens.

"I reckon you got your sister hidden back there somewhere?"

Slim's shoulders slump and he turns to run. Dr. Curtis is out of the car and takes three long steps toward my brother, catching him by the length of his hair, drawing him back and to his knees. Slim is crying.

"Baby," she calls from inside the car. "Come on, Baby. It is time to go home." She is so pretty, sitting in the glow of the car. The car looks so safe and quiet.

I stand up from where I am crouched in the ditch, pulled by an invisible thread.

2

PART TWO
May : Present Day

Stacy

Breathe. Breathe. Breathe.

I draw air in and release through my nose, standing in mountain pose, my arms at my side. John snores, his arm flung over his face, blocking the glow of my iPad from his eyes. The girls sleep, past the living room, at the front of the house. I don't go to the living room because I would wake the dogs, and they would wake the house. It is just a few minutes of time for me before my life belongs to everybody else. I move from one pose to the next in our bedroom, trying not to wake John. My eyes roll over him as I fold down until my hands touch my toes, and I pop my legs back to plank, aware of the small rustle of motion from the bed. Breathe. Breathe. Breathe.

Along the rim of the window, there is a glow, heralding the coming sun, and I follow the tiny woman on my iPad through the rest of the morning routine, letting my muscles relax into each pose until I feel loose and hot in the morning chill. The quiet moments settle my mind—my ever-pacing, fretful mind. "It's six," I say, leaning low over John. He groans, and I leave him fumbling for his phone to check his first-morning emails.

The girls are still asleep, but not for long, as the dogs both prance and spin in their kennels. They are Boston terriers, the kind of dogs John had as a kid. They are black and white and stocky, snorting with the effort to breathe. I let them out, and they jump and circle, their claws tapping a cadence on the wood floors. I open the sliding door to the back yard and let them bound into the morning.

Feet shuffle down the hall, past the bunnies in their cage, snuggled together in a ball on the ledge, and Sophie stops at the edge of the counter, bleary-eyed, waiting for me to speak.

"Good morning, Soph," I offer, pulling her close for a hug and a ruffle.

Sophie groans. She is nine, but so much older than nine.

"You could have slept a little longer."

"When I'm awake, I'm awake," she says, sounding twelve, or thirteen, or thirty.

"Yes, I know." It's in the blood. I am the same, just like my mother, just like my brother Darren—we are all early risers. I have never owned an alarm. "You get that from Grandma, you know."

Sophie nods, too tired to care, to play along. She climbs onto a barstool and folds her head down on crossed arms.

"Breakfast?" I offer, and another groan rumbles from the small lungs.

I pour coffee, letting her get around to it when she will, half listening for the shower to start. I put together her lunch, tucked into a too-mature lunch bag that she fell in love with at Target. It's a grown woman's lunch bag—no singing mermaids for Sophie, no pale mountain princess in blue, just a subtle pattern on a coral background. They grow up so fast. Sophie finally draws her head up, heading to the pantry for cereal. I walk down the hall to wake my youngest daughter.

Four-year-old Shelby stretches across her bed, one foot pushed through the slats of her railing. The sheet tangles around her torso, but the comforter is pushed up in the corner.

"Shelby," I sing, leaning close, my breath whispering through her curls.

When she was a baby, she slept so soundly that we worried about SIDS. Sophie had always moved and moaned through her nights, restless as a cat, lighting the baby monitor every time she shifted, but

Shelby would drop into deep caverns and not make a sound for hours. I whisper again, running a finger along the small jawline, feeling her heat, relieved, even now, when Shelby draws an audible breath and cracks an eye.

Back in the kitchen, the girls talk, and I listen with half an ear. Sophie chews, talking between bites, "I thought it was a nether portal, but it wasn't... but it was obsidian. There were these sheep, and the guy was counting the sheep." She laughs.

Sheep, I latch on, I understand sheep. "How many sheep were there?"

Sophie looks around, rolling her eyes. "It's not about the sheep."

"Oh, is this about Minecraft?" I ask, passing the look right back to her, letting my last syllable draw out long and creaking the way all the kids do these days.

"Yes, Mom." She is so perturbed, so much the omen of the adolescent she will be that I bite the inside of my mouth not to smile. She is going to be a handful.

"But how many sheep?" Shelby asks, because now she, too, wants to know. I have to laugh. Shelby is always on my side. I pass her a small high-five, my comrade, my teammate, my precious Shelby.

"Mom," Sophie groans.

"Seriously, how many? Inquiring minds want to know."

John's arrival saves Sophie from having to explain. He is dressed and combed to perfection. His hair is dark, like Sophie's, with the same tendency to curl. He keeps it short and contained, but I remember when we were younger, and there were those hot, dark curls hanging long. I reach out and touch the smooth back of his neck, missing those curls, missing those days.

"Morning girls," he says and leans in to kiss the top of each of their heads. I pour coffee into a tumbler for him, and he kisses me, as a matter of course, the way married people do after children have changed them from lovers to a family.

"Do you have a busy day?" I ask.

"Courthouse steps. It's foreclosure day." He says it like it's a holiday, not like it happens once a month.

"Oh, that's right," I say, nodding. I should know his schedule by now, but my mind is like Swiss cheese, and he knows it. Raising kids is exhausting; it makes me scattered, he knows.

"It won't be late," he says, heading to the door.

"Good. I'll cook." A look passes between us, amused, born of familiarity. I always cook, which is not to say that John always enjoys my cooking. The look says "yippee," and I imagine confetti exploding from his head. I cock an eyebrow, in a challenge. He closes the door behind him—no way in hell is he rising to that.

The girls work through their morning routine. Talking about how many days of school remain. "Eight, after today," Sophie concludes.

"So nine days," Shelby says, beaming with pride that she already knows one more than eight is nine.

Sophie groans at her sister, for adding the day back into the count. Sophie finds everybody frustrating and uncool.

Was I ever too cool like that? I wonder, watching the smooth grace of Sophie walking to place her bowl in the sink, her head at a slight tilt as if she could throw out gang signs at any second. They are too exposed to everything. All the kids are these days, strutting like teenagers before the first nubs of breasts are even on the horizon. We've been good about keeping the programming in the house at what we think are appropriate levels, but once they go to school, they just learn stuff.

The girls dress, and I brush Shelby's hair, pulling her strawberry locks into a high curly-top ponytail, like a fractured halo atop her head. We head into the cul-de-sac, and the other neighborhood moms are coming out. The bus picks up at the end of the street, and we join the other mothers and children. Conversations start and roll. Sophie walks ahead with Willow and Spruce, the twins from next door. Willow is Sophie's best friend, and Spruce's real name is Bruce, but nobody calls him by his real name. He peels off to join Jace when we pass his drive.

Jace's sister, Julia—Shelby's favorite friend—climbs into the jogger with Shelby, and bits of their chatter comes through the top mesh.

Mona, like me, is dressed for a workout. We are both still trying to lose the "baby weight" from our four-year-old babies.

"Do you like the new studio?" I ask. Mona does cross-fit and jumps from one studio to the next. "I need to feel challenged," she had explained, sounding frustrated that nobody could help her get rid of the little bit of bulge remaining.

"It's tough. You should join me."

It's a mantra, the "you should join me," but I prefer to exercise solo, without criticism. I've never been one to enjoy being yelled at. I avoided team sports like the plague and, even now, almost never allow arguments to escalate to a raised voice.

"I don't know... shoving tractor tires sounds like fun and all, but... you know."

Mona nods, having expected nothing different. We've reached the end of the street. Shelby and Julia climb from the stroller and head toward the retention pond, where some geese are skirting through the water. The girls squat near the water's edge, but not too near. The bus pulls to a stop, blocking traffic, and the school-aged kids line up and climb the steps, waving back at parents left behind, or not, too focused on the importance of their moment in time.

When the bus is gone, and when we've let the girls squat a little longer at the water's edge, Mona calls them to us, and they bound, free of the stroller, back toward the cul-de-sac.

"We'll play later, okay?" Julia says as we get to their house. Mona and I share a look at the maturity of the question.

"Yes," Shelby agrees, reaching out and giving Julia a quick hug. I envy my children that—the easy way they hug people, the comfortable way they are with touch. I've tried to be huggable, but I'm not. People can feel it, and even if I manage to get the motions right, the small pat on the back, the minute squeeze of the biceps, they can still feel the awkward stiffness in my frame. John says it's like hugging a fish, and I think he's generous. I'm only good at hugging my girls.

"Have a good day!" Shelby calls, and my heart presses a hard beat. I love her so much, both my girls, and there are moments when I feel my love for them is too big, that my body can't contain an emotion so strong. I pat my heart, and Shelby climbs back into the stroller. I take the rest of the street at a slow jog, warming up for the run to her school.

I was depressed after Sophie was born, legitimately depressed, postpartum, and John had made me go to the doctor and get meds to level me out. They had helped, and the drastic swings dissipated, and when I stopped taking them six months later, the swings hadn't come back. I didn't go through that with Shelby, not to the same degree. But now and then, the melancholy washes over me, and I have to close the door on it or get sucked in.

We have a few minutes before we have to leave to get Shelby to school, so we sit together on the couch, and she tells me about the dream she had last night. A horse with wings, flying to the moon. Of course, Shelby, my moon fairy. By the time she finishes talking about the dream, it is time to go, and we head out through the garage, with her iPad clutched to her chest. I don't know if she really dreamed it, but she loves the act of telling stories, and often she frames them as if they are dreams—her stories impress her more if they come to her in a mysterious way, I think.

"Off like a herd of turtles," I say as we careen down the slope of the drive, and Shelby squeals.

3

Stacy

My life, when the girls are not home, is a series of completing small tasks that nobody ever notices. I sweep the house, clean the dishes, wash a load of laundry. I dust the coffee table and television because it is Tuesday. Then I heft the bunnies in their cage and take them out to clean, also because it is Tuesday. The girls love their rabbits, and usually, they help with the cleaning. It teaches them responsibility. But this morning, their cage smells, and I don't want to wait. I place the bunnies in their outside hutch, in the shade of the big tree in the front yard. The sun is already hot, burning down against the black pa vement of the road, and soon it will be to hot to be outside. That's how it is in north Florida, cool at dawn and hot by nine. Sweat drains from my face, my hair damp, the tips of my ponytail sticking along my shoulders.

I am almost finished with the cage when my phone buzzes. I drop the base of the cage, wiping my hands on my shorts, to get to it.

"Hello."

"Stacy?"

"Hey." Darren, my brother, doesn't call me in the mornings. He doesn't call me, ever. We almost never talk on the phone. "Is everything okay?"

"No. Not really." His voice drops, and I know he is trying to hold himself together, my sensitive, sweet brother.

"What happened?"

"Well, you need to come home." The noise in the background drowns out his voice, and Darren says, away from the phone, "Dad, what do you need? It's okay; it's okay. I'll get it." There is shuffling, and I wait, feeling the nervous tension building the longer I stand motionless. I pop my feet to mountain pose and stretch out through my core, letting each nodule in my spine snap into place, feeling the individual muscles and tendons connecting, pulling, and I tilt my chin to the sky. "Sorry," Darren says to me, and I drop my face back forward.

"Is everything okay?" I ask, and hear the shuffle of him stepping into another room.

"It's Mom." There is a crack around the edges of the word.

"What about Mom?"

"She's gone." My brother gasps and snuffles before pulling himself together again. What does he mean gone? To the store, on a walk? "She didn't wake up."

"Are you sure?" I ask, realizing the stupidity of the question even as it is coming out of my mouth. "I mean I talked to her yesterday morning, and she was fine, talking about planting the garden . . ."

"Yeah, I know. She wrote it on the calendar."

I see her then, answering the phone and turning to the wall, the ever-present Audubon Society calendar, noting the time, writing my name.

"Oh, okay," I say, turning and pressing my free hand to the rough stucco of the house, leaning, feeling the weakness starting at my feet. "What happened?"

"She just didn't wake up," he says, and I hear the strain in his voice. I think he already said that once.

"How is Dad?"

"He's in shock," he says, "I think." I hear the doorbell on the other end of the phone, and Darren is on the move again. "I'll get it, Dad. Dad. I got it."

"I'll let you go," I say, hearing the chaos erupting around him. "I'll head out this morning."

"Good." The phone is already moving away from his face, but I hear, "Hi, thanks for coming." The last words fade, and I can envision him opening the front door, sunlight streaming in. The call ends, and I stand, watching as a family of geese fly overhead.

I press the phone, and John's face flashes across the screen.

"Hey," he says, talking through the wireless system in his car, sounding echoed and distant.

"Can you be home by the time the bus comes?"

"What time is that? Are you okay?"

"Three. Yeah, um, I'm okay, I just got off the phone with my brother."

"Is everybody okay?"

"No. Mom passed away." I say it quick, matter-of-fact, not wanting to dwell on the details of it.

"Oh, babe. I'll come home."

"No, John, just be here at three. I'm gonna head up there." Then I add, "Dad sounded very confused." We've known for a year that his memory was slipping.

"Might be a blessing."

"Yeah, maybe." I stand, watching the geese as they disappear past the trees. I'm irritated that he can say that. My father having dementia is not a blessing.

"What can I do?"

"Nothing. I just need to go. I'll take Shelby with me. I can take Sophie, too, but she's got her big test on Thursday." If only it were next week, it wouldn't matter if she missed the last couple of days.

"Do you think she could go to the neighbors if I'm not right there?"

"Yeah, that might be better. You have foreclosures. I forgot. I'll talk to Dee, and she'll get Sophie from the bus."

"Okay." I hear the relief in his voice and am instantly annoyed.

"I know it's inconvenient." I snap, clenching my jaw.

"I didn't say that," John says, using his let's be calm voice.

"I don't know when the funeral will be."

"You can let me know." He has reached his destination: the courthouse steps. I can tell by the shuffling, the bonging of his car as he opens the door—and then the key sliding out and the wireless disconnecting and the signal transferring to the phone. "Do you want to take the Mercedes?" he asks.

"No. My car is fine." My car is a point of contention between us. It's twelve years old, and he's been trying to talk me into a new car for years, but I like mine; it is just fine.

"All right," he says, resigned. "I'm sorry this happened."

"It's just such a shock. She was fine yesterday."

"At least she didn't suffer." There he goes again. I roll my eyes, feeling angry . . . How can he say that? Of course, she suffered. She suffered enough to die.

"Yeah. Well, I'll work it out with Dee."

4

Stacy

My mother is gone. How am I supposed to feel? My mother, who told me every day that I was terrific and that I could grow up to do great things. My mother, who encouraged everybody to do great things. She was a woman people wanted to keep. People to whom she had sold houses years ago would still send Christmas cards, like family.

"Who are these people?" I had asked one day when a photo card came in the mail—a man, a woman, and three red Irish setters.

She glanced at the card and smiled. "That's Julian and Evie Donas."

"How do you know them?" I questioned, almost annoyed, the way of teenagers.

"I helped them buy their house when they first got married." I picked up the envelope and the return address was Lake Oswego, Oregon.

"In Oregon?"

She laughed, that tinkling sound, like bells rolling down a stream. "No. They moved to Oregon about ten years ago." She had taken the card from my hand, and I could almost see the connection she had built with these people.

"They still send you a card?"

"Sure. They are a lovely couple."

People love my mom.

~ ~ ~

I am brought back to the present, yanked out of my memory because my phone vibrates.

"I'm here," I say into the phone when it chirps.

"Where are you?" The strain is palpable in Darren's voice.

"I'm at the house," I say. I've just pulled up the drive.

"We're at my house. Remember?"

"Yeah. I know. I'll be there in a second. Just wanted to stop here for a minute" I try to keep my voice steady, to not rise to his assuming I wouldn't remember. Of course, I didn't remember, and that annoys me, my weak mind, my faulty memory. "How is Dad?"

"I don't know. I don't think it's registered yet." He pauses, waiting, weighing something he wants to say, "Do you remember where my house is?"

"Yes. I remember." I let out a long breath. "I'll be there soon." We disconnect, and I look into the back seat, where Shelby has been asleep but is now waking. "Hi, honey," I say, and she stretches.

"Are we there?"

"Almost." I reach out and squeeze her fingers. "Let's get out and stretch."

Shelby and I walk around the side of the house and through the gate to the back. The yard rolls down to the lake, which spreads out in front of us.

"I 'member this," Shelby says, excited because she knows now where we are. "Grammy and Grandpa's house? Right?"

"That's right." We walk down the stretch of the back yard and stop in the gazebo overlooking the lake.

Shelby puts her hand in mine, and when I glance down, she is looking up at me with way too much understanding for a four-year-old.

"I'm gonna miss Grammy," she says with a too-grownup sigh. I nod, and we look back out over the water. "She makes the best cake."

I choke out a laugh and spin down to her, wrapping her in my arms, the first tears of grief slipping over the edge of my lashes. I squeeze her little body, and she wraps her arms around my neck, one hand patting the back of my head, unable to comprehend the depth of my sadness, but knowing all the motions—the ones I use on her when she is sad.

Minutes pass, and when I have pulled myself together, Shelby and I pass back through the yard to the car. I send John a text, telling him we've arrived.

~ ~ ~

Darren opens the door before we mount the steps to his porch, and he reaches a hand out to draw me into his embrace. "Are you okay?" he asks, and I nod against his shoulder, needing him to let me go. "Come in. Come in. Dad's lying down." We follow him into his home.

The house is neat, the way of homes where there are no children or pets. Darren is fastidious; he is tidy. He has always been, but this seems even more pristine than Darren's norm. He offers coffee, and I sit at the table while his Keurig spits out the brew. Darren doesn't acknowledge Shelby, which would annoy me in anybody else, but he is weird around kids; he usually pretends not to see them. He does not address his discomfort. Darren was an old man at ten, and he hasn't changed except for his receding hairline.

He proceeds to tell me the details from the morning, how he had called, and when nobody answered, he had driven down to check on them. He had found Dad sitting out back in his pajamas, and Mom had been in bed. "I don't think he understands."

"Of course he understands," I say. How could he not? He isn't a child.

"You don't know. He's gotten a lot worse since you saw him last."

"Mom told me he's doing fine."

"Mom says what she needs to believe. He can't be left alone. He walked out of the house last month, and we had to have the police out looking for him. Found him in Peachtree City at the Best Buy."

"So?"

"He walked there. In his pajamas and slippers."

"Oh." That's a little different picture. Peachtree City is only minutes away by car, but there are no walkways between here and there, so that means he either walked through the yards and neighborhoods to get there or he walked along the main highway. "Why would he do that?"

"I don't know."

Shelby sits on my lap, and she turns her face up to me, whispering that she needs to go to the bathroom. Darren points the way, and I walk with her, but she closes the door between us, "Privacy, please." She's a big girl and very proud that she uses the potty alone.

I wait outside the door until she opens it again. "I can't reach the sink." I lift her, and she washes her hands, using Darren's monogrammed towel to dry them.

When we come again to the living room, Dad is standing in the doorway from the kitchen. Shelby squeals and runs for him.

"There's my girl!" he says, scooping her up and squeezing her to his broad chest. He hasn't changed. He is still a handsome man, with his shock of black hair sparked with white. He is stubble-cheeked but freshly showered and dressed. I rush to him and wrap around him and Shelby.

"Hi, Daddy," I say, a catch in my throat, pulling at my words.

He drops a kiss on the top of my head, and I think that Darren must be exaggerating.

"Where's my other girl?" He looks around for Sophie.

I explain that she had to stay for a test on Thursday. "She and John will come up on Saturday."

He nods. "Well, what brings you up this way?" He sets Shelby's feet on the ground, and I look at him, then at Darren, who shrugs.

"We came up to see you, Dad."

"Well. Isn't that nice." He musses Shelby's hair. "Well, come on back to the house. Grammy will be glad to see you. She'll have a cake out of the oven shortly."

Darren jumps in with, "Dad, Mom's not at the house. Do you remember?" Dad is moving toward the door, and Darren catches up to him before he can open the door. I stand there, watching, a little dumbstruck. How can he know Shelby and not know what happened this morning?

"What are you on about?" Dad looks at Darren, irritation creasing his brow. "What am I doing here? I got to get back home."

"Dad. You can't go home right now."

"Your mother will wonder where I've gone. You know how she worries."

"Mom isn't at home," Darren says slowly, like he is talking to a dimwitted adolescent.

"Well, where has she gone? Is she out for a walk? Gone to the store?" I hear the faint echo of my questions earlier, and I understand that Darren has been dealing with something while I've been off living my life.

"Mom died. Dad. She died. Do you remember?"

His face contorts, from shock and annoyance to disgust. "What are you talking about?" Dad looks at me, and I see the vacant place in his pale eyes where understanding should be, where knowledge should live.

"It's true. Dad. I'm sorry. That's why Shelby and I are here." I touch his shoulder, and he shrugs free of me, pushing past Darren, opening the door, and stepping out into the sunlight.

5

Stacy

Darren leaves it to Shelby and me to follow Dad, so I hitch Shelby onto my hip and set out after him. Darren closes the door behind us, and I imagine him sighing in relief now that he has a few moments away from the family drama. We walk down the street, past the house where Darren's best friend, Diego Martinez, used to live. The house is overgrown and looks abandoned. Giant evergreens line the road in front of the house, blocking the view. Shelby and I walk past, and I glance through the trees to see if there is a car parked in the drive, but there is none. What happened to him? Where did he end up?

Darren's house is at the end of the street, a dead-end cul-de-sac. The lake stretches out behind the house in a long curve, turning up toward the spillway. The view from his home is different than the one at my parents'. He sees houses across the lake; he sees the long line of shore. My parents' house sits at the best vantage, so they only see the far edge of the lake, the spillway, and the houses off to the side. We grew up on this street, and Darren never left. Dad is a few paces ahead of us, walking with long strides and determination.

I don't call out to him. I just follow, pacing him, and when he walks up the drive to the house, Shelby and I pause.

"Maybe Grammy will be here," Shelby whispers.

"I wish, baby."

"What kind of cake would she make today?"

"An upside-down one," I reply, because everything about this day is upside down.

We follow him and stand at the bottom of the steps as he goes to the front door. He turns the knob and pushes, growing instantly angry when the door doesn't open. He shoves his finger against the bell, and the chimes ring through the house. He pounds the door, his back rigid, and I stand with Shelby clutched tightly to me, not sure what to do. I have never seen my father weak, and the foreignness of it is crushing. This cannot be happening. This whole day cannot be happening.

"Doris!" he yells, his face pressing against the door. Then he slams the heels of his hands against the wood, in one sharp staccato hit, and leans against the door, his forehead resting on it, his shoulders dropping, the tension in his back subsiding. I stand frozen, but Shelby squirms and I set her down. She climbs up the steps and slips her hand into his, looking up at him with all the open-eyed beauty in her soul. I follow her and watch, awed by this little person, the beautiful little girl who came from my body and is already better at being alive than I am. There is so much I could learn from her. My father's face tilts, from directly facing the door to looking sideways and down at Shelby.

"I'm sorry, Grandma went away."

"How can she be gone?" he asks, and there is something of a child in his voice.

Shelby shakes her head; even she, with all her wisdom, doesn't know the answer.

Dad kneels down in front of her, pushing a strand of hair out of Shelby's eyes. "I need her," he says, and for the first time, I think he does understand what has happened and has just been denying the truth.

"I know," Shelby says. "But we're here now."

Tears are draining from my eyes... How does she know? How can she possibly understand? I swipe my arm across my face and join them on the porch. Dad looks at me, and I swear he is suddenly an old, old man, his face slack and with jowls. His eyes are milky, pale and haunted. He stands again, and I almost hear the creaking of his bones.

"Don't you cry," he says, and I hiccup because, for the first time since we left Darren's house, I see my dad, the man who was always in charge, the man who understood what he needed to do and was willing to do it.

"I'm so sorry, Dad." I press into him, and his arm folds around me.

"I know you are, sweetheart."

We make our way into the house, using the hide-a-key from behind the bench on the front porch. The house is so familiar that I feel like I've dropped back into some version of the past. If not for Shelby being here, I could imagine that I'm sixteen again, riddled with acne and tormented by insecurity, taller than everybody, like the hideous giant in the land of fairies. I straighten my shoulders; I am not that girl anymore. I am a grown woman with children of my own, a handsome husband, a lawyer husband. I am a woman. I am a woman without a mother.

There is something in the stoop of my father, as the reality of his altered future dawns through the webs and fogs of his tired mind, which makes the modified facts of my own life loom stark. He is wifeless; I am motherless—we are both made less by her passing. The house smells dank, like it has been unoccupied for weeks, not hours, and the gloom of the foyer dispels as I make my way through the living room, opening the blinds to let in the sun. The lake beyond the back yard spreads, and I stand for just a moment staring out at it, as I so often did when I lived here, trying to find my bearing.

The sun sparkles across the tips of the small undulations, and all the nerves wrap themselves in their cocoons, and when I turn back to face my father, he and Shelby are sitting on the sofa, and he is scrolling through television channels, looking for something they can watch together. "Merida!" Shelby laughs, and then says again, "Merida!"

"What is this Merida?"

"Go back, go back, Grandpa. Merida is brave, like me. Brave. Right there." It is her favorite movie—in fact, maybe mine, too. I was so excited when they produced a princess movie that didn't involve the handsome prince transforming the princess. I loved the theme of "brave," the independent, wayward daughter bucking against the proper mother. I had been Merida at one point, with less beautiful skin, but with all the struggles against the old guard, all the rebellion.

Then I went and married a man who is just like my father, and now I catch myself saying the same things my mother said to me. Is there nothing new under the sun? All that teenage angst… is it just a thing, a stage we have to go through, thinking we are so different when we are all the same?

My father has figured it out, and he and Shelby sit side by side as Merida follows the wisp toward the witch's cottage. I stand, leaning one long-fingered hand on the textured leather of the couch, watching my father and daughter.

How can she not be here? I turn away and go into the kitchen, with its marble island clean and uncluttered. Coffee. I clean the dregs from the French press and put a kettle on to heat, sorting through the flavored coffees in the bread bin. I finally find the simple Folger's and ready the press. How many conversations have I had here in this kitchen, watching my mother watching her kettle heat? Too many.

Not enough.

When my mug is hot with steaming coffee, I rouse myself; there are things to be done.

Shelby and Grandpa are still watching Merida. "Watch, watch." Shelby says, grabbing his hand, and I realize that the mother is in the midst of her transformation from woman to bear. Shelby is clearly entranced.

My parents' bedroom is dark and cast in gloom, and I pull all the shades to let in the early afternoon light. The bed is rumpled, and I pause, looking down at the dent in her pillow where her head last lay. I touch the hollow, hoping for some remembered warmth, but it is cold, empty, not living. Something akin to anger washes through me, and I throw back the comforter and strip the sheets and pillowcases from the bed. While they are soaking in the washer, I remake it, neat and tidy with fresh linens.

My phone vibrates in my hip pocket, and I step out onto the deck before answering.

"Hey, babe" is the response. His voice is warm, a little muffled and I know he is at the courthouse steps waiting for the next foreclosure sale to start. He is surrounded, using his I'm with people; I can't talk now voice.

"Hey. You at the courthouse?"

"Yeah. How are things?"

"Strange." The word breaks in my throat, and I stop. I was going to tell him about the odd, disconnected way my dad is, but suddenly there are no words.

"How's Shelby?"

"She's good. They're watching a movie."

"Good. Did you get in touch with Dee? This could run late tonight."

"Yeah. I packed her an overnight bag. She can stay there if you're too late."

"Oh. Good thinking. That's a good plan."

"I'm glad you approve." The dry tone of my voice may not stretch across the line; if it does, John chooses not to mention it. Good plan, I think. I love John, but there are times that absolutely everything he says irritates me. He is always pronouncing judgments, looking for flaws, seeing the failures, the breakdowns.

There is commotion on the other end of the line, and I'm glad because my snarky comment has sat too long unanswered. But John is distracted; he is talking away from the phone, muffled.

"Yeah, yeah. Just gimme a second." To me, he says, "Look, babe. I gotta go."

"I know."

"I'll check in later. When's the funeral?"

"I don't know; we haven't talked about that yet."

"Why not? That's why you're there, right?"

"We're working on it." I clench my jaws tight against my anger. He is not the enemy; it's just his way.

"All right. I'll talk to you later." His phone clicks to silence, and I spread my hands wide-fingered on the deck railing and lean as far as I can out over the yard. The wind coming across the lake catches my hair and lifts it, cooling the heat on the back of my neck, and I let my head loll. He's right. There are things to do, and we're just hanging out. Washing linens. Watching movies. I call my brother.

"What do we need to do next?"

"What do you mean?"

"I mean, funeral arrangements. What's next?"

"Scott's coming home, so he can sit with Dad. I don't think he's really up for going, do you?"

"I don't know. I feel like he should, don't you?"

"He doesn't even know what has happened," Darren says, and I walk down the deck, looking through the windows where Shelby and Grandpa are laughing. On the screen, the boys are leading the men on a wild bear chase through the castle.

"Probably right."

"It would just confuse him."

I nod, forgetting that he can't see me. "Okay. So when's Scott going to be home?"

"He's on his way now. We'll be down as soon as he gets here."

Darren had come out of the closet when he was seventeen and had fallen in love with the foreign exchange student visiting from Norway. Oleg was nearly seven feet tall and, as far as I knew, he wasn't gay. Darren was gobsmacked, though—utterly smitten. I don't know that he ever talked to the tall Norwegian boy about his affections, but he did tell my parents.

"Okay," my mother had said in her quiet, reserving-judgment voice, "what do you want to do about it?"

"What do you mean 'do'?"

"Do you want to tell him or not?" she had said.

Darren had deflated, all the hackles on his back lying down, and I understood then that he had planned for a battle. He had expected our parents to throw him out or, at best, force him into therapy. My mother acted as if he'd found a stray dog he wanted to bring home, which was not an unusual thing in our foster-friendly home. He got more of a fight from Dad, but even that was unimpressive. It took Dad longer to process, longer to come to terms with the facts. Really, though, I think we all had known that Darren was gay.

I don't believe Darren ever told the boy, who had gone back to Norway at the end of the year, but Darren had transformed. Once Darren admitted his sexuality, he had relaxed into himself. If our parents could accept it, then so could he. I don't know what he had expected—some high drama he had seen on television—but our parents were not the "high drama" type. They were the "live and let live" type. When Darren brought Scott home from college two years later, it was like Scott had always been there.

By the time Merida is covering her mother, who has transformed once again into a woman, with the tapestry after the rising of the dawn, Scott and Darren are coming up the drive. Scott is a good-looking, blond-haired man, thinning a little on top, but handsome in the way models are. He told me once that his own coming-out had been of the high-drama variety, and the last I had heard, his father had still not spoken to him. "He is missing out," I had said, putting my hand over his. Scott had smiled, looking sad and resigned.

"Hey, Dad," they call in unison as they come through the door. A look passes between them, an inside joke; they often say the same thing at the same time.

"Well, who is that?" Scott says, peering down at Shelby, sitting curled around her plate of PB&J sandwich and carrot sticks. Dad has already finished his food and set the plate on the coffee table.

"I'm Shelby, Unca Scott. You know me." Her mouth is thick with a wad of sandwich, and Scott rubs the top of her head.

"Of course you are, darling. Aren't you fabulous?" He reaches out and takes the plate from her lap, setting it aside. "Let me see how big you've gotten." He lifts her over the arm of the couch and stands her up in front of him.

"I was this big last time you saw me."

"No. I don't think you were. You didn't even have any teeth."

"I had teeth!" She looks over at me, to confirm.

"I'm sure you didn't." He picks her up and squeezes her. "They sure do look good on you, though, except that one, right there… got some peanut butter on that one." Shelby giggles. If ever there was a man who should have been a father, it's Scott, and I let the thought run, as it so often has, about his choice to always be relegated to uncle. I know it's not a choice, the being gay thing, Darren has told me that often enough, but it just seems sad that Scott will never have a daughter of his own to make a fuss over. It's funny how different they are, Scott and Darren. Like John and me, I guess… like Mom and Dad. A balanced set.

"Dad, Stacy and I need to go take care of a few things. Okay? Scott's going to stay with you."

"I want to stay, too," Shelby says, taking Scott's hand, now that he has set her again on the ground, and dragging him toward the couch. "Unca Scott, we're watching movies. What's next, Grandpa?"

"I don't know; let's look."

6

Stacy

Funeral Saturday at 6. Visitation at 4. I send the text as we walk out of the funeral home. We have chosen a casket. We have discussed the music. We have even arranged for a string quartet to play through the service. We've written an announcement for the local newspaper, and Mr. Follett, the owner of the funeral home, is, even now, arranging for its run in the paper. Darren holds the folder full of insurance information; there are also notes written up along his forearm.

"I called the attorney; they can meet us tomorrow to read the will."

"Everything goes to Dad, doesn't it?"

"It's just a formality." We've reached his car. "We have to run probate."

My phone vibrates, and I look down to see a text from John: Good job. I tilt my head and close my eyes, trying to convince myself it's not a judgment.

"I need to call and check on Sophie." I dial Dee's number, and she answers on the first ring. "Hey, how's Sophie?"

"She's good. We're sitting out front. They're riding bikes."

"What did you tell her?"

"Nothing, really. Just that you had to go up north for a day or two. What should I tell her?"

"No, that's good. Can I talk to her?"

Dee calls out, and Sophie takes the phone. "Hi, Mom."

"Hey, love," I say.

"Is everything okay? Is Grandpa sick?"

"No, honey, Grandpa's fine. He's looking forward to seeing you."

"Cool." She is distracted, and I have a moment of panic that maybe I shouldn't tell her—it will ruin her evening.

"It's Grandma." I hear the creak of my voice and clear my throat. "Grandma passed away this morning."

"Oh." Sophie is back, attentive. "Mom, I'm sorry."

I'm melting, tears washing down over my cheeks, feeling unreal. I fold my hand over my mouth to keep the sound away from my daughter.

"Are you okay?" she asks, her voice so much older than nine, more prepared for life than I ever was.

"Yes, honey. I'm okay. Are you okay?"

"Yeah, Mom. How is Grandpa?"

"As best as he can be, considering. You and Daddy will come up on Saturday, okay?"

"Okay. I love you."

"I love you, too," I say in front of a sob that is forming. I choke it down.

Dee is back on the line, and I confirm that John is probably going to be late, so it might be better if Sophie stays the night.

"Absolutely. You let me know if there's anything I can do."

"Could you check the dogs?" And as an afterthought, I add, "And the rabbits?"

"We've already taken care of it." I hear her smile across the line. "That's the first thing the girls did."

"Thank you."

"Anytime, Stace. Be strong."

I disconnect and stare out the window. That was not the conversation I had expected. I had thought to hear some hint of the devastation I feel, but Sophie is a matter-of-fact, pragmatic—she is strong. Children are resilient.

We are driving, and I can feel Darren watching me from the corner of his eyes. I would not have reacted like that as a child. I would have fallen to the floor in a heap, pathetic and broken. Or I would have thrown something and screamed. I was not a resilient child. But Darren doesn't know me, not anymore. I'm not the volatile, angry girl he remembers. I'm not the girl that slept on the floor in her closet one whole weekend because I thought somebody was looking in my window.

"Scott seems good," I say, clearing the air.

"He is. He just got a promotion."

"Another one?" Because last I had heard, he'd been promoted to managing a team. He works at Wachovia in the Fraud Protection Department.

"Yeah. He now has four teams under him and manages the managers."

"Wow. That's incredible," I say, feeling proud of Scott and his accomplishment.

"He's good at it."

"How about you? How's the real-estate industry?"

"It's good. You know." His voice falters. Mom was in real estate, for years, and when she retired, she passed all her leads on to Darren. They'd been working together for ten years by then anyway. "I got my broker's license. I've got two agents working out of my office."

"You have an office now?"

"Well, virtually."

"That's great," I say, and I mean it, even if I feel a little jealous of all this forward motion in their lives. I love my life, even if it feels like a lot of standing still. I'm not doing anything big, just washing laundry, sweeping floors, raising kids. I don't miss working. I don't miss sacrificing hours of my day to achieve somebody else's goals. John and I agreed when we decided to have kids that I'd stay home with them, and it feels like hitting the jackpot. I have so much me time. When I first quit my job, I had secretly hoped to start writing again, maybe even finish the novel I started in college. I like the idea of being a writer, but it was like all the interests I'd had growing up—something I started but never finished. Starting projects was my best hobby. As soon as it got tough or I had a setback or I got overwhelmed or burned out or just disinterested,

I'd find some other thing to start. Mom always said it was the "flash in the pan," meaning that my interests came and went, like the glimpsing of gold only to be lost again by the cascade of dirt.

I didn't start writing again, never even thought of a story. "Folding laundry takes so much time," I say to myself, but the reality is I'm just not interested. My life is a series of completing boring tasks that nobody ever notices unless left undone.

"Dishes from breakfast?"

"Look at that dog hair."

"Wow, did you see that cobweb in the bedroom? It's huge!"

The litany of criticisms, observations, rolls through my head, and I slide my tongue over the rim of my teeth and turn to look out the window—how mundane my life is, how boring.

"So, how's John?" Darren asks when we park at the florist's.

"Oh. Good. He's doing great. I think he'll make partner this year." We head toward the front door.

"That's good." Then, as if he's been poking around inside my head, he asks, "You been writing at all?"

I laugh, wishing I hadn't told him, years ago, that was my goal. "Nah. I got nothing to say."

"I bet you do. Whatever happened to that thing you wrote in college? You were pretty serious about that for a time." There were vast stretches of time through my adolescent years where I wrote feverishly, chunks of time that I disappeared entirely into the words. When I later read the pages, I could never remember having those thoughts. I didn't even remember the characters' names; it was like reading something written by someone else.

"Yep, for a time, I guess." I shrug, just a flash in the pan. "I don't know, just seems silly now. I'm raising people and all. It takes so much time to fold the clothes."

"Trust me, I know." I look at him, thinking about the pristine house at the end of the street, about his monogrammed hand towels and I wonder if he, like me has a basket, or two, or three, of laundry sitting in the bedroom, waiting for folding.

The flower shop is just on the east side of the downtown square, where residential and commercial meets. We are greeted by the tinkling of a bell overhead as I follow him through the door. The shop is dark, lit mostly by the light coming from the windows. The corners offer gloom, the shade of my soul.

"Oh, Darren." A lady comes from the back of the shop and bustles past the counter, her eyes fluttering against the sun.

"Hi, Sue," Darren says, and she stops in front of us, not even seeing me.

"I wondered if you would be coming in today. I'm so sorry about your poor mother. We all just loved her."

"Thanks. It's been a shock. You remember my sister, don't you?"

I straighten to my full height, pressing my shoulders back until I stand a whopping six inches taller than Sue Bellefonte.

"Of course. Stacy." She smiles and waggles her fingers at me. "Good to see you. Where are you these days?"

"We're down in Florida." I let my hand rest with my index finger on my lip, putting my two-carat diamond-crusted wedding ring on full display. Sue Bellefonte used to call me Spaghetti back before her hips spread to the width of a Volkswagen Beetle. She was the most popular girl in school, and I hated her for it.

I see the moment when her eyes catch the spark of my ring and feel immediately like a shit. I drop my hand, embarrassed. "How are you?" I ask, trying to put genuine interest in my voice.

"I'm good. My youngest will be going to kindergarten next year. Can you believe it? My oldest is gonna be in junior high. They call it middle school now. Isn't that the silliest thing?" She is friendly, and I remember her in the hallways at school, turning all the heads. Everybody was in love with her.

"I guess." My voice sounds flat inside my head, and I glance at the window to see that my reflection hasn't transformed back to the Emo Girl I used to carry as a shroud. I haven't; I'm still me, clean and pulled together, a "mom" to a tee.

"Well, it's so good to see you both." She puts her hand on my elbow, as I pass her into the shop. "I wish it were under better circumstances." Darren and I nod, and she leads us over to a table where several photo albums are stacked. "Do you have an idea of what you'd like to do? Or should we just look through some books?"

Less than half an hour later, we've chosen a wreath and two large double-ended sprays for the sanctuary, with mixed flowers in blues and whites. Sue has managed a stream of small conversation, asking if I have children, asking about Scott, asking all the right things to make us feel cared for. She is very good at managing people. Sue will take care of everything, coordinating the deliveries to the funeral home and the cemetery. By the time Darren and I are heading back to the car, I feel somewhat better than I did. Sue made me feel comfortable, like I didn't have to wear a mask, and that's a pretty unusual thing for me. Her being so nice and genuine has me embarrassed by the stunt I pulled, showing off my ring as if that makes me something. Somebody married me, so I'm okay. Some guy thought I was good enough. It was such a junior-high thing to do. She's probably not the same girl; she was nothing but kind, there in the store. The world could use more "kind." Sue and Darren, and everybody else, have figured out how to be an adult, and I'm still checking windows to see how I look. Coming back here has made me backslide.

"Stacy," Sue is behind us, calling from the door of her shop.

"Yes?" I turn back and make a step toward her, curious what I may have left behind.

"Well, I was thinking, that if your youngster wanted to come have a playdate with my Jack, it might be nice."

"Really? That would be nice. She'd like that, I'm sure."

"Let's make that happen, then." She nods, wrinkling her nose.

"All right. Let's do. You have my number," I say, heading back to Darren as Sue Bellefonte bobs back through the door to her parents' flower shop. I glance down at the card I have in my hand and see that it's not Bellefonte anymore; it's Miller—and I realize that I never asked her a single question about herself.

7

Stacy

Wednesday morning dawns gray, and the mist over the lake floats heavy, like phantoms hovering above the water. Shelby and I spent the night in my old bedroom, which is now one of two guest rooms. My old twin bed was replaced by a queen years ago, and the last time John and I visited, the girls had slept in the adjoining room, with the glass doors open. I try to remember when Mom exchanged the wooden French door with glass. I try to remember when she started leaving the doors open. I can't remember. I let it go. My memory has never been my strength. That's why it worries me to hear that Dad's memory is slipping. Is that what's wrong with me? Have I got some strange variation of dementia the starts when you're just a kid? I've never been able to recall things, almost like I have amnesia or some disorder that prevents me storing memories.

Shelby sleeps like a wild animal, all feet and knees, and elbows. When she lands a knee against my kidney, I roll off the bed and place a pillow in my space to keep her from falling off. I walk, with quiet feet, down the hall, past my parents' room, past my snoring father, through the living room, and out onto the back deck.

The cacophony of frogs down by the water's edge is deafening in the otherwise silent world. A dog barks somewhere in the neighborhood—somebody's lap dog yipping at nothing and everything.

I stand in mountain pose, tall and straight, calming my breathing from the chaos that hit when I passed my parent's room, aware that only my father sleeps there now, conscious in the starkest way that today marks the first day without my mother at all in it. Something I had almost forgotten.

Breathe. Breathe. Breathe. My heart slows and calms, and the black doom slides down and away from my mind. Standing on the deck, in the dark side of dawn, watching as the pale mist on the water shifts and dances as night gropes toward the day, I feel less like a woman about to erupt from her skin. Since Darren's call yesterday morning, I've had that strange crawling sensation under my flesh that I remember from when I was coming through adolescence when my hormones were in flux, and the faults in my mind were becoming more evident. Thirteen had hit me with the force of something needing to be set free.

I let the calm wash over me, listening to the frogs. Of course, I haven't been that girl in years. I have learned how to be alive. I make lists now, keeping notes to help me remember the things that happen in my life. I don't drink; I practice yoga, which helps to calm the crazy in my head. I went to a therapist for several years after the break, and I have better ways of coping now. I learned a lot, although I never remembered how I'd ended up in the psych ward. Where had I gone for the three days I was missing? It wasn't the first lost time I'd had, but it was the longest stretch, the darkest black hole in my memory filled with such holes. I have no idea where I was or how I ended up walking into the hospital, blood dripping from my wrists as if I'd punched through a plate glass window, not remembering how I had gotten there, how I had been injured, who had dropped me off, where my shoes were. Maybe I had punched through a window, which is the story I tell now when people notice the scars and need to understand. Surely I wasn't trying to kill myself, without even knowing it.

Breathe. Breathe. Breathe. I push the thoughts out of my head, these disjointed memories. It's just the loss, I know . . . the loss of my mother that has set me on edge. That and being back in Georgia.

It had been a Friday when I went missing, and the last thing I have ever been able to remember was walking to Cassie Carter's house to spend the night. Did I make it there? Yes. I know I did because they said I was there. I vaguely remember opening the door to their house and walking in, the party already in progress. But that could have been any other night when I'd gone to Cassie's when her parents were not home. I don't know if it is a memory from that night. When did I slip?

There was a young man there. I don't remember the young man. Later, when I had been missing and then found, everybody said they had never seen him before. He had come to the party saying I had invited him.

I don't remember inviting anybody. I hadn't even been planning on going until I went. Did I leave with him or just wander off on my own? A sharp edge rises in my mind, as it does so often when I try to think of the dark places.

Yoga helps. Having the girls helps. Knowing that it isn't all about me, helps. Grounded. I don't have to risk anything; I just have to do my small part and help to raise good people, who will take my place in the world when I, like my mother, dance out across the lake. I am safe.

Why safe?

I watch the fog rising from the lake and push down the small, sharp pain in my mind. It is better not to think on those things. Better to not try to remember what is in the darkness.

~ ~ ~

Dad is sitting in the kitchen, without any lights on, when I come in. The chill from the early morning air seeps under my skin; the tips of my hair are damp from the moisture coming off the lake. The kitchen is dark because the clouds are dense in the sky. He doesn't look up, and for a second, I hesitate, wondering if maybe he is asleep. Does he sleepwalk? Does he sometimes wake up and not remember how he got there? Shelby does. I do.

He turns toward me, seeing me in the doorway. "There you are." There is relief heavy in his voice, too heavy just for me. Does he think I'm my mother? Surely not—we never looked alike.

"Hi, Dad." I sit at the bar with him and fold my hands on the counter in front of us.

"It's gonna be a rainy day," he offers.

"Yes, looks like it."

"That Shelby . . . she's something else, isn't she?"

My lips spread, and pride reels in my heart. At least I've done that one thing well. I have amazing children, even if there are three baskets of laundry waiting at home. "She's pretty special."

"How is Sophie?"

"She's good. Sharp as a tack."

"I bet." We sit, letting the silence fold around us as the room lightens with the force of the sun, even as it is hidden in the shroud of dark clouds, rising over the hemisphere.

"How is John?"

"He's good. We think he's gonna make partner this year. He's worked hard."

"Are you happy?"

I laugh. "Yeah. I'm happy." I let out a sigh. "I have a great life."

"Yes, but that doesn't mean you'll always be happy."

"You're right. 'Happy' maybe isn't the right word." Actually, "happy" could never be the right word for me. I am always too serious, too tinged by melancholy for "happy" to apply. "I think I'm content. I'm peaceful."

"Content is good." I glance at him, wondering where he is today. Does he know that she is gone, or has he forgotten again? What happens next for him? Should I invite him to come and live with us? Should he move in with Darren and Scott? Should we get him a home-health person to stay with him during the days? "So, will John and Sophie come for the funeral?"

"Yes." I reach out and put my hand over his, tucking my fingers into the warm space of his palm.

"Good. I'd like to see them."

"Sophie's gotten big. She's tall."

"Like you," he says, and I nod.

We sit until the clouds outside crack open with a great clap of thunder, and water slashes in sheets against the windows. We both jump at the thunder, and then we laugh, in that nervous way people do when they feel their mortality.

"I'm sure gonna miss your mother. She was a hell of a woman."

I squeeze his hand, and we hear Shelby shuffling down the hall, her little voice sleep-filled, calling for me. The thunder must have woken her.

"Hey, baby. I'm here." I reach her and carry her back into the kitchen, turning on a light, dimmed, and she leans toward Grandpa. I pass her over.

"Coffee?" I ask, cleaning the silver press into the trash, rinsing the last grounds down the sink.

"I don't drink coffee," Shelby says, shocked and appalled.

"That's good. It will put hair on your chest," Grandpa says, and Shelby giggles.

Dad's fine. I thought yesterday that maybe Darren was right—that he was struggling with dementia—but today he is just like his old self. He was just stressed and in shock yesterday. Who wouldn't be?

The phone rings and I reach for it. "Hello?"

"How is everybody?" Darren asks, and in front of me is the Audubon calendar, with my mother's distinct handwriting: Stacy. 9:30.

"We're good—listening to the rain." I turn away from the calendar, swallowing hard against the crush of emotions rising. How could we have just been sitting here a minute ago, talking like it was a typical day, speaking as if everything was going to be fine and dandy? How could we have just been acting like the bottom hadn't just fallen out of the world?

"How is Dad?"

"Good. He's teasing Shelby."

"That's a good sign." His pause feels heavy, and I realize he's getting ready to bring up something he thinks I may not like.

"What is it?" I ask, walking through the living room, holding the phone to my ear, waiting for him to speak. I stand at the back door and look out over storm hammering down on the world.

"Well, are you okay . . . there with him? I kinda need to go to work today. I've got an open house and—"

"Of course. We're fine."

"You sure?"

"Seriously, Darren, I am an adult. I think I can handle hanging out with Dad for the day." My voice has frozen over, and lightning blazes up from the center of the lake. The small hairs on my arms stand up, and the phone line to crackles and hisses.

The thunder crashes, and I jump back from the glass, feeling the reverb of it in the cavity of my chest. The boom drowns Darren's apology.

"I'll call you if I need you," I say and hang up.

I stare outside for a full minute, while the hairs on my arms slowly lie down, listening to the little ebb and flow of conversation from the kitchen.

8

Stacy

I'm in the attic because Dad swears the discoloration on the ceiling in the living room is new, and when I climbed up on a chair and touched it, I couldn't say that it didn't feel damp. I couldn't say that it did, either, but it did feel cool, so I pulled the string to drop the stairs, and I'm up here looking for the part of the roof that would be over the living room. My bearings are turned around in the jumble of decorations, boxes, and suitcases. I stand and look at the roof line, trying to orient myself. In my head, I see the layout of the house, and I move through a path until the subfloor is gone and the remaining area is covered only by insulation.

"I see it!" I call out when I notice the glistening line of moisture coming down one of the beams, riding a grove before gravity forces it to drop. I pick my way along the trusses, careful not to step off, because surely I would go through the sheetrock. I take the bowl and place it to catch the drips, wishing I'd brought something to mop up the water.

There is plenty of stuff I could use up here, I realize, and head back to the subfloor where I start pushing through boxes, looking for something to put around the bowl to catch splashes. There are curtains; there are boxes full of Christmas decorations; there are boxes of old clothes that she couldn't bear to discard. One box contains toddler clothes—mine, I assume when I see the tulle and flowered patterns. I dig through, looking at the little bib overalls and realize that these would all fit Shelby. A small flutter rises, and I smile. Mom saved everything. I remember outgrowing favorite outfits and her saying she'd put it away for when I had kids. She must have forgotten. I muscle the box up in my arms—my goal of finding an absorbent cloth forgotten—and manhandle the box, precariously, down the ladder.

"Look what I found." I laugh, setting the box down in the hall, calling out for Shelby to see.

They both come. "What is it?"

"Old clothes, from when I was your age." I smile and glance at Dad before looking back into the box. I look back up, trying to understand the faraway look on his face.

"You were such a skinny little thing when we got you," he says, catching my eyes, and I laugh.

"I was always a skinny little thing."

He nods and turns, walking with a shuffling step down the hall, looking old.

"That was odd." I mouth the words but don't say them aloud. Shelby is digging through the clothes, and I leave her to take a towel into the attic to put around the bowl. When I come back down, Shelby is nearly chin deep in the pile of clothes she has pulled from the box.

"Look at this one." I laugh and pull out a tulle purple skirt.

"Ooooh," Shelby says, her eyes glistening, excited.

"It will probably fall apart if I wash it." We laugh, and I call out, "Dad, is it okay if I run a load of wash?"

"Sure." He comes shuffling back down the hall, to show me how to use the washer. I let him demonstrate, although it's the same washer that's been here for years. I learned how to wash clothes using this straightforward washing machine.

"I forgot Mom saved all this stuff."

"She saved everything." He looks at me for a long second before shaking his head. "I think I'm going to go lie down. I feel a little tired."

"Are you okay?"

"I'm fine. Just feeling old." We've had lunch, and it's closing in on Shelby's nap time as well. Even though the excitement of the box of clothes perked her up, she still looks a little droopy around the edges.

"I think Shelby's tired, too."

Dad looks down at her, and she nods. "You can come nap with me. When we wake up, maybe your mama will make us hot chocolate."

"Sure." Shelby can be bribed with chocolate to do just about anything. I wonder how my dad knew that—it's not like the girls are growing up next door.

Shelby waggles her eyebrows at me, feeling like she's gotten the better end of the deal. She follows Grandpa to the bed, and I have a moment of panic, realizing she is going to lay her head on the pillow my mother died on, that she is going to sleep just as my mother did and maybe never wake up. I shake my head. I know I have issues, morbid thoughts, depressive tendencies, hypochondria. I force myself to let it go.

It would seem crazy to insist on a different bed or to refuse to let her nap with Grandpa. I clench my teeth and force myself to be still. I don't want to pass my issues on to my children. I finish filling the laundry tub, adding my old clothes, wondering if any of them will survive.

When I peek back into the room where my dad and daughter are lying, I hear them talking, Shelby's arm outstretched, pointing to the ceiling. My father chuckles at something she has said, and she flops her arms down across his neck, hugging him to her.

"You okay?" I ask, moving on quiet feet to the side of the bed, almost holding my breath.

"I love Grandpa," Shelby whispers, and Grandpa's grin deepens, but he doesn't open his eyes.

"Me, too, sweetheart." She rolls on her side, takes a deep breath and closes her eyes, ready now for her nap. I leave them to it and find my calm in the kitchen, with my hands around a reheated mug of coffee.

I let my mind wander, rolling through my life, slipping past the dark days when my eyeliner was thick, and I preferred my chokers leather and studded. I see pictures from that time and just can't reconcile it with me. How did my mother stand it? I hope my children don't go through that phase. It was a mask, all that eyeliner. I understand that now, after the therapy. Hours spent sitting across from the shrink, trying not to talk. My hour of lying. It was an accident. I hadn't been trying to commit suicide, but the scars on my wrists suggested otherwise. I didn't take the sleeping pills to die. I took the sleeping pills to sleep. If I'd told her I was trying to shut up the voices in my head, she would have locked me up again. Somehow, even the trying not to talk had helped, and along the way, the voices calmed and the anger subsided. Maybe it just scared me, realizing how close I had come to dying. I'd like to say that everything was better after that—that Mom and I connected and understood each other, but we never really did. Not until after Sophie was born.

I feel the melancholy like weight, dropping down over my shoulders. I head back to the washer, checking on Shelby and Dad as I go. Their hands link across her stomach, and I snap a quick picture to send to John. Then I send it to Darren, too, so he can know that everything is fine.

My phone buzzes with an unknown number. Local. "Hello?"

"Stacy?"

"Yes." It doesn't feel like a telemarketer call, but I'm ready to hang up at the first sign.

"This is Sue."

"Oh. Hi." I lean against the washer, folding one arm across my stomach, resting my elbow on the wrist, a prop.

"So I was wondering if Shelby would like to have a playdate?"

"She's taking a nap right now. When are you thinking?"

"Well, Jack doesn't have daycare tomorrow, so he'll be at the shop with me. We have a playroom in the back."

I tilt my head, squinting my eyes. "Well, why doesn't Jack come here? They can play outside if it doesn't rain, and Shelby would love that."

"Oh. Are you sure?"

"I can't leave Dad, you know?" I don't know if she does know, but it's better than me saying that I don't let my kids play at other people's houses. You just can't trust anybody these days.

"Oh. Well, maybe it's not a good idea."

"No, why don't you bring him by tomorrow after lunch, or we can come get him, and they can have the afternoon?" It feels too complicated, and I wish she hadn't called.

"I didn't mean for you to watch my kid."

"No, of course not, but it just makes more sense. It would probably do us all good to have a friend over."

"If you're sure?"

"Of course. Shelby would love it. We all would."

"Okay," she concedes, and a small sigh comes across the line. It hits me that maybe the years after high school have not been kind to Sue. "He would love that. I'll bring him by after lunch. Are you sure?"

"Absolutely." My voice is all benevolence and calm. It's the right thing to do, and since I'm not going to have to go pick him up, it will be fine. She'll bring him, and then she'll come get him. Shelby will have a new little friend. It will be good. Maybe Sue can have a few minutes to herself—what a luxury that must be to her, with all her kids and her work.

"All right. Tomorrow then?"

"Tomorrow." We disconnect, and I stand for a moment before I swap laundry from washer to dryer and scoop the last of the clothes out of the bottom of the box. I scoot it to the side of the hall, out of the way until I can break it down and take it to the recycling bin.

A knock on the front door draws me down the hall, and I rush to the door, not wanting whoever it is to ring the bell for fear that they will wake Dad and Shelby from their naps.

I fling the door wide, ready to tell the Jehovah's Witness to be gone, but it's not a solicitor with pamphlets for a church… it's Cassie Carter. Cassie, who had been my best friend until I went off the deep end. She looks so nervous and uncomfortable that I almost laugh.

"Hey, girl," she says, and just like that, I feel sixteen again.

"Wow! Cassie Carter."

"Hernandez, now. You remember Theo?"

"Theo Horn-andez?" I step out onto the porch and hug her. Theo was a popular football star back in the day and always had the best-looking girls trying to get with him.

"Yeah." She blushes, knowing what I'm thinking.

"You married the Horn-Dog?" I laugh, not meaning anything by it.

"I sure did." There is pride in her voice, and I remember my manners, inviting her in, explaining that Dad and my little girl are napping. We make our way to the kitchen, and I offer to make a fresh pot of coffee.

"He's the county sheriff now," she says. The pride in her voice is thick and sincere.

"Theo?" I ask and then laugh. I hadn't meant to sound incredulous, but seriously... Theo was not the guy I thought would grow up to be the county sheriff. Back in high school, he was the next to best resource for quality dope.

She must guess my thought process. "He found his straight-and-narrow."

"I'd like to hear that story sometime."

"You remember Billy Cohen? He was deputy for years here in town."

I shrug, not remembering much from the town. I left a long time ago. There were police, so surely a deputy, so I accept her word for it.

"Well, he put out a scholarship for Theo to go to college. He said it was because he liked to watch him play ball. Theo had to be part of the Big Brother program and to volunteer at the department when he was home from college, but never had to pay any of it back."

"Well, that's cool." I'm impressed. Deputy Cohen must have been a special kind of guy to do something like that. Or a creep—he may have been a creep. People aren't always what they seem. What did he get out of it?

"Yeah, it was. Billy was a good man." The reverence of her glazed eyes suggests that Billy is dead, and I've had quite enough of that melancholy subject to last this week, so I don't ask, just let her comment fall and hold on to the exciting bit, that Theo "Horn-Dog" Hernandez made good.

"I'd rather have a glass of wine," she says when I hold up the silver coffee press.

"Ha. Not in this house." I shrug. "I thought you gave it up."

"Yeah. But a glass of wine every now and then." It had been quite a hullaballoo when Cassie's parents sent her to rehab. I don't know if she had a problem, really—everything with Cassie was so much show. She had been on a path, though, and it seems like rehab maybe wasn't a bad idea. "Theo's a purist, you know. Macronutrients and purified water. I'm hard-pressed to slip a bottle of wine past him."

I laugh. The idea of Theo being a health nut is completely at odds with the boy I remember from high school.

"Sometimes I just miss the party," Cassie admits, wistfully.

"Yeah. I guess." I don't miss the party, though. I love my life, quiet and peaceful, raising my kids, loving my husband. I could never have dreamed how simple and good life could be.

"You must have found your straight-and-narrow, too," she says, leaning her shoulder forward, as if she wants to touch me. We were wild children, Cassie and I, trouble and troubled, and putting on a hell of a show. Occasionally, I catch a glimpse of that old self creeping around the corners in Sophie, and I don't look forward to the coming clashes, I hope I can handle it with as much grace as my mother.

I nod. There is a fine line for me, with alcohol. One or maybe two, and I'm okay, but any more than that makes me feel out of control, uncomfortable. When Cassie and I were teens, experimenting, testing the limits, I sometimes heard voices. I sometimes found myself in places without remembering how I got there. I sometimes lost entire days and had no memory of where I had been or what I had done. Blackouts I understood, but when it started happening without alcohol, it was different, more frightening. I think I broke something, or maybe we let something through Cassie's Ouija board when we were convinced we wanted to be witches. It took me years to be right again. That time was chaos, disruption, dark. It's hard to reconcile that girl with who I have become. Maybe that's what being a teenager is like for everybody, with all those raging hormones and body chemistry in flux. I don't know for sure.

There are still moments when I find myself in a room and don't remember why I am there, but that's normal. That's raising a family. That's sleeping with one eye open.

"I was sorry to hear about your mom," she says, shifting to a topic that makes us both less uncomfortable.

"Yeah, it's a shock."

"How's your dad?"

"I don't know. I think he's still a little shaken."

"I always liked your parents." I nod. I start to say that my parents always liked her, too, but it isn't true, and she knows it. They blamed her for what happened in our sophomore year; it was her house from which I had disappeared. It was her party. Even now, all these years away from it, I want to ask her again about what happened that night, I want her to tell again about the boy—the man, really—who arrived at the high-school party, the man I'd apparently left with. We've been through it before. The police even did a composite sketch of the man, but nothing ever came of it. I couldn't say I was kidnapped, and everybody said that I seemed to know him.

"They're good people." I say, feeling the catch in my throat. She was my most significant influence those years, leading up to my break, and I wonder what her life has been like, really like, since high school

Cassie was theatrical, and her drama was huge. Most of it was a show for her, calling out to get the attention she didn't get at home. It wasn't her fault; I know that in my mind, but when she opened the doors, talking about contacting the other side, wanting to escape, I just kind of fell through. I had identity issues, like all teens, I guess, and depression was always on my shoulder. She was strange back then, sleeping with her tarot deck under her pillow, cleansing it in the moonlight. When the voices started after that, when I started losing time more and more often, I thought I was possessed by somebody we had contacted. If we hadn't opened the door, would they have stayed quiet?

When I had told her about the voices, she played along; telling me that she heard them too, and I'm still not sure if she just didn't want to be left out or if she did. She had admitted when she came to the hospital, when I was there the second time, that they didn't talk to her anymore, and the way she said it made me think that maybe they never had.

Cassie didn't punch holes in my head; she just helped show me the path. It would have happened anyway. My therapist said my break came from some emotional crisis in my childhood. But I'd had a great childhood, and there was nothing I could point to that even constituted upheaval, let alone crisis. We never found an answer.

But where had I gone that night? Where was I for those three days? I shake my head, yanking myself forward through the years. There is no point in dwelling on that. The year after was a nightmare, and most of it lives in the dark holes of my mind. I know I'd raided my mother's prescriptions, even if I don't remember doing it, which landed me in the hospital a second time. It seems like it was somebody else, somebody I watched in a movie, not like it was me. Not like it was real.

That's why I stopped writing, because I had to listen to the voices, and they were never kind.

They were so loud by then, and they hated me so much.

9

Stacy

The next morning dawns bright, the sun splashing through the kitchen windows with blinding intensity. The decorative curtains do nothing to shade the room, and I squint against the light.

"Are you excited about your playdate?" I ask. Shelby is sitting at the island, a plate of bread and honey in front of her.

She nods. "I miss Julia, though."

"I know. We'll be back home next week. It'll be okay."

"What's Jack like?"

"I don't know. I've not met him."

"What if he's mean?" she asks, crinkling her nose.

"I'm pretty sure he won't be mean. His mama was a friend of mine from high school." Which is not true, but close enough. I don't think Sue could raise a mean kid.

"What is she like?"

I think about Sue, meeting her at the shop, seeing her as a different person. "She's nice. She's one of those people that tries to make other people happy."

"Oh."

"It will be fun. We can play outside, if it's not too muddy."

"Can we go swimming?"

"Do you have a hook-up on a pool?" I ask, because while we have one at home, pools aren't as easy to come by in Georgia.

She shakes her head, looking sad. "I miss Sophie."

"Me, too."

"And Daddy."

"I miss your bunnies." I reach around her and squeeze her, seeing her little lip pucker out.

"And Bonnie and Brisky." We've made the list and missed them all. A playdate will be good, and I'm grateful that Sue followed up, because I wouldn't have. I would have let my daughter be lonely and sad before I had reached out to Sue Bellafonte for anything. Being in this house has sent me backward, like all my hormones have gone pubescent. Just because I've lost my mom doesn't mean I cannot take care of my family. Life goes on, and I'm not a child anymore. I don't have the luxury of only worrying about myself.

~ ~ ~

Sue arrives with her redheaded son. She looks like a yellow balloon with her huge breasts pressing against the buttons of her slightly-too-tight lemony shirt. Her jeans are those stretchy denim look, not even blue-jean material, and her rolls are contained like sausages in a skin. Then she smiles, that beautiful smile I remember from high school, and all the weight and my ugly mental commentary slips away and I see again the girl she used to be. I think I hated her so much then because I wanted to be her, or at least, be like her.

Shelby bounds against my hip, "Hi, I'm Shelby. You are Jack."

He nods and tucks just a little behind his mom.

"He's a little shy," Sue explains.

"Oh, my sister is shy, too, and Julia . . . she doesn't talk to anybody but me. Come meet my Grandpa." Shelby takes his hand, and he lets himself be drawn away.

"He'll be okay. Shelby's really good with people," I say.

She hesitates; I see the pause, the hesitation in her standing on the front porch. I open the door wider, realizing I've not invited her in. "Come in, if you have a minute?"

"I have a minute. Mom is at the store."

"How is your mom?"

"She's good. Still makes pies for the diner."

"That's right! I forgot she used to do that. Her rhubarb pie was the best."

"Still is." We laugh. "It's just so great to see you," she says, like it is a truth.

"You, too," I say, believing my own words.

"So, what have you been up to?" I say, intent on asking her about herself and not only thinking about me, the way I had at her shop. We turn down the hall and catch sight of Shelby and Jack standing next to Dad, where he is watching the news. Shelby is doing introductions, and my father is looking at her the same way I sometimes do, like she is some fairy child sent to us on loan, with too much awesomeness for one little body.

"Oh, you know . . . I married John Miller right after college."

"I remember John. How is he?"

"Oh, he's fine. We got divorced two years ago. He moved to Atlanta."

"I'm sorry. I didn't know." I feel awkward, so I do what my mother always did—I offer coffee.

"Don't be. I'm all right. Surprising how life turns out, isn't it?" She settles on one of the stools. I nod. "But you look great. Haven't changed a bit."

I laugh. "I've changed." I hope I have changed.

"Can we go outside?" Shelby asks, bounding into the kitchen with a smiling Jack on her heels, fast friends.

"Sure, we'll come, too." I glance at Sue and see the relief on her face. The concern that her child would not be accepted here, that he would not get along, drains out of her face. Isn't that always what we worry about for our children—that somebody won't be kind to them?

The years spread and lengthen as Sue and I sit on the back deck, talking about everything, and all the awkwardness washes out of me. We are like long-lost friends, catching up. "I was so jealous of you in high school," I say after we have laughed and gotten comfortable with one another.

"Nothing to be jealous of there." A wistful smile parts her lips.

"You were fabulous. Star of every spring musical, cheerleader."

"Homecoming Queen," she adds and laughs.

"Twice," I confirm.

"High school was my kingdom." She is still smiling, but there is sadness in the tilt of her head.

"And now you are the queen of the flower shop."

A low, rumbling laugh escapes her, and I am relieved because the small press of sadness has evaporated.

"Let's not even talk about what I was in high school," I say. High school was not my kingdom.

"You were a Cindy Crawford."

"Hmm," I say, unsure what that means.

"You know . . . she talks in interviews about how she was a wallflower in high school, how people just didn't see her." We turn and look for a long minute at the kids. Shelby is chasing a ball Jack threw out toward the lake. "You transformed after high school."

"You have no idea." The voice coming from my lips is low and sultry. I clear my throat and laugh, feeling unhinged, disjointed. "I hope I'm a better person now than I was then. High school was tough for me."

"I remember. I've wondered about you, and was so happy when Darren told me how well you were doing."

"You and Darren are friends?"

"Yeah, I'd say we are friends. He buys a lot of flowers."

"He does?"

"For open houses. You know, gives a house a pop," she explains.

I nod, and we watch as Shelby overtakes the ball and turns back.

"Now, you're married to an attorney."

There is a sharp ridge in my head that feels almost like pain, the beginning of a migraine, riding high and shiny in the dark meat of my brain. It's been sitting all morning, just like that, pressure behind my eyes, but not culminating. It's how it was when I was a teen, before I'd step out and lose time. It's a nether portal, I think, remembering Sophie's conversation from the other morning. It was a mistake to come home. I feel like somebody else is sitting inside of my head, like the door from the Ouija board is open again. It's just a sense of being off, off-center, out of balance. I know that's all it is—with the loss of my mother, coming back here without all of my anchors.

Nobody else lives inside my head.

But I can feel them, trying to push forward, knocking on the nether portal. It has been so long since I have felt that, the revolving door in my brain.

"'Attorney' is just a job," I say, refocusing, staying connected.

"It's a good job."

"It is, but it's a lot of long hours. There are a lot of evenings with just me and the girls."

"At least you got a man." She sighs, and our conversation rolls, grounded again in the present, kids, relationships, safely away from that other me from so long ago.

"Do you remember Cassie Carter?"

"I do. You two still in touch?"

"No. Not really. She stopped by yesterday, out of the blue. It was strange to see her. It's strange to be here." Our attention draws to Jack and Shelby, watching as they run toward the lake in pursuit of the ball. We are both prepared to launch to our feet if they get too close to the water's edge, but the ball slows and stops, cradled in the root of one of the river oaks.

"I never thought she'd stay in town."

"Me neither. I thought she had 'Hollywood' written all over her."

"I know. She had some drama. She seemed good, though. Not so . . ." I shrug when I cannot find the right word.

"Strange?" Sue offers, and I laugh, the ridge in my mind easing, slipping back from my eyes. "You know she married Theo Hernandez?"

"She mentioned that."

"Dang. He was good-looking back then, wasn't he?" We laugh like schoolgirls, and the shade begins to tilt across the deck. An easy hour passes, then two, almost three, and the sharp pain in my mind recedes.

The kids play, and we talk about life and the path we've each taken, the journeys our old classmates have made.

I turn and check on Dad, finding him napping at one point, changing channels at another.

10

Stacy

"Doris?" His voice echoes down the hall, and I start, rolling out of bed and placing a pillow beside Shelby in one motion. It is the art of waking up on full alert, a skill learned by parenting. He calls again, and I rush from my room and see the hulk of his shape shuffling down the hall toward the living room.

"Dad," I call in a loud whisper, not wanting him to wake Shelby. I reach him and touch his arm. He jerks away, then sees it is me.

"Where's your mother? She isn't in bed." He raises his voice again, calling her name.

"Dad. Stop. You're going to wake Shelby." He is like an old steam engine, chugging forward with determination, through the living room, through the kitchen, down the hall, and to the front door. I can do nothing to impede his progress; I am a fly on the butt of a hippopotamus, an annoyance but not a hindrance. He opens the front door wide and bellows into the night. "Doris."

I grasp at his hands, his flailing agitated hands, and force him to look at me.

"Stop. Mom isn't here."

"Where the hell did she go?" He pulls free of me and is shuffling down the steps. Panic flares in my chest, fluttering like a caged bird. I can't leave my daughter alone in the house. I can't let him go off on his own.

The door is standing wide open; if she wakes up, she'll find me. I have to keep him on the front lawn. He bellows again, and I cringe, rushing down the drive to catch up to him.

The moon is high, half a face, and deep shadows fall under the trees and under my father as he marches determinedly to the street. A dog barks in the distance, and I wish I had grabbed my phone. I need Darren. I can't do this on my own. How am I supposed to get him back into the house? I can't leave my daughter. I need my phone.

I've reached him. He has finally stopped moving and is looking from one end of the street to the other.

"Dad, what would Mom be doing out here in the middle of the night?"

"Well, where is she?" He is nearly prancing, needing to move but unsure of where to turn. "Where is she?" he demands and calls her name again. Lights begin to flicker on in the neighbor's house. The caged bird I'm my head loops, I'm torn, I can't leave my daughter. He's causing a scene. We are waking the neighbors.

The pressure builds behind my eyes, blooming, impeding my vision, blurring my thoughts, then . . . Pop.

I am standing back on the front porch but can see myself standing in the driveway with him, my nightshirt fluttering in the breeze, my hair lifting and falling.

11

Shiloh

"She's dead," the voice hisses, cold and clear.

My face is frozen, a mask, my brows low and close. He's a foolish old man, causing a scene.

12

Stacy

"She's dead."

I hear it, but from the distance across the yard.

I am standing on the porch, watching.

The woman standing with my father is straight and lean, the flat of her back braced and tight. I see the recognition on his face, the moment the words sink in, and the meat of his hand smashes into her cheek.

It's me. I know it's me standing there, but it's also me standing here.

The impact brings us back together and I am again just one woman, feeling the jarring of the impact of the slap throughout my whole frame. I stumble back and land with a thud on the rocks of the drive. "Holy shit, Dad," I gasp, my hand flies up to cover my face. He has turned away and is starting into the road. I scramble to my feet and stand out of arms reach of him.

"Where is she? Where is she?" He mumbles like the words are rolling through his mind and falling free, unbidden, a waterfall of confusion.

"She went to visit Aunt Mari. Remember?" I try this tack. The side of my face is stinging, on fire, and my eye is watering.

He turns slowly toward me, and I can almost see the thoughts, the acceptance that maybe he has just forgotten.

"Oh. She did?"

"Yeah, remember? She'll be back in a couple of days." The lie rolls off my tongue. Should I tell him when she will be back? Should I tell him when she left? How am I supposed to lie to him when it isn't about something I don't remember doing? I lied to them all through my teen years, about drinking the family liquor, about taking his truck, and always it was with conviction because I never remembered any of it. I don't like this, fabricating stories, because I'm afraid I won't be able to remember what I've said later.

"Oh." He still looks confused, but he is shuffling out of the street and back toward the driveway. He climbs up the porch steps. From the corner of my eye, I see the man next door standing on his porch, watching us, and I give him a small wave, indicating that everything is fine. Nothing to see here. I'm scared that he will call out and break the spell I'm casting with my words.

"Mari is putting up jellies this week, remember? Mom went to help because Mari has such a hard time getting the seal on tight with her arthritis." It's all plausible; it's all true... but from somewhere in the past. It is the familiarity of the story that draws him back, and when we finally make it to the house, his agitation is gone. "Why don't you go on back to bed. The sun won't be up for hours. We'll give her a call in the morning, and you can ask her when she's coming home."

He nods, and I leave him at the door of his bedroom. Should I walk him to his bed? The way I walk with the girls after they've had a bad dream. Should I make sure he settles? I am not entirely comfortable following him, but I do. I pull the covers back over him.

He's a grown man, and I'm not sure what he needs from me. But he is scared; I know that well enough. I lean down and kiss his forehead, whispering, "I love you."

But I think he is already back asleep, and I wonder if maybe he was never really awake.

~ ~ ~

Shelby is still asleep when I get back to our room, wrapped around the pillow I had left, lying sideways across the bed. I let out a long sigh, looking at her, cast in luminescence from the moon through the half-circle window high on the wall. The light makes her glow, and I lean then slide down the wall to sit on the floor, watching the bow of her mouth as she dreams, unwilling to wake her.

I put my hand up to my cheek, checking for damage—just a slight warmth for the memory. I won't sleep again tonight. My soul spasms. I review the moment when my mind popped, when I was standing on the porch, watching him with the woman who was me but was not me. I'd heard her words from across the yard, and the words, spoken cold and hard, had yanked me off the porch and back into my body in the split second before he hit me. What had she said? I can't quite catch them, her words, but the tone was clear, cold and hard and angry.

She is me, and I am her. This is not the first time I have watched from a distance as someone else worked my body, used my lips. More often, when it happened before, I felt myself squashed down inside myself, hearing my words but not being in control of them, feeling my body move but having no power to do anything different. It has been a very long time, though, and my stomach churns that she is back, that I am, again, not alone inside my skin.

What had I, as that other me, said? I had heard it, but now the memory is gone, and I can only see them, us, standing, words passing between them, us, then the arc of his hand making contact, and I was back inside of my body just in time to feel the blow, landing on my backside on the gravel.

I try to settle myself, the spasm in my soul, for all my lost memories. I probe into the dark space, trying to calm the racing of my heart. The moment he struck me, there was a flash of memory, of being hit like that some time before. Not just a déjà vu moment, like the harkening of a dream at waking, but the real and substantial memory of a hand across my face and that familiar, unfamiliar blinding pain.

What had I said, out there in the yard?

I shake my head, pulling away from the dark hole.

He was just agitated; maybe I hadn't said anything at all. Of course, that's why I can't remember. I hadn't said anything.

A little voice inside my head whispers, "Fool."

There were plenty enough nights when I heard such words when I was self-destructing, during that long, horrible year after the break.

My mind cycles back, and I know I've been hit like that sometime before. I remember. Was there some boy who had hit me for some vicious thing I said? I was good enough at provoking anger back then.

I shake my head. It wasn't a boy.

In my mind's eye, the face attached to the hitting arm is my own.

13

Baby

Mama is mad. She's so mad. My face stings where she hit me. She is screaming at Slim, because she knows that he's the one who pushed out the window, and she thinks he made me go with him.

Slim is bleeding. His lip is busted, and I tried to make her stop, but she hit me and made the angry face, and I ran down the hall to get way, hearing her scream as she hit him again.

I am crying, but I can hear Slim, whimpering, and it's my fault. He would have got away if I hadn't followed him, but now she's going to kill him, and then she's going to kill me.

My lip puckers in and out of my mouth, spit spraying. I am back in our room, past our cage, and scuttle into the closet, where it is dark and quiet and I can almost not hear.

I fold my face onto my knees, trying to make myself small and invisible in the closet. Maybe she'll forget I'm here. Maybe she'll forget I was ever here.

He's gonna be so mad. When she is done with him, he will come to get me, and then I'm going to be in real trouble.

14

Stacy

"Mama?" the voice comes from far away.

I shift in my sitting position, opening my eyes to darkness.

I am folded over my knees; my body aches from sitting up. My muscles are tense, even in sleep I strained with my arms wrapped around my knees, my bony butt on the hard wood of the floor. Pain shoots through my core as I unfold.

I am completely disjointed, confused.

"Mama?" The voice comes muffled by the door between us, by the fabric of clothes hanging from the rod.

I push my hands up over my face, pressing the sockets of my eyes.

"I'm here," I call back, wiping crust from the corners of my mouth, pushing forward, past the trailing garments, reaching up for the knob of the closet door. I feel stunned, shell-shocked, waking up in a closet.

Shelby giggles, seeing me come out of the closet, and I make a silly face, so she won't see how wrong everything is.

"What were you doing?"

"Looking for Narnia," I answer, and I'm surprised the by easy tone of my voice, that easy response, the easy way the lie tripped off my tongue.

"Did you find it?" Shelby is instantly excited. She doesn't really understand the movie—it's too slow, too complex—but she did appreciate stepping into a closet and out past a ledge into a winter wonderland.

"I think I may have," I say, spilling onto the bed with her. She squeals and wraps her arms around my head, squeezing with all her might.

How long has it been since the last time I found myself in a closet? It was well before the girls.

I should never have come back here.

15

Stacy

The sun is streaming through the kitchen windows, and Shelby is eating a bowl of oatmeal. I have Darren on the phone, relaying to him the events of the night. In the light of day, it's easy to pretend that it happened the way I tell it. It seems silly to have been so panicked. I don't mention my moment on the porch; I don't say that he slapped me. I only tell him the story of Mom being at Aunt Mari's, canning jellies. I certainly don't tell him I woke up in the closet, because that's just weird.

"That was smart," Darren says.

"He's really bad," I whisper, turning away from Shelby.

"Sometimes," Darren agrees.

"I didn't know what to do."

"It sounds like you handled it well."

"Does that happen often?"

"I'm not sure how often, Mom didn't like to talk about it. So I don't know."

"What are we going to do? It was frightening."

I hear Dad shuffling down the hall, heading toward me, and I tell Darren I have to go. I turn to face him, scared of which person I will find there. He walks behind Shelby and ruffles her hair. "How's the big girl?" he asks.

"Good." She puts her arms up to hug him, and his eyes land on mine, light and comfortable, until I look away. Does he think Mom is at Mari's today, or does he know she is gone? How am I supposed to do this? Do I just wait until he gives me an indicator? Does he remember slapping me? Does he remember what I said to him? What was it that I said? I stretch back but find only the image, the silent movie reeling in my mind.

"You look tired," he says, coming toward me. I feel the muscles of my legs twitching to step back, and I force myself not to move. He lifts a hand to my cheek, not quite touching, but I can feel the heat from his palm. On my jawline, there is a slight purpling, probably at the point where his ring hit. I put my hand up, covering the spot, turning away.

"I stepped into the door going to the bathroom last night. I'm fine. Toast?"

"That would be nice." He sits down next to Shelby. "How is that oatmeal today?"

"Berry good!" She giggles, then laughs. "Get it? It's berry good because it has strawberries!"

"That's very punny."

They guffaw, and I listen, smiling away from them, waiting for the toast to pop, waiting for my father to let me know where we are today.

~ ~ ~

"I'll ace it," Sophie says, in the quick conversation I get with her before she heads to school. Pride and confidence electrify the airwaves between her phone and mine.

"Excellent." My heart swells. My amazing Sophie, who is so grown up and proud of her abilities. Did I ever make my mother feel like that, or was I always fighting with her about something? I try to remember conversations, but it all comes up as a void. There was always contention between us, some battle. I wish I could step back in time and remember why I was mad at her. What had she done? What was it? What was wrong with me? I wasn't like that with Dad, just with her—the nicest woman I probably ever knew. "I miss you."

"I miss you, too. Dad says we're coming up in the morning. They gave me an excuse to be absent; I don't have to go to school."

"Good." Relief washes over me, I can wait one more day to see her. I can survive that long. I should have known that I would need both of them here to ground me, to keep me in place. Tonight is just one more night, and I can get through it, whatever it brings, knowing that John and Sophie will be here tomorrow.

Dad never does let me know where he is mentally, so I am careful not to mention anything that might trigger a response. It's like walking on glass.

Shelby takes him out to the lake in the afternoon, and they find a shallow with a dozen or more tadpoles. I watch from the deck, my coffee mug warming my hands. Dad shuffles to the shed and brings back two fishing poles, and they sit in the gazebo, casting hookless lines into to water. I leave them. Shelby will do him more good than I can.

Later, I take ice water out to them, and they are rooted in conversation about the importance of being kind. "So I just told her that if she wants people to like her, she has to be nice." I catch the inflections of her sister in her voice, and I wonder if it is her story or Sophie's story, retold.

"That was very smart of you." He reels in his line, and she does, too, imitating his motions with sincere effort. "How did you get so smart?"

"I don't know." She shrugs, casting her line, mature and nonchalant.

Dad glances at me and probably sees the well of tears in my eyes. I smile, my vision going blurry. No matter how poorly I was made, my children are extraordinary. I offer the water.

"That sounds nice." He compresses his lips and nods, accepting a glass. What his eyes are saying is, "Good job. You're doing a good job," and I hastily wipe the tears before Shelby can see me crying and turn back up toward the house, finally letting them fall, feeling blown apart.

I miss my mom.

I stand for a long minute, letting the grief wash through my soul, filling the corners of my heart, recognizing that I will never again be able to call her and ask her how to make something. "Mom, do you remember that goulash you used to make?" "Mom, what kind of crackers do you use in your meatloaf?" "Mom, how do you make fried green tomatoes?"

The laundry timer goes off, and I head down the hall, still sniffling, still thinking about all the food I'll never be able to cook like my mom did, and I trip over the box from the attic that I should have already broken down for recycling. I swap the laundry from the washer to the dryer and pick the box up on my way back to the kitchen.

"No time like the present," I say, hearing my mother in my mind.

Something slides in the bottom of the box. I tip it up, and a dark brown envelope slides out and onto the floor. It lands with a thump. It is nearly an inch thick.

Brown packing tape seals the flap. I study it as I head toward the kitchen, toward the light streaming through the windows. There is nothing written on the outside. A small hollow pit grows in my stomach, and I feel the weight of the envelope increasing. What an odd thing to find at the bottom of a box of old clothes. It feels like a gift, just when I was missing her so much. Will the papers inside show the moments when I made her proud, the times I got it right growing up? Surely she was sometimes proud of me the way I am proud of my children. Will this be the answer to why my mother always stood by me, why she still fought for me when I was so busy fighting against her? I'd put her through so much.

I slide a knife along the fold of the top flap, anticipation sending a quiver through the tips of my fingers. A packet of papers slips out and onto the counter, followed by another sealed envelope with the initial "S" in a corner. Newspaper clippings are also in the first envelope, yellowed and brittle with age. "Children Found in Dog Kennel." The bold-type words span two small columns of print.

The story reads:

Two children were removed from what authorities described as a "filthy" White Springs trailer home, where a four-year-old girl and a nine-year-old boy were discovered in a wire dog kennel, police said Thursday. White Springs officers went to the home late Wednesday after receiving an anonymous call asking that police check on the welfare of the children living there, Police Lt. Andrew Torley said.

When officers entered the trailer, they were met with the stench of trash and feces throughout the home. An officer discovered the children in a back bedroom inside a 54 x 36 x 45-inch wire dog kennel. "The children were filthy and asleep on a pallet of tattered blankets, inside the crate," when they were discovered. The door was locked with a padlock.

One adult was present at the time, a woman claiming to be the mother of the two children. Dr. C. R. Montelbaum, prominent local psychiatrist, owns the property, and when questioned, he was unaware that children were living there. Kristine Moony, who rents the lot and trailer, age 24, is a patient of Dr. Montelbaum, and suffers from mental illness. This story is developing.

The next clipping, also yellowed and brittle, shows a bone-thin woman with stringy, blond hair and wide eyes staring from hollowed sockets. "White Springs Woman Pleads Guilty to Child Endangerment."

A White Springs mother pleaded guilty and was sentenced Wednesday to endangering the welfare of children. Kristine Moony, 24, who deals with mental health problems, explained that she locked her children in a dog kennel to keep them from climbing out of the trailer window, which was broken and would not latch. She signed court documents, relinquishing parental rights to the children after receiving counseling from the Department of Family Services. The children will be placed in foster care until permanent placement can be arranged. Ms. Moony will be sentenced next month in the case, and until then remains in county custody.

I drop the clipping from my hands and draw my fingers to my face to the back of my head, tangling them in my hair. How horrifying. Those poor children. Bile sits low in the back of my throat. I shuffle out the last contents of the envelope, a series of photographs of the two bone-thin children, ribs pushing through their skin, hollow-cheeked, hollow-eyed.

At first, that is all I see, the parts of the images—the curve of a skull under thin, matted hair, the overlarge eyes, dead and hollow. The knobs of folded knees, the long, narrow length of a forearm, the ridge of a wrist. Then the image blends, and I don't see the parts; I see the shape of the face, the arch of the brow. I see Shelby.

My skin erupts in gooseflesh, and I drop the pictures on the counter and push away, feeling the surge of my blood coursing through my veins, feeling the heat in my lungs, the obstruction in my throat, blocking air from passing. I am gasping for breath when I get to the front door and burst onto the front porch. The fresh air washes over me, and I breathe deeply. My skin is crawling. Under my hair, my scalp is rippling, and I spin down the steps and onto the sidewalk. The afternoon is settling in long shadows across the yard, casting the trees as silhouettes.

I try to calm myself, the roiling of my stomach, the charging cadence of my heart. I snap my feet to mountain pose and try to concentrate on the air passing through my lungs and into the world, but the breaths are coming in sobs, and the name that is coming from my lips is "Slim." It is whispered and desperate, and I know that name because the face that was Shelby's wasn't my face—it was the boy, the brother.

16

Shiloh

I am the one who belongs. I should be here, not Stacy. It was me with Mama and Slim, not her. Doris took us away from Mama, and she needed us, needed me. Mama needed us, and Doris stole us and then wouldn't give me back, and I never saw Mama again. Except for the once, when she came here to take me home, and Doris wouldn't even let me see her. Mama needed me.

Anger floods through my veins and my lip curls above my teeth, feeling the set of them, recognizing the braces are gone. I always expect there to be braces.

Doris is gone now, so Stacy can't push me away anymore. Slim got back to her, somehow, some way he got back to her, but he wasn't her baby. He wasn't the one who made her smile.

She had such a beautiful smile; no wonder all the men loved her. That's why we had to be quiet, when the men were there. They didn't want brats. They only wanted Mama, and they wouldn't come back if they knew we were there. Dr. Curtis most of all—he really didn't like us being there, and he was the only one who knew. He only liked Slim, though, and always took him away, and when he'd bring him back, Slim would be mean and hateful, but he'd smell like the most delicious food. I remember waiting for him to fall asleep just so I could turn and smell his breath.

Poor Mama! Pain blooms in my chest—loneliness for her. Even when she was angry, making the angry face, slapping out to catch me or

Slim, she was so beautiful. We were bad, Slim and I. We made her act like that, like the day we ran away and she found us. She was so angry then. Dr. Curtis was so angry, said we'd nearly "blown it," even though I didn't really understand that part. It was Slim's fault. He hurt her so bad by running away. She said he was old enough to know better, but I didn't know what that meant, and not long after that, the men came and broke through the door and made Mama scream and cry. Slim turned his face away from her as we were carried out, but I had looked at her, her face crumpled in on itself—not beautiful, for once, but so sad, so hurt.

Stacy doesn't have to stay now. Doris is gone.

My left eyebrow cocks up, and I raise my arms to the sky. I am out. Energy is burning in my blood, and I stand for a long minute, enjoying the air on my skin.

I could just leave, disappear.

Secrets. All the dirty little secrets.

I don't have to stay here, living the life that Stacy made. It is a revelation; it is power.

Stacy is in my head, screaming.

What did you think Doris would have? School papers, locks of your hair? I want to ask, but she isn't listening, just screaming and screaming and screaming.

I turn out toward the road. I could just walk away and leave all this behind.

I don't know why I don't.

When I look back at the house, Stacy stops screaming, and I just know it's not the right time. I can't leave yet, so I take a deep breath and walk toward the house. I have nowhere to run. It has been a very long time since I've been out. It is better to bide my time. There are people I need to find, first.

17

Stacy

I am at the front door, my hand on the knob, halfway through a turn, and I feel jarred. What am I doing out here? Was I just standing in the yard? I turn and glance to the yard, half expecting to see another me still there, like last night, but the grass stretches out to the road, vacant, empty. I take a deep breath and push the door open.

I'm just so tired.

Time is slipping. I have to keep a better hold on it, or everything will fall apart again.

Suddenly I remember the horrible envelope with its contents splayed across the counter and I rush into the house. I shouldn't have left it lying out. What if Shelby had come in and found those images, her face etched on the scrawny boy's countenance?

Secrets, secrets, all the dirty secrets, whispers in my head, singsong, like a child's rhyme.

I feel guilty, low in the pit of my stomach, like I was doing something I shouldn't have been doing. Everything feels off, and I'm only coming back to where I was in stutters and stops, remembering things in chunks. I wasn't doing anything wrong, I was about to break a box down for recycling, and this envelope—this packet of horrors—was in the bottom. It was just there, like it was waiting for me, like it was waiting for me to find it, to open it, to know its secrets.

Where are the school papers? Where are the baby pictures, where are the notes about me learning to walk or potty train? There is nothing here but a horror show.

Secrets, secrets, all the dirty secrets.

Shelby and Grandpa are coming in through the back door, and I slide the contents back into the envelope as I turn to face them, feeling the stretch of my skin into a smile that feels more like a grimace.

Shelby launches, and I catch her and lift her to my chest, folding in around her. "Did you catch anything?" My voice sobs out of me, and I shudder, trying to contain myself. I don't want to scare her. I'm okay; I have to look okay. At least the papers are tucked away, hidden, gone.

"No." She laughs, not feeling my distress. "We didn't use hooks," she whispers, and I wonder if she thinks that was a mistake.

"That's all right," I whisper back.

"Yep, we didn't want to catch any fish."

I sob, unable to contain it.

Shelby squeezes my neck, her hot little body melting into me. I scoop the envelope off the counter and carry it, along with my daughter, back to the room we are sharing.

"Good fishing?" I call to Dad as I pass him in the living room, where he has just picked up the remote for the television.

"She's a natural." There is laughter in his voice, a small happy in a week of tragedy.

I set Shelby on the bed we shared last night and wipe my eyes.

"I'm sorry you're sad, Mommy," she says. She cannot comprehend that I'm not just "sad." I am destroyed... I am blown apar... I am fragments spreading to the far corners of the earth.

"I'm okay. I just need a big Shelby hug." I squeeze her again, pulling all my far-flung pieces back to me, stitching the shards of my shattered soul back together. When I feel that I can release her without coming apart all over again, I do and then tuck the envelope into the zippered pocket of my suitcase. A thief hiding my contraband.

18

Stacy

Friday morning finds me back in the attic, ostensibly checking the damage from the leak. I spend a good minute feeling around the beam where I had found water draining during the storm, and the wood is now dry. When I am satisfied, I go to the boxes, stacked and leaning, and glance inside those that are easiest to look in without rearranging, without making a noise that might give away my snooping. I want pictures, documents, proof that the images and materials found in the envelope cannot pertain to me. I need to find a picture of my mother pregnant, holding Darren on her hip, the way I carried Sophie when I was expecting Shelby. I see a box of old photos and take it down the ladder.

"Shelby?" I call, letting the ladder go up, slamming it home. "Shel?" I head down the hall. She is standing with dad, hand in hand, at one of the four full-length kitchen windows.

"We have babies," she whispers, shushing me with her tone. I set the box of pictures on the table and join them peering through the glass. A pair of geese are coming up from the edge of the lake into the side yard, followed by their seven progeny. The babies are little more than puffs, and I stand, awed by the power of small creatures to restore the world. It's what having the girls did to me, grounded me, gave me purpose. All the chaos in my soul ebbs, and the cyclone of emotions that started raging yesterday, with the opening of the yellow envelope, suddenly sputters and dies. The sharp ridge of strain behind my eyes recedes, and for the first time in hours, I don't feel that I am clutching the insides of my head, holding myself together.

We stand at the window, the three of us, watching the small family edging nearer the drive, the father on alert, the mother with her head nudging through the grass, the babies following, letting her teach them the small things for survival while the male keeps a wary eye.

"How was the roof?" Dad asks when the family has moved to the front of the house, blocked from our view by the bushes lining the drive.

"Oh, it looks good. I think it was just the one. I'm sure John can fix it." John worked his way through college doing construction, and there's no doubt he'll know how to repair the leak.

"Good," Dad says.

"I found some old pictures. From when we were little," I say, indicating the box I've set on the table, and Dad looks confused.

"What pictures?"

"I don't know, just from when we were little." He processes my comment into a coherent thought, looking irritated. I am not sure if he is annoyed that I am snooping or annoyed that he hadn't understood.

"You found them in the attic? I reckon you'll find a lot of stuff when you move me into a home."

"We're not moving you into a home."

He snorts as if he's caught me in a lie.

"We are not moving you into a home, Dad," I repeat, my voice filling with as much annoyance as I dare, trying to convey how ridiculous it is for him to think we would ever put him in a home.

He harrumphs but doesn't look at me. "I'm gonna go lie down for a bit." He ruffles Shelby's hair and shuffles down the hall without looking back.

I watch him go, irritation sparking through all my nerves. I had expected the pictures to be something we could look through together. He doesn't know what I am looking for, and I had thought it would be fun to look back with him, over our life together.

It's too soon maybe. Maybe he can't look back because his loss is too fresh. Maybe none of us can. Now that I look at the box, thinking about seeing my mother as she was, I feel how overwhelming the box is, and I leave it sitting on the far end of the table, unopened. Whatever answers I am searching for, I can't find them there, not yet.

19

Baby

We are sitting in the living room, surrounded by Barbie dolls, some of which are naked. Sometimes when everything else is quiet, and the little girl is playing, I get to come and sit with her, and Shiloh and Stacy both leave us alone. I used to get to play with the older one, too, but she doesn't want to play with dolls very much anymore, and sometimes she looks at me like she thinks I am green, and that makes me uncomfortable. The younger one, Shelby, seems to think it's okay for me to be quiet. She talks enough for everybody. I have one doll of my own, but I can never find it. I don't know where it went or when I lost it. Mama is also gone. I don't know where she is—maybe my doll is with her. I think it's okay for me to be here. She wouldn't have left me where I wasn't supposed to be.

The girl talks a lot, and because she talks so much, I don't ever really have to say anything. I like to play with her. She's nice, and she's pretty. I like it here, because it's quiet and Slim isn't here. He's still mad at me, about getting him caught, but I don't know where he is. It seems like I haven't seen him in a long time. Maybe he's with Dr. Curtis, who is trying to train him. That's what Dr. Curtis says when he comes and takes him from our room. "Come on, boy. It's time to train you."

Slim used to fight, and he'd say horrible things when Dr. Curtis would come to get him, but then he just stopped and now he just climbs out of our cage, if we are in lock-up, or gets up from his mat and follows Dr. Curtis to the door and down the hall. When Dr. Curtis comes, Slim never looks back at me, and Dr. Curtis doesn't see me, either. Maybe I am invisible. Dr. Curtis owns our house and lives in the house next door. He is helping Mama. I thought he was going to be my Daddy, but he only wants Slim. About once a week, he comes and takes Slim for training. I don't know what training is, but Slim always smells like food when he comes back.

"What is Slim training for?" I ask mama when she lets me sit with her while Slim is at Dr. Curtis's house.

"Dr. Curtis is taking care of Slim. He's taking care of all of us." When I still don't understand, she says, "You know Mama has some problems, how I get real sad and loose myself sometimes?"

I nod, because Mama is really sad sometimes.

"Dr. Curtis is trying to make sure Slim won't ever be sad like that."

"What about me?"

She squeezes me, "Oh, Baby, you'll never be sad." That is all she will say, and she turns up the television. She lets me sit on her lap with the television so loud, and I know that if I ask too much, or if I make it so she can't watch her program, she'll make me go back to my room. Sometimes, though, I am sad. Don't they know that sometimes I'm sad, too? I want training and to come back smelling like chocolate.

The girl, Shelby, is putting clothes on the dolls, changing them from one dress to the next and some of the dresses don't fit. Why don't they fit? They all look the same size, with their hair frizzed and matted.

"That one would be pretty with that blue dress," Shelby says. I nod and start trying to put the dress on the doll.

I like Shelby.

"Where'd they all come from?" I ask, my voice a whisper.

"The dolls?" She does something with her lips, like a pucker or a quiver, and shrugs. "I don't know. Grandma just always has them."

I nod, and we sit, putting clothes onto the naked dolls, and I wonder what it would be like to have a grandma.

Her sister and her dad arrive, and I have to leave, and I'm sad because I was happy playing with Shelby, sitting on the floor with all her grandma's naked dolls.

Stacy

They've brought hot pizza, and I feel a little disoriented passing through the door and out onto the porch. "You're early," I say, rushing down the steps.

"No, it's noon. I told you we'd be here about noon."

True enough, my watch says 12:15, and I just thought it was much earlier. My legs are cramped, and I have a flash, seeing myself sitting on the floor with Shelby, and even though it doesn't make sense, I'm grateful to at least have a sense of where the past two hours have gone.

Shelby is at my side, leaving the Barbies in a heap. Grandpa is a few paces behind and seems irritated, annoyed. He has a right to be ill-tempered; his wife just died. It doesn't have anything to do with us. It isn't about the pictures I brought down. He just lost his wife—of course he isn't happy.

There are two of them, the Others, living inside my head. I even know their names, and I think they are kind of me at different times. So, the one who was just here, that I always thought of just as Baby, she's very young. During the year of half-truths, when I was seeing Dr. Martin, Baby left scribbles and rough crayon drawings all over the pages, between the angry pages filled with words like DIE and HATE that the other one, Shiloh, left.

Shiloh refused to write coherent thoughts in the notebook, but she wrote reams and reams of stories, typed on Dad's old typewriter. I should probably find those, the stories and the notebooks. My thoughts are pushed aside because I've reached Sophie, and I fold around her, feeling all the core pieces of my soul finally settling into alignment.

Sophie is in my arms, thin and lean as I lift her from the ground. Her fragile bones compress, and I have a flash of those children with their bones sticking through their flesh, the knobby knees, the hollow eyes. I bury my face in her hair, breathing in the scent of her. I don't want to let her go. She's grown taller this week, grown up while I was away. I missed her life for four days, and I feel it like a wound.

All too soon, she is pulling away, standing up on her own, giving Grandpa a side-armed hug, and I see me in her, that stiff-bodied posture saying, "I love you, but don't touch me."

John leans in to kiss me, and I wrap my arms around him. He hugs me back, but I can feel the surprise at my expressive hug in the slow melting of his muscles around me. He was prepared for my cold-fish hug, but when I wrap around him, I hear his breath draw in, feel the moment before he relaxes into me, feel for an instant what I am to hug. I have missed him so much. He is my ballast, and now that he is here, now that Sophie is here, I know I will be myself again. I need all of them to keep me in place, the way they have for all these years. Shelby pushes against my hip, breaking us apart, and John catches my eyes with a cocked brow before leaning down to his youngest. He carries Shelby on his hip, back onto the porch, and shakes hands with my dad.

I walk Sophie to the guest room. She is carrying her backpack, and she talks a mile a minute. "Daddy bought one of the houses from the sale this week. He took me over there. Mom, it is a total zombie house." She rolls her eyes. "He says he's gonna gut it. What does that mean? It sounds gross."

She wrinkles her nose, and I'm surprised that John bought another flip property without even mentioning it to me, especially one that will require gutting. Maybe he did mention it and I just forgot—me and my Swiss-cheese memory. We were due to buy another; he tries to do at least one a year. Most of the houses he buys are cosmetic fixes and quick to turn, but a full gut will take time and money and will be a harder sell because we'll need to recoup more costs.

"It just means he's going to remodel it. Do you remember the house we lived in when Shelby was born?"

She shakes her head. She was only six at the time—so, it doesn't surprise me. I don't remember anything before I was six, when we moved into this house.

I say, "Well, that was one of his 'zombie' houses." Then, because I'm curious how far back her memory stretches, I ask, "Do you remember when Shelby was born?"

She nods. "Why?"

"I just wondered. You would have been five." So she remembers the big event that year, Shelby being born.

"I remember Bobby Fuller who lived next door; I guess I remember that house. It had pink floors in the bathroom?"

"Yes. That's it." I am feeling more grounded, more solidly inside my skin now that they are here, and I let out a sigh. "Do you remember the first time we went to Disney? Before Shelby?"

Sophie nods. "You threw up on the Pirates of the Caribbean."

"So, not quite before Shelby," I say, remembering that I was pregnant and hadn't quite made it out of the morning sickness. Sophie is already turning away, taking out her belongings, taking her toothbrush and toothpaste to the bathroom. She is meticulous. Just like her daddy.

But she would have been four at Disney, and she remembers that. I try to reach back in my memory for something from my younger days—before age six—just to see how far back I can go, toward the dark holes. My skin prickles as I try to remember and that small edge of pressure in my head builds. I come up blank. I pull myself out of my head, and Sophie is already leaving me behind, calling out to Shelby, "Let's go see the lake." Shelby scampers from John's side to follow her into the sun.

The back yard is shaded around the edges and sunny down the middle. I love the dark, gloomy spaces overlooking the lake. My mother always struggled to find the perfect garden spot. I remember her coming in angry when the tomatoes failed to ripen because they were too hot. Another section was too wet from the underground springs that run through the neighborhood, or there wasn't enough sun. There was no perfect spot for her garden. Finally, Dad built her raised beds on a trailer so she could roll it around the yard with Darren or me helping. What had she done when we left home?

Well, Darren stayed close. He stayed here to help. Every day this week, I've been out moving the trailer—into the sun for the morning and into the shade for the afternoon—struggling against its weight, trying to figure out how my mother handled it alone. She wasn't alone, though. Darren was here. Dad was here.

I lift the hitch, pushing the cart back toward the dark edge of the yard, now that the sun is high in the sky, heating up and bearing down. I don't know why I'm bothering; she would have just planted, and I doubt that Darren will keep it up once I leave. Regardless, I angle it and place it again in the shade before I head out to the gazebo. The girls are sitting cross-legged, pointing at the geese gliding along the edge of the lake. I sit behind them, joining them without permission, and finally, I feel my breath coming normal. My heart finds its cadence as I listen to them talking as if I am not here.

My children. I breathe, feeling the sun on my face. How could I breathe at all without them both here with me?

"You guys gonna eat out here?" John says, coming up behind us, his feet quiet in the soft grass.

"Yes!" Shelby squeals, and the goose that had come nearest the shore shifts course and heads back into the middle of the lake, taking his small family with him. John has come prepared with four slices of pizza on paper plates.

He slides in beside me, pressing his shoulder against mine, passing around plates. "You okay?"

"I am. I think." I want to tell him about the envelope stashed in my bag, about the story about the two children found in dog kennels, but of course, I can't say anything here, not with the girls. I may never be able to say anything.

I sit, leaning against him, watching the lake, watching the girls eating their pizza. The joy of having them here, back around me, my family, my protective gander and our goslings, is like the sun to me, bright and shining, refreshing, clearing away the gloom of the past week. When the girls have finished their pizza, when they have eaten the slice that John brought out for me, when we have sat even longer still, feeling the breeze coming from the lake, I finally glance back toward the house.

"What was Dad doing?" I ask.

"He said he was going to go for a walk."

I nod and continue to look at the house, feeling a quiet, thick unease rising. Remembering the disconnect I felt in my dad earlier. Remembering the night out by the road.

"I'm gonna go see if he's back."

I let the unease draw me forward at a trot through the back yard. I open the door of the house and step inside, my eyes blinking to adjust. "Dad?" I hope to hear him moving somewhere in the house. I go through the kitchen and the dining room, past the living room, and down the hall, listening for his breathing. Hoping he is here, in the bathroom, getting a glass of water, sitting on his bed staring out at the lake... hoping, to no avail. His room is empty. I call out again and hear only silence. I walk through the front door, down the steps, and along the edge of the drive, looking down the street for him.

"Dad?" I call, hearing the frantic rise in my voice. I shouldn't have left him alone. It's my fault. I should have thought about it more, but I was so happy to see the girls and John that I just forgot to think about Dad's new reality. Darren had warned me, and even after seeing it myself the other night, I still hadn't taken it seriously. The terrible things that happen in the night tend to fade from thought when the sun is bright and high. I lift my phone to call Darren, trying to calculate how long we have sat in the gazebo. How long has my father been walking? How far could he be by now? Could he make it to the Best Buy in this amount of time? Is he walking out on the street? Is he out by the highway? "John?" I call out, and he and the girls head toward me.

"What's wrong?" John asks, reading my distress, familiar with my panic.

"Dad's not here," I say. "He should be back. Has it been an hour? An hour and a half?" I am asking because I don't know. I could have spent the whole of a day sitting in the peaceful bubble of the girls in the gazebo and not noticed time slipping. I explain, keeping my voice low, trying not to alarm the girls, who are watching me with intense interest.

"Would he go to Darren's?" he asks, and I shake my head. Darren would still be at the office. "I'll drive through the neighborhood. He can't be far."

"Should I call the police?"

"You think that's necessary?" His voice says that I am going too far, that there is no need for my near hysteria.

"I don't know," I squeak.

"Okay. Relax—don't overreact."

"I'm not overreacting." I refrain from stomping my foot, the way Sophie does when she is frustrated, feeling accused unjustly.

"Okay. Okay. Let me drive through here and see if anybody has seen him. If I don't have any luck, we'll call the police. Okay?"

I nod and pick Shelby up, putting her on my hip. "Sounds good," I say, reaching for Sophie's hand and drawing her close while John gets in his car and heads out. We watch him go, my guilt like weight, like an anchor holding me moored.

"You know, I saw a soccer ball in the garage," I finally say when Shelby tucks her head into my shoulder, and I notice her thumb moving stealthily toward her mouth. She doesn't suck her thumb, but when she is nervous, she tucks it between her lips and pushes against her front teeth. "Sophie, why don't you go get that, and we'll kick it around?" I can't lose it, for their sake, so I mention the soccer ball and give Shelby a small squeeze. Sophie nods and goes through the house to reach the garage. Of course, she knows something is wrong, but she's keeping it quiet for Shelby's sake.

While they kick the ball, and Sophie keeps an eye on me, I call Darren and tell him that I've lost our dad.

20

Stacy

Darren doesn't wait for John to come back without our dad before calling the police, and when it's all timed out, Dad was missing for over two hours. The girls and I kicked the ball until Shelby melted down in a fevered mess, in need of her nap.

We go in, but I keep looking out the front window, hoping to see him walking up the drive. Time stretches, and Shelby, still sobbing, folds into her bed and hiccups into her pillow until she falls asleep.

"I didn't mean to kick the ball that hard," Sophie says.

"Oh. Is that what happened?" I ask, letting my hand rest on the top of her head, feeling the heat of her on my fingertips.

"Yeah. I'm sorry."

"You didn't do anything. She's just tired. Poor baby."

"Is Grandpa okay?" Sophie asks, always one to get to the point.

"I hope so." I drop my arm around her shoulders.

"Where do you think he went?" she asks, and I shrug. "Why did he go?"

"He's not thinking clearly."

"Because of Grandma?" She is so astute.

"Maybe." We step out onto the front porch, waiting for anybody to come home. "So you think you did well on your test?" I ask, needing conversation but not able to talk about my parents.

"I did. I totally aced it." She is confident; it resounds in her voice, in her words and mannerisms.

"I'm really proud of you. You are so smart." Tears well in my eyes, and I blink them away, drawing her close in a side-armed hug.

~ ~ ~

John comes back, looking tired and strained. "Why didn't you tell me?" I look him in the eyes, feeling accused. "You should have told me."

I nod, understanding and not willing to disagree. He's right. I should have said something. I should have thought about Dad, but I'm so used to John just taking care of everything that I forgot it was my job. The girls are mine, but pretty much everything else John handles. He's the planner, the precise one, the thinker with a side of OCD. It's just easier for him to be in charge, less chance of him not approving of my decisions. Less chance of something disappearing into the holes of my mind.

Darren comes up the drive minutes later, looking relieved. "They've got him," he says, parking behind John's Mercedes.

The relief is palpable.

"Where was he?" I ask.

"Two neighborhoods over. The homeowner came home and found him sitting by the pool. Called the cops."

"I'm so sorry, Darren," I say, knowing it is not enough.

"I told you we can't leave him alone."

"I know I screwed up. But he's been okay the past couple of days, like normal." Except for the other night. I see the thought crossing his mind, and he quickly looks away

"Yeah, well, clearly he's not." He reaches out and shakes John's hand. I look at him, trying to find the shape of his skull under his hair, trying to find some semblance between my stocky, stable brother to the long, dark-eyed boy I had seen squatting in the pictures from the folders, and then I understand. That boy was not Darren, Darren has blue eyes. Darren has Dad's eyes. I turn away, feeling invisible.

Sophie follows me in, and we make our way back to the bedroom, where Shelby is still sleeping, and I try not to let myself cry—not in front of Sophie.

I wish my mom were here. I really need to talk to her. Sophie and I climb onto the bed with Shelby, scooting her in toward the wall, with Sophie in the middle. I fold in toward them, drawing the blankets up, and tuck my head into the warmth of the pillow. Sophie puts her hand up to my cheek and rubs my jawline, where the small purple bruise is covered over with powder, the way I've always rubbed her face when she was worried or sick. I don't know if she sees the bruise; I don't know if I should explain it or just say nothing. In the end, I don't speak, because if I open my mouth, I do not know what may come out. Would I tell my daughter, who seems so much older than nine, things that no nine-year-old should know? I smile through the sadness and look her in the eyes, afraid that all the shattered shards of my soul will show.

~ ~ ~

I am alone when I wake, with nothing except Shelby's stuffed bunny keeping me company. The room is dark and shadowed, with the muted sounds of conversations rolling toward me down the hall. There are no words, just sound, and I stare up at the ceiling, wondering how long I can pretend to be asleep.

Sometime later, when I have fallen again off the edge of wakefulness, John comes in with the girls. I hear him tucking them into the other bed; I feel him drawing the bunny from my hands. I hear him telling them goodnight. I hear him closing the door again behind him.

In the morning, I wake, and the light in the room is golden. John is beside me, his arm thrown over his face. Across the room, through the open doors, I can see the girls. Waking is like coming out of a fog, out of the depths of a murky lake.

Today we will bury my mother. I try to contain the sudden puckering in my soul, biting hard on my lip to stay still. Today I will bury my mother, who was not my mother.

The words from the first newspaper clipping float in my head, then the pictures of the knobby-kneed, emaciated children. Me and my brother. My brother and me.

21

Stacy

The funeral home is packed; people loved my mother. The potted plants and arrangements sent by people who live too far away to attend dwarf the sedate flowers Sue brought and set in displays. Does the couple from Oregon, with their red retrievers and hair, have an arrangement amongst all of these? I am tempted to look, but I am stuck between John and Sophie in the receiving line, with Shelby on my hip. Darren and Scott are on the other side of Sophie, and then there is Dad at the head of the line. He is shaking hands, thanking people for coming, and I watch out of the corner of my eye, wondering if he understands why we are here, wondering if he remembers that she is gone. My kinship with him is so much stronger, now that we share this one thing—this loss of time, of memories not retained.

Cassie, my old friend from high school, is working her way toward me, down the line. She hugs my father as if they are old friends. Beside her is a square-shouldered man with a dark mustache, and I recognize, with a jolt, the high school jock that Cassie married—Theo. He had narrow hips in high school, muscled but lean. Now he is thick, like a brick wall.

Cassie reaches me, making eye contact with my girls, shaking Sophie's hand and then Shelby's in a show of seeing them as adults. Shelby folds her head down to my shoulder, shy of the attention, that little thumb heading to her mouth. But Sophie accepts the attention as her due and says, "Thank you so much for coming." I smile, in spite of everything. I am impressed by Sophie's ability to mimic.

"Yes, Cassie, thank you so much for coming." I lean in and hug her, taking Shelby with me.

"Of course. I love you, girl."

I nod, unable to speak.

"Theo," I say, stretching out my hand. He clasps it, and my hand completely disappears into his. When he touches me, I have a confused memory of an awkward fumbling at buttons, like déjà vu. Did Theo and I once have an encounter at a party that ended with me throwing up in a potted plant? It's vague and fleeting, fuzzy and sputtering, like the film on an old-time movie reel when it spits off, something from one of the dark holes. I hold my face steady, keeping my eyes from darting away, keeping my forehead from wrinkling, keeping my hand from pressing against my eye socket. If I remember right, and that is a big if, he ended up face-down on the stairs, I think. Maybe he doesn't remember the encounter any more than I do. Maybe it's not a dark hole, but just the effect of being a teen, working through the angst.

The six months leading up to my break and the year following is mostly absent, as if I wasn't participating in my own life, and more than once, I felt myself, the core of myself, pushed down or out. I watched, from inside or outside, as my body continued functioning, often doing things that I wouldn't normally do.

"Stacy." We nod at each other, and I wonder if he would have any information about the kids in the crates, but there is no mystery—it was all there in the paper. Even the name of the mother. The only secret is who the children were and why my mother had kept clippings of the story. It seems like a social worker might be a better resource for information than a policeman. I bite my tongue and let them pass down the line.

It should have rained as we lowered my mother's casket into the ground, but it didn't. In fact, there wasn't a single cloud in the sky the entire day. The sun shone bright and happy, which would have suited

Doris Alexander just fine. She loved a sunshiny day, and she would have been severely displeased had this day been marred by rain.

When we arrive back at the house, Dad changes out of his suit and settles on the couch. "Shelby, our movie is on," he calls. The girls and I are in the guest room, changing out of the dresses and putting on pajamas for them, shorts and a t-shirt for me. Shelby jumps at his call, squeaking, knowing what movie he is talking about, and barely has her pajama dress down past her rear before she is scampering down the hall to join him.

"Brave," I explain to Sophie, who rolls her eyes.

"But, Mom," she drawls in her best Merida imitation, "it's just m' bow." We laugh, and she heads down the hall to join her sister and Grandpa.

I find Darren, Scott, and John sitting around the kitchen table when I come back. The box of pictures, that I never actually found time or courage to look through, is pushed to the far end.

"I agree," John is saying, and I slide onto the bench next to him.

"What do you agree with?" I ask, lifting out a picture from the box and studying it. I'm probably ten, a string bean with dark-blond hair pulled up in a ponytail. Darren is sitting astride his bike, and I can see the clothespin connecting the playing card to the back tire. When he rode the bike, it purred, and a small chuckle escapes as I pass the picture down to Darren, who glances at it but has more important things on the agenda than walking down memory lane.

"We think Dad needs to move in with us," Darren says.

"When did you decide this?" I ask, feeling prickly.

"We've been talking about it for some time."

"You didn't mention it to me." I look at him with slightly narrowed eyes. "I've been here a week, and you haven't mentioned it to me."

"It just didn't come up." Darren shrugs, looking at Scott for backup. Scott raises his eyes to him, a look that says, "I told you so."

"He's not going to want to give up his house."

"Well, what would you like to do? You gonna move up here and stay with him? Because hiring somebody to stay with him is gonna be expensive."

"Well, no. I can't move up here." I look at John, who is looking into his coffee. "Have you talked to Dad about this? Or are you just making his decisions now?"

"We've mentioned it."

"What did he think?"

Darren shrugs. "We can't afford to hire somebody to sit with him twenty-four hours a day."

We sit in silence, letting that sink in. "You gonna sell the house, then?" I ask, feeling hollow, like a conspirator.

"We could rent it. We'd hate to sell it," Scott says, and I'm annoyed that he is even part of this conversation, although he's been part of our family since sometime shortly after my breakdown—longer than John. But it's not his dad, and apparently, he is more in on the decision-making more than I am.

"I could come for the summer," I say. "The girls and I could come for the summer."

John looks at me, his brows drawn together, not liking the idea.

"You're never home, anyway," I counter. "It'd be just a couple of months. We could help sort through stuff, you know?"

"No," John says, adamant. "You're not moving up here for the summer."

"Excuse me?"

"No," and in his tone, there is a warning. "It doesn't make any sense."

"Wow." I roll my tongue over my teeth, feeling a fight, but then I look around at the men circling the table, and I close my mouth. Darren and Scott are both looking away from me, expecting an explosion, but John is looking at me with steady eyes.

"You're exhausted, and you've been here a week with only Shelby to worry about."

"My mom just died." I say, low and tight almost under my breath. Of course I'm exhausted. Of course I'm stretched thin. But he is right, and even as I want to offer myself to care for Dad, I know, especially now, that I am not the best option.

"We can talk about it, but I don't think it's the answer."

"All right. We'll talk later," I say, a promise, a threat, even as relief blossoms through my chest. I let a pause settle there. They all feel the shift and again—Darren and Scott look at us, Darren's eyes, particularly, study me. Something about what just happened struck him as odd, or different, and I try to imagine who he really thinks I am, who I am in his memory. Obviously not someone who discusses, not someone who acquiesces. "So, if he moves in with you guys, where will he be?" Darren reminds us that the basement of their house is a guest suite, a complete apartment, with windows that open out to the lake. "What about when you're gone? You have to work."

"I can work from home most days. We can hire somebody for the days I have to go in," Scott offers.

"What about this house?" I ask.

"We can rent it out for now," Darren says, and I think he may have said that already.

I nod because this decision is made, and I am only coming to the table after the fact. "All right, then. It sounds like you all have a plan." I pass a look around the table. A small smile presses my lips, tight and controlled but not disingenuous. I'm glad they have a plan. I'm glad I don't have to make a decision. I leave the kitchen to join the little party watching Brave in the living room. I failed miserably this week. I nearly let him walk out of the house one night, and barely a day later, he wandered off. I have no reason to think I could handle moving up here even for the summer. Darren is doing the right thing, and Scott—bless him—is willing to sacrifice a big part of his day to make sure Dad is safe. That's more than I can offer. I'm exhausted, and all I can think is how much I want to get back home and start living my life again. Darren is the one who is here. He's the one who has come down to fix leaky pipes and help tend to the garden. He's the one they've turned to since the day I left for college, and even before that.

To the right of the television is a montage of framed photos, several smaller pictures circling the central family picture. Mom is sitting on a couch, with Dad to her right, his hand resting lightly on her knee. I am sitting in front of her and Darren in front of him, both of us on the floor with our legs out to the sides. Darren is thin in this picture, with none of the gut that has found him as he matured. I guess Darren to be twelve in this photo, and I was nine. I am Sophie's age and not at all unlike her. It's not so much that Darren and I couldn't be related; it's more that they—Mom, Dad, and Darren look so similar—and I look so different, with the sharp angles of my knees, the long stretch of my legs, the pale hair and dark eyes. I am the only Dodo in this nest.

Dad reaches out and pats me on the shoulder, and when I look at him, he smiles. I smile back, feeling so many emotions that don't make sense that I can't do anything else.

Is there anything else I should have done? Should I not have fought for John to take the job in Florida? Should I have encouraged him to stay nearby to help with our parents as they aged? Probably, but when Florida was offered, I nearly insisted that he take it. We argued for a week, because his parents were in Savannah and a job was waiting there as well. In the end, he relented, and I got Florida. Why had I been so determined? Why was it so important? I felt compelled. I didn't think about my parents aging. I never thought about John's parents or his brothers. I never even cared that Florida wasn't what John wanted.

22

Stacy

John goes to leave on Sunday night, loading his overnight bag into my Civic. "I'll just feel more comfortable," he says, explaining why he is taking my car and leaving me the Mercedes. The girls and I are staying another day or two to help get Dad settled at Darren and Scott's.

"Yeah, the old Civic is a comfortable ride," I say, mocking him, as if I don't understand.

"I'll just feel better knowing you and the girls are safer," he says, but doesn't rise to my bait.

"I hear ya," I say. "I better not come home to a different car."

"You'll be ready for a new car after driving mine."

I blow a breath through my nose and roll my eyes. It is such an old conversation. We are standing out by the drive, the girls and I, sending him off, back to Florida. He has early appointments tomorrow, and I am almost relieved to see him go. I need some space to process everything, and I can't do that with his eyes watching every move I make.

"You'll see," he jokes, folding his arms around my waist. "Are you okay?"

I nod, forcing my body to relax, forcing the tension out of my frame, leaning toward him instead of pulling away. I smile, but can't quite meet his eyes. "I'm good." I tilt my head to his chest, so I don't have to look at him.

"Okay." His lips press, light, against my head, and he releases me, turning toward the girls, lifting them each in turn. He's a great father, affectionate, engaged. He's a great man. Why can't I ever just relax around him? Why do I always feel like he's watching to judge?

It is only when he has left, and after the girls have bathed and are in bed, that I feel the tension ebbing from my shoulders. Dad is sitting in the living room, watching a John Wayne movie, some western, but I don't know which one. I sit down next to him, and his hand drops down on my knee.

"Dad?"

"What honey?" he says, but doesn't look away from the television.

"Was I adopted?" I keep my voice steady, not wanting to betray the heaping emotions the question covers.

He is quiet for so long that I begin to wonder if I only asked inside my head, but then he turns and faces me. "Why do you ask?"

He doesn't say, "No." He doesn't say, "Of course not." He asks me why I wonder.

"I was just looking at that picture, how you all look so similar. I just wondered, where did I come from? Nobody in our family is tall like me."

"Yep. You've got some height."

"Was I?"

"What?" he asks.

"Was I adopted, Dad?"

"Well, you know, that's complicated."

"How is it complicated?" What about it is complicated? Either I was or I wasn't. There is no shame in being adopted. A family down the street from us in Jacksonville has adopted three kids. They love them the same as I love my girls. I know that. There is no shame in adoption, and I admire people who have done it, opening their hearts to a child in need and all that. But admiring others and recognizing that your story is different from what you thought are two entirely different things.

Dad has turned back to the television, reabsorbed in the western.

"Dad?" Exasperation tinges my voice, poisoning the air between us.

"What?" He does not look at me.

"Was I adopted?"

"Of course not."

"Oh." The level of deflation inside my stomach doesn't make sense, relief and sorrow warring. Of course I'm not that little girl. Of course not. I let out a small laugh, relief washing through me. Of course I wasn't adopted.

He pats my leg and stands up. "I think I'm going to turn in. You staying up?"

I shake my head. "No. I'm tired, too." I follow him down the hall, turning off lights and the television in our wake. He turns into his room, and I go on down to where the girls are already asleep.

I change into my pajamas and sit on the bed, looking out across the room at the girls. I pull out my phone and send John a text: Heading to bed. Drive safe. Love you.

He texts back, clearly not driving safe: Half hour. Love you.

I slide under my blankets, listening to the girls breathing, listening to the house shifting. "You were such a skinny little thing when we got you." The words bounce in my head. That's what he had said when I'd come down with the box of clothes. Who says that when you bring a baby home from the hospital?

I scramble across the floor to my suitcase and take the envelope out, flashing past the newspaper clippings, pushing the disturbing pictures back into their folder, and I lift the unopened envelope. I hadn't even looked at it before. It sits in my lap, the small "S" winking at me from the glow of my phone. I find my pocket knife in my purse and slice through the crease at the top of the envelope. Sliding the contents out before I can change my mind. What I see first is a series of photographs of the same blond-haired boy and girl, but less bone-thin, less hollow eyed, but still serious, intense children.

Then another picture of three kids, and Darren is unmistakable—smiling at the camera—between the sullen boy and girl. I squint at the picture. It's a birthday party, a cake in front of Darren, and candles lighting the faces of the kids. The girl is me; I know it because she is wearing the tulle skirt that I washed from the box of clothes I brought down for Shelby. Not just that, but she looks like me, when she's not so skinny, so dirty and hollow. I recognize my sullen, angry face. When did I stop looking like that? I shift through the photos, until I come to some in which the blond-haired boy is missing, and it is only me and Darren, at another birthday party, me smiling, glowing as six candles burn on a cake. I recognize in the background the kitchen before we remodeled.

My whole life has been a lie.

When the photos have been shuffled through, dropped one after the other to the floor beside my knees, it is only a stack of papers that remains. I skim the pages and my heart skips a beat. Birth certificates, pristine and unfolded, with the seal of the court—Stacy Ann Alexander, Daughter of Andrew and Doris Alexander. The birthdate is listed, but no hospital, no time of birth. It isn't the same as the birth certificates I have for my girls, but I am already numb and just shift through the small stack until I come to the first page that is different, and at the top of the page are the words "Decree of Adoption" and all the other words blend together until there are no spaces between the letters.

I gather it all and shove it back into the envelope, putting it in the zippered pocket of my suitcase. I can't deal with this. I can't cope. I can't breathe.

What difference does it make? The voice whispers through my head and I don't have an answer. What difference does it make? I'm a grown women with children of my own. Why does it matter how I came to the family that raised me? It doesn't matter. I know that it doesn't. Nothing inside that envelope changes anything about who I am, although suddenly I see what was missing. What happened to the boy? Where did he go?

My eyes fall on my girls. What would happen to them without each other? Would they grow up angry? The way I did? Would they grow up feeling a loss that they couldn't explain? I crawl across the floor until I am beside their bed, peering at them, one and then the other.

What happened to the boy?

I climb into the bed with them, squeezing between them, needing them, and Shelby rolls toward me, tucking her forehead against my shoulder. Sophie groans in her sleep and turns her face toward me, her mouth puckered, like a kiss.

What happened to the boy?

23

PART THREE
July and August

Stacy

The search bar reads "Slim Moony." I've been staring at the name for minutes, it seems, unable to request the search. Ridiculous. No child is actually named Slim. I've typed this name into the search window a hundred times since the girls and I came back to Florida, and every time, I stare until my eyes cross, and I close the browser. I am Pandora and pressing "search" will release all the evils into the world, because just maybe there is one boy who was given such a name.

I change the search to "Kristine Moony," and stare at that name for a while. The sun is hot, brilliant in the Florida sky. I am sitting in the overhang of the back deck, and before me, the pool is overflowing with kids. Shelby and Julia are afloat in the hot tub, above the rest, and the bigger kids are splashing and jumping from the edges, yelling "Cannonball!" as they hit the water. Dee is next door mixing a new batch of margaritas. Music is echoing against the back fence, something by Sia, I think. Something inappropriate, I'm sure, but the kids aren't listening, and Mona is swiveling her hips, feeling the heat of her margaritas and the echo of her youth not so far behind her.

"Where are you?" Mona asks, dancing past me.

"I'm here." I look past my phone, out to the kids, counting, letting my eyes fall to each of my own for a second longer before moving on.

"Yeah, but not here." She sits down in the shade beside me, breathing her margarita breath out in a long sigh.

Dee comes out of the house, the plastic pitcher sloshing with the foamy green nectar. She refreshes Mona's drink and refills her own. Dee is red-faced already, either from the heat or the alcohol.

"What are you talking about?" Dee asks, settling on my other side. I shake my head and shrug.

"Don't you think she's been a million miles away since she came back from Georgia?" Mona asks, and Dee widens her eyes.

"Well, she did just lose her mama." She looks at me, patting her hand on my knee.

"I know," Mona says.

"Seriously, I'm here. I'm just a little distracted." I hate when they talk about me like I'm invisible.

Mona keeps pushing. "Is that it? I mean, you and John are okay, right?"

"We're fine." I roll my eyes and reach for my glass, water. Then I set it back down without drinking from it and open the pictures on my phone. I scroll to the image depicting the yellowed newspaper clipping, the first one, and hand the phone to Mona. The secret has been riding high in my chest for weeks now, catching me at unexpected times and sending me spiraling into dark holes. I can't hold it inside myself any longer, and Mona and Dee are my closest friends. I trust them with more of my soul than even John.

I watch the kids as she reads, unable to look at her, my jaw clenching and pulsing. Dee steps around behind and peers over Mona's shoulder.

"Well, that's just horrible," Mona says, handing the phone to Dee.

"Isn't it, though?" I say, my jaw still clenched.

"Yeah," Dee says, handing the phone back to me. "So?"

Leave it to Dee to cut right to the point. "I think that's me," I say it light, without any tone in my voice. I say it like I say "I have blond hair" or "I am tall."

The only sound is the rhythm of the music, the sound of the kids splashing, my breath passing through my nose, my heart ricocheting against my ribs.

"How do you mean?"

"I think that's me," I repeat.

"How?" Dee asks, leaning in, her hand brushing a strand of hair out of my face.

"Why do you think that?"

"I just know." I flip to the next picture, the rest of the story, and Mona takes the phone out of my hand. I let her, but don't really want to let her. She slides her thumb and finger across the screen, enlarging the image of the two children, the skinny, pitiful children with Shelby's face. I reach for the phone; I wasn't ready to share that. It's too private, too embarrassing. She draws the phone away but then realizes from my expression that I need her to give it back, and she hands it over, looking meek and chagrined.

"Stace," she says, and it sounds like pity.

"Don't do that," Dee says, hearing the tone in Mona's voice. "Why do you think this is you?" Dee asks, getting to the meat, digging in for details, ready to tear away my fear that this is really me.

I tell them. Starting with the box of clothes from the attic. "Then my Dad said I was a 'skinny little thing when we got you.'" I did air quotes on the last bit and let that hang in the air, tucking my phone under my leg, getting the evidence out of sight.

"That's odd," Mona agrees, her voice far away.

"Yeah, but didn't you say your dad was kinda losing it?" Dee's skepticism annoys me, even though it is what I want from her, precisely. I want her to tell me this is crazy. I want her to put it to rest.

"He is, kinda, but I'm telling you, it felt like the most honest thing he's ever said to me."

Shelby has climbed up on the edge of the hot tub, calling to me, and I watch as she yells "Cannonball!" and splashes into the big pool, bobbing to the surface with the aid of her floaties, snorting with laughter.

"Good job, baby." Willow grabs her by the front of her floaties and spins her in the pool, passing her over to Sophie, and Shelby giggles until they reach the edge of the pool. She climbs out and trots around to the hot tub to do it all over again. I cringe as she runs, but refuse to call out. They will fall, they will bruise themselves, and it's okay. I want them to be fearless. It isn't going to kill her to have a skinned knee.

She doesn't fall; she doesn't scrape her knee. She clambers back into the hot tub, confident and secure.

"Well, what are you going to do?" Mona asks.

"I don't know." I sigh, feeling better now that the tension of telling is gone, and it is now just knowledge. "I found my adoption decree."

"Oh, wow." Dee says, taking a long drink from her margarita.

"I know. They even changed my name." It had been such a shock, seeing the name-change affidavit attached to the adoption decree. Such a simple form to erase an old life.

"Shiloh Cheyanne Moony. Isn't that horrible?"

"I think it's pretty," Dee says, sounding dreamy, licking the salt from the rim of her glass.

"I can't believe they never told you," Mona says, leaning back. "You know Gina Simpson?"

I nod. They live down the street and have three adopted kids.

"When they got their kids, they had to sign a form saying that they'd never keep the adoption a secret."

"Got," I whisper, proof that what my dad had said meant something.

"That's right... they did," Dee says, picking up the thread. "She said that they've found that kids who know their birth story all along have an easier time adjusting."

"Yeah, kids who don't find out until later really struggle," Mona adds.

"You think?" I say, sarcastic, feeling like my head could explode.

We sit in silence for maybe a minute. The music loops. The shouts of the children rebound back to us.

I've been better since coming back to Florida, more grounded. I haven't lost any time since I left Georgia, at least I don't think I have. Of course, I've found myself standing in a room and not remembered what I came for, but that's not the same as losing time. That's not the same as what was happening right after I found the envelope, when I felt so unhinged. Being distracted isn't crazy, is it? Isn't that normal—something to be expected when you lose someone you love?

"What about the boy? That your brother?"

"Not Darren." I tell them that there were pictures of the three of us, and then the boy just disappeared. I fight the impulse to bring the envelope out, to share it all.

"Dude. You gotta find him," Dee says, always one to get to the bottom of a story.

"You think?"

"Oh yeah. You have to. How can you not know what happened?"

I nod, letting that sink in. How can I not know what happened to the boy?

24

Stacy

John is late coming home, and the girls and I have dinner together. I put them to bed while the sun is still high in the evening sky. They are worn out from the afternoon in the pool, and their sunburned cheeks fall to their pillows. Shelby is likely asleep before her head touches down.

I put the dogs out one last time and watch them as they romp through the back yard, out past the pool, under the swings. I leave them and go in to clean the kitchen, putting everything away. I feel better after sitting with Dee and Mona this afternoon, less like I'm going to explode.

When the kitchen is clean, I open the envelope and sit at the table, waiting for the dogs to come scratching at the door. I bypass the pictures; they are seared into my head anyway. I read the adoption paperwork. It's a straightforward thing, and my other mother, Kristine Moony, isn't mentioned. This document only pertains to the relationship created between my adoptive parents and me. All ties to my other mother were severed before this document, and Kristine Moony is not mentioned. Neither is her son, my brother. There is nothing in the text saying the adoption should not be kept secret, and I wonder if that's something new, something they've come to understand about the way adopted children mature.

Reading the decree offers no answers that I didn't already have, and I shuffle the paperwork back into the envelope and pull out my laptop.

I search first for my birth name. Shiloh Cheyanne Moony. The search results come back with a Facebook hit for Cheyanne Shiloh, a woman living in San Fransisco, California, who has a photo of her backside as a profile picture. A quick glance through the profile convinces me Cheyanne Shiloh is perhaps not a natural woman as her "About Me" section would have you think. She is stunning, regardless.

Facebook isn't what I need. I need John's search engine, the one he uses to research people involved in lawsuits and divorces. Human nature is not always honest, especially when a divorce looms, and digging up dirt about the opposing spouse is just legwork, the necessary evil to being a civil lawyer. It's dirty work; he doesn't enjoy it.

The computer logs on to the site, and I'm grateful that John saved his logins.

I type in "Shiloh Cheyanne Moony," and it comes up empty. Then I type my name, Stacy Ann Alexander, and wait while the computer churns. Has John ever looked me up? I'm sure he has; it would just be his way. I'm feeling anxious, and then the search comes up with a couple of name matches. I scroll until I find the one that is me. It lists only my marriage and a couple of addresses. Of course, my break happened before I was eighteen, so I guess none of that would show. Anyway, it's not like that was a legal problem. I just had an episode. A "fugue state" is what Dr. Martin had termed it. I am more relieved than I should be, and a small splinter of guilt pushes under my ribs and lodges near my beating heart, because John should know all my secrets.

I type in the name "Kristine Moony," and I get several hits—different women all across the country. I scan until I find a mug shot I recognize. She has two, actually. The first I recognize from the newspaper, her long, stringy hair and wild eyes. The second shows an older woman—clean, at least—arrested for trespassing. Looking at the image glowing from the screen is like looking in a magic mirror that shows the past or the future.

A flash of memory erupts from a day when I was twelve. I am walking down the hall, hearing my mother's voice, sounding angry and scared. I come behind her, where she is at the door, holding it only partially open, blocking it from opening further with her foot.

"I just want to see her," the voice beyond the door says, pleading

"You have no rights here."

I've stepped far enough to the side that I can see the woman standing on the step, her blond hair tied back in a low ponytail. The woman sees me, and her hand flies to her mouth, and my mother understands suddenly that I am behind her. The woman's face contorts, and my mother pushes me back, closing the door in one swift, decisive motion.

"Go to your room," she snaps. At the moment before she closes the door, I glimpse the blue car in the drive and a boy sitting in the driver's seat, his long, blond hair brushing his shoulders, his face closed, jaw clenched, facing forward, not watching the scene on the steps.

"Who is that?" I ask, but Mom is pushing me toward the hall, and when I look back, I see the woman with her face contorted in agony, pressed against the glass panes beside the door, tears streaming down her cheeks.

I try to fill in the memory, to stretch out the moment when I had seen her, the moment when she had seen me. She didn't look like a wild woman. The boy, sitting in the driver's seat… was that Slim? Or was that a man, grown, whoever came along to fill the shoes of the most recently departed man who tried to "help her?" Did Slim end up back with her, the woman who locked him in a cage? Did he get to go back to her? She gave up rights—how could he have gone back to her?

I went down the hall with my mother, and she drew the shades down on the windows and closed the door to my room, leaving me alone with my questions and confusion. I could hear her on the phone, and although I desperately wanted to look out the window to see if the woman was still there, terror gripped me, and I sat rocking on my bed, unable to stand, biting the tip of my tongue until the metallic taste of blood filled my mouth. I saw when the light of the police car arrived. I could hear the low confrontation.

"Who was she?" I asked when my mother finally came back to me, after the police, after the small scuffle on the drive.

"Just a poor troubled woman."

"What did she want?"

Mom shakes her head and pulls me into a hug, one of my uncomfortable, stiff-bodied hugs. The only kind I know how to give.

I come back to current and realize that I am staring at the dog kennels in the corner of the room. I am staring at them in a vacant way, as you stare at something that has always been a part of your life, a part of your furnishings. I leave the table and walk to the kennels. Kneeling down, expecting some rush of memory. How can I not remember being padlocked in a dog kennel? I should have some rush of emotion, some intense response, but there is nothing. I stick my head inside of one, then my shoulders, and soon I am inside the kennel from my hips up staring up through the wire.

Nothing.

I am disappointed. I am insane; I had hoped for a flood of recollection, even horrible memories, if they could bring some understanding. I would welcome the understanding. I squirm out of the cage and hear the dogs finally at the back door. I let them in, and they run straight for their kennels, and I watch them spin and lie down, panting a little from their outdoor exertions. Safe and secure in their cages. Was she keeping us safe? Did we feel safe? Was she really protecting us from going out the broken window of the trailer?

I sit back down at the computer, her face still glowing. It's the same woman, smeared and then clean, staring at me from the screen. I open a new search and type in "Slim Moony."

Nothing.

I remove "Slim" and do an advanced search for male, last name "Moony." The screen comes up with about thirty hits. I scroll past the seventy-four-year-old man from Tucson, Arizona, arrested in 2004 for public indecency, past several others that are forty or older. I look at a couple who are the right age but wrong ethnic blend. It's a dead end. None of these Moony men are the boy I knew as Slim. If he has any criminal activity since becoming an adult, I haven't found it. He probably isn't a Moony anymore if he was adopted by some other family and he is somebody entirely different. Disappointment floods, and I feel remorse that he is really gone, that I will never find him, never know what happened to him. I don't know his first name, I don't know his last name. I am hopeless to find him.

I open the Bing browser and type "Moony," and go through the same routine, filtering through results until a name makes me pause, Shane Moony. That feels strange and familiar. Shane—could his name have been Shane? I click on the link and a row of photographs spreads across the screen under the heading "Employee of the Month." The page contains pictures above the names of Employees of the Month for Lake City Automotive in Lake City, Florida.

My eyes immediately find the name. "Shane Moony, Service Department – May" is listed beneath a picture of a handsome young man. I squint at the picture and let the memory overlay the image. It could be the same boy. The man's hair is darker than the boy's in the pictures. His hair is a chestnut brown. Of course, the man is less hollow-cheeked than the little boy in the images had been. He would be. He is thin, though. He is smiling for the camera, handsome. Could he have been called "Slim" when he was little? My heart jars in my chest. Could this be my real brother, my biological brother? His eyes look dark in the picture. Did my brother have dark eyes? Maybe it's just a shadow. I want this to be him; I want him to have a good life, to be doing good things. Is this the face of a boy who was locked in a dog kennel until he was nine? Could that boy ever grow up to do good things?

I had. I grew up to do something useful—raising kids and taking care of my family—but it wasn't an easy road to get here. I had a lot of support along the way, and then John, with his ambition and rigid expectations. He gave me a framework that I lack within myself. I had never thought of it like that before, and suddenly his small criticisms and observations have a different meaning to me.

Is this my brother, though? I take in the rest of the page, noting the dealership. Lake City, Florida, is just down the road. I dial the number for their service department, and a woman answers.

"Lake City Auto. This is Beth. How can I help you?" I'm surprised they answer, but it is only eight o'clock, so... not late.

"Hi, Beth. I, uh, have an old Civic. It needs... well, to be serviced." I stumble over my words, having not prepared myself for actually speaking to someone.

"Great, we can help with that. When would you like to come in?"

"Tomorrow?"

"How about ten?"

"Will Shane be in?" I ask, trying to keep my voice steady. It feels illicit, sneaky, to say the name, foreign on my tongue.

"Yes, Shane will be here." I hear the smile in her voice. She has mistaken me for a lovesick girl, asking for him like that.

"My husband says he does good work," I add.

"Great. So you've been here before?"

I stammer and hang up the phone. Stupid, stupid, stupid. I blow a puff of air across my teeth and close the laptop, shaking out my hands over the farce of calling the dealership, asking for him.

It may not even be him.

Of course, it's him. A cold shiver rides down my spine. Is that fear?

I sit back down at the computer, and my stomach rolls over on itself. I click on the tab with Kristine Moony. I tear my eyes from the photo and scan the article, the same clipping from the envelope, but what was missing from the clipping is present here. The newspaper is the Florida Sentinel.

White Springs is in Florida. My vision narrows, blacking out the kitchen, and I close my eyes until the dizziness passes.

When I open them again, my sight is clear, but the pressure behind my eyes is mounting. The next entry is the trespassing arrest. I press the heel of my hand into my eye socket, trying to push down the pressure, reading the subsequent records with one eye. The last one indicates that she changed her name to Kristine Yaw.

I switch to the Bing browser again and search for Kristine Yaw, and what appears is a husband and a wife, both smiling, looking like a pair of Hell's Angels, standing in front of a sign that says Yaw's Paws Rescue, which strikes a chord. The sign, the lettering, is familiar. Then I glance at the address, and my stomach rolls in on itself. Yaw's Paws Rescue is in St. Augustine, just down a different road. He's in Lake City, and she's in St. Augustine. I'm in Jacksonville, and the trailer we were rescued from was in White Springs. If you drew a line between the three of us we would make a square—a perfect cage.

I stare for the longest time, trying to reconcile the images I have in my head with the image on the screen. She is thin, her face taut with sun, her hair braided in two plaits alongside her face, a child's style. She is dressed in a black t-shirt and faded Levis. Her thin arms wrap around the man's waist. They are proud and happy in their mangy sort of way. She has squinting eyes and a broad smile. She looks rough, maybe, in a biker chick way, but she doesn't seem like the type of woman who could lock her kids in a dog kennel, even if she thought there was a good reason.

I open my phone and type in the address for the rescue. St. Augustine is one of my favorite places, and John and I looked at a lot of houses there when we first moved down, charmed by its quaint history, the almost-island feel of it. I've not been back to St. Augustine since the girls were born.

Eight years ago, Sylvester and Tina Yaw opened their no-kill shelter, Yaw's Paws Rescue, on the A1A. Thirty minutes from my house. What are the chances that we would end up in the same area?

I get up and rush to our closet, dropping to the floor, opening the safe. How did I not notice what state the adoption was filed in? I slide the contents out, shifting through to the decree and clear as day... State of Florida.

I push Darren's number on my phone. "Hello?" He answers on the second ring.

"Hey. How is everybody?"

"Good. We're watching a movie; Dad's asleep. What's up?"

"Where did we live before we moved to the lake house?"

"Florida. We had a house in St. Augustine, a block from the beach."

"Oh."

"You okay?"

"Yeah. I just wondered. Well, I'll talk to you later." My mind flashes. I had practically insisted that John take the job in Florida, even though it required him to pass the Florida bar, even though it meant we'd be moving away from both of our families. Then I had dragged him to every listing I'd found in St. Augustine. Oh, my God, and it is a prayer, help me understand. I brought myself back here, to where it all began.

Holy hell.

25

Stacy

The summer rolls. Dad has settled in at Darren's, and Darren says it is working out. I try to check in at least once a week, and every phone call provides the same report. I put away the envelope containing my history in the bottom of the safe, where we keep copies of our wills and property records. There is nothing else I can do with it; it's just an albatross.

John is wrapped up in a big-money divorce case at the office, and his time at home is mostly after dark. I used to get jealous before the girls were born, and I always thought he was having an affair, but I don't think he was, not then. He just always loved his work and had a good work ethic. It's one of the reasons I fell in love with him—his intention to do the right thing. Four days out of the week, I am asleep when he comes home, curled in our bed, unaware until I wake in the morning that he ever arrived. He used to wake me in the night when he would get home, but since the girls wake me so often now, he has stopped, feeling like I don't sleep enough.

We are cohabiters in life—roommates raising children together.

~ ~ ~

The girls are in bed, and I am sitting out back, watching the moon rise over the pool—with only the screen closed, so I can hear them if they call. The light from the kitchen flashes on, and my shadow leaps into the pool. I swipe at my eyes, trying to put away the tears.

"I'm out here," I call, waving a hand over my head, not turning to face the light, not wanting him to see. He comes out to me, carrying a freshly opened beer. He squeezes a wedge of lime down into the neck of the bottle and pulls over a chair to sit next to me.

"Long day?" I nod at the beer.

"Long day," he agrees. "Don't ever divorce me."

"I'm not planning to." My voice wavers, a traitor.

"You all right?" John asks, his hand falling on my shoulder, squeezing.

I nod but cannot speak.

"Have you thought anymore about a support group? I don't think it would be a bad idea."

I shrug.

In the shadows, his eyes are dark pools. I'm wearing on him. My depression, this funk I've been stuck in, is frustrating to him. He's a fixer, and he can't fix me.

"Did you eat?" I ask, changing the subject.

"Yeah, we ordered in. That new barbecue place on Lafayette."

"How was it?"

"A lot of gristle. Too sweet." He makes a disgusted sound in his throat. "Gave me heartburn." I can hear the relief in his voice that we've changed topics.

"That's too bad."

John always has a criticism. Nothing is ever just good to John; it's never just okay. It makes him excellent at his job, but sometimes it is exhausting for me. Sometimes I just want to hear that something is good. I reach out and touch his hand, needing to be connected. He squeezes my fingers but then lets go and leans forward, putting his elbows on his knees.

"It was a rough day. People are just vicious. In divorce." Something must have happened that hit hard, he doesn't usually talk about his cases, almost never. "We had the police at the office today."

"Why?" I lean forward to see his face.

"Dumbass," he says, a low snarl in his throat. "My client." His jaw is flexing, and I see now that he is angry, legitimately angry.

"What happened?"

"He assaulted her. Right there in the conference room. I had stepped out for a file, and when I came back, he had her down by the throat on the floor. He's a bastard."

"What did you do?"

"I called the police and dropped his case. It took both of us to get him off of her."

"Both of you?"

"Her attorney was in the room. What a dumbass. He's gonna lose everything he's built."

"Is that the 'big' divorce?"

He nods. I know he has several divorces running right now. People with kids hold on until school is out and then file, thinking it will be less disruptive in the summer. I know who he is talking about, the "big" case. The man is a well-connected land developer down here, and she filed against him, claiming domestic abuse. "So now he's going to have an assault charge?"

"Yeah. I'll probably be called to testify."

"Wow. Could he go to jail for that?"

"Theoretically, yes. But I doubt he will." We sit in silence, him drinking his beer, me watching the moonlight on the water. "He should, but he won't. It does strengthen her case, though." John is opposed to all forms of violence and is particularly intolerant of the strong preying on the weak. Another one of the things I love about him—he has a soft heart.

I am tempted, at that moment, to tell him what I learned while I was in Georgia, to show him the file, the pictures, the evidence of my adoption. What a relief it would be to lay it out like a dinner spread. What a relief it would be to have him on my side. I am tempted, but I don't move. I don't speak. He has so much on his plate already. How would he respond to such information? Would he become angry and demand justice against my abusers? Would he suddenly find me distasteful, tainted by such neglect? Would he want to drop my case, or would his need to protect overwhelm me and smother me? I hold my tongue.

"She'll probably just use it in the divorce, to prove his violent tendencies. I helped her file the restraining order."

"Oh. Are you representing her now?" I keep my voice neutral.

"No. Not in the divorce." I'm relieved, even though I don't think I'm jealous anymore. I know the wife involved in this case, and if any woman could turn a man's head, it would be her. But I trust John, I remind myself, ashamed that for a moment, I didn't.

"Want another?" I ask, noticing that the bottle is empty, with just the wedge of lime circling the bottom.

He nods. "Do you mind?"

"No. I don't mind." I head inside and prepare John another beer, slicing the lime, squeezing it down the neck of the bottle. A familiar yet foreign motion.

I went to a couple of AA meetings after the incident with the sleeping pills—the ones I don't remember taking. Cassie was out of rehab by then and doing the meetings, so for a month, I sat next to her, talking and not talking, but strangely comforted by having her around again, even if we would never be the friends we once were. There was too much water under that bridge.

After a month of listening to the addicts talk about their powerlessness over their addictions, I stopped going. Dr. Martin, my therapist, thought I should continue, and even "insisted" that I continue. No matter what my other issues were, after the month, I was convinced that alcohol was not one of them. It was a relief to sit with all those people and feel so different. I had no pull toward alcohol. I didn't crave it. I couldn't remember ever even drinking. I didn't belong. For Cassie, it was an hour-by-hour struggle against drinking, as was true for many of them. Their thoughts were consumed by alcohol—how to get some, what kind, when they could sneak a bottle home, where they could hide it. Even if they weren't acting it out, it was in their minds, looping, repeating. I had other things looping in my mind, conversations being spoken just out of range of hearing. Well, I knew that I had drank, and to excess, but for the life of me I couldn't remember doing it. It wasn't a total waste, though. I learned the twelve steps, and there was some value there, and in my own way, I worked them. There were definitely things I was powerless over, even if I didn't know exactly what they were.

It had been a year of self-reflection, even if I didn't know quite how I'd ended up there. While I sat in Felicia Martin's sterile office, it was hard to remember the voices I had heard, hard to explain how I sometimes seemed to stand outside of my body and watch from a distance. I still lost time that year, and Dr. Martin recommended I keep a daily log, a journal of sorts. I've started making notes again, since my mom died.

It's been quieter since I came back from Georgia, as if I left the Others there in that house.

So why, as I head back toward John on the patio, do I just want to slam the beer, after all this time? Why do I smell it suddenly as an invitation? I turn my face, so the scent doesn't hit me and pass the beer over. I sit again in the seat next to him, feeling the twitching of the muscles in my jaw.

Breathe. I lift my head, opening my throat, and force my jaws to relax. I arch my shoulders and drop them, allowing them to fall away from where they have been hovering around my ears.

We don't speak. We listen to the sound of the crickets, to the croak of the stray frog out in the yard that has somehow found us instead of the retention pond it was probably searching for, sounding just like a child's scream.

26

Stacy

"My name is Stacy, and I just lost my mom. I'm having a hard time getting past it," I say, when it is my turn. We are sitting in a large circle. All the empty chairs have been pulled out and set aside. I'm sitting low in my seat, my hair in a messy bun, tucked up under a ball cap, and I look young in jeans and a baggy t-shirt. I had expected to be able to sit in the back of the room, the way I had in the AA meetings, passing notes with Cassie but otherwise anonymous, but the circle makes us face each other, and I keep my head low, letting the visor of my cap shadow me.

I had woken at four, sweat pilling on my lip, my stomach roiling. John snoring beside me. I rolled to my side, slipping out of bed, afraid I would be sick. The room spun but righted itself as my feet touched the ground. The kitchen was a mess. John's vodka bottle sitting opened and half empty on the counter, the cap resting in the sink. A single glass upside down in the strainer, not two. My head throbbed when I tried to think back, but the last thing I could remember was sitting by the pool with John, listening to a screaming frog. I capped the vodka and put the bottle away. I washed the glass and dried it.

Ibuprofen and three glasses of water later and finally my head stopped pounding, and the furry sock stopped masquerading as my tongue. I sat in the kitchen, in the dark, waiting for the day to start. Writing down the odd morning in my journal, feeling the hint of lost time, but waiting to see if John knows anything. Maybe he was drinking in the night, and I just have a touch of the flu. But I remember very clearly how the scent of his beer had affected me, how I had felt almost compelled to drink it myself.

The girls woke up, John woke up, and everything was normal.

John didn't mention me drinking, and he would have if we had done it together. He would have said something if he had known. "I still think you need to think about a support group," he had said, the last thing before kissing me goodbye. That's why I am here, still half queasy from a night I don't remember. I have to do something. I feel like I'm sliding deeper into darkness, and I'm afraid that, at some point, I won't be able to see the light.

I wish I knew what I did last night.

"Was it sudden?" the man who opened the meeting, Leon, asks.

"Very." Tears prickle in my eyes, and I blink to clear them and then compress my lips, unable to say anything more.

"We're glad you are here," he says, and I want to scream, *This isn't helpful!*

I say nothing else; I sit, sullen-faced, burning.

"Do you have something you'd like to share?" Leon asks, his cigarette burning low to his fingers.

"No. My mother just died, and I'm having a hard time processing it. That's all." I close my mouth, my teeth clacking together.

He looks at me, questioning, judging, as if to say, *I know there is more.*

Do I have to say more? Can I not just sit here and be not alone? I shake my head, looking away toward the concrete wall.

"Thank you for sharing," he finally says.

"Thank you for sharing," the cult of sufferers recite.

The next person tells his story, about a son who died in a car accident. His grief makes me feel worse. I want to leave. I need to get back to my children. It's the natural way of things, to lose your mother... but to lose a child? His sorrow is overwhelming, and I wish I were the hugging kind.

The meeting goes on, and by the end I feel less alone, less isolated in my sorrow. Leon finally asks, "Is there anybody else who would like to add anything?" Heads shake around the circle, and he offers a prayer. "We are here every week." He smiles around at all of us, and I realize that he is the only person who did not share his story. "It's a good idea for you to connect outside of the meeting, have a friend you can call." There are nods and murmurs around the room.

When others begin to rise and shuffle together in small pods, connected by their time in the group, I bolt. I am nearly to the steps before a voice calls out, "Stacy, wait."

I pause and turn back to see the man, Leon, coming through the doors. "Yes?" I ask, my voice clipped.

"Glad you came."

"Yeah. Me, too." Although I am not, and now I just want to get back to the cul-de-sac and collect my girls from Mona's and Dee's houses. I just want to fold around them and crawl into a hole.

I want to crawl into a dog crate.

The thought jolts me, and I cough, having been mid-swallow when it hit.

"You all right?" he asks, patting me on the back until I step away.

"Just swallowed wrong." My voice comes out in a croak.

He nods, his hair falling over the arch of one eyebrow. "I felt like you had more to say in there. I just wanted to offer myself, like an ear. I know how it is, coming in from the outside."

"No, really, I'm fine."

"I'm sure you are." He nods, knowing. "Losing a parent is hard. If you want to talk, or just want to listen to somebody breathe, I wanted you to know I can do both, listen and breathe." He flips his hand and presents a card, a magician pulling a rabbit from a hat. I take the card, although I don't want to. My hand reaches for it, and then it's between my fingers, closed, cupped, protected, sheltered.

Centered on the card is the name "Leon Freak," and beneath that is a phone number.

"Freak, huh?" I ask.

"Not my real last name."

"That's probably good. That would certainly have set you up, wouldn't it?"

He grins a wide, toothy grin, showing stained teeth. "Yeah, we all are, though, aren't we? 'Set up,' just wired a certain way, and that's who we become."

"Maybe." I agree because I certainly feel wired that way.

"Anyway, I just didn't want you to leave without having a resource. I don't sleep, so call anytime."

"If I wanna hear somebody breathe?"

"That's right." He chuckles, and for a split second, I can almost see the young person he had once been—cocky, sure of himself, before he got lost in the haze of whatever his life has been, before it stole his gifts and wrecked his body. Because he is a wreck of a man now; I notice as he walks away with the slightest of stoops, the smallest of limps. His work boots look too heavy for his narrow frame to carry.

Maybe this is all I need—to be connected to others who are struggling. Maybe it's all just part of the grief. Are they always in control of their souls? Of course not. Is everything that has been happening to me just a normal part of life? Is this how everybody is? I envy people who own their flaws—people like Leon Freak. What sort of man claims such a moniker? What name would I choose, to describe the circumference of my soul? Stacy Mother? Stacy Rabid? Stacy Frightened? Stacy Lost? Stacy Caged Girl? Who am I?

Others slap Leon's hands as they pass through the doors, heading up the steps from the church basement.

"It works if you work it." The phrase runs in my head, an echoed memory from the AA meetings I'd attended with Cassie. Nobody just said that; it just came from inside of my head. It feels strange, because even though the voices have been quieter since I came back, I have still felt that odd creeping of my skin, like I was outgrowing it, bursting free from a cocoon.

As I step into the sunlight, pressure builds behind my eyes, and I hear somebody screaming.

Shiloh

"You okay?"

I open my eyes, and I smile. I'm tempted to cup his face in my hands and kiss him. That would blow his mind. Not because he's cute—although he is—but because I am out and Stacy is very far away. I remembered, finally, how to get back out. You have to sneak up on her, quiet and stealthy, when she's not expecting it. Ha!

"I am now."

"I'm sorry about your mother," he says.

"Yeah, whatever." I turn on my heel, thinking that he has no idea. The car is parked, and I dig through our purse until I find keys.

When I leave the parking lot, I turn south, and I drive until I come to the A1A, which slices across the top of St. Augustine. I drive to the address and park in the lot next door. I get out of the car and walk toward the building, intending to go inside, to find Kristine Yaw. Will she recognize us, after all these years? Will we recognize her? I press my face against the darkened windows, trying to shield the light from the outside with my hand.

Guilt washes in my heart at having left her when I knew how much she needed me. I tried to get back to her, I really did. There is a counter and, behind it, two racks of bagged dog food. The room is empty. I change my angle, and the door behind the counter opens. Startled, I almost jump back. She is tall, with a long, blond ponytail that swings over her shoulder, and she glances toward the window. I drop out of sight, my pulse racing, terrified suddenly that she may be mad. She may not be happy to see me. She may be angry that I never came home. Will she still be hurt that I didn't get away from the new family and find a way back?

I'm going to talk to her, I promise.

But not today.

Stacy

I am rushing across a parking lot, and nearly stumble when I realize it. Why am I running? I stop and turn, trying to get my bearings. I expect to see the church, but it isn't there. I am in a parking lot, and the metal building behind me says Yaw's Paws Rescue and Shelter across the front windows, and my stomach lurches.

I run again. Why am I here? I jerk my car door open and slide into the seat, feeling a high, breathless panic. I crank the engine and put the car in reverse.

Then I glance back at the building, and my foot hits the brake. I sit, not breathing. Seconds pass like minutes. The door opens, and she steps out onto the sidewalk in front of the building and lights a cigarette. I watch her drawing the smoke into her body, the ember end glowing.

I'm crazy.

How did I get here? Of course, I know. I've lost time. Damnit! I've lost time.

My heart wars, equal parts longing and terror and remorse.

~ ~ ~

The girls were clamoring to swim when I got home, and Willow and Julia with them. Other kids will come as the day passes, but for now, I am folding laundry on the patio table, watching the girls play with only one eye, letting my mind roll. When the laundry is folded, sitting neatly in the basket to be put away later, I pull my notebook onto my lap, unopened. The girls will play, and when they are tired of being wet and in the sun, they will come inside, and I will let them watch a movie. It's okay. I'm okay. I still feel like my skin is crawling off, the way it does when the Others come, but less so, The card in my hip pocket with the name "Leon Freak" settles in like a talisman.

John's liquor—the vodka, the Gold Label whiskey, the Anejo rum—calls to me, and the soles of my feet itch to walk into the house, to stop at the counter to slam a shot and then another. I stay seated cradled by the webbing of the patio chair, refusing the call. I listen to the kids. I force myself to be grounded.

I have to be vigilant. I know now that it was Shiloh who drank John's vodka and left me to deal with the hangover. I have to be more aware. I can't let her do what she did today, taking over because I wasn't paying attention.

How do I write what happened today? I have to be honest, to not filter it. I have to admit everything, even what I don't remember—or keeping the notebook will be no help. I drove while she was here, and I don't even know if she knows how to drive. This is different than finding myself standing with the refrigerator open and not remembering what I was getting. The pages that have gone before are clipped together, and I don't look at them, but every day, I make notes about what I do. I've already written that I woke up sick this morning, about finding the vodka on the counter. I write about going to the meeting, about Leon Freak, the only person who didn't share his sadness. I remember all of that well enough. I've drawn a square on the page for the time I can't explain and write 11:00-11:30. Then, thinking that I need to make a note about where I found myself, I write YP, which will only mean something to me, Yaw's Paws. It feels red to me, that missing time, like anger and confusion and heat. I flip through the clipped pages and see all the similar blocks, mostly for short amounts of time, mostly with small notations saying, "Home" or "Grocery," or in one instance, an hour-long block that ends with "Shelby's room," and that day felt kind of orange. I am losing more and more time; I realize it now, looking at all the small blocks. I keep thinking that it's been quieter since I came back, that I'm having less lost time, but now I am not sure. The pantry is full of cookies and sweets that I don't remember buying, and clothes hanging in my closet that I would never wear.

I need to break the cycle. I don't remember driving to St. Augustine. I don't remember going to the pet rescue. I just remember running across the lot feeling panic chasing me. I think of the glowing cigarette and the moment when she glanced toward my car. Had I gone inside? Had I spoken to her? Would the people at the grief support group see this as a reasonable response to my sorrow? Would Leon Freak think this was normal?

When Leon had looked at me, I felt seen. What does that mean? Did he recognize me because he is like me? Did he really see me, or was he just being sympathetic and I'm projecting?

I wish there were a twelve-step program to find all of my lost time. Three time-blocks already this week.

Did she know me? What did I say to her? Did I go inside?

When she looked over at my car, the tip of her cigarette glowing, I had shrunk down in my seat, peeking through the steering wheel. But I know she saw me. I half expected her to walk toward to me, to drag me from my car, to steer me into the building and into a kennel, placing a lock to secure me. I half wanted her to, just to release the chaos mounting in my soul.

My heart hammers in my ears, and Shelby calls, "Watch me!" I look up, smiling as she jumps from the hot tub into the pool. She rebounds to the surface, spluttering and laughing.

"Good job, Baby."

The gate opens, and Mona and Dee come through the yard. "Can we come visit?" Mona asks, and the tension in my frame relaxes.

"Absolutely," and it almost sounds like a plea. Please let me feel connected.

~ ~ ~

Hours later, John rolls into bed beside me, carrying the slightest hint of the whiskey he had shared with Franklin and Jonas, the men who own his firm, and the new associate, Janice, as he sometimes does after a long day. I slip toward him, feigning sleepiness, but alert and charged. The need to be connected, to be seen still stampedes through my soul.

I touch him and kiss him, tasting the remnants of his whiskey on his tongue. We have sex for the first time in weeks, months maybe. For the first time in maybe a year, we make love in a passionate, hungry way, and I only vaguely wonder if it is me or someone else here with John? The lines are getting blurry.

27

Stacy

"Look, you need to come back up here and get some of your stuff." Darren's agitation, his annoyance, is palpable across the airwaves, and I slip down in my lounge chair, sliding my hips forward, ready to fight. "I mean the attic is full, and it's mostly your stuff left, and there are boxes in your closet. I don't think I should have to go through your junk." It is a speech he has practiced, probably on Scott, over this last week. Scott is perhaps sitting there, listening, giving him the courage to tell me what for.

"Okay," I say, my voice low, letting the fight wash out of me. There is no reason to fight. Darren and Scott are taking care of Dad, and I'm sitting by the pool miles and miles away.

Shelby squeals and jumps from the hot tub to the pool, and I have the urge to cover the phone to keep him from hearing, feeling guilty for the luxury of my leisure. Mona is sunning herself not far away, and I catch her eye and point toward the pool and then the phone, indicating that she needs to be on kid patrol for a few minutes.

"It's just too much. I mean, my whole life has been disrupted, and you've just gone back to the beach."

"Your life has been disrupted? It wasn't my idea for Dad to move in with you." As soon as the words have left my mouth, I wish I could bite them back. Darren could always get my hackles up.

"Well, you weren't offering to have him come live with you." There is satisfaction in his voice. This is what he had expected, the script he had prepared.

"Like that would work. We don't have room for another person. I have a family, kids." It feels like a low blow. "I mean, he'd have to sleep on the couch, or the girls would have to double up. It would have been too traumatic for him, to make that kind of move, don't you think?" I add the last hoping to mitigate the judgment in my voice, as if I had thought about these things when the time was right. I hadn't. It was never a question in my mind that Darren would take care of Dad, that my life would not be upheaved by my father's change in circumstance. When the words are out I hear how they sound, suggesting that without kids his life is purposeless, that his life is extravagant. It's just like showing off my rings, this using my kids, my family, to justify my failure to rise to a need. Dammit, I don't want to fight, but he gets under my skin. "Look, I don't want to argue. If you say I need to come up there and clear my stuff out, I will come up and clear my stuff out. Okay? I would never ask you to go through my junk."

"Well, you just left and expected it to get done." His voice has risen to another octave, and I remember how I used to call him "Old Woman" when we were kids, and I'm tempted to say it now, just to hear his head explode.

"I'm sorry. I just didn't realize you'd have renters so soon."

"Well, it can't just sit empty. I can't afford to pay for that."

"Okay, that's fine. I'll come. I'll talk to John and see what I can work out."

"Okay. That sounds good. Let me know when you're gonna be here. I need to arrange for cleaners."

"All right. I'll call you back."

~ ~ ~

John buys me a ticket for Friday evening, and he and the girls drive me to the airport to see me off. I wanted to take the girls and drive there, but the house has already been cleared out, and there wouldn't be anything for them to do. "There's just a cot and all your boxes," Darren had said, sounding annoyed, again, that I hadn't understood the magnitude of his effort, his sacrifice.

"Okay. I'll come alone." I felt guilty, when I'd told John that I couldn't take the girls, explaining what Darren had said, what the project will require. The girls are my job, and I feel like taking time away from them is a failure.

"That's fine. We'll fly you up," he had said, his voice sounding light across the phone line. He was in his office, and his voice still holds the small bubbles that come with laughter. John has a beautiful laugh, resonate and solid, and a small jealous piece of me wonders who he is sharing it with. Whomever it is, is still there, because he muffled the phone for a second to say something before coming back to me. "We'll just buy you a ticket. The girls and I can go to the zoo or something."

"You sure? We could take sleeping bags." I desperately wanted to take them. I need them to ground me.

"No. It'll be fun. You need to do this without distraction. Don't you agree?"

I shrugged, not convinced, which doesn't translate across the phone line, but he knows me. He knows.

"Do you have any friends who might come help?"

"Yeah, Cassie will help. I'll let her know I'm coming." I say Cassie, but it's Sue Bellefonte's face that looms in my mind's eye. She would be more likely to come and help, although I have no real intention of asking for anybody's help.

I fly into Atlanta, feeling the weight of Florida lifting from my body as I travel, being replaced with the different weight of Georgia. I have found myself at Yaw's Paws Rescue seven times since that first time. I never remember driving there, but I am obsessed with the thought of catching sight of her. The girls have been in the car three of those times. I would never put my children at risk, but Shiloh doesn't seem to care.

I take an Uber down to Peachtree City and have him drop me at U-Haul Storage on 34 to pick up the truck John has arranged. I pull out onto 34, feeling high up and a little dangerous, without a clear understanding yet of my parameters. It's not a huge truck, and by the time, I turn off of 34 and onto Oak Dale, I'm feeling more confident.

I send Darren a text: I'm here.

He texts back as I'm unlocking the front door: Good. But he doesn't offer to come meet me.

As Darren had said, the house is vacant. The furniture from the living room is completely gone, with only small piles of debris along the edges to indicate that this house was ever a home. The dining room and kitchen, likewise, are void of furniture. I am relieved to see the kettle sitting on the stove and, beside it, Mom's French press. There is one lone mug sitting on the one dish towel beside the sink. "Thank you, Darren." Whatever else Darren may be, he is thoughtful. In the bread cupboard is coffee. I'm pretty sure I couldn't make it through the weekend without caffeine.

I set water to boil and stare out the window over the sink, where twilight has already made the shadows dark and long.

"The house is so empty," I say to John when he calls. "It's so sad."

"I'm sorry, babe."

"It's all right. How are the girls?"

"Getting ready for stories. They said you're reading Huck Finn?"

"Yeah, I think we left off at chapter five."

"Really? It's a little... advanced, don't you think?" I'm irritated, but, in truth, it is a little advanced, especially for Shelby, but I read it with enthusiasm and paraphrase where I need to for it to work.

"No, it's a great story. It's an adventure."

"It's a little racist, don't you think?"

"I'm skipping over anything that isn't appropriate." I bite my cheek. Of course, he would think I would read them the whole of it.

"I think I'll leave that for you to finish."

"Probably best," I say and let the silence hang, feeling judged and criticized, feeling the need to defend my parenting choices and refusing to. "Can I talk to them?"

"Sure. Sophie first."

"Hey, Mama," Sophie says, sounding younger over the phone when I can't see her animated features testing out new personas.

"Hey, Soph. You guys doing all right?"

"Yep. We had Jimmy John's for dinner."

"That's nice. Big pickle?"

"Yeah. How is Grandpa?"

"I haven't seen him yet, probably not until tomorrow."

"Oh. I love you."

"I love you, too. I miss you. Is Shelby ready?"

"Here she is." She kisses into the phone, and I reach my hand up to catch it.

"Hey, Muffin."

"Hey, Mama."

"How are you?"

"I don't like the pickles," she whispers into the phone.

I laugh, and all the tension of my travels washes down my arms. Neither of the girls like the pickles at Jimmy John's, but John insists on buying them and making a big fuss about them, and they don't have the heart to tell him the truth. "I know you don't," I whisper back.

"Give Grandpa a hug."

"I will do it when I see him."

She yawns loudly into the phone, and in my mind, I see her jaws stretching in that sudden quest for oxygen. Shelby is a master yawner.

"I love you, Mama."

"I love you, too, Shelby-fi. You get some good sleep, okay. I'll see you on Sunday."

"Okay. Bye." I envision her handing the phone back to John, and I feel the absence of my children like a great chasm in my chest.

"Let me get them to bed," he says.

"All right. Love you.

"Yeah. You, too."

I stand for a long minute in the dark, looking out at the lake that is turning black.

I feel hollowed out, like the house.

I walk down the hall, past my parent's bedroom, which is like the rest of the house—completely barren—and I step through it to the bathroom, remembering when they remodeled it and put in the heated floor like it was yesterday. The closet is empty of my father's clothes, but still full of my mother's clothes. Her slacks and shirts still hanging there. What am I supposed to do with her clothes? The thought of donating them, of some stranger wearing them, makes me feel weak. I'll bag them up. I'll take them home. I run my hand along the fabric of her blouses, and in the motion, I smell her. Grief washes through me. I wonder how long they will smell like her? Like this house? I bury my face in a tangle of silks and cotton and rayon, wishing I had been a different kind of daughter. Wishing I had told her how much I love her instead of always keeping her at arm's length.

My foot hits on an object, solid but not hard, and the object shifts and falls to the floor. I kneel to see a set of two violin cases, one small and one large.

"Wow." I can't believe she kept them. An almost hysterical laugh escapes me, and the skin holding all my cells in place feels suddenly very fluid. When I was young, I wanted to learn violin. I had wanted to learn violin for almost a year before she bought me a quarter-sized violin for my seventh birthday and got me lessons. For weeks we went to classes, and when we came home, she would use my quarter-sized violin to learn what the teacher had taught. She learned to play "Twinkle, Twinkle, Little Star" so I could hear how it should sound. When a full-size student violin went up for sale at the studio, she bought it and started working her way through my Suzuki book. By then I had lost interest, annoyed in equal parts that she was better than I was and that she was excited about playing. We worked through the whole of that book, her learning far ahead of me, and me being sullen and taciturn because I didn't want to practice.

She kept playing long after I had quit lessons, although she only played when she was home alone, never feeling confident enough to let anybody hear.

I hug the violins to my chest, bulky in their cases, and wish I could bring her back. I would be a better daughter if I could do it over.

28

Stacy

I start in the attic, bringing down boxes that are easy enough to manage and setting them in rows down the hall. The violins sit in the guest room on the cot that Darren and Scott had set up for me. Every time I come down the ladder with a new box, I see the cases, and they pull me. I wish I had kept at it. I wish I had done that one thing with my mother. Would that have changed the whole course of our lives together, if we had been able to share music like that? I have a flash of the music circles she took me to when she was trying to keep me interested. People gathered together, each playing the same song. "Orange Blossom Special," "Rocky Top," "Wabash Cannonball." I remember sitting like a lump, watching the happy people, their wrists flying, their fingers flailing, seeing my mother's urge to dance, like an embarrassment. It all felt obscene to me, such displays of exuberance. It felt so country. I was such a stubborn child. How would my life have been different if I had let myself connect?

It is nearly eleven when I make my last trip down the ladder, dropping the box onto another. I am weary, my legs stinging from the up and down on the ladder, from the loads I have carried down, my lungs are drawing for air. The last box skitters as it lands and topples off the one box, landing on one of its corners. The flaps spring open, and the contents spread out across the hall. I laugh.

Suzuki, Book One. Suzuki, Book Three. Book Two, Book Seven... they are all here, with my mother's handwriting in notes along the margins. I gather the books and head back to the hall, feeling the omen, the serendipity of those books falling out when I'm already feeling sentimental. I unzip the case of my mother's violin, still strung, and when I test the strings, they sound nearly in tune. Had she played all her life? I spend a few minutes finding and downloading a tuner from the app store and fine-tune the violin, wondering if anything at all will come back to me.

I play, from the first book, the well-rehearsed and much-hated "Twinkle, Twinkle, Little Star" in its variations, then move through the book, letting the remembrance of the strings come back to me. I squawk and squeak and make a terrible racket until my neck feels cramped, my shoulders aching from being raised.

"Ha!" I say, finishing with a flourish, and set the violin back in its case. That poor instrument probably never felt more violated.

Grief is like the ocean, crashing in waves and ebbing. Being in this silent house is like being submerged. I search through my room. I ache—the feelings are bursting through my skin, and I feel like my flesh could burst into flames with the intensity of it. The circling in my head is cyclonic, a hurricane washing through my memories.

I miss my mother.

The boxes in the closet, all things I have left behind—notebooks and journals and sketchpads. I settle to the task at hand and pull the first of the boxes from the closet, half terrified at what I might find. I paw through old clothes, a bundle of notebooks, junk left sitting for twelve years. My finger grazes against cool glass, and I close my hand around the neck of a bottle of Jim Beam. Odd. Surely I am the one who stuffed it there, wrapped in the cotton of a Destination 312 concert shirt. There is just no explanation for it being here, no memory in my mind of ever purchasing or owning or finally hiding a bottle of Jim Beam. Of course it's mine, though—here from the year of half-truths. Nobody else would have buried it in a box of forgotten things.

I want my mother back.

The bottle is unopened, sealed. Maybe it's a gift from my younger self to my older self. Tonight, if ever, I could use a little numb.

"Just a drop," I answer aloud, as if someone is there to pour, to offer, because, yes, we could use something to take the edge off. Normal people would have a drink on a night like this. John would have a drink on a night like this.

Nobody will know. It won't hurt. I think about the man who had given me his card when I went to that first grief support group, when I felt like all my parts were coming unglued. Wouldn't it be a better option to call him, a stranger, to help me through my grief? Leon had said I could call him if I needed somebody to talk to or just to hear somebody breathe. I should call him. I should pour this bottle down the toilet, or better, take it down the street as a gift to Darren.

But I don't want to hear somebody breathe.

I want to be numb.

I want to be normal.

The lines inside my head have blurred, and I sometimes see myself doing the things I don't know I do. I sometimes see myself as somebody else, wearing clothes that I would never wear.

I hear her, always, talking, talking, talking, talking.

Just a drink to dull my mind, so I can process all this shit and go home.

It's no big deal.

I just want my heart to stop aching.

"That's right," I say to my reflection in the mirror, without moving my lips.

I pour the rest of my coffee down the bathroom sink and fill the bottom of the mug, gauging an ounce, two?

"That's right, Stacy, run and hide. I'll take care of all this for you." Shiloh whispers in my ear.

The odor is strong, and the cup is on my lips before I know it, before I decide. I watch myself from the outside and from the inside and reflecting in the mirror, all at once, slamming the liquor, coughing, gagging, eyes watering.

Then I am back in my body, looking up into red-rimmed, teary eyes reflected in the mirror.

The heat comes, that heat, radiating from my core to my fingertips, so familiar yet forgotten, like an electric charge.

I take a deep breath and then let the fumes out, remembering this like the touch of a lover long lost.

I pour another slug into the mug, as if even my hand has a mind of its own.

The roaring in my head slows; all the gears relax and settle.

My phone vibrates, and I skitter to catch it. John's face lights the screen, and the enormity of what I've done hits me. I am wholly inside my body, pushing the voices down and away.

"Shit," I say, and my voice sounds slow and unwieldy. I let the call go. It's only when I hear my voice, slurred, that I realize how much time has passed, how many boxes I've gone through, the contents spread across the floor, in an arc around me. It's only when I hear my voice that I notice how much more of the liquor has been drained from the bottle. How much time has slipped? Enough for my voice to be thick, enough for my mind to be infinitely numb.

Shiloh is laughing in my head. Hysterical, knee-slapping.

I'll call him in the morning. Tell him I was already asleep.

Heading to bed. Hope you are okay. His text comes through as if he knows something is wrong, and guilt washes over me. He doesn't know about the break, or the therapist, or my little voices. None of this would make sense to him. None of this would be acceptable to him.

I almost respond to his text but realize that then he'd call back. Then he would hear my slow and unwieldy speech, and he would know. He would be worried and call Darren to come and check on me.

I let the phone go dark and sit on the floor, rocking, surrounded by concert shirts and studded collars, crying for what I've lost, feeling the thin sloshing of the alcohol and coffee in my stomach. When I stand up, the world spins, and I have to lean on the wall to keep from falling. I pour the remaining contents of the Jim Beam bottle into the toilet, hating the way I feel, dumb and thick. I push my hand down my throat, purging the rest from my body. Retching until my stomach is dry.

Shiloh laughs and laughs and laughs, even as my head pounds with the pressure of the retching.

The alcohol still sloshes in my blood, but a good part of it is gone.

I stand in the shower until the water runs cold, still feeling the liquor in my blood but the diminishing of it. When I am clean and dressed for bed, I take the bottle and put it in the trash, burying it under a wad of paper towels.

That felt dirty, not like the times I had cocktails with John, wine over dinner. This was something different, drinking to be numb, drinking to get through something ugly. Something gritty rolls under my eyes when I close them, and I think it may be shame.

29

Stacy

I wake at four, sweating the rest of the alcohol from my body. I've been up twice in the night to pee, having tried to flush my system with water after purging. There is nothing to give away what I did last night but the burning of my skin. My face isn't swollen; my eyes are not blood shot. There is nothing to tell the world about my dirty night, but the guilt still churns in my stomach, as if I've harmed someone. I feel like I've done something horrible and that the secret will come out in the daylight.

I shower, again, and when I get dressed, my stomach feels hollow with the need for food and with my unsettled sense of guilt. I set the kettle to heat and open the pantry. Darren left me crackers. While I stand at the island, I type my old therapist's name into the search engine of my phone. Felicia Martin. She is still practicing up in Atlanta. Would she remember me?

All my pieces are flying out away from me; my memory is faulty and misfiring. Last week, I found myself sitting on Shelby's floor, playing with her stuffed animals when she wasn't there. All of the glassy-eyed animals were staring up at me like I was their god. I'm losing it. I'm cracking up.

It's almost five, and I have gnawed my way through half a sleeve of saltines and am almost finished moving the stack of boxes from down the hall to the front door, the staging area, before I will carry them out to load them in the van.

My phone rings, and I set the current box down and go to answer. "Hey, love," I say, out of breath from exertions, planting a smile on my face as if he can see me.

"Hey. How's it going?"

"Good. I'm just moving boxes." I look out the window above the sink, watching the light from the house across the lake coming on, seeing the faint silhouette of movement behind sheer curtains. When I lived here, I used to watch that house and imagine terrible things. I had made up a story about a man who murdered his wife, and the kids across the lake had witnessed, from this kitchen window, the murder, and they go on a sleuthing mission to expose the killer. I was in a mystery phase and had planned for a whole series, The Shoal Creek Capers. Of course, I never wrote them. I just thought and planned and imagined.

"I tried to call last night."

"I saw that when I woke up. I was pretty worn out."

"Yeah, I figured." There is no suspicion in his voice, no hesitancy. I bite my lip to keep from unloading my guilt.

"How are the girls?"

"I haven't been in to check on them yet, but I think they're awake. I hear movement."

"Good." We laugh, and I can almost see him stretching in the way his voice thins. "It's strange to be here, without anybody else."

"I bet. You okay?"

"Yeah, I'm fine." I turn away from the window. "I found the old violins. I think I may learn to play it."

He chuckles. "Really?" He knows I am fickle; I get excited about things, and when they get hard, I move on to something else to be excited about.

"Yeah. I think I will. It would make my mom proud."

"Your mom is already proud of you."

"I know." That knot rises in my throat every time I speak of her. "Maybe one of the girls would want to learn. I'm gonna bring them both home."

"Good. I work a lot." The amusement is thick, teasing me. He knows me even if he has never seen me the way Leon Freak had upon first meeting.

"Shut up," I say, laughing, but he is right. The violin is a difficult instrument to make sound good. It takes practice and perseverance. It takes dedication. I hear the last almost from outside of my body, my mother's voice coming back to me on the loop of memory. I almost turn to look through the room, hoping to find her standing there. I hold myself steady, watching out the window.

"So are you gonna be able to do this?" He feels guilty for not coming with me, for not helping.

"Yeah, it's mostly boxes. I'm not going to go through everything. I'll just put it up in our attic, and the girls can go through it when I die," I say, meaning it as a joke.

"You should probably go through it, don't you think? Instead of bringing a bunch of junk you don't want back here?"

"Yeah, I'm going through it. I was just kidding."

"Hm."

My phone vibrates, and I glance to see Darren is calling through. "Darren's calling. Talk to you later?

"Okay."

"Give the girls some love," I say, but the line has already been disconnected, and I push the button to answer Darren's call. Surely, John will give them my love.

"Hey, Darren."

"Come on down for breakfast. Scott's cooking."

My stomach rumbles. "Great. I'll be right there."

~ ~ ~

Walking into their home is like stepping into a Hallmark movie. Their house is clean and airy, light. The aromas of bacon and pancakes float toward me as I stand at the open front door. It's almost like a dream. I hug Darren, turning my face away, hoping that the toothpaste and mouthwash have rinsed away any last remnants of the alcohol. Guilt rides on my shoulder.

I walk with him to the kitchen, and Dad is standing at the waffle iron, waiting for the light to turn. I go to him, and he gives a side-armed hug. "You look great." It's true; the gaunt hollows in his face have filled in, and even the dark circles beneath his eyes are less.

"Scott is fattening me up."

Dad seems to be having a good day, and we stand around the island, only Dad sitting on a stool, to eat. We eat the bacon from one platter, almost as quickly as Scott can lay it out. We eat waffles with blueberry compote, probably homemade, and powdered sugar. My blood shifts gears and slows with the influx of sugar.

When the food is gone, when we have eaten our fill and I feel, finally, at last, wholly normal, Darren asks how it's going at the house.

"It's good. I was pretty tired last night, but I was up at it this morning."

"I'll come down and help, after we get the kitchen clean."

"That would be great. But don't feel like you have to. It is all my stuff." I don't look at him, feeling petty, manipulative. I gather the empty plates and move them toward the sink. His words had come as an admonishment, although he probably meant nothing by it. "There are some boxes in the attic that I'm scared to bring down by myself," I say, trying to soften the edge of my comment.

"Yeah. I'll be down, probably an hour or so. There are big trash bags under the sink. I thought you might want to sort through some of it for Goodwill."

"Sounds good." I can stand here longer and talk about what needs done, and continue dreading it, or I can get up and head that way and just get it started. "All right. I'll see you down there, then. Scott, breakfast was divine." I squeeze him and kiss his cheek, no longer worried that the scent of Jim Beam clings to me. I smell like bacon and sugar.

I hug Dad, and Darren walks me to the door. He promises it won't be long, and I wave as I'm walking back down the street, "Whenever. I'll be there."

I feel like a kid who has gotten away with the cookie from the cookie jar. Did it not happen because nobody knows? So what if I had a drink last night? It isn't a crime. I wasn't out driving; I wasn't hurting anybody. So why do I feel so guilty? People drink all the time when they are under stress. It's not a big deal. But I remember last night—every dirty little detail. There should be no shame in it. I'm an adult; I can choose.

Normal people would talk about it. If I were normal, I would have answered the phone to John last night and said I'd found a lovely bottle of Jim Beam. Or I would have told Darren, "Guess what I found in one of those boxes?" I would have given him the rest of the bottle for his liquor cabinet. That's what normal people do. It's dirty because it's a secret.

It's dirty because I am not normal. If nobody knows, will they think I'm normal?

What is the sound a tree makes when it falls and nobody is around to hear it? Just because nobody heard it fall doesn't mean it didn't.

30

Stacy

The morning slips past, and between the two of us, we get the attic entirely cleared. I plan to load everything on the truck and deal with it at home, regardless of John's recrimination. "I'll sort it there," I say to Darren when all the boxes are down from the attic. I had dreamt, the night Darren had called to insist that I come, of sitting in my driveway in Florida while the kids are riding bikes in the cul-de-sac, going through one thing after another. The dream had ended with a gasp and a small scream when I reached into the box and pulled out a heart tangled in hair, still pumping, still warm. But the image of going through the boxes with the girls nearby sticks with me and feels warm when I think of it.

Darren blows out a breath, throws his bottom jaw forward in a theatrical gesture. He rolls his eyes and kicks one meaty hip out under his hand.

"What?" I ask, confused by his posture.

"You haven't needed any of this stuff for twelve years."

"So?"

"You don't need it. You should tidy up."

I laugh, almost hysterical. Sometimes Darren is such a woman. Who in the world uses the word "tidy"?

"Seriously, if it doesn't bring you joy—and I guarantee none of this is going to bring you joy—you should set it free."

It is doubtful that joy is what I am going to find in these boxes. What I am going to see inside these boxes are scraps of paper where I wrote dark thoughts, clothes that I will be embarrassed for my girls ever to know I wore. They will laugh, I know; they will not be able to imagine me in all the short skirts, the studded, badass jackets. Especially Sophie—it will give her power when she rebels to say, "It's not as short as what you used to wear." These are glimpses of the roughest years of my life, and I am none too confident I ever want to open them.

I certainly don't want to face the contents right now. I need my children near when I open them, to keep me grounded, to claim the studded collars for their stuffed pets, to normalize my abnormal adolescence. I have the most unnatural feeling that if I open them here, without the girls, I will be sucked into them like a genie into a bottle and disappear entirely.

I push the thought out of my head, a small laugh at Darren's expense still bubbling on my lips. I am feeling light; the physical work has done good things for me, and I am relaxed, at ease. Shiloh had tried to take over, to claim me, but I forced her into silence. I did not give in to her... well, in the end, I didn't. I remember almost everything that happened in the night, not with pride, but with power. It is not a black hole. I have power over Shiloh. It's not like when we were teens, and she could push me out with a whisper. I've been an adult for a long time now, and whatever made her is a long way in the past. Isn't it just an excuse, blaming it on Shiloh? Isn't it all just me, trying not to take responsibility. "Avoidance issues"—isn't that what Dr. Martin had said?

Darren is talking, and it takes me a second to catch up. "...It totally transformed my life."

"What did?"

"The book! Do you never listen? I read this book about tidying by this woman from Japan, and now I just can't tolerate clutter."

"Sounds like a powerful book. I'll have to borrow it." I'm teasing him, but he doesn't see it.

"I'll loan it to you. Then, when it has transformed your life, you can pass it on to some other sucker who thinks things matter."

"So, if things don't matter, what does?"

"Joy. Only joy. You should fill your space with things that make you joyful and nothing else."

"I guess I can get rid of the stove, then."

He quirks an eyebrow but doesn't add anything more, surely remembering some of my first cooking attempts, one of which prompted the insurance-funded remodel of the kitchen.

We work hard through the morning, bringing everything down from the attic. We are hot and sweating by the time Scott calls to ask us back for lunch. We are happy to make our way down the street.

"Do you remember a boy we called 'Slim'?" I'm not sure which of us is more shocked at the question. I wasn't even thinking about the boy. I feel ridiculous, saying the name aloud—an adjective, not a name. I wish as soon as I hear the name on the wind that I could draw it back and eat the words. Darren stops in his tracks, and when I turn around to face him, he has gone three shades of pale. Red splotches grow on his cheeks and chin, amidst the unnatural pallor left when his blood leaked away, and it takes a moment before some semblance of his normal color drains back into his face.

"Do you?" he asks in a very thin voice. It is an admission, and I almost cheer.

"Not as such," I admit. "What happened to him?"

"He probably ended up in jail. Bastard." He says it like he is spitting. It is vulgar language coming from Darren, and I regret my part in making him say it.

"Why's that?"

"What all do you know?" he asks, finding his feet again, and we continue our walk toward the cul-de-sac.

"I know I was adopted. That the boy, Slim, was my brother? I think. I'm not sure. I think we were in pretty bad shape when we were taken."

The word "taken" echoes in my head. Why hadn't I said "rescued"?

"How did you find out? Mom thought you didn't remember anything and made us promise not to bring it up."

"I don't remember. I found some pictures and paperwork. The last time I was here." I keep my voice steady, trying not to show the turmoil that the information has caused, the tailspin, the nosedive. He looks at me with raised eyebrow, and I explain about the envelope in the bottom of a box of old clothes. He has regained his composure and nods.

"I wouldn't mention it to Dad."

"Why not?" I ask, annoyed by all the secrets. My life is full of dirty little secrets.

"The little bastard tried to kill him." We have reached their drive, and he starts up it.

"Wait! What?"

"Yeah. Dad woke up with a knife in his chest."

"I'm the man of the house." The words echo in my head, and a flash of memory, of the skinny, blond-headed boy leaving my bedroom with the knife held at his side, determination in every joint of his body. I see him in living color, and my memory of that night opens like a rear-facing window, my life before rolling out in rapid succession. It wasn't this house; it was from before we moved here.

"He did something to you, too. What did he do to you?" My hand is covering my lips because in my memory, I can hear Darren snuffling from across the hall, weeping. What had happened? What had he done?

Darren's face closes, and he spins in a small circle, a dog looking for a place to rest.

I reach out and touch his arm, but he jerks away.

I know in a flash what he had done, because I suddenly remember Slim's ownership of me, his emulation of the only man who knew we were there, who came and took him sometimes and brought him back smelling like food and untouchable. What had happened to that boy? I have the sudden urge to spin around as well.

My skin crawls and feels like it wants to skitter free, shedding my soul in the process.

Darren walks away from me, his back stiff, his shoulders strangely out of alignment. I try to grab hold of the memory so I can begin to put together the pieces, but it evaporates, and where there was color before, there is now only an opaque fog.

"I didn't know," I say, calling to him as he edges up the drive, walking away from me, looking tucked and folded. "Darren, please stop."

"What?" He does stop and turns to look at me, his face closed and his eyes hard.

"I didn't know anything. I just found out." I explain myself, try to return to the comfort of the morning. "It's all so confusing!" My voice cracks, and I feel like I am going to cry, but I blink hard and keep the tears at bay. "You're the only person with any answers."

His shoulders relax, and he steps toward me, becoming again the man I know, shuffling free of the shuddering memories with each step forward.

"You were adopted. They tried to adopt you both, but... that didn't work out. You came from a bad situation, but I don't know what it was. That's everything I know." The questions scud across my mind too rapidly to pluck one, so I stand with my mouth open, staring at him in disbelief. "We'll never talk about him again. You understand? Never. He was a monster."

I nod. "I didn't know." A single tear breaks free and rolls down my cheek. I didn't mean to hurt Darren, my brother.

"Well, now you do." His voice is cold and closed.

"I'm sorry." I say, swiping the tear from my cheek.

He pauses and turns back to face me, placing gentle hands on my shoulders, looking so much like my father that I want to curl into his arms like a child. "No, I'm sorry," he says. "I never thought they should have been so secretive about it, but they did what they thought was right. I wish I had answers for you, but I don't. You probably know more than I do. When we moved up here, you started talking and you never mentioned him or seemed like you had any memory from before."

"What do you mean?" He looks blank and I clarify. "What do you mean by 'started talking'?"

"Yeah. You didn't say a word for the first six months you were with us. Then we got rid of him and moved here. You were like a different kid."

The door opens, and Scott is standing there, his apron dusted in flour—the host with the most.

"I don't remember ever living anyplace else."

"That's probably for the best."

I nod. "Okay." I walk up the steps and close a door in my head as I hug Scott.

"How is it going down there?" he asks into my hair.

"Making progress. I'm famished. That smells good." I've lived my whole life not knowing, and I can't do anything with what I've learned today. I am determined not to know again, at least through lunch.

When I smile at my father, it is as if there had been no conversation, as if I'd never found pictures, as if there was no dark and hideous devil living inside my soul. I hug him, one of my stiff, cold-as-a-fish hugs, and we make our way to the kitchen while Darren and Scott stand to talk on the front step.

31

PART FOUR:
Fall

Stacy

Labor Day is our favorite holiday. John always saves some of the Fourth of July fireworks for September. This year the men carpool to buy more. It's been a long, hot summer, and the hint that change is coming is welcome and celebrated.

Everybody who lives in Durbin Creek knows that the best fireworks of the year happen at the end of Afton Lane over Labor Day weekend. The party starts around three in the afternoon, and by six, nearly everybody in the neighborhood has been in one or more of the neighborhood pools. Alcohol is flowing, and the music can't be loud enough. Dee is already dancing, in her most seductive way, gyrating her hips, pulling an imaginary rope to drag her most recent boyfriend out to dance with her. He can't keep his eyes off of her, for sure, but he'll need a lot more to drink before he joins her hips in the driveway. She doesn't care. We all love her, and she knows it. She's the prettiest woman here.

As long as nobody vomits or tries to take the wrong man home, there is no foul. Mona is the real dancer in our group, and although we've all secretly attempted to master her moves, only she has Shakira hips.

Through the evening, families migrate down the street, setting up their chairs in the cul-de-sac. Shelby and Julia are riding their bikes, training wheels popping and scraping as they hit the pavement. I scan the growing crowd and find Willow and Sophie, standing with a small group of girls, and I recognize one of the adopted daughters. I try to remember her name... Margot. No... it's Maggie. I watch her, all of them, but especially my daughter, who is standing with one hand on her hip in a pantomime of adulthood. I smile.

"Wow. You've got quite a turnout. Are you charging admission?"

I laugh and turn, facing the speaker. "I'm Gina." She offers her hand.

"I know. I've seen you at the bus stop." I nod toward our girls. "You're Maggie's mom?"

"Yes, I am." The pride in her voice is unmistakable. "This is Emily and Tommy." She indicates the girl and boy standing still with her, unsure about the party in progress.

"This is your first Labor Day with us, isn't it?"

"Yeah. We moved in at Thanksgiving time last year."

"I remember. I'm Stacy." I extend a hand, a little late.

"This is incredible," she says, surveying the mob in the cul-de-sac.

"This is nothing. Wait till Halloween." My smile spreads. "Welcome to Afton Lane."

"Thanks!" She smiles as if they've hit the neighborhood jackpot. "My Maggie thinks Sophie is the bomb."

"The bomb?" I let my brow rise in question.

"Her word, not mine."

We laugh. Oh, our sassy kids.

John passes by, red-cheeked, his hand grasping the meat of my rear as he goes, a wink, joining Dee's boyfriend, glass in hand. Our fingers touch for a moment, and I breathe a sigh. We've been better since I came back from Georgia the second time. Maybe cleaning all the garbage from my parent's house was what I needed to let it all go, even though it's now stuffed into my own attic. I've been more myself. We're closer than we have been in years, it seems—at least since Shelby was born.

The stress of that trip, driving the U-Haul full of unsorted boxes, has ebbed. Darren didn't, in the end, share his copy of the Magic of Tidying, or whatever the book was called, saying that he realized he still had work to do. The truth, I think, is that he didn't want me to have it; he wanted to punish me for what I'd brought up. We never quite got back to comfortable footing after the revelations on the driveway, but we came close, and I've made an effort since then to reach out to him, ostensibly to check on Dad, but really to check on him. I'd opened a Pandora's box for him, there on that driveway.

The trip to Georgia was a reset for me, and the obsessive cycling of my mind has calmed. I've had fewer headaches since I got home, fewer lost-time events. I'm back to doing my yoga; I am finding my calm. I erased all the search histories from John's computer and my phone, and I have not driven down the A1A since. I haven't had an empty box of unknown time added to my notebook. I wonder if the tidbit Darren gave me was enough, if just the acknowledgment has released me.

Gina's kids, Tommy and Emily, go to join their sister, Maggie, with Sophie and Willow, and I notice that they are now standing with a couple of boys, two older and one younger. I search the crowd to find John and catch his eye, nodding in Sophie's direction. I watch him discover her, watch his face as the scene registers. He begins the slow migration toward the small pod, and I pass the responsibility over to him. We know the boys; they're decent kids, but, still... things happen. Kids test the limits. They grow up too fast in a rush toward adulthood.

"Come with me. Looks like the margarita supply is running low." I say to Gina. Dee usually manages the margaritas, but she is preoccupied, and the last batch she did was definitely on the heavy side. I lift the jug from the cooler, and we make our way through the kids gathered in the driveway.

When we are alone in my house, and the music is just a low thrum, I say, "So you adopted?"

It's not what she expected, but she smiles, "Yeah. We did."

"Why?" I ask, feeling too blunt, but needing to understand.

"Well," she says, her voice low, slow, and I can feel her trying to decide the version of the story she should share. "Truth?"

"Why not?" I ask. "I respect adoption."

"I've had a complete hysterectomy."

"No shit? Why?"

She laughs, a robust, throaty laugh, "Because I had cancer." Of course, a complete hysterectomy wouldn't be something you would just choose.

"Oh, I'm sorry." The Labor Day party is one of the few times in the year that I drink, and John and I shared a shot not an hour ago. It's singing in my blood, and I'm feeling loose, uninhibited. I feel a little off-center and have the outside-of-body moment, watching myself from across the room. Alcohol was never my problem, but it did make it easier for time to slip. I am still sort of watching from across the room, and I try to pull back into myself, but I am unable to shift my vision from being on the outside looking in. I'm not losing time, this is different—I'm just not inside myself.

"It's okay." She puts her hand up, touching her forehead.

"I didn't know."

"It's okay. I mean. It's not what you would choose, right? But it's good. I have a great life."

"Yeah." I pull the ice out of the fridge and fill the pitcher a quarter of the way, pouring tequila to the half and then a little more, feeling daring, adding the sticky sweet mix to top it off. I blend. "So now?"

"Cancer-free," she says, triumphant. Suddenly, my vision swirls, and I am looking at her, not the two of us standing, talking, but from inside myself again. I've pulled myself back in, and the wash of triumph is like a warm shower or a summer rain. I want to cheer and have a momentary urge to hug her, rejoice in my private conquest. Then I visualize the absurd action, the reaching out in my awkward, stiff way, leaning in, patting her, a dead fish flapping.

"Adoption is great," she says, smiling.

"Yeah. I guess so. Do the kids know?"

"That they're adopted? Oh yeah, certainly. It's not something you want to keep a secret. Everybody should know their birth story."

"Even if it's a bad story?" Why did I say that?

"Well, Maggie's story isn't great, you know, and we've not told her all the details. She's too young for that, but she knows how she came to us."

"That's awesome," I say, wishing my parents had done that—let me know, so that I could have incorporated it into my being somehow. "I was adopted."

"Really?" she says, and I pour two glasses from the pitcher and hand her one.

I sip the other. It's strong. I leave my drink on the counter to lift the pitcher in both hands and start back through the house.

"My parents, my adoptive parents, never told me. I found out in May after my mom died."

"Wow, that's hard," she says, and her hand lands softly on my forearm. Her brow furrows and concern stamps across her face.

"Why is that? I mean, what makes it harder?" I sincerely want to know. If a child can assimilate their life story, why can't I, a grown woman, with a thinking mind and at least average intelligence?

"Oh, well, because it shatters your frame—at least that's the theory. We grow up and have context for our lives, but when you find out later that things aren't what you thought, it can blow apart your framework." She shrugs, dropping her hand free. "At least that's the current ideology."

I nod but don't say anything.

"How has it been for you?" she asks.

"It's been rough." I smile, but I know she can see the turmoil in my eyes, the strain. "I feel like my frame has been blown apart. Absolutely."

"I'm so sorry." She reaches for me and draws me into a hug, and for split second, I fear I will melt and start blubbering. I hold myself together, my hand tense on the handle of the pitcher, and she squeezes until she lets me go. There are tears in her eyes, and I wonder why she is crying. Is she imagining her children growing up troubled and broken when the ideology changes and she finds out she did it all wrong?

Her face is open and sympathetic, and I see that she is only sad for me. She understands something about the deceived childhood, the lost mother. I want to peel off my skin for her, so she can see the tiny creatures that live inside of me, my little hat-trick of crazy. Would she understand? Would she sit down with me and tuck them all back into their corners and zip me back together? Would she read me a story and tell me everything is going to be okay? Or would she run from the house, screaming, knowing that she had seen a monster?

"I bet. Are you okay? I mean, they say it can cause major problems when it comes to you later. There are all sorts of studies. They made us sign documents during the adoption, agreeing that we would not keep it a secret."

"Yeah, I'm okay," I lie, shrugging as she holds open the door. The laughter in my head is low and chuckling. I feel the spin of being pushed out of my body again, but I keep my grip and focus until the feeling abates.

"Well, hey, if you want to talk, I'm just down the road." It is an honest offer.

I nod, feeling grateful for the offer but overwhelmed, too.

"I haven't told John yet, you know, so don't mention it, okay?" Her eyes widen, and I see her perspective shifting. Why would I tell her this when not even my husband knows? I can't answer that, not aloud, anyway.

You can't tell John because then he'll know what a fraud you are, and he'll leave you. Shiloh is chuckling, leaning forward from the dark corner I squashed her into.

"Well, you'll figure that out. You have to find your way through it, I guess."

"I guess." We make our way through the throng of people, adding the margarita concoction to cups. Gina stops with Dee, giving me one last smile, and I pass on through the crowd, doing my best Scott impersonation—the hostess with the most-est.

I'm on the far edge of the cul-de-sac, and the pitcher is nearly empty. From a distance, I catch sight of a man watching me, tall and fair-haired, the lower half of his face shielded in a tidy beard. He is maybe not looking at me but in my direction. It is too dark to see him clearly, but I am almost certain he is looking at me. He's clean cut, with a tie loosened around his neck.

My stomach flips because there is something in his posture, in the tilt of his head that is very familiar. I know him, like I know my own reflection. I catch his eye and make my way through the crowd with determination. Is he one of the neighbors? Is he someone I've met once but forgotten his name? Why, then, is he standing in the shadows, almost like he is hiding? Why isn't he here in the street, sharing in the festivities?

"Hey, Stace, I'll take more," a voice calls, and I slow, halted in my progress but unwilling to take my eyes off of him. He is straightening, and I see the arch of his brows. I see the shape of his cheekbones. One brow cocks, and he lifts his hand, pointing at me, his fingers a gun. He narrows his eyes, and his hand rocks, like a bullet has left the chamber.

The pitcher slips from my hands and shatters on the pavement, shards of plastic splintered, slick with margarita. The liquid sprays over my feet, and chaos erupts in the small group near me. When I look back, he is gone.

I scan the crowd, all the men and women, all the children with their mouths open, laughing and shouting, eating hot dogs and chocolate bars. There are too many people, and I am not even sure now that I saw him at all. I head back into the house with the pieces of the shattered pitcher gathered together in the bowl of the largest of the shards, stopping to kiss the top of Shelby's head, to wink at Sophie, where she is testing out the earliest form of flirtation. I bump John's shoulder, raising the remains of the pitcher.

"What happened?"

"Slipped out of my hands."

"That's it. You're cut off," he says, laughing, leaning toward me, kissing my lips.

"I hear ya." I continue toward the house, smiling at everyone as I go. Inside and alone, I dump the drink I'd left down the kitchen sink, half convinced that my mind was playing tricks when I saw the man in the shadows. John's right—even though he meant it as a joke, even though he doesn't know anything about what is happening to me. He knows, on some level, that even one drink is too much for me right now. Even one makes all of my lines blur together. I crumple the cup and dump it into the trash on top of the pitcher shards. My hands won't stop shaking.

I'm dirty with it, dirty with all my secrets.

32

Stacy

I'm losing it. I'm breathless; my throat feels burned and raw; and tears are floating along the lids of my eyes. I'm losing my mind. Hallucinations, voices, out-of-body experiences, lost time. My chest is constricting. I can barely breathe.

I am flawed and separate from all the revelers filling the cul-de-sac. My fingers scrabble through my top dresser drawer, and for a moment, I think it is gone, that John has found the card and thrown it out—or worse, called the number. My vision starts to tunnel, and the low pressure in my head begins to swell, dough rising above the edge of the pan. The sounds of the cul-de-sac become muffled, and my heartbeat is a skittering thud, thud, thud.

My fingertip touches the edge of the card, and my vision expands. The sounds in the cul-de-sac return to their proper pitch. The cadence of my heart still skitters, a rolling snare in my ears. Relief washes over me. I glance down the hall, making sure I am alone and dial the number.

"Leon Freak here."

"Hi, Leon. You probably won't remember me, but you gave me your card at the grief support group a couple of months ago." I'm talking too fast, breathless, whispering, fearful of being caught.

"Of course I remember you. How are you?" he asks.

I chuckle, low. I'm insane; nobody can help me. I am alone; there is nobody who would understand.

"No. No. I just..." What? I just what? Why can't I just say the truth... that I feel myself slipping, that I am on the slope?

"Needed to hear somebody breathe?" he asks.

My breath rushes out in a gasp, a sob. "Yes."

"I can do that." He does breathe, and my breathing calms. My heart stops racing. The fire in my throat continues to burn, but the swirling in my mind settles.

"Do you ever think you see somebody who isn't there?" I ask, hearing my voice like a stranger's.

"All the time."

"Really?" Relief washes through me. I knew he would understand.

"Sure."

I want to tell him about the man in the cul-de-sac, but I suddenly don't need to. He already understands.

"Thanks," I say when we've sat listening to each other breathe for what may have been minutes or hours.

"Anytime. You okay?"

"Yeah. I think so." A small laugh escapes, at the absurdity of me sitting on the lid of the toilet, hunkered down over my illicit phone call. "You know, I'm not crazy. I'm just having a hard time, you know."

"Call me anytime. Grief is a powerful emotion."

"Who did you lose?"

"My father," he says, and I hear the clip in his voice, the tension in the words.

"I'm sorry."

"Yeah. Me, too."

We sit in silence for another long minute before I rouse myself. "I'm not sure why I called you." I laugh, a small skittish sound, nervous.

"Because you wanted to hear somebody breathe."

"Yeah. That's right." I have the impulse again to unzip my skin. Would it heal me, to share my secrets, to share about Shiloh and Baby and how sometimes I'm not entirely myself? Would this strange man understand?

"Well, you've got my number on your phone now, so don't hesitate to use it."

The low burn in my stomach flares, and heat ratchets through my veins, feeling connected, linked. "All right. Thanks."

The first bottle rocket whistles into the air and explodes. I disconnect the call and sit, listening to the cheers outside, feeling calm, no longer panicked. I'm sure it was just an illusion, a trick of my mind.

I find Shelby, who is sitting with Mona and Julia. I lift her and hug her close to me, scanning for Sophie. She's on Dee's driveway, surrounded by her friends. I make my way toward them, just needing her to be close, and I sit in a spare chair with Shelby in my lap. She is tired. I can feel it in the way she is leaning into me, watching the fireworks but not responding. I see John, in all his glory, handling the rockets, selecting the next display.

I'm going to call Felicia Martin, my former therapist, on Monday. I remember sitting across the room from her, her lacquered nails tapping lightly on her knee, knowing that I was hiding things, but patient, waiting. What if I were to tell her everything I've found out? Would she be able to help me? Why didn't my mother ever tell her? Didn't she think it could be messing me up, all the secrets?

~ ~ ~

I'm waiting for John to come from the shower. I've brushed my teeth and braided my damp hair, and I wait. That moment of feeling connected when I was on the phone with Leon has left me with an empty hole that I now feel the need to fill. I need to feel linked, attached, part of. John has no idea what I am missing. He doesn't see me. We've already gone through the easy conversation, talking about how great his fireworks display was, about the kid's attempts at karaoke, about Dee's dancing.

That was not enough to reconnect me, and I am desperate to get safe. I feel Shiloh just at the edge of my thoughts, waiting to spring forward, to claim her place. I don't know what that would cause. Would he see the shift, the moment when the woman he married transformed? What does it look like? Is it a blink, a shifting of features, a subtle change of mannerism? I want to know, but how can I know what it looks like? I focus, intent, studying the small wound at the base of my fingernail.

He can't know that I am fragmenting.

How do I keep him from seeing?

Keep him happy, whispers through my mind.

What does that even mean?

Maybe "happy" isn't the right word. Maybe what I'm looking for is "satisfied." John's desire has always been enough. Maybe I just don't know what all the fuss is about. I think I'm broken. Other women talk about their orgasms, how life shattering they are, but not me. I can never just let go.

Sex isn't a simple subject inside of my mind. I enjoy sex, I guess, as much as most women enjoy sex, but I think I could go the rest of my life without ever being touched again. Sometimes the idea of sex makes me feel guilty, like I've done something bad. It's more than that—it makes me feel dirty.

~ ~ ~

"You all right?" John asks when he finds me still awake as he steps out of the bathroom. I am standing behind her, myself, where she is patting the bed, beckoning him. She is better at all the sex stuff. I realize how often of late that I've found myself, just like this, standing over my own shoulder. I thought I wasn't losing time because I remember, but it's still not right, not normal. I try to pull back into my body.

"Yeah. I had fun tonight." Her voice purrs, low over her teeth, and she is powerful, like a goddess.

I am stuck on the other side of a glass, watching as my husband. He jostles into bed, fluffing his pillow, getting settled.

She rolls toward him, the way I never do, propping up on an elbow.

He cocks an eyebrow. "How many did you have?"

Does it say something that he thinks I have to be intoxicated to initiate sex? I wonder from my place behind her.

She licks her lips and offers a small smile. "Hmmm." I watch as his eyes follow her tongue, seduced by the woman who is not me.

"You all right?"

"Yeah, just in the mood," she purrs, and I'm embarrassed by her boldness, her wanton desire.

She leans forward and kisses him, and I slide down the wall, angry and disgusted that he can't tell the difference, that he thinks she is me. His arms come around her, catching her heat. I glance at the door, wanting to escape, and notice that the knob is turned, locked, not remembering. Did I lock the door? Did she, before I knew she was even coming?

Then I am pulled in, and his lips are on mine. I need him to be connected to me; I need to bring him back home. Does she know that? Does she know that I couldn't draw him the way she did. Confusion rockets in my mind as the two of us, Shiloh and me, fill the same space. I don't know who I am, but my body is moving in ways that are unfamiliar. I straddle his hips, and the startled look on his face makes me wonder why I never did this before, why I never let him know how much I wanted him.

"What did you do to my wife?" he asks, his voice husky with desire. His hands grasp my hips, confident and practiced.

I lean forward and whisper in his ear, "I sent her away," and I don't know if it is me or her who said it. Then I let my lips close around his earlobe and gently tug before pulling away.

"Damn," he groans.

I wonder if Shiloh knows how to orgasm.

~ ~ ~

Morning comes with the light in shafts through the window and the pounding of Shelby's small fist on the door. I jump out of bed, pulling clothes on, catching John's squinted eye and smiling at him, but feeling strange remembering the disjointed night. Are we becoming the same, integrating? I remember standing over her shoulder, watching the seduction, and then suddenly being in my own skin again. He grins like we've had a secret rendezvous.

"I'm coming," I say, pulling on the t-shirt, which brushes against my too sensitive nipples. I glance back at John to ensure he is covered and open the door. Shelby wraps around my knees.

"Why did you lock me out?" she whines.

"Oh, honey, I didn't mean to lock you out." I lift her and carry her back to bed with me, snuggling her in on my side. "Is Sophie still sleeping?"

"Uh-huh." She snuggles in, a spoon, and I blow a wisp of her hair out of my face. John rolls toward us, and I'm relieved to feel his PJs between us. He pushes against me, and I force myself not to move. A flash of memory, my legs spread over his hips, astride him, and my face flushes. The black hole of the night shifts and churns until I remember, in a disconnected way, waiting for him in bed, reaching for him. "What did you do with my wife?"

It's not a coherent memory, but pieces of a puzzle left on a table.

"Why are you up so early?" My voice is light, not betraying the turmoil in my soul.

"It's not early. The sun is up. "

"Indeed it is." I squeeze her.

"Can we have pancakes?"

"Pancakes?" I squeak as if she has asked for ice cream and chocolate syrup. "You want pancakes?" and I tickle her sides. "I want riblets." I clack my teeth together, and she giggles, squirming but not trying to get away.

"Pancakes, pancakes, pancakes," Shelby chants.

"Riblets, riblets, riblets," I respond, and John joins in, folding around me, adding his tickling fingers. Shelby squirms right out of bed, toppling to the floor in a giggling heap.

"All right," I say with a huge sigh as if I am the most put-upon woman alive. "Pancakes it is."

I scoop her into my arms and smile at John. I carry her through the living room to the destroyed kitchen. "Big party last night," I say, pouring melted margarita from cups down the sink.

33

Stacy

By the end of September, after the flurry of shopping and orientations subsides, we settle into the mundane routine of another school year. Sophie is in the fourth grade, and Shelby is in pre-K 4; next year, she'll be in kindergarten. My babies are growing up.

They are the about the same age my brother and I were when the police took us from Kristine Moony.

It's hard to adjust to the quiet house, and for three weeks, while they've been gone I have run through the neighborhoods, down past the schools, filling in the hours, so I'm not tempted to go searching in dark corners for people I don't want to know. When we first moved here, before the girls were born, I spent many long days on the beach. It was a place of peace and calm. I liked it early before the crowds came. I would take my running shoes and run along the packed sand with the sun beating on one side of my body as it rose over the ocean, sending my shadow long and tall across the white sand. It was a solitary pleasure, something I did to fill the long hours of the day while John was away. I've gone to my car several times to take myself to the beach, but each time I came back inside without ever starting the engine. I am afraid that if I go anywhere, I will end up back at the shelter on the A1A. So, instead, I run through the streets, down sidewalks, and past other joggers and bicyclists.

Now it is Saturday, another Saturday of John working, just like last Saturday and the two before it, and the girls and I try to fill our day.

I am restless like a cat, pacing the house, anxious. I keep picking up Mom's violin, as I often do, playing some half-remembered song, hearing my mother in the notes. It calms me, touching her violin, the wood of the neck, pressing the body up under my chin, putting her rosin on her bow. It helps my skin to stop pulling from my bones. The day is stretching out like an eternity. The tension of holding pressure on the small, dark door in my head that keeps all the half-remembered memories hidden is exhausting.

It's been a hard morning, and I can't stop crying. I'm pathetic. Washing dishes after breakfast, and I'm sniffling. Wiping down counters, I'm moaning. Catching sight of Merida's mother as she transforms from bear to queen beneath the stitched-together tapestry, the sun rising over the standing stones, I'm sobbing. Not just tears, but snot and hiccups and gasps.

Shelby pats my hand, and I laugh, a sticky, wet sound. I am absurd. I try to keep myself together so that the girls won't see. Maybe it is better that they know how hard life can be, but I don't want them seeing me so pathetic and weak. I'm embarrassed at myself. I don't want to mess up their lives. Why can't I stop crying? When I cry, they take note, but they don't panic. They don't overreact.

"Mama, why are you crying?" Shelby asks, now with her hand folding into mine. "She's back. She's not a bear anymore."

I nod, smiling in spite of my sorrow. "I'm just sad, baby." A shuddering breath. "I miss Grammy."

She nods, so grown up and knowing, and I lift her into my arms. "It's okay to be sad," she says, words I have said to her a hundred times. She tucks her face into the hollow of my neck. Her arms close around me.

"I know it is." I bury my face in the ringlets of her curls and breathe. The scent of her begins to knock away the cobwebs in my mind, and the depression ebbs. I feel lighter, with the two of us wrapped up like this, her holding me together. I wish my sorrow were just for the loss of my mother—that would be easier—but my sadness is for the dawning realization that I am broken. Now that I have some inkling of what had happened to me, I can't seem to find balance. I can't seem to keep all my fragments in one place at any given time.

I've made it through the worst of it, I hope. She's been gone for almost four months now, and surely I'll start getting used to it soon. I have made it through the loss of my mother, through the discovery of my origins, and I didn't fall entirely off the dark ledge into despair, although I've skirted close and reckless for a time.

I've lost a lot of time... hours I don't recall while the girls play.

I'm taking care of them, though. All the laundry is finally put away; the house is cleaner than it has ever been.

It gives me something to focus on, while I'm trying to hold all my pieces together.

I've so lost it, but nobody seems to know but me.

Nobody else knows how crazy I am, but I'm exhausted from the effort. I've done it without calling Leon to listen to him breathe, except the once. I've done it without a therapist, although I did leave a pathetic message for my old therapist, Felicia Martin, asking for a referral in the area. She hasn't called back. I have so many questions for her. She always suspected my problems stemmed from some repressed experience, and I finally have an idea of what that was.

If I just keep walking, sooner or later, I'm going to come out the other side. I'm a grownup, and this is what grownups do. Everybody is a little crazy.

"What shall we do today?" I ask when I have breathed her in and I feel almost whole again. "Shall we go to the beach? One last time before the water gets cold?"

Shelby wrinkles her nose.

"Nobody loves the beach as I do," I complain.

John doesn't like sand and has made such a show of it that Sophie picked it up, always looking to be just like her daddy. Shelby learned it from Sophie, wanting to be just like her sissy. The highest form of flattery is mimicry. Nobody wants to be like me. It's good that they want to take after John; he's so steady. I laugh at Shelby's wrinkled nose. "I know, you don't like the sand." I put my lip out, large and exaggerated.

"I'm sorry," I say, pressing my forehead to her forehead, and she becomes a cyclops baby in my foreshortened vision. I'm sorry because this one, even with her daddy's blue eyes, this little one here... she is the spit of me, no matter how much she may want to be like her sissy or her daddy.

"We could see if Dee and Mona want to go?"

Her cyclops eye blinks, and I see her thinking about it.

"Okay."

I squeeze her tight, holding her for just moment longer until I feel her need to be free.

These long days heading toward October are still hot in the cul-de-sac. Not quite like it is in the summer, when being outside feels like standing in an oven, and if you stand too long on the hot pavement, your shoes will begin to melt into it, but hot like summer in normal places. We are tired of the pool. We are tired of television. We have watched all of our movies at least once, and I feel like a caged animal. I need to get out of the house.

Must get out of the house. Beach? I send in a group text to Mona and Dee, and within minutes, the day is shaped. Willow slept over with Sophie last night, and they are still asleep when Shelby and I come to wake them. I flounce down on Sophie's bed, and the girls bounce and shriek. "Rise and shine, little people. It's a beach day." Sophie groans, but after a few, exaggerated moments, she rolls out of bed to rummage for her suit.

"You, too, Willow. Your mom has the van loaded." The cheeriness in my voice grates on them, and it makes me happy to hear their groans.

Shelby and I change, drawing beach cover-ups over our bathing suits, talking about what we should get for lunch. Sophie changes and goes with Willow to get ready.

We leave Afton Lane in a convoy and converge on Publix, where we pick up hummus and pretzel thins, breakfast bars, and sandwiches from the deli. Dee buys a bag of ice. I buy water, and Mona buys wine coolers, like high-school kids get, when they are just testing out their taste for alcohol. I smile at her, realizing that I had completely bypassed that phase of my development. Maybe if I had started with wine coolers, I would have ended with wine and would have appreciated alcohol as something other than a dampener, an escape so I wouldn't feel my emotions.

~ ~ ~

I am sitting under the umbrella, just past the reach of the surf. Sophie and Willow are walking along the beach in loops. They go back and forth, their legs looking unbelievably long in the sun. They are so close to being teens, and for Willow, puberty already claims a ridge of small bumps that have erupted over her eyebrows and along her cheeks. Sophie will be soon to follow, and I only hope that her adolescent years are not as confusing as mine were.

Dee flounces down beside me, and the scent of her spritzer clings to her like sand. Mona is stretched back, her face turned toward the sun.

"You realize it's, like, ten thirty," I say, not in judgment, but just in case she has lost track of time.

"Pshaw." She flutters a hand, waving me off. "There are no clocks at the beach."

"That's true," I say with a laugh, and she leans back, her turquoise bikini top cutting a sharp line through her flesh. She broke up with the boyfriend after the Labor Day, but she hasn't told any of us what went wrong. We didn't ask. Most often, with Dee, it's because she met somebody new. John calls her the BBD, not to her face, but in conversations with me, he'll say, "What's the BBD up to?" It's true; she is always looking for the "bigger, better deal," always flirting with the next man.

"I noticed you had a visitor at your house last night."

"Uh-huh." She drops her eyes.

"New fella?"

"Uh-huh." She doesn't offer anything more, and I don't push it. Dee cycles her boyfriends, and sometimes a late model comes back around, so we are all careful not to get too invested. I noticed the car because it was a BMW. Most of the men Dee meets are blue-collar—not in a bad way, just working men... carpenters, mechanics, landscapers. Dee doesn't attract men who wear suits and drive BMWs, as a rule. Men who wear suits aren't looking for women with soon-to-be teens in the mix. Even in my head that sounds like a stereotype, and I don't like it, but still think it's true.

"Nice car," I say, noncommittally. "Beamer, wasn't it?"

She is looking at me out of the corner of her eye, a slow grin spreading. "Guess what he does?"

"What?"

She faces me square, sitting up and reaching for my hand. "He's a therapist, like a psychiatrist, you know?"

"Really?"

"He's very smart."

"Maybe I should schedule an appointment," I say, laughing.

"Seriously, right? So, I was talking to him about your story, you know?"

"Yeah?" Heat blooms across my skin, thinking about her talking about me to her new man, lying in bed, talking about the crazy woman next door.

"Hypothetically, of course, about, you know… well, he says that after age eighteen, all your records would be opened, and all you'd have to do is make the request, and you could know everything."

"I have the adoption decree. I pretty much know everything." I shrug, feeling the power of speaking it out loud. There is no shame in being adopted. Maybe there is shame in what came before, but that shouldn't be mine to carry.

"But he says there is no shame in seeking therapy, to talk through things."

"Of course not," I prickle. It's like she read my mind. "Why would there be shame in that?"

"I didn't mean it like that," she says, sitting up, looking at me square, as if to make sure I understand that her intentions were all good.

"You can't talk to people about me, you know," I say in a low voice, glancing around to see if anybody is listening. I haven't even told John what I'd discovered. What would happen if Dee pops over in her way and starts talking to John? Or worse, her new boyfriend feeling it's his obligation to help now that he knows? A ridge of panic swells, and a dimple of sweat erupts on my lip.

I turn away from her and find the kids out by the surf, jumping over the line of water as it moves in.

"I didn't tell him anything particular, you know. Just asking questions about adoption in general, and how people cope when they find out."

"So you didn't tell him about the pictures? How we were found?"

"No, of course not." She presses her hand over mine, looking distressed that I would think it. She is lying. I can hear her talking about me to her new boyfriend, telling him secrets that aren't hers to tell.

"Of course not." I nod and give her a tight-lipped smile. For a split second, I want to punch her. I want to grab her by the hair and drag her across the beach. The vision is gone as quickly as it appeared, and I am left only sitting in the sand, staring into her face in a vacant way.

My mind returns to the here and now, the moment. I feel the soothing presence of the ocean, and I try to let myself soak it in. But Dee will not allow me that luxury. Or maybe it's me.

"I'm sorry. I just felt like it was weighing on you. Don't you want to find out what happened to him? Your brother?" Dee's voice drops on the last word, the way people say "cancer" in an almost whisper, as if to mention the word was to invite it into your home, a vampire, to wreak havoc and destruction.

There is a pull in the thought of knowing what happened to the boy, but it is not enough for me to go seeking again. I remember Darren's response and the flash of memory—the boy with the knife at his side. Darren was whimpering from across the hall. He may not be somebody I want to find.

It's hard to reconcile that memory with Employee of the Month Shane Moony. It probably isn't the right Moony. My brother, Slim, probably isn't even Moony anymore, if he was ever adopted. I have nothing to go find him with, just a child's nickname and a last name that was surely changed when he was adopted. If he had been adopted.

"Meh."

"So you're okay with everything? It seemed like it was stressing you out."

"It was, but I don't know how much I want to know." I turn out to watch the kids, letting the sea calm me. "I'm kinda over it, you know?" I say, meaning I am over the trauma of finding out my secrets. "It was just a shock, finding out like that. But I don't know how it could have been different. There would never have been a good time for my parents to tell me," I explain. "They thought I didn't remember, and they were afraid that if they told me, it would bring it all back. I get that." I've tried to imagine telling my children something like that, if their histories were like mine. "There never would have been a good time."

"Did you know Gina had to sign papers saying they would not keep the adoption story a secret?" Dee asks, and I can tell she thinks this is valuable information.

"Yeah. She told me that." Everybody keeps telling me, like it's somehow relevant, like it makes a difference in my life.

"I guess they figured out how damaging it is to keep secrets."

"Ya live and learn." I shove a mound of sand up around my feet. "But, listen, you can't be talking about me to people. I mean, John doesn't know yet. My kids don't know. I'm still processing it. You understand, don't you?"

"You haven't told John?" There is something in her face that I suddenly don't like, the hint of an ambulance chaser, the glow of a dog with a new bone.

"No, and he better not find out from anybody else." I put as much threat in my voice as I can.

The gleam fades from her eyes, and she looks a little offended. She turns to face the sea.

"I would never tell your husband your secrets," she says in a quiet voice.

"Good. Don't tell anybody else either, okay? Not to be a bitch, but this has thrown me, and I'm not ready for it to be public knowledge. Okay?" I reach out and put my hand on her arm, trying to soften my words.

"I get it." She nods but doesn't look at me. She tilts her bottle to her lips, and I watch her throat move as she works the liquid into her stomach.

"We good?" I ask when she is again staring out at the kids playing.

"Yeah, we're good." She turns and smiles at me.

I nod, not at all convinced, but I leap up from the sand, peeling my cover-up off as I go to join the kids, splashing in the surf.

34

Stacy

I am sitting with Dee in her driveway while the kids ride their bikes in the cul-de-sac. They've been playing since they came home from school, and Dee has talked nonstop about the latest boyfriend, the therapist. His car was parked overnight again last night, and I had noticed his vanity plate "MNTLBM" and thought it looked like initials for a personal ad. I don't know why I'm feeling so uncharitable about him. It would be great for Dee to meet a man who could take care of her and the kids. It's always been a struggle and the twins' father has never been a part of the picture.

I know I'm just irritated that he knows something about me, even if she didn't tell him it was me. I just feel like he'll see me and know that I'm the person she was talking about—and I know she told him about the photos and how we were found. It would have been impossible for Dee to leave that cherry out of her conversation. I'm still annoyed that she talked about me. It feels like such a violation. I'm still listening, though, the way I always listen, not retaining any details because I know, in a short matter of time, there will be a new boyfriend, and he'll have the same or different qualities, and it won't matter then, either—because nobody lasts in Dee's dating zone.

My phone vibrates in the cup holder of my lawn chair. The initials FM flash on the screen, which is how I'd saved Felicia Martin's phone number. It's been two weeks since I left my last message for her, and I expect it to be her receptionist, telling me Dr. Martin can't speak to me right now. But maybe they'll have a referral, and that's all I want anyway.

"I need to take this. You okay?" I ask Dee as I get up, already moving toward my drive. I glance out at the girls, trying to catch their eyes, so they see that I am just going to our house, but only Sophie looks at me, a frown creasing her forehead.

"Hello."

"May I speak with Stacy Alexander, please?"

When I had left my message with her receptionist, I remembered to use my maiden name, so she would hopefully recognize it.

"This is she." I am breathless with anticipation.

"Hi, Stacy. I was surprised to hear from you." Her voice is low and modulated, and I remember how infuriating her calm tone was to me when I was bouncing off the walls.

"Hi, Dr. Martin, thank you for calling me back."

"How are you doing?"

"Good, well, I don't know, really. I don't know how much you'll remember about me, but you used to tell me that there was something in my childhood that was causing me to act out."

"Of course. I have your file in front of me." I can almost see her, in her serious tweed blazer, her fingertips tracing the edge of the pages within my folder.

"Did you know I was adopted?"

She is quiet for almost a full minute, and I hear the pages of my file flipping as she searches for that tidbit of information. "No, I don't recall that."

"So, my mother never told you?"

"No, she did not." She breathes in, whistling. "And you are certain?"

"Absolutely," I say wondering why she would doubt me, but then I remember that not everything I said to her during my year of half-truths was true. Some of the halves were the beginning of extravagant, fabricated stories that no sane person would ever believe.

"How did you come by this information?"

"My mother passed away in May, and I found a folder."

She breathes a long breath, as if something is suddenly coming clear in her mind. "I'm sorry she passed. Are you seeing anybody?"

"I'm married," I say, feeling disjointed. Why would she ask if I was seeing someone?

"No, dear, a therapist. Are you seeing a therapist?" There is laughter in her voice, just a small chuckle that makes me think she might be a good person to know outside of the office.

"Oh... no." I laugh, feeling self-conscious that I could have mistaken her meaning so badly.

"Are you still losing time?"

"You know about that?"

"That's why you started coming to see me. Your parents were very concerned about your 'incident.' You had a three-day lapse in time and memory, if I remember correctly. A 'dissociative fugue' is the term we use."

Of course. The three days I was missing. Was that the first time?

"Are you?"

"I think, maybe." A weight lifts off my shoulders. "Not like that, though, just small moments where I don't remember what came right before."

"Do you still hear voices?"

I don't know if I hear voices. I don't know if the conversations in my head are normal or something different. Doesn't everybody talk to themselves sometimes? I am silent long enough that Dr. Martin continues.

"How can I help you, Stacy?"

"I'd like a referral. I'm in Jacksonville now."

"Oh. There are several very adequate therapists in that area. I have thought of your case for many years and often wondered how you developed. There has been so much progress with our understanding of your disorder over the last several years."

"My disorder?"

"Well, of course we never made an official diagnosis, but I did have several theories. Do you still have out-of-body experiences?"

"Sometimes."

"Hmm." I can almost see her making a note in her notebook, the way she used to do.

"What were some of your theories?"

"Well, schizophrenia displays some of those characteristics, and that's what I thought in the beginning. But you were pretty connected to reality most of the time, so I ruled that out. In the end, I suspected dissociative identity disorder, D-I-D."

"What is that?"

"It used to be described as multiple personalities, but we understand it a little better now. It's not so much different personalities living in one body as it is one personality unable to assimilate all the different sides of itself. Think Sybil."

Sybil was a movie about a groundbreaking study back in the fifties regarding a woman with multiple personalities. "That ended up being a fraud, didn't it?"

"Well, yes, the story was debunked, but it did open the door for legitimate study and progress in understanding."

"Is that what's wrong with me?"

"It's not wrong, Stacy. It's just a coping mechanism. Do you understand? The human mind is incredible."

"Yes." My vision is tunneling; I can no longer feel my legs or hands.

"I will call you back in an hour with a referral."

"Okay."

"It's good to hear from you, Stacy."

I wish she would stop saying my name; it's jarring to hear it over and over.

"Thank you." The phone goes dead, and I stand at the counter, my hands splayed, staring down into the sink.

She had never said "multiple personalities." She never gave me a diagnosis. Why not? Has she confused me with some other patient? I pull myself away from the counter and open the browser on my phone.

I read through WebMD's definition of dissociative identity disorder, previously known as multiple personality disorder, and discover that the condition is likely caused by "severe trauma during early childhood." I also learn that most people have experienced some level of dissociation, such as daydreaming. The disorder aspect is believed to be a coping strategy when a person cannot assimilate an experience that is too violent or traumatic.

Like being locked in a kennel with your brother for a short lifetime.

There is some conflict among the psychiatric community as to whether it is even a legitimate disorder.

"Mom?" Sophie calls, and I jerk, dropping my phone, startled.

"I'm here."

"I need a drink," she says.

"Oh, okay." I had forgotten my children were outside. I had forgotten I had children. I had forgotten everything. My hand trembles as I reach into the cupboard for a water bottle and fill it. Shaking, spilling,

"Mom. Are you okay?" Sophie asks, standing next to me, looking at my hands.

"I'm sorry, baby." I hand her the bottle, and she tightens the lid. "I'm fine. Just—" My voice trails, and I look at her. "Am I a good mother?"

Sophie laughs, a hoot. "Well, yeah."

"You sure?"

"Yeah, Mom. Is this about Grandma?"

"I guess so. I just miss her." I do miss her, so it isn't a lie, but I am also angry with her, simmering on a low boil. She did this to me. She set me up. When I was a teen, and the voices started getting so loud and I started losing time, why didn't she tell me the truth? Was my therapy a failure because I didn't know my past? For all I knew, I had a perfect life—no trauma, good parents. It was just me. I was the wreck. I was the trauma. I had no point in time, no one experience, that I could go back to say this is what is upsetting me, this is why I am so angry.

If I had known about my past, I could have talked to Dr. Martin, opened up more, told more truths. Maybe. We could have made progress.

"I'm going back out," Sophie says, checking to make sure I'm okay, and I smile, telling her I'll follow in a minute.

Some emotion shifts inside of me, and I realize I'm not scared. If there is a name for what is wrong with me, then it can be fixed. If I know what's happening, I should be able to stop it. I laugh. And laugh some more. Joyous almost. If it's just parts of my personality, then I'll just pull them all together. They are not other people; they are not ghosts or demons. They are just pieces of myself that I haven't come to terms with. The voices are just my thoughts, my insecurities.

The laughter stops.

My head splits.

"My name is Shiloh." The words ratchet out of my mouth in a near scream.

"Who is the other one?" I ask, but the words are only in my mind.

"That's Baby. She's the one who remembers."

"How do I get rid of you?" I ask, but only in my mind, because Shiloh has pushed me back and down, and I can feel her panic, her fear that I will rip them out.

"You can't. I was here first. How do I get rid of you?"

It feels more like a promise and a threat.

We go outside, and Shiloh runs into the cul-de-sac with the kids on their bikes, springing like a gazelle, and somehow I am stuck outside myself, watching, and, at the same time, pushed down deep inside, feeling the heat of the sun on my skin, feeling the thump, thump, thump of my heart. I am disconnected and connected, myself and Shiloh, and for now, I am okay with Shiloh being in control, taking the reins and giving me time to process all the information I've gained. While I try to figure out how to get rid of her, how to merge her into myself.

Maybe Shiloh was here first and I, Stacy, am the usurper.

35

Shiloh

"You need to look at those brakes. You told me you were going to do it last week," John says, his voice is annoyed, coming across the line.

"I know. I will."

"You were supposed to have it done all summer."

"Okay." I drop a plate into the sink with a loud clatter. "Let me go, and I'll call now," I snap.

"All right." His irritation stretches across the line, rebounding on my own. He's not used to me talking back. But Shiloh is in charge now, bitches. He disconnects without saying goodbye, without saying, "I love you."

"I'll get my brakes looked at; I'll get my brakes looked at." Singsong words, and a quick search through the phone's browser provides a list of repair shops near me. Duffy's, Carmichael's Tires, Earl's Quality Car, Simpson Nissan Motors, Lake City Motors, Sterns Automotive. The farther down the list I look, the more distant the business.

My heart thumps hard in my chest, and my thumb hovers. Stacy pushes hard, trying to take her place but I'm in charge now and have been for days, ever since Dr. Martin called and left a list of therapists she would recommend. I'd written the list in the crazy-girl notebook: Suzanne Heffner, Charles Johnson III, Pamela Mendelsen, Matthew Montelbaum, and Aria Zane. Dr. Martin had reached out to each on the list, and all had agreed to accept Stacy as a new patient if she chose.

I've not left long enough for her to choose one over the other, and it's getting easier to keep her pushed down.

"Maybe it's time for me to take my place." I've spoken aloud, and the kids are both looking at me. "I have to get my brakes looked at," I say by way of explanation and raise exaggerated eyebrows. The little one giggles, but the big one rolls her eyes and goes back to eating her bagel.

I let my thumb touch down, and the browser opens to Lake City Motors. I scroll down to the service department. Is it too early to call?

"Lake Motors Service. This is Angela. How can I help you?

"Do you do brakes?"

"Yes, ma'am."

"I have a crappy old Civic that needs the brakes done. Could I come in today?"

"Yes, ma'am. We have an opening at three. Will that work for you?"

"Do you have anything earlier?"

"No, ma'am. Not for today. Would you like for me to look for tomorrow?"

"No. Three will do." I give her Stacy's name and tell her the year of the car.

I wish they'd had something earlier; the kids will be out of school by then, and I'll have to take them with me.

Oh, joy.

~ ~ ~

The girls are in the back seat, flipping from argument to play, and I've turned the radio on then off again. Stacy is having a major meltdown, and I have to concentrate to keep her pushed back. If the damn kids would just keep it down, maybe I could hear myself think.

"Guys! Can you just shut up? You're driving me crazy."

It's louder than I intended, more hysterical. But it does the trick, and they shut up.

"They are fine," Stacy hisses. "They are just playing. We want them to play together."

I think they may have heard that, because the big one asks, "What?"

"Nothing," I snap, and turn back to drive. Within minutes, they are talking again, and with every outburst of laughter or complaint, my hair stands on end.

I should have left them with the neighbor. Or just at home. The big one is nine. That's old enough, isn't it?

We pull into the lot, using the GPS from the phone, burning through the data, and I follow the signs to the service department. It's a large dealership, and the service intake area is inside the building, through giant uplifted garage doors. We pull in the line, one car ahead of us.

"Good afternoon," a man says, stepping out from the main building. We pull forward as the car ahead is taken by a technician, around to an open service bay.

"Good afternoon," I climb out and open the rear door, leaning in to unbuckle Shelby. Sophie is standing, hunched over, waiting to get out this same side.

"What are we doing for you today?"

"Brakes, and can you rotate the tires? I'm sure they're due."

"Sure. Have you been here before, Mrs. Linde?"

"No. First time." I have the girls out of the car now and standing beside me, night and day children.

"Well, we're glad to have you." He trades me the keys for a tag and puts paper sheets on the floorboard of the old car. I would laugh at the idea, protecting it, but my nerves are jangling as I try to keep Stacy pushed down, not in charge.

I can see through the small glass into the service bay, where men are moving around cars, bending into the hoods. I know who I'm looking for, but I can't see enough to find him.

The man, with his wax-tipped handlebar mustache, rises back up, out of the car. He points to the door leading into the main building. "There's a waiting area inside there. Coffee and water, and there may even be a few juice boxes in the fridge in there. Help yourself. If you ask Lori, the lady there at the desk, she'll change one of the TV channels to something your kids will like."

"Awesome. Thanks." We head inside, and I almost lose my control when the little one puts her hand into mine. It's moist and slightly sticky.

My nerves fray, and then they rethread, wiring my head a different way. We find seats, and the girls set out their stuffed animals; each of them has three. Big-eyed, multi-colored animals, that Sophie calls "Beanie Boos." They play, with Sophie telling Shelby what to say, how to do it. I let my mind drift away, my eyes watching but not watching the cycle of news running on the television.

"I'm gonna get some coffee. You want a juice box?" They nod but continue their game. The Keurig is just ten feet away, in full view of the girls, I can walk ten feet away and let them play. I put a hazelnut pod in and wait as it dribbles into the cup, checking the fridge beneath and picking out two juice boxes before turning back.

That's when I notice the Employee of the Month wall. Glossy framed pictures of the best of the best for the given month mounted on a wall leading toward the service department.

There he is. Handsome and dark blond with a sideways, cocky grin. My stomach flips like he is an old lover. My blood washes through my head in a wave and leaves me feeling dizzy, unsteady on my feet. Is that him, fine-boned and so handsome? I glance around and see the girls, sitting around the chrome and glass coffee table, playing their game, but Sophie's eyes are on me over her sister's head. She is still moving the small stuffed animal, her mouth speaking, but Sophie saw something in me that caused her to go on the alert. I can tell. She feels like she needs to keep an eye on me. I give her a quick smile, the wave of dizziness passes, and I turn away from the wall to rejoin the children.

I should have brought along one of the pictures, not the horrible ones, with the knees atop the rods of bony calves, but the one with the cake. Was he smiling like that, cocky and lopsided? The picture rises in my mind, line by line, overlaid by shadow and light. No, he wasn't smiling like that. He wasn't smiling at all, but rather staring into the lens with a cold, narrowed compression of his lips, a burning in his eyes.

My coffee has cooled enough to drink when the receptionist, Lori, calls me up to the front desk. "Mrs. Linde?"

I step up, motioning for the girls to join me.

"The service technician would like to show you something. Could you meet him? Right through those doors." We entered the lobby from the intake area, and the doors she points to now lead past the glossy portraits toward the service bay.

"Is something wrong?" Is the rear axle rusting through? Is there a problem with the U-joints? Stacy doesn't know anything about cars except how to put gas into them.

"No, ma'am, nothing is wrong. He just wants to show you why he's making the recommendation he's making."

"Okay. Just through these doors?"

"Yes, ma'am. Your kids can stay with me."

"No. The kids go where I go." I reach out, and the girls take my hands, and we walk together down the hall toward the service bay. At least the little one's hands aren't sticky anymore, thank God.

I don't turn back around to see the expression on Lori's face, but I know I sounded paranoid, like I thought she might run away with the precious children. The fact is, if I leave them behind, I don't think I could keep Stacy down.

A heavyset man meets us at the doors and leads us through the service department without so much as a word. We stop at the raised Civic, and the man dealing with the repairs turns to face me. He has dark hair with a full beard, hefty, solid, not fat. I am relieved. My heart has been pounding since we stepped toward the door. What if Shane Moony was the man working on the car? Yes, I came here to find him, I realize, but that doesn't mean I am quite ready to meet him. What if he is really my brother? What words could I possibly say to him?

My eyes scan the room, searching for him, listening to the technician explaining that he will need to replace both rear rotors, showing me the grooves on what should be a smooth surface.

"Both?" I ask, and he takes us around to the other side, showing me where the grooves are also present.

"Your front is okay. Just need the pads up there."

"That's good. How long? My first question should have been "How much?" But I don't care. John will pay for it.

"It's a pretty common part. We have them here, so... not long. I'll work you up an estimate."

"Whatever." I flutter my hands, looking past him, trying to find Shane before I have to go back to the waiting room. I catch a glimpse of the expression on the technician's face, which is confusion.

"I don't need an estimate; just do it. I brought it in to get it fixed, right?"

"Yes, ma'am." He raises an eyebrow, and I draw a hand up through my hair. I see his eye catch the ring and understanding dawns. He thought I was one of those people that would have to arrange payments.

I drop my hand, laughing. Stacy would be embarrassed like she was with that cow, Sue Bellefonte. Should we be embarrassed that we don't have to worry about the money because John works hard to take care of us, that we get to stay home with the kids and know that he'll pay the bills? The old Civic gives a different impression... like we are driving a cash car because we can't afford it, like we are driving a cash car because we spent too much money on a ring. If I were in charge, we wouldn't be driving a cash car, that's for sure.

I turn away from him, looking down, reaching for the kids' hands, and almost run into the man walking past. "Sorry," I say, looking up.

The man's hand shoots up, out of the way, as startled as I am and cautious not to touch me.

"Shane Moony," I whisper, and there is recognition in my voice, like I know him. Is he too young? How does thirty-six look? John is thirty-five.

It's not him.

He's definitely too young, too broad in his jaw line. He's too pretty. He's too short. Slim would have grown up to be tall, like me, but this man is no taller than I am.

He's too soft. I roll my tongue over the ridge of my teeth, disappointment warring with relief.

I recognize him, yes, but from the Lake City Motors website, not from the birthday picture of the non-smiling boy. This one's too clean, too nice.

I wanted it to be him; I'd planned to confront him about the days in the kennel that I only sometimes remember.

I wanted to get proof that our beginnings are not the sum of who we are, that we are not a fraud hiding behind John's gifts.

He has blue eyes.

Shelby has blue eyes. Did Slim have blue eyes? No. He had the same dark eyes my mother had, the same eyes I have.

"Do I know you?" I ask, and his eyes flash to Sophie and then catch on Shelby, and I see him taking in the blond hair, the smooth features of her face. Does he recognize her? Does he see himself in the lines of her face?

His brows are too flat; he is not my brother.

"I don't know. Do you?" It's a challenge, said with a cocky grin. It could be him after all.

"I don't think so." I cock an eyebrow, meeting the challenge. "I saw your picture. Employee of the month. Congratulations." I say it, wrinkling my nose, like it is no accomplishment at all, in his menial little job.

Stacy cringes and yanks, pulling me down and in when I wasn't expecting it.

Stacy

I push up, like surfacing from the depths of a murky lake. "That's very cool," I say, without hardly missing a beat and smile, my most genuine, kindest smile. The look of confusion and insult on his face eases. He steps aside to let us pass.

I glance back at the technician and say, "I would like to see an estimate, after all, if that's okay?"

The mechanic frowns at my indecision, but shrugs and says, "Yep. All right."

We leave the service bay, Shelby in front of Sophie and me behind. I haven't lost time! I remember everything. It was like a switch. As if by being aware, knowing, I have some power.

When I glance back before I hit the door, I see him, Shane Moony, Employee of the Month watching us, his forehead puckered in doubt, and I wonder if he is trying to figure out if I was some bar conquest and Shelby the product. What is he thinking? Am I wrong? Is it him? Is recognition sparking through him? He was older, nine when they took us. Does he remember? Does he know me? I should turn back and ask him, point blank, and be done with the wondering. But we are at the door and through it, and the opportunity is gone.

Is he the same boy that came to our lake house all those years after we were taken from the kennel? Does he remember waiting in the car while she begged to see me?

Could he be the same kid who walked away from me, carrying a knife at his side, his back set with determination to set us free? Free. Free from what... a home with food? Free from a home without cages? How did he end up with her again? That's the question I want to ask. How did she get him back? Or is that moment, that memory of seeing the boy sitting in the car, all part of the faulty network in my mind and just something I'd created?

36

Stacy

"Why would you drive all the way to Lake City?" John asks, his voice so heavy with disdain that I feel small under the weight of it.

We are still in the lounge at Lake City Motors. The girls are no longer playing with the big-eyed animals and are now staring gape-mouthed at the SpongeBob cartoon Lori had put on while we were in the service bay. I didn't ask her to, and now the little sponge's laugh is grating on my nerves, the few I have remaining. I want to get the car back and go home to our cul-de-sac so I can write in my notebook. I have to remember.

"It doesn't make any sense," John says, still waiting for an answer, sounding more annoyed by the minute.

"I don't know. They could do it today."

"And Duffy's couldn't?"

I don't respond. I won't lie, because he would know. He always knows. So, instead, I stay silent, letting my jaw clench and flex. What would he do if I told him the truth?

"You know they're gonna screw you."

"They are not." I turn toward the windows, looking out over the flowing traffic.

"I think you need to take it to Duffy's."

"They're already putting it back together. They're almost finished."

"Well, I want to see the old rotors."

"I saw them; they have ridges."

"I want to see them."

"You think I don't know what ridges look like?" This is unfamiliar territory. I don't argue. I don't fight.

"I don't understand why you drove all the way to Lake City. We've never had work done there; I want to see the rotors. Do you understand?"

"Fine. I'll have them put them in the trunk."

"Are you okay?"

"I'm fine."

"You've been a little off. Are you sure you're okay?"

Silence. "I'm fine, John. Just... you know." He doesn't know, of course, but the idea of telling him anything real is daunting. "Well, let me go so I can get the rotors."

"All right." He disconnects, and I slip the phone back into my purse, irritation rolling in waves through my body. I'm not a child. What difference does it make where I take the car? He makes me feel like I'm foolish, always, and I hate him a little because of it. How can he not know that there is stuff happening inside of me? How does he not know?

"Because he doesn't look at you." The voice is loud and doesn't sound like something in my head, and I turn to see who has spoken, but nobody is there... nobody except my kids, staring up at the laughing sponge, like zombies.

"No. He looks. He just doesn't see," I say under my breath, answering the comment. Oh, John looks at me, all right. He looks to see if my hair is brushed and if my clothes match, if my bra strap is showing. Am I holding the right countenance on my face? He looks at what I've done. Are the girls clean and dressed in an acceptable manner? Is dog hair on the floor, or has it all been swept away? Is water tracked from the pool through the house? Did the groceries get put away? Are there dirty dishes in the sink? Is there something sticky on the counter left over from breakfast? Who left their shoes in the middle of the floor? He looks and looks and looks, but he never sees.

I go to the desk and tell Lori I need the rotors to take home—my husband wants to see them. I keep my voice steady as if this is a reasonable thing to ask, as if I am not saying my husband thinks they scammed me, a stupid girl.

She smiles and nods, no big deal, and picks up the phone to call back to the service department to relay my message.

I return to my girls and sit between them, scooting Shelby over to make room, and watch as SpongeBob, who lives under the sea, tries to get his driver's license. I watch like a zombie, letting my mind go dull and slow. The four-second flit of the cartoon soothes the worry in my soul and silences the screaming woman in my head.

~ ~ ~

"Are you sure these are from your car?"

We are standing in the driveway. It is late evening, and the girls have already been bathed and put to bed. I met him in the garage to show him the rotors, and we've stepped out into the remaining light of the day to inspect them.

"Yes." I let the word draw out like floss through my teeth. I am seething.

I smell the whiskey on his breath, and I turn my face away from him, a flush rising to my cheeks, my anger flashing.

"Well, they wouldn't have been in such bad shape if you had just taken it in when I first told you to." He drops the rotor into the trash, and the other behind it. He turns and walks through the garage, and I bite my lip, feeling the small nodules under my skin compressing.

~ ~ ~

I walk through the house, past where he is already sitting in front of the television, tuning in and tuning out, and I go to our room, stripping out of my clothes and pulling on running clothes. I haven't run since the day I talked to Felicia Martin, the day Shiloh pushed forward and kind of took over.

I shake my head and clear the thoughts. It's been an emotional day, and I need to get some of the emotion out of my blood before I explode.

"Where are you going?"

"It's a beautiful night. I'm going for a run."

"Okay." He sounds annoyed, offended.

"What?" I stop, turning to face him, ready to come unhinged.

"I just thought we'd spend some time together. I just got home."

The screaming woman inside of me nearly erupts. "I need a run." My voice cracks, and for a moment, I'm afraid I may cry. "I feel like I put on some weight." There is nothing I could have said that would have set me free quicker than that. John has disdain for obesity; he finds it repulsive.

"All right." He turns back to his show, dismissing me, Al Bundy with his hand in the band of his pants. I find him repulsive. Does my opinion count? Is my opinion as valid as his?

I run down the drive, not even bothering to warm up, just feeling assured that my body will remember what to do and will handle it fine. It does. The muscle memory sets a comfortable pace, my breathing finds a rhythm, and I wonder how long I could be gone before he would think to look for me. Would he look for me? Or would he just hire somebody to fill the shoes I wear in our home?

It is only then that I realize why my anger flared. It wasn't the criticism; it wasn't his doubt that I would do the right thing. It was the smear of pale lipstick on the edge of his collar. When was the last time he came home before the girls were in bed? Is he coming back home late more often or is it just that I am only in my skin some of the time when he does?

~ ~ ~

He is asleep when I come back, lit by the glow of the flashing images on the television. I walk in my socked feet toward him, expecting him to wake, but he doesn't. I lean close, smelling him, trying to catch the hint of something else...

And there it is. Something sweet, and then the tang of sex, or is it just my imagination? I narrow my eyes, focusing on the smear on his collar, the very lip-shaped smudge, and I know that he is sleeping with someone else. No, that's wrong. He is only sleeping with me; he is sexing with someone else.

I lift my phone, opening the camera, and I take a picture, close and precise, of the pale pink spot on his shirt, catching the bruised-looking space of skin just above it.

Son of a bitch.

37

Stacy

Going to the support group makes me feel less alone, although I never speak and feel almost invisible. I sit and listen to the tragic stories and convince myself that I'm going to be okay. I wave to Leon each time as I come in, but only sometimes do I stop and talk to him. There are always so many others around him, circling him, like he is their god. I sit with the group, listening as the tormented souls share their stories.

"It's been five weeks since my husband died."

"It's been six years since my son committed suicide."

"It's been three years since my fiancé..."

They are all the same, the stories they share—tales of how the grief overwhelms them. They all speak of their loss as if it is a living, breathing demon, hunting them through their lives. "It's been one hundred thirty-eight days since my mother died," I could say, standing up in a meeting, looking for affirmation, but I seldom speak in the meetings. I listen and then get up as Leon closes, and I leave, convinced once again that I am not alone.

On Wednesday, I go to the support group, which I've been a regular at since school started again. Leon isn't there. I call him on Thursday when my feet are too tired to run any further.

"How are you?" he asks.

"Crazy," I answer, my most common answer with him.

"More so than usual?" he asks with a little hint of laughter, his most common response. We've gotten to know each other, a little, since I started showing up regularly at the meetings, and there is something comforting in the familiarity.

"No. Not really. Missed you at the meeting yesterday. It's been a strange week."

"I was going to take a ride out to the beach. Want to join me?"

I think about it only for a minute. "I have to be back by eleven thirty."

"That's fine."

"I'll pick you up?"

"Okay. I'll meet you. Publix on Racetrack?"

Ten minutes later, I'm in the parking lot, watching for him to arrive. I don't know what car he drives, so every car that pulls in sends my stomach flipping. I don't know what I'm doing. If I were going to have an affair, it wouldn't be with Leon. I would never do that, though. I never thought John would have, either. I push the thought out of my head. He isn't. It was probably just a smear from a hug. His women clients always hug him; he's that kind of guy. Even if he has found someone else, can I blame him? I've been distracted and distant for months.

I wasn't expecting a motorcycle, so when the bike sputters to a stop beside me, I only glance over because it is there. I am startled to see Leon peering at me from the upraised faceplate of his helmet. He pulls it from his head, and his thin hair is wet with heat and stands up in unruly spikes.

He cuts the engine to his bike and rocks it onto the kickstand. "Thought that was you."

"Hey," I say, after rolling up the window and climbing out of the car. "Taking a bike, huh?"

"Sure. It's like freedom."

I know he is right. I dated a man in high school who rode a motorcycle, and the best memories I have of him are on the back of his bike. That was before I stopped participating in risky behavior. It was before I stopped stockpiling razor blades and tequila, in a one-to-one ratio.

He unstraps a spare helmet and hands it to me, and I peer inside, looking for remnants of another woman's hair, checking for lice or cooties. "I haven't been on a bike in a long time."

"I'll be careful. Hop on."

I do. Even as I climb on the back, I see the headline: "Local Woman Killed in Fatal Motorcycle Accident, Without Her Husband." I am stupid; this is a mistake. But I'm on the bike now and I let my legs fold toward him, in the old familiar way of riding on the back of a motorcycle, and with the push of a button, the engine roars to life and the years drop away. We fly.

He is not reckless, and it is not the same as I remember it being. I am sober, and this may be the first time I have ever been so on the back of a bike. I am aware of how close the pavement is, and I am aware of the roar of the wind around me. By the time we reach Mickler's Landing, I have finally relaxed, and the tension has washed out of my body from places I didn't even know. He parks in lot 9, and we walk down the edge along the sand until we reach the boardwalk that will take us to the beach.

"Ah." I draw in a long breath and expel it, letting the salt in the air cure all that ails me. I pause and slip off my shoes, folding my socks down into the toe of one. Leon watches, waiting. "You aren't going to take off your shoes?" I ask.

"No." He wears heavy, steel-toed work boots, and I ask him what line of work he is doing. "I do a little construction." That explains the heavy boots. "But really, I'm a poet."

"A poet?" I smile up at him, rising to my feet. "Is there money in poetry?"

"No." A smirk spreads on his lips, a sardonic compression of the lips, humored but not amused.

"So, tell me a poem."

He does, his voice rebounding off the sand, an orator's voice. I stand, gaping, not sure how to respond to the rhythms rolling around me. His voice takes me, but I don't understand what he is trying to convey. I'm not smart enough to appreciate poetry. I never know how I'm supposed to feel about it. I need clarification; I need direction and explanation.

"Wow," I say when he finishes, and we start our forward march again. "You did that well."

"I do a lot of open-mic nights." That explains the booming voice, the emotional inflection, the practiced narration.

"Impressive." We walk. "But—and don't be offended—what does it mean?"

"I don't know." He shrugs, and I laugh. "I know what it means to me, but it's not going to mean the same thing to you. That's what is great about poetry. It's a jumping-off point. Every flight is different. It's like dropping acid."

I had never thought about that—that a poem could mean different things to different people. That's not what I'd learned in college. Meanings are meanings; alternate interpretations are invalid. "I never thought about poetry like that," I admit.

"That's the only way to think about poetry," he says, and there is still some inflection left over in his voice, the rhythm and cadence of his poem lingering.

"I used to write."

"Why 'used to'?"

"It was in my self-destructive phase," and I have the strangest urge to show my scars, but I keep my wrists turned down. The scars are ugly and stark, white lines slightly ridged by scar tissue. I told John I had gone through a window when he had noticed them, way back when we were just beginning to date, back when he was still looking at me to see.

"Writing can be therapeutic."

"Yeah, or not." I am not convinced that the writing I did, ever, was therapeutic.

I can feel him watching me, and I wonder what he sees. Does he see through me? Into me? Does he see how screwed up I am?

"What's your story?" I ask.

"Probably the same as yours, Stacy. We both lost someone who mattered."

I laugh. "I guess. But you never share."

"Most everybody has heard my story."

"Not me," I insist.

Leon's limp is more pronounced in the sand, and we stop, sitting, as the heat rises around us. I wish we had shade. Sweat is already pooling along the ridge of my bra, along the top of my jeans.

"All right." He clears his throat, and I expect the orator to come out when he speaks again, but his voice is quiet. "You familiar with golf?"

"Sure."

"Well, my dad was something of a big deal in golf. Won the Masters three times, the Players twice."

I've heard of the Masters, having grown up in Georgia. "That's impressive," I say, and Leon nods.

"Yeah, he won a lot of that sort of thing. There was a time when he was supposed to be the best." He stares out at the water like his mind is rolling through the past, and I hesitate to draw him back. "I was his only son. Of course, he wanted me to follow in his footsteps."

Of course. It's that old familiar story. "So what happened?"

"Well, I was good. Not as good as him maybe, but I was getting better. It looked like all my prospects were in line."

"You were a pro golfer?"

"For a while." He clears his throat, looking down at the tips of his shoes. "Then, one night, I drove under the back end of a semi. That kinda ended it for me."

"Drove under a semi?" I think of Chevy Chase in Christmas Vacation, the hilarity of his realizing he had driven under the trailer, the panic in the car, the risky escape from one catastrophe to the next.

"Well, more 'into,' I guess. Traffic had stopped, and I was distracted, checking my phone, whatever. I had just won the qualifier to get me into the Masters. It was a big deal."

"I bet," I say to fill the long silence. "Were you drunk?" My jaw clenches, the words press through my teeth, and the bitter taste of bile rises.

"Nope. Not at all." He stares out, letting that reality sink. "I still don't know how it happened. I looked down at my phone and clipped the semi. My car flipped and landed on the car beside me. Killed the whole family. Three people died. Should have been me."

"Oh shit, Leon." I want to touch him but can see the barriers around him, the brace of his shoulders, the tension in his neck, and I know that if I reach for him now, he will unravel.

"Yeah. Oh shit. The firemen cut me out of my car, and three days later, I woke up with a metal rod in my leg and a metal plate in my head." He pushes back his hair, and I see the scar. He pulls up the leg of his jeans, exposing the mangled, scarred flesh of his lower leg. "I lost everything, checking that phone."

"That's horrible," I say, meaning it. My story doesn't feel as big; it doesn't even seem to be about me.

"Yeah. I'd never play golf again, for sure." He lifts a handful of sand and lets it stream between his fingers. "My dad never spoke to me again."

"Why not? It was just an accident." It seems too harsh a judgment since he wasn't drunk. "Accidents happen."

He shrugs. "I let him down."

We sit in silence.

"Maybe I never spoke to him again, either. Maybe we just stopped knowing each other," Leon says, as if it's a new thought, a new way of looking at what happened.

I don't know that I can follow that story with mine. It will feel like a one-up. Like trying to compare our tragedies, and I feel petty because, really, mine has a happy ending. Beautiful people adopted me, and they gave me every opportunity I could hope to have. How had I repaid them for all of those possibilities? By fighting about everything, by being difficult, by hating them for what I didn't know. That is the sum of who I have been—an ungrateful child. Who cares about the rest? Nobody, not even me.

I never caused anybody to die.

"When did he die?"

"Two years ago." He compresses his lips, and I wonder if he tried to fix the divide. Had he tried to rebuild their relationship, or was it just a lost cause?

"I'm sorry."

He nods, and we sit steaming on the sand. "So what's your story?"

"It's nothing, really, compared to that."

"Just because it isn't filled with drama doesn't mean it isn't tragic."

"Oh there's some drama," I say, surprised how I feel insulted that he would think my tragedy is just run-of-the-mill.

"I didn't mean to imply..." His voice trails off when I hand him my phone, showing the only picture I'd kept on there—the two bony children staring from lost eyes, their skulls pressing against their flesh.

He groans, looking at it. "What is this?"

"That's me and my brother. We were locked in a dog kennel when they found us."

"How old were you?"

"I was four, and he was nine." I glance at Leon, and his face is blanched white under a sheen of sweat. "I was adopted after that and had a great life. But my parents, my adoptive parents... they never told me."

"How'd you find out?"

I tell him the story of the envelope.

"Have you asked your dad about it?"

I shake my head and explain that Dad has dementia. "I did ask my brother, but he wasn't able to say much." I remember Darren spinning in a slow circle in the middle of the road when I'd mentioned Slim.

"That's horrifying," he says.

"Isn't it, though?" I agree, meaning it.

"No wonder you're having such a hard time." He puts his hand on my shoulder and, for once, every muscle in my body doesn't jerk at being touched.

"It makes me feel guilty."

"You have nothing to feel guilty about. These things were done to you. You were just a child."

"I was a horrible teenager. I put my mother through hell."

"That's what teenagers do." He arches an eyebrow and tilts his head, looking at me. Suddenly, I am ashamed for walking around feeling like I have a corner office on personal tragedy. Is it true that it is just the way of teenagers? Was I no worse than others? He's right—I was a child, and those things were done to me. I should have no guilt for what I did not know.

But Leon has guilt. I can see it now, etched in the too-deep crags of his face. How has Leon lived? How would you live, knowing that somebody else died because you were checking your phone, not paying attention? Distracted driving—that's what they call it. It's as bad as being drunk. It was his fault, and Leon has guilt. I was just a child.

"Your story puts things in perspective," I say.

"Yeah. It has that effect." He presses his tongue against his teeth, the way you do when you are trying to get a foul taste out of your mouth.

"How have you moved on?"

"Have I?" he asks, tossing a shell out across the sand, with force, like he is throwing it intentionally away from himself. "Good therapist."

I don't know why it surprises me that he has a therapist. "Yeah, I'm wondering if that would be a good idea, for me."

"Probably. I think everybody should have somebody to talk through their shit with. Dr. Monty is great. He's really helped me a lot. I'll send you his number if you want it."

"Thanks. I'm not sure I'm ready, but it's good to have options, right?"

"Yep. Good to have options."

"Thanks for sharing," I say, using the words he says at the meetings, trying to lighten the mood. But I mean it, too. I'm glad to finally know his story, to understand what somebody else carries. My weight feels lighter than it did when I woke up this morning.

"You, too."

We sit again, another long stretch before I become aware that the sun is high in the sky and it's probably close to noon. "We should probably head back," I say, and he looks down at his watch and then pushes himself awkwardly up from the sand.

~ ~ ~

We are sitting at dinner, on a rare evening when John is home, when Leon's text arrives with the name of his therapist. M. Montelbaum, and there is a phone number. Something clicks in my head, something in the name is familiar, and I think it may be one of the names from the list that Felicia Martin sent. John doesn't know that I spent the morning with Leon, and when he raises his eyebrow about the text, I simply roll my eyes and shrug, as if it's something from Dee or Mona, something of no importance. It's not that I'm trying to keep my morning secret; it's just not important enough to share. Leon is just somebody from the support group, and John would be glad to know that I've found someone who understands, someone who can help me find a way through my grief.

John and I have so many secrets between us that this doesn't even feel like one. He'd be relieved to hear, and he'd hope that maybe I'd get over it sometime soon, that someone else would help me through my grief, a fellow traveler in tragedy. But the result of spending that time on the beach, of hearing the story of Leon's broken life, is a snapping in my head, springing me out of the depths of my self-pity.

I never think John notices me, but he is very perceptive.

38

Stacy

This morning, I woke with my mother's voice in my head, telling me a story from a long time ago, about her and Aunt Mari when they were young. An adventure on a camping trip that left them treed by a pair blue tick hounds. I stand at the counter, writing the words out longhand, waiting for the girls to wake, for the day to start. It is satisfying, feeling the words sliding through my fingers, but also not. The words are hard to get down fast enough, and I realize that what I want is my old typewriter. I want the rhythm of the keys.

I wait for John to leave for work, and I get the girls off to school, driving Shelby instead of pushing her in the stroller. When I get back to the house, I pull out John's old laptop, feeling anxious until the apple lights up and the machine boots. Leon says that writing can be therapeutic, and I am in desperate need of therapy. I have circled the name Montelbaum in the list that Dr. Martin gave me—two recommendations are better than one—but the dread I felt looking at the name nearly overwhelmed me, and I closed the notebook without making the call. I may need therapy, but I'm not quite ready for it. I need the black space inside my soul to recolor, I need to stop feeling half dead, invisible.

I open a new document and put my hands on the keys, waiting, watching the cursor blinking, and then I type, "I was the girl in the kennel."

I backspace, erasing the words. There is no place to go from there. If that's all I needed to say, then it's been done. I've admitted that; I've internalized that. Yet, I am more broken every single time I shed my identity and someone else claims my body. It didn't make me well to show the pictures to Dee and Mona. It didn't make me well to tell Gina, or Leon. It isn't just about that one last moment that I have knowledge of—the moment the police broke into the trailer, stormed through the halls, discovered us. My memory peels back, and I see his face, the officer who kneeled down and peered into our cage. He had jerked back when Slim reached to wrap his long fingers around the wire. "Oh my God, there are children here."

Where is the backstory? There is a whole lifetime that happened before that moment. How did they come to find us? Did somebody see us running across the back yard and called the police when the memory of us stayed in their head until they had to do something? Did they come to the trailer asking about the children they saw running across the back yard? Did they get turned away, and after that encounter, did they then notify the police that there was something not right? I think about my girls, the same ages as those children when they were found. I can't even imagine them confined in such a way—sending them to their room to "think about it" is as close as I can imagine. Was it a one-off, us being in the kennel? Was it because we had run away and she was punishing us?

How did it begin? How did it get to a point that locking children, even disobedient children, in a dog crate seemed like a rational idea? I could never imagine that. Nothing could make that okay. I would never put my children in such a situation. Why would she? The newspaper said she suffered with mental illness. Is that something different from the voices in my head? Was her illness more extreme? Dr. Martin had said she thought I was schizophrenic, but she eventually ruled it out because I seemed connected to reality. Did Kristine Moony not understand that she was locking her kids in a kennel? Did she think instead she was sending them to play in a meadow? Was she delusional? All of my questions stop with her. I cannot understand until I understand her.

The blank page glows from the screen, feeling like an accusation. It needs to be filled.

I take out the notepad that I had written my mother's story on and transcribe it. I copy the document and send it to Leon.

The cursor blinks.

I am not satisfied. How did I ever write, when I was a teen? How did I do it?

Maybe I didn't write. Perhaps it was Shiloh, and that's why I never recognized any of the stories.

I close the laptop and walk around the house, pushing dog hair toward a corner in the kitchen with the dust mop. The dogs are out back. I join them, feeling restless, feeling like my skin is just a hair too tight. The sky is gray with fat clouds shifting lazily across, pretending to be winter.

I should have run this morning. I have too much energy. The dogs follow me back into the house, and I take them with me for a run. At first, they pull, and I tug, and they cross their leads, and I try not to trip over them, but soon we find a rhythm, and they run with their heads up. We make it to the end of the street before they peter out on me. It's too much for them; they aren't used to running with me. We turn back, them panting, me perspiring, unsatisfied.

I open the laptop again. I have nothing to say, sweat crawling down my forehead, cooling in the air-conditioned chill. I close my eyes and let my fingers fall. This time, I will not look at the words I type.

"Do you have something you want to say, Shiloh?" I ask, and it feels dangerous, opening the door to her like that.

I let my mind drift as my fingers rattle over the keys. There will be typos, and I don't care. There will be mistakes; there will be secrets. I type until my breathing steadies, and when I open my eyes, I am looking above the laptop, not seeing the words, but seeing the tree and the bushes beside the driveway next door, seeing the sky gray and looming. I listen to the rhythm of my nails clicking on the keys, and I breathe. Something slows and steadies inside my soul, and the strange shifting of my skin over my vessels stops. The call to be set free—Of what? From what?—is answered, and I breathe.

My eyes wander around the room, landing on the clock on the microwave, telling me it is 12:05, and I type, my eyes stuck on the numbers but my mind flying free, my fingers typing, clicking. 12:06.

Oh shit. Shelby gets out at noon. What am I doing? I glance at the screen, and the words "hurt me" glow out from the white background. I hit the red dot in the corner of the page. "Do you want to save?"

I scan the screen again, looking for the words "hurt me," but in all the flowing together of the words and sentences, with all the typos, I don't see those words. It looks like something a drunk person would write.

No. I don't want to save, and the thoughts—maybe they were Shiloh's; I don't know—evaporate and disintegrate with the lost document. For the first time in hours, I feel almost sane.

39

Stacy

"Mama, where were you?" Shelby asks, her eyes wide and tearful. I am always one of the moms waiting when the door opens, so my not being here was a big deal for Shelby. I scoop her into my arms, whispering how sorry I am, telling her that I got sidetracked walking the dogs. The lie comes easily off my tongue, as if it is more justifiable to have lost track of time because I was doing something for the dogs than to have been doing something for myself. What if I had said "Mommy was trying to figure out what is wrong with her"? Would that have made it okay? To me? To her? It doesn't matter. I should have been here, and I wasn't, and I feel like a horrible mother.

I have no identity. I am John's wife. I am Sophie and Shelby's mother. My impact in the world stops with the three of them. I am invisible. I am Caged Girl. I squeeze my eyes shut, hidden in her hair. Dark thoughts in my head, now that my fingers remember the rhythm.

She squeezes my neck. "It's okay. Guess what?" she says, pulling away, her face glowing in front of me.

"H-What?" I ask, putting my "h" first in an exaggeration.

"Okay, so, Lucy is learning to play the piano, and I told her that I'm learning the violin, so when we grow up, we can be in a band together."

"Oh, well, that sounds like fun."

"Can you teach me? You have Grandma's violin, and you can teach me, right?"

"I don't know, Shelby Honey. Mommy's not very good at the violin." I regret again that I gave it up. Oh, how I would love to be able to teach her. "But we can get you lessons."

"No. I want you to teach me. Lucy's mom is teaching her."

"I'm sure she is." I have a flash of recollection of the pristine, fastidious woman that is Lucy's mom. Of course she would be capable of teaching her child an instrument.

We have reached the outside, and the heat rises, residual from the sidewalk. The sky is still gray, and far away, I hear the rumble of thunder. I had driven the car, being so late, and now settle Shelby in her seat, buckling her. We pull out onto Flora Branch and turn left, toward Racetrack Road and into the gas station across the street. Gina's husband, the father of all the adopted kids, manages this store. I look through the dark windows to see if he is there, to do the neighborly thing and wave, but a young man is behind the counter, and I don't see any other employees in the store. A car pulls into another stall, and a tall man gets out to pump gas. He nods at us, and I nod back, getting out of the car, sliding my credit card into the machine. I stand with my back to the man, the stranger, blocking Shelby from his view.

Shelby has rolled down her window and is watching me, catching my eye with the flutter of her hand.

"Please, teach me."

"Okay. Okay. I'll teach you what I remember, and then we'll get you a proper teacher." I reach through the window and catch her little long-fingered hand.

"Nope. Just you," she singsongs, and I finish pumping gas and go around to climb into the driver's seat. I glance across the pump and see the car that pulled in beside us, and only now does it register that it's the car that has been parking overnight at Dee's for the last few weeks. Damn, I should have paid attention! He has his back to me, tall and lean, clean-cut, professional. I am so happy for Dee. I think she caught a good one this time.

Shelby is singing, "Just you, just you, just you."

"Just me, huh? What about when you get better than me?"

"I'll never be better than you. You're my mom." She says this as if there is some truth to it.

"I've got you fooled," I whisper under my breath, but I don't want either of my girls to figure that out yet.

~ ~ ~

We make our way back to the house, and she is so excited about the idea of learning to play the violin that she isn't even interested in lunch. "Lucy says it's not a violin; it's a fiddle."

"I think they're the same thing."

"She says they're different," Shelby insists, and irritation sparks through me at know-it-all Lucy.

"I don't think so. I think it's the same instrument, just played differently."

"That doesn't make sense." She takes a bite of her peanut-butter-and-jelly sandwich and looks at me with one eye narrowed to a slit, a very John look.

"It does. It's just like down here we call soda 'coke,' but up north they call soda 'pop.' Understand? Fiddle playing is more country, like bluegrass. I think 'fiddlers' play more than one string at a time. I don't remember." I fetch the violins from my closet and set about the task of tuning. "Either way, you're welcome to learn."

How do you teach somebody music who doesn't even know how to read yet?

How did my mother do it? I try to think back. I was seven, though, so I could read. Shelby knows her alphabet—isn't that enough? I start by giving her the violin and teaching her how to do long bows. How to draw the bow across all the strings, one at a time, in one long motion. I talk to her about how the bow needs to be straight across the strings to give it a good sound, and she squeaks and squawks with fantastic enthusiasm.

She laughs at the sounds coming from the instrument, squeals of delight. "Is it supposed to sound like that?"

"It always did when I played it," I admit, and she laughs, catching the meaning. How did she get so smart, so observant and aware? She is too young to comprehend, just nearly four years old is too young to understand my meaning.

"Teach me a song."

"How about I teach you the beginning of a song?"

"Okay."

I try to remember how my violin teacher taught me the strings, the notes, and I start her on the opening measure of "Theme," known to the rest of the world as "Twinkle, Twinkle, Little Star."

The opening measure is four notes, A, A, E, E. Second string open, twice, then the first string open, twice.

This is exactly what I needed, after my morning of reflection and dissatisfaction, I needed to connect, and Shelby gave me that connection. When I was feeling like everything was wrong and confused, she pulled me back from the ledge and suggested I not jump by offering me an alternative. What a blessing it is to have my kids. How could anybody lock them up?

I will never understand. I realize it in a flash, and the pressure that has been rising and rising and rising in my soul recedes. I will never understand it. I will never understand it because it doesn't fit in the realm of normal behavior. I will never understand it because there is no way for me to ask why she did the things she did. There is no good that will come to me by dwelling on it.

She squeals, hearing the beginning of the song, recognizing it. We work through the first line. "What's next, what's next?"

"Next we walk down to get Sophie."

We go out through the garage, and she clutches the violin. I should make her leave it; it could get broken. But she's so happy and I feel so light that I let her take it. It doesn't matter; if she wants to learn and the violin becomes damaged, I'll get her a new one. She already has a better appreciation of it than I did.

Is it the flash-in-the-pan, though? That trait of mine—high excitement to burn quick and fade. How many things was I intensely interested in before the age of twelve?

I haven't seen that in Shelby. Sophie has a touch of it maybe, but not Shelby. Sophie rotates through her favorite things, asking for input each night as to which animal should receive her favor of the twelve she keeps on her bed. But Shelby is steadfast, she has loved her stuffed rabbit best of all her stuffed animals since the day we got it. The first line of "Theme" is coming from the stroller as we walk, and I hear her beginning to experiment. She finds the next note, then the following, and soon she is working from the beginning; she is hitting the tones intuitively.

We stop at the end of the road, where all the moms are converging, some in cars, but mostly on foot.

I kneel down in front of the stroller, watching as Shelby finds the next note, plays, goes back, starts again, plays, adds another note. She is talking every time she finds a new note— "Oh, that's it"—and then playing some more. It isn't smooth or practiced. The bow still squawks and squeaks across the string, but she is finding the right tones, the right movements through the song.

I close my mouth, then say, "You have an ear." Isn't that what they call it, when a person can pick notes from the air and find them on an instrument? I am awed.

"What do we have here?" Mona asks as she and Julia come alongside the stroller.

"A virtuoso." I say, laughing, proud.

Shelby sets the violin aside, careful, and I help her climb out to play with Julia.

Mona and I watch the girls, as they trot toward the pond. "When did she start taking lessons?"

"She didn't. She just picked it up today." I tell her how I had shown her the basics, from what I remember, how I had helped her through the first part of a song, and how she started adding notes as we walked. It feels like magic. Shelby is my little elf, my little moon fairy.

Mona isn't as impressed as I am, and I let the conversation roll toward her. "He absolutely hit on me," she whispers, and I follow her nod to see Gina's husband, Boyd, the lone man in the sea of women.

"No," I insist. Surely she misunderstood.

"He did. I swear it."

"I don't doubt you. All that cross-fit will drive a man to distraction."

"Yeah, well, he's lucky I didn't tell my husband."

"What would he do?" I don't even try to keep the laughter out of my voice.

"We have a gun," she says, her voice so severe that I look at her to make sure she is joking. I'm not sure. Her brows are drawn down, low and close, like she has some legitimate reason to be offended.

"Is he gonna shoot a guy for hitting on you?" I laugh it off. "Ah, Mona, take it as a compliment. He didn't mean any disrespect. Did he touch you?"

"No, but still."

"Okay. Why do you work out?"

"To be strong. To be healthy." She grins, understanding my point.

"To be attractive," I insist.

"To be attractive," she agrees, her cheeks flushing a little.

"Then why would you be offended? Somebody appreciated your efforts. That's all." I glance back at the man, "He's pretty into his wife." She nods, and I know that it was more of a thrill, him "hitting" on her, than she wants to admit, which is why she mentioned it. The bus rolls up. I watch as Boyd's three adopted children come down off the bus, right after Sophie and Willow. I watch, from half-lowered lids as the younger two make a mad dash for him. A man who can make a home for other people's kids can't be wrong in my book.

When we get home, while Shelby is showing Sophie what she has learned on the violin, I step outside and call my dad, just to hear his voice—a man who could make a home for someone else's kid.

40

Stacy

The days are gray and gloomy, with dense clouds scudding across the sky. It's a change, and something we've all needed, the slight chill in the air. Florida has two seasons, at best—a prolonged summer and not-so-summer. We've finally reached not-so-summer. Georgia gets a little closer to winter than Florida does, but even there it is a slow shift from hot to not so hot. I can count on the fingers of one hand the number of times I've seen snow. The dark days match my mood, and my notebook is dotted with days I find myself places and don't remember getting there. I am at the beach one cold morning, waist deep in the water, gasping as a wave tumbled me and took me under. The water is frigid this time of year, and the search for my car leaves me with chattering teeth and rigid muscles. Another day, I find myself on I-10, heading north, with no idea of my destination. I had thought I was through the worst of it, and it's true that the black holes in my mind aren't as black. Often little pieces of memory come to me later from inside those dark spaces, but it's almost like I'm losing the war to control my body, and Shiloh is taking over.

Today, though, has been a good day. I have been wholly myself all day, and this evening, our house is full of our neighbors, here to plan the annual Thanksgiving party. We do a potluck, and this year, we're doing it on the Saturday after the holiday. It's Scott and Tammy's turn to host, but Tammy was just diagnosed with breast cancer, so we're going to have it here, again. John likes a good party, and he likes being the host. The front of the house is overflowing with kids, and Sophie is in her element, managing games, setting boundaries.

I find Mona in the living room and slide onto the couch beside her. John catches my eyes and winks. I don't want the party here, but I can't tell him that. It's been almost six months; I can't keep using Mom's death as an excuse to not function. So, I'm doing my part, working my way around to get the menu planned. "Hey," Mona says, leaning in toward me. "Where's Dee?"

I shake my head. "I don't know. She said she was gonna be here."

"I haven't seen her in weeks. I thought maybe she was moving in with her new guy."

"Have you met him yet?" I ask. We've all seen his car parked in front of the house, but he is scarce and gone by morning.

"No."

"Where did she find this one?" I'm trying to remember which of her dating sites hooked this catch, but I don't think she ever told me.

"I think she just met him, like at the grocery store."

"Over produce? How organic."

We laugh a little, at Dee's expense.

"Maybe he's the one," Mona says, shrugging. It's hard to imagine Dee finding "the one," but we both want her to settle down, to find someone who will be good to her kids and to her at the same time.

"I don't know; she's so cagey about him." We sit, listening to John and Scott plotting the turkey, the bourbon, the cigars.

"Man, I'm gonna hate it if she leaves us," Mona whispers.

"Me, too." We bump shoulders, feeling supported.

The first notes of "Lightly Row" come from the front of the house, and my spirit floods warm. Shelby loves the violin. Some days she spends an hour or more working out transitions, teaching herself the notes on the page, going from my handwritten page to the book, and writing in the names over the notes on the staff. She only knows the alphabet, but she's teaching herself music.

I think she is a prodigy. She talks all through her practice sessions, exclaiming when she finds the right note or when a melody blossoms from the strings. She has mastered all the variations of "Theme" and even moved through the rhythm work with an innate sense that makes me wonder who she was in her past life. She plays "Lightly Row" and "Song of the Wind" and segues into compilations that only she knows.

"Listen," I whisper to Mona, and we both lean in the direction of the music. When Shelby finishes the first song, she transitions into "Song of the Wind" and then "Go Tell Aunt Rhody," and she plays the slurs that I could never master. When she finishes, and the violin stops singing, the front of the house erupts in applause. It wasn't a perfect playing; it wasn't a virtuoso, but it was good, and Shelby's only four.

"Shelby?" Mona mouths, and I nod.

"She loves it. Her grandma would be very proud."

"I'm sure she is," Mona says, putting her arm around my shoulder, squeezing me.

"Shelby's birthday party is on Saturday... can you make it?"

"Pool?"

I shrug. "Doubtful. We'll see if I can get the water warm enough. Bounce house, though." It's not unusual for us to manage a late-season pool party for Shelby's birthday, but without the sun, it's iffy.

~ ~ ~

Saturday is perfect. The sun breaks the clouds by nine, and for the day, it feels like summer again. I've run the pool heater for a week, and the water is at least tepid, warm enough for kids. They are splashing in, then climbing out, shivering in the coolish air. A loop of sugar-pop hits—Meghan Trainer, Taylor Swift, a couple of old favorites from Pink—is playing on repeat, each song handpicked by Shelby.

The grill is heating up, and John is sitting with the other dads, looking handsome and young. His blue eyes catch mine, and I smile at him. We're going to be okay. If I'm okay, we'll be fine. It's true that in the last few days, I've felt the gray fog of depression lifting. My notebook is dotted with half memories, but only one true lost time event last week, down from four the week before. At least I wasn't driving that time, or neck deep in the sea. I was just sitting up in the tree house, cross-legged, not remembering how I got there. I knocked some spider webs down before descending the ladder, as if that had been my purpose all along.

Dee comes through the back gate, led by Willow and Spruce, her hands laden with a pitcher, and I rush to help her. "I'm glad you made it!" I squeeze her, careful not to cause spillage. Her skin is hot under my hands. "Where have you been?"

"I've been busy." She winks and gives me an air kiss.

"When are we going to meet him?" I ask in a whisper, urgent.

"He's not ready."

"What's wrong with him?" I ask, because she has never been hesitant to introduce her men before. The look on her face, though, says there is nothing wrong with him.

Dee's kids, Willow and Spruce, launch toward the pool, and a great splash rises when they cannonball in together.

"Thought we'd need some margaritas," Dee sings, and I push my questions away, just glad to have my friend back amongst us.

"Sure. We always need margaritas," I say, smiling, although it's not really appropriate to bring alcohol to a five-year-olds birthday party.

She air-kisses Mona, who has just now seen her and motioned from the other side of the pool. When did I became one of those women—those women who air kiss and flirt with my friend's husbands? That's what Dee is doing now, flouncing past me to offer the gaggle of men red cups and nectar. The string of her bikini cutting a line through the skin of her back, her full breasts barely contained by the small triangles. It is chilly for a bikini; I'm not even wearing a suit. My Bermuda shorts and Polo shirt are staid and matronly by comparison. Even with her breasts nearly bursting free, I am so happy to have her back. It's been a long stretch of dark days, and Dee's presence makes the sun shine a little brighter.

A couple of the moms from Shelby's school look at Dee with disapproving glances then look to me, as if I have some explanation. I shrug, rolling my eyes, shaking my head. I don't care what these women think; they don't know me or Dee, and when our kids split out from the academy, most of them will be in a different district. They are all so sedate, dressed in khakis and button-downs, so LL Bean. They don't have to have any margaritas, but their husbands are enjoying the show. Dee is my friend. So what if she came in her tiniest bikini, bearing alcohol, to my five-year-old's birthday party? Dee and Mona are my closest friends, and I'm certainly not going to dis either of them for the likes of these wannabe soccer moms.

The kids are out of the pool, shivering, wrapped in towels, and we serve hot dogs and hamburgers. I bring out the cake, shaped like a violin, and Shelby squeals. There are no gifts at this party. Shelby insisted that everybody donate to the animal shelter instead of bringing her a gift, something Sophie did for her birthday as well. I'm proud that I'm not raising people who prize things. They have big hearts, and they, like me, feel strange about accepting gifts.

We sing; we eat cake. The kids jump back in the pool, leaving small skins of oil on the water. It is a perfect day.

After the guests go, and the girls are showering, I feel the little core of my center humming, happy and whole, and I wonder if I haven't turned a corner toward a more positive space of being. Maybe tomorrow I won't wake up feeling like a stranger in my own skin.

Shelby's birthday ends with hugs and firm kisses from my girls, their skin pink from the day in the late season sun and warm from the shower.

As I am tucking Sophie into her bed, I glance through the slats of her blinds and see that Dee's boyfriend is back. He is just getting out of his fancy car, tall and lean, his hair closely trimmed, his beard a shade darker than the hair on his head. His neck is cased in a collar, and I wonder if he just came from his office, from seeing patients. I crane, trying to catch sight of his face, my curiosity distracting me from Sophie.

"His name is Dr. Matt," Sophie says, tilting up on an elbow, looking through the slats.

"You've met him?"

"No, but Willow says he's getting divorced or separated, and that's why he won't let Dee bring him around."

My mouth drops open in an O," understanding now why Dee's been so cagey. No wonder she hasn't done the introductions. I glance at Sophie, and when I look back out the window, I see the front door opening toward him, and he is gone.

"Hmm. Well, that's interesting."

I finish our nighttime rituals and head into the kitchen to finish cleaning up. When the dishes are in the dishwasher, when the table and counters are clean, when the remaining pieces or cake are put in Tupperware and placed in the fridge, I finally join John on the couch. He has followed the margaritas with bourbon. When I fold down beside him, he drapes his arm over my shoulders, and I settle close.

"Dee's fella is back," I say.

"Oh yeah?" His fingers trace a line from my elbow to my shoulder.

"Sophie says that his name is Matt and he's married. Getting divorced," I say the last with air quotes because that's what all cheaters say when they have affairs. "That's why we haven't met him."

"How does Sophie know that?" He cocks a brow, moderately interested.

"Willow told her."

"Think it's true?"

"She's never hesitated to introduce us to anybody before. It seems a little odd."

"It's probably not true."

"I hope not," I agree.

He tugs, drawing me over and into his lap. His eyes are low lidded, and he kisses me, familiar with the stiffness in my frame. I try to relax, to fold into him, and my body remembers, finally, how to be held. We make love on the couch, like teenagers, waiting to hear the parents returning.

"Wow," I say when we have finished, and our clothes are put to rights. "What was that?"

John shrugs and turns up the volume on the television. I remember Dee's breasts pressing against her bikini as she leaned forward toward the men, and a little pulse of jealousy erupts. If I wasn't her friend, would John be fair game?

"Where'd you get that appetite?" I ask, trying to sound flirty, not critical, not judgmental, not jealous.

John looks at me, his eyes dulled by alcohol and sex, and a slow smile spreads across his face.

"I came home to eat, didn't I?" He squeezes my breast and turns back to the television. He doesn't mean to be a pig; it's something we've always joked about, that the appetite comes from everywhere. But I remember the lipstick on his collar. I remember the smell of somebody else on his body when he has come home late and thinks I am already asleep. He doesn't always come home to eat.

"I reckon you did." I sit for a long minute, feeling dirty and violated.

His hand rests lightly on my knee, not knowing that we are at odds, not understanding that I am angry, that I am upset, that I am insecure. He's just a man; he doesn't get it.

"I'm gonna head to bed," I say, leaning in to kiss him, not wanting him to know what is going on inside of me.

"All right, babe. Good party today. I think Shelby had a good day."

"Yeah. I think so." I rise, my back straight, my shoulders rigid, and make my way to our bedroom and the shower, where I wash the scent of him off of me. The little core of peace destroyed like a private nuclear holocaust.

41

Stacy

Looking at her is like looking in a distorted magic mirror that shows the future. We are facing one another over the counter, and I've just found myself here. Her eyes skitter off of me and back to the couple in front of us, the ones holding the leash of a giant gray pit bull, as they work through the last of their adoption paperwork. I step back, trampling Shelby's foot in the process. She squeals, and I turn to hug her, apologizing, checking my surroundings, checking the girls... Sophie holding Shelby's hand, a half a step away now, watching me, her dark eyes wary, alert.

"Hey." I reach toward her, and she shifts, the slightest, almost imperceptible, pulling away. Damn Shiloh. "What if we don't do this here?" I whisper, leaning down toward them, and they let me draw them close. "We can just go," I say to the girls, panic racing through my veins, my heart thudding, my hands collecting my children, shuffling toward the door. That look on Sophie's face terrifies me—that she has seen something, that she knows I'm slipping, that Shiloh has done something to them while she was here.

"Mama, we haven't given them the donation!" Shelby says, pulling free, holding up the check, facing me. The print on it is small and precise, with a slight backwards tilt. The "Pay To" line is filled out to "Yaws Paws Rescue," the signature is signed "Stacy Linde" in that same backward slant. I don't write like that.

Damn Shiloh.

She set me up.

I stand up, straightening my shoulders. "Let's just leave it on the counter." I reach for the check, but Shelby pulls it away.

"No, Mama. You said we'd see the dogs." Tears well in her eyes, and I kneel down in front of her, rolling my head forward, releasing the tension building. "You promised."

"Okay. You're right. I promised." Apparently, Shiloh's now making promises to my children on my behalf. I don't understand how it works—how sometimes I am semi-aware and other times it's just blackness. This will be okay; she doesn't know me, this Kristine Yaw. She hasn't seen me since I was four. She won't recognize me.

Except that my daughter looks unerringly like I did at that age.

Except that I am the strange woman who has been watching her front door over the summer and into the fall.

Except that she was standing in the park across from the church when John and I got married.

Except she was at my high-school graduation, standing in the crowd.

Was she? Really?

I'll just tell her I've been scoping out different shelters for months, as we were trying to decide which one for our donation. That would sound legitimate. Normal people would do that, right?

Her mouth is slightly open, then closes with lips pressed firmly together when I turn back to face her. She has seen me, the small disruption caused by my stepping on Shelby's toes, the minute exchange, has drawn the couple's attention as well. I smile a tight smile and nod to them, an apology for making a scene, for interrupting their adoption process.

Does she falter? Does she know me? Does she recognize me as the person who has been sitting in the silver Civic in the late mornings, watching the building, sometimes walking up and down in front of the building, on the sidewalk, seeing but trying not to be seen? Or does she know me? My scalp crawls. Bumps rise all down my arms.

Damn Shiloh.

"Mama?" Sophie says, feeling the ridge of panic arcing. She feels the odd vibrations in the air. She puts her hand in mine. I squeeze, and when I look down at her, I see that her distance has melted—the aloof look in her eyes—but she is still wary, cautious, worried.

"It's okay. We're almost done," I say, low and under my breath.

She nods and squeezes my fingers. The woman is not looking at us; she is still working with the people in front of me. Did I ever call her mama? The dog turns to look at me. His tail wags, and it almost looks like he is smiling.

I tilt down, facing Shelby.

"Almost our turn," I whisper with mock enthusiasm, the best I can do, and reach to take her hand, too. I try not to look at the woman as we wait.

We watch the couple with their new pet as they each sign the paperwork, touching the dog in turns. When I look back to the counter, Kristine Yaw and I make eye contact, and my panic ebbs because her face is utterly calm. There is no hint of recognition, no fluttering of her eyes. She does not know me. She is just a gentle, skinny woman, trying to help animals find their forever homes.

My reason takes over, and I nod. Standing up, putting my arms protectively around my children. She doesn't know me, not from the parking lot or another life. It wasn't recognition that I had seen—the compression of her lips when she looked at me—it was just a mannerism, just a way of doing things.

How can she not know me? I would know my children forever. There is nothing that could erase them from my memory. I could be wrong; maybe it isn't her at all. Just like the man at Lake City Motors was not the brother I was searching for—just a familiar name, maybe a familiar name. Just me grasping at straws. But then I remember John's search program and the trail that led me here. She has to be her. The program connects and traces everything—police records, social security numbers, names. But it doesn't make sense. A woman who locks her children in a dog kennel doesn't go on to rescue dogs, does she? Unless she is trying to salvage her soul. Is this her way of making amends for the damage she did?

Her hair is long and straight, a shade lighter than mine, with streaks of gray beginning at the temples. Her brows are thick, not groomed, not bushy but natural, over dark eyes. Or are they brown? Or black? I can't tell, and I try not to look at her, try not to see similarities. I drop my shoulders and close my eyes.

Damn Shiloh.

Breathe. Breathe. Breathe. I pull my shoulders back and straighten my core, feeling Mountain pose like a coat of armor.

The couple moves past us, with their new adopted dog, and out the door. Smiling at each other, at us, down at the new dog, who smiles at the entire world.

"I'm sorry to make you wait," she says, and we step forward. Is her face closed? Are her eyes cautious?

"No. No worries. We support pet adoption. We support all adoption." Why did I say that? I blow out air, pulling myself together, trying to reconnect with my mission at hand.

"Wonderful. How can I help you? Are you looking to adopt?" The rescue is her domain, and she takes charge.

"No. No. We already have two dogs." My voice is stilted, jangled, frayed at the edges. "Shelby, my daughter, just had a birthday."

"Oh. Well, happy birthday, sweetheart," she says, looking from one girl to the other, and I realize that what I've said doesn't explain anything.

"And for my birthday, I just wanted everybody to donate to the Human Society," Shelby says, sturdy and dependable where I falter.

"Humane Society," I explain, correcting Shelby's mispronunciation. "So, we have some money to donate to your shelter."

"Well, isn't that wonderful?" the woman says, leaning down toward Shelby. "That's a wonderful thing to do. You must be an amazing little girl."

"I did the same thing, at my birthday," Sophie says, not wanting to be outdone by her little sister.

"Really?" The woman smiles, her eyes crinkling.

"I did. We donated a hundred and seventy-five dollars last March."

Her eyes tilt to mine, then slip back toward Sophie. "I think it's wonderful that you donated to the shelter." She smiles, glancing at Shelby, and back again, "Do you have any idea how many dogs your donation fed?"

"No," Sophie says, but looking proud.

"Well, I don't either, but it was a lot." She smiles, her large front teeth stained by the cigarettes I've watched her smoke.

Sophie likes her, and she laughs, happy with the attention.

"Did you donate here?"

"Well, to the Humane Society. We didn't know about your shelter then. We love what you're doing," I explain.

"Well, you understand, we are not part of Humane Society. We're an independent no-kill shelter. We do what we can." She is looking at me, but not seeing me, not remembering me.

"We understand," I say.

"How did you find us?" She is looking down and away, but the question feels heavy. Is that just a question she asks everybody, to find out where their marketing dollars are working?

"I've been scoping out different shelters, all summer long," I say, and it works. It sounds legitimate. It justifies me parking outside her rescue, just in case she does recognize me. I'm stuck in the loop in my head and feel sweat breaking out on my lip as I watch her hands folding together on the counter.

"I think you came to my school," Shelby says, breaking the loop in my mind, bringing me back to where I am. I hadn't known she had come to their school.

The woman smiles and nods at Shelby and then me, and I see that aged mirror reflection again. "Which school do you go to?"

"The Academy at Julington Creek."

"Aw. Yes. We came to your school last February, I think, around Valentine's Day, maybe?"

Shelby shrugs, not remembering when, but remembering this woman, the dogs she brought, the story she told.

"We do a lot of school outreach," she explains to me, with a small, self-conscious smile.

"Do you?" I ask.

"We do. If we can get the children, we can get the parents." I catch her eyes, and I look away. Does that mean something more? Of course not; it's just a turn of phrase. Besides, it's true. It's the very reason we had disconnected from cable, the commercials instilling wants as needs, creating little consumers in a throwaway society.

"You came to my school, too," Sophie says, and I glance at her. She is not usually one to crave attention, but this is the second time she has stepped up.

"Which school?"

"Julington Creek. I was in Mrs. Mattis's class last year. That's third grade. You brought a German shepherd to our class."

"Yes. That would have been Sheba. That was in March. You know, if I remember right, Mrs. Mattis adopted Sheba."

"She did," Sophie hoots, thrilled that this woman remembers. I'm impressed. Could I tell you anything I did last March or anything from last week?

May. I could tell you about May. My mother died in May, and I found out that I am not who I thought I was.

"Well, let's go meet the dogs you'll be helping." She reaches out, and Shelby takes her hand, I push down the urge to draw her back and away.

"Okay," Shelby says and glances at me over her shoulder, her hair bouncing, strawberry-blond where it catches the light from the windows. I follow with Sophie's hand in mine as we pass through the doors to view the animals on display. I try to silence my sense that everything is wrong—there is no real reason to think everything isn't right. I am crazy.

"This is Bobo," she says at the first cage, and a dog with gray eyes and a square head looks up at us, his whole body wagging with his stub of a tail. He is brindled, and there are scars on his chest. "He was used in an dog-fighting ring, which is illegal," she explains to Shelby. "He was in terrible shape when we found him." Her voice is thick with emotion. She passes her fingers between the wires, and the dog's tongue folds around them. Was he thrown into a ring with another dog, both of them half-starved and terrified, to destroy or be destroyed? Tears well in my eyes, and I want to take him home, with those wide, soulful eyes and his scars. The next dog is much the same, different stories, but all with the same response to Kristine Yaw, excitement and enthusiasm, affection.

Ridiculous—that's how I feel. Ridiculous that I would think any tall stranger might be the woman who had kenneled me. I feel confused now, having watched her for so long from outside, and I know I have to be mistaken. She would have given something away if she had known me. There is no way, even with the physical similarities, that this gentle woman would have locked her children in a kennel—her filthy, underfed, emaciated children. It's just like the trip to Lake City Motors, a wasted effort, and I feel both disappointed and relieved.

"How did you get started doing this?" Sophie asks.

"Oh, well, my husband was always in rescue, and when we got married, we decided to start this facility."

"How did you meet?" I ask and watch her shoulders rise and fall.

"You know, the way people generally meet." She glances at me, a wink in her eye.

We walk through the rest of the shelter, and Kristine Yaw keeps up a steady monologue as we meet one dog after another. She tells each dog's story, how it came to the shelter, how she and Mr. Yaw rescued it. I want to take them all home, me and my bleeding heart. Bobo and Frosty and Daisy and Norton. I want to have them all and keep them safe. That is the danger of visiting shelters, of going to PetSmart on adoption day.

She explains again that this is a no-kill shelter and that any animal lucky enough to be registered here will not be destroyed for lack of a home. They will be sheltered and cared for until the right family comes to find them. She makes a big point of expressing how vital Shelby's donation is. "Donations are what keep us in business."

"How long have you been here?"

She turns back to look at me before answering. "Oh, about eight years, I'd say."

"What about before that?"

"Oh, Mr. Yaw worked for the county, before that. He pioneered the prison-based dog-training program. Are you familiar?"

I nod. "I've heard of it." Is that where they met? Was she in prison, one of the inmates?

"Everyone deserves a second chance. Don't you agree?" she says, looking lovingly down at the dog still rooting his nose against her hand.

I nod again. I desperately want it to be her; I could give this woman a second chance. A split-second image of me climbing into one of the dog cages jars me.

I want answers, dammit! How can she stand here and not know me? Am I mistaken?

The trail led here. John's search database cannot be wrong. It would not have led me here if this is not the same woman who locked me in a kennel. Was it just a mistake, us being in the kennel? Some game we were playing? A one-time thing?

There is something about her that I like—the throaty laugh, the smooth spread of her lips into a smile. Is she someone who laughs quickly and often, or is she serious like me?

It had to be a mistake, a misunderstanding. The image of the kids found in the dog kennel swirls in my mind. There is no way to reconcile the state of those children with the well-fed animals here. A woman who could let her children suffer would not be a woman who would make her life's work an animal rescue. She is doing good in the world. Everybody deserves a second chance. Is this her second chance? I want to like her for the kind way she is talking to my kids, making them feel important, adult-like.

The conflict is making my head hurt, and I press the heel of my hand into my eye socket, trying to push the pressure back, and I see her catching the motion, from the corner of her eye, but enough. Shiloh is pushing up, and I'm afraid of what she may do if she gets out.

Kristine Moony, Kristine Yaw, stumbles, her words falter and skid on the concrete. Her eyes go wide, and there it is, what I have been waiting for, what I came here hoping to find.

"Do you have kids?" I ask while she is unbalanced, off her center. My voice is flat, toneless. I can't let Shiloh push up.

She looks away. "No. Not anymore." Her lips compress. "They are grown," she clarifies. These guys are my kids, now." She regains her composure, and I can almost see doors and locks slamming shut behind the black of her eyes. Her lashes flutter, then rise. Her momentary discomfiture wiped away in a blink.

"You're doing a good thing here. It's a great rescue." The hostility that was surging in my blood just a moment before wanes and evaporates.

"Thank you. I just believe everybody deserves a second chance." There is something in the way she says it that makes it sound a little like a question.

"Well, thank you for the tour." I put out my hand, and she hesitates. Is that fear in her eyes, or just a shadow? She stretches her hand to mine, our long-fingered hands fitting together like a matched set.

"Thank you for the donation."

"We have more birthdays coming." My lips spread into a smile, and our hands separate from each other.

"Indeed," she says. Now her hands are falling on my children's heads, touching their hair in a most familiar, fond way. We have come again to the front, and the door closes to the dog runs, muffling the sound.

"We do a lot of adoption events; maybe we'll see you around sometime."

"Maybe." I hold the door open for the girls, and she makes the last show of shaking their hands, telling them how much the money will help, how impressed she is with their gift.

When Shelby and Sophie are buckled into their seat, and I am behind the steering wheel, Shelby leans over to her sister, whispering something that I cannot make out, and Sophie nods. I see it in the mirror.

"What was that?" I ask, putting the car in reverse.

"Nothing. Shelby just said how much she looks like you."

"Did you think so?" I ask, pretending I hadn't noticed.

The drive back up the A1A feels like flying... or fleeing.

42

Stacy

"Why would you want to do that?" John is stretched flat on his back, one hand folded under his head, the other on his flat stomach. He is watching me from the corner of his narrowed eye. Is he irritated that I am keeping him awake?

"You should have seen the dogs; they've been through so much. I just think I could be useful."

"You can be useful here. It's not like we don't have dogs."

"But these dogs need help," I say, feeling my resolve folding in on itself. It's been almost a week since the girls and I made our trip to the rescue, and I've felt the pull to return ever since. I want to get to know her. They always need volunteers, she had said. I could help and get to know her. She was good with the girls; there has to be some explanation for what happened.

"I think you'll be wasting your time."

"I need to be busy." I try to say the right thing, but know by the exhalation of air that it was the wrong thing.

"Well, the house could certainly use some cleaning." He sits up, turning away from me. "How long has that laundry been sitting there?"

My anger flares then quiets. He is right. That basket has been sitting there, with clothes rotating in and out for most, if not all, of the fall. There was about a month, when I was feeling so unhinged, when the black holes were dotting my mind like Swiss cheese, when the house had been immaculate. I had tightened the ship, and by keeping the house in order, I felt somehow still in control. The moments of absolute lost time have diminished ever since I spoke with Felicia Martin, and she told me about her preliminary diagnosis about my condition—as if having a name for what was happening solved some of the problems. I know that's not entirely true, but I do feel less frightened by the moments when I wake and don't remember getting to wherever I am.

How do I explain without explaining? John knows nothing about what has happened since my mom died. So, instead of telling him that I think I have found my birth mother and that she may have answers that could be helpful, I say that I want to do something that has some reward at the end, unlike cleaning the house. I could spend hours every day putting clothes away, washing clothes, folding clothes, hanging clothes, and nobody would even notice. More hours doing dishes and sweeping floors, mopping floors, waxing floors. Hours and hours of meaningless time spent on something nobody will ever see. "I just feel like I need something outside of the house, you know."

"Volunteer at the schools," he says, problem solved. "That would make more sense than wasting time at a dog kennel."

I watch his back as he gets up and leaves the room, dismissing me, finished with the conversation, satisfied that he is right. He is always right.

"You're not my father, and I am not a child." The words roll in my mind, but I don't dare say them aloud for fear that he will hear. I get out of bed and empty the folded clothes onto the bed from the basket and start the monotonous task of putting them away. He is right. Of course, it isn't about me keeping busy, but there is no way I can explain what it is about without telling him everything. I watch the door and hear the television coming on in the living room. For just a moment, I imagine the conversation if I could tell him the truth. It ends much the same as the one we just had. If anything, John, in my mind, after hearing the whole of it, is even more opposed. I am disappointed that I was not able to create a better ending, even in my imagination.

I can't help it, but I want to give her a second chance. I want to know what her life has been since we parted ways.

When I have finished putting the clothes away, I go down the hall to check on the girls. Sophie curls on her side, the way she does, and Shelby is spread-eagled, one foot sticking through the slats of her toddler bed. I push the little toes back through the bars, and she groans, drawing her foot up, flinging her body toward the wall, emitting a small snort in the process. I walk back to my room, and glance at John, sitting on the sofa, lit by the glow from the television, looking glazed and numb. The sound is low, so I can't hear the show; apparently, it is something that doesn't need words.

I step toward him, and he only looks up when I stand above him. "You're right. It was just a thought." He reaches his hand up to me and draws me down on the couch. I glance at the television, expecting some version of soft porn, but what I get is a man on a boat, casting a line.

"I just don't want anything to make you not available for the girls, you know?"

I nod against him, sliding down and resting my head on his leg. His hand folds over the curve of my shoulder, and all the anger washes out.

He hasn't forbidden me to do it; he just thinks it's a stupid idea. If I had really wanted to do it, I wouldn't have mentioned it. I would have done it and told him somewhere down the road when it was only part of the shape of our lives. It was a doomed conversation from the start. By suggesting that I was "thinking" about volunteering, I opened the door for him to help me decide.

He's right, of course—even more so, if he were to know the whole truth. I got off easy the first time, but stepping into Kristine Yaw's world would not be good. It's a bad idea; I would have come to that on my own, had I not been told it was stupid. I relax, letting all the tension ease out of my muscles. It was just a thought, anyway—a flash in the pan. The logistics would have gotten sticky at some point.

43

Stacy

The next morning, after Sophie is on the bus and after I've run Shelby to school, I take our dogs for a quick walk to the end of the street and then leave them free in the back yard, able to come into the sunroom through the dog door. The sky is dark with the threat of a late-morning cloud break.

I haven't been to the support group in a couple of weeks. My sleep was fitful, and I woke with such sadness in my heart that it felt like lead.

I don't bother to shower; I don't want to be late. My mind is quiet; nobody is talking to me today as I drive down Afton Lane. When I stop at the end of the road, I glance in the mirror to see Dee's boyfriend in his pretty BMW behind me. His eyes are shaded by aviator sunglasses, and he is handsome, although most of his face is shadowed by the beard. I'm tempted to step out of my car and introduce myself, but I don't. Dee doesn't want us to know him yet, and I don't blame her if he's married. It makes me think of her differently, the fact that she's seeing a married man. It makes me see all the harmless flirtation differently. It makes me think of her as a home wrecker. If she and I weren't friends, would John have been a target?

I know John finds her attractive—everybody does. Could he have been seduced into an affair with her if she had really set her attentions on him? While sometimes I do think John is having an affair, I have a hard time reconciling the idea with my rule-following husband. After all, don't I have a shade of lipstick the very color that was on his collar?

Couldn't one of his clients have hugged him for a good outcome and smeared her lip on his collar, an accident? John doesn't respect cheaters; he always says that you should finish one thing before you start something else. But isn't that better in theory than in practice? If he suddenly found himself interested in somebody else, would he throw away our family for what may be just a fling? Wouldn't it be more practical to have the illicit relationship and then know if it was worth throwing away the family?

My mind is on a low hum, listening to the radio, thinking about John having an affair, in an abstract and distracted fashion. I pass John's office on the way to the support group, and when I look in my rearview mirror, I see the nose of John's Mercedes preparing to pull out onto the street. Two cars pass the office behind me before John pulls out, followed by another car which follows from John's lot, directly behind him as if they are connected by a bungee cord.

My small edge of distrust settles along the soft lobes of my mind, amidst my musings about his fidelity. He didn't mention plans to be out of the office, but would he? Do we do that? I haven't told him that I was going to a meeting.

I pull into the church and watch as they drive past, on down 13—John first, followed by the pretty associate in her black coupe. I am tempted to turn around and trail them, my thoughts still humming with the hypothetical of John having an affair. Janine, the pretty associate, came on board last fall. What color is her lipstick? What perfume does she wear? When did I first start thinking he was seeing somebody else in a real way? When was the first time he smelled like perfume?

I sit, letting all the little clues over the last year settle down around me. The small smears of lipstick, the odd bruise along the ridge of his clavicle. The late nights, the missed calls. I wait for the rage to snare me. I want to feel the heat of righteous anger flowing in my blood, but I feel nothing. I'm not numb; I'm just indifferent. I don't care if he is with somebody else. I don't want to be touched; I don't enjoy sex the way I should. I'm not like other women. There is something wrong with me. Suddenly, it feels like a relief, a blessing.

I don't want to know. If John is having an affair, I hope it's just a fling. I'd hate to lose the structure in our lives. I walk through the lot and stand at the edge of the road, looking in the direction he had driven. I could have followed him, found out where he was going, but I didn't. Let him satisfy his appetite somewhere else. From the corner of my eye, I see something else, and when I turn to see it clearly, the BMW that followed me out of the cul-de-sac shoots past, the engine gunning.

That's odd. But I'm probably wrong; there are probably a hundred BMWs just like that one in Jacksonville, probably more than a hundred. The car turns at the light and disappears out of sight.

Leon is dark-eyed, pouring coffee when I come down into our basement meeting room. I join him, and he offers me the cup. The lights are dim, only some of the fluorescents turned on, and I nod and say hello to a few of the regulars I've talked with over the past several months.

"You look rough," I say to Leon as I approach him.

"Yeah. I'm all right. I'm feeling a little Floyd Mayweather today."

"Rich as shit and unbeaten?" I offer.

"I'm just saying I can't keep on taking life's shit. I'm gonna fight back and damn the consequences." There is that quality of oration in his voice, like the day at the beach—not loud but punctuated, punched. "Fire all the guns and charge over the hill and take it to the bastards."

I nod, not sure of how I should respond. There is an edge here, a sharp and jagged point that is unfamiliar. I thought I knew Leon; he's always steady and calm, thoughtful, predictable, breathing into the phone when I need him to.

He leans close to me, his breath brushing along my cheek. "I've been there, in war. In some other life, but I've been there. Honor truly belongs to the fallen." He taps his finger into the bones of my chest, light but intense. "Courage is facing your fear and continuing with no regard of the outcome." He rolls his tongue along his teeth, and I touch my hand to his elbow. "Death is my friend who prods me slowly forward." He ends with a flourish. Is he reciting some play, a monologue, or one of his poems?

"You okay?"

"Yeah. I'm just groovy." I've seen him before when he is in the depths of despair, but never here, never at the meetings. He is always pulled together here, offering his card to first-time attendees, manning his station as facilitator. It's a little frightening to see this Leon here. Does he suffer with a chemical imbalance, or is he just prone to bouts of depression? Is he like me, housing more than one inside the smooth interior of his skull? Did he suffer brain damage in his accident, where the metal plate protects his gray matter? When his lows hit, there is nothing anybody can say to bring him out. The world is all darkness for him then, and there is no hope.

Laughter erupts inside of my head, and it's so loud that I turn to see who it is. Nobody is there, or rather, a lot of people are there, but none of them are laughing. I smile, catching on, Shiloh thinks it's funny that I should be so critical and uncomfortable, when I am the one losing time. I am the one with brain damage. I doubt that Leon has ever found himself someplace and not known how he got there.

"You know I'm here."

"Yeah." There is something cold in his eyes, and I step away, giving him space, feeling that he, like me, is unknowable. I can't fix him; I don't know how to offer hope. Before I can think of anything, he says, "My dog died."

"Oh, I'm sorry." I hadn't known he had a dog.

"It was a long time ago."

I'm off balance by the shift in thinking the dog's demise was the cause for today's melancholy, not just a fact in the past. Where did that even come from? I'm so confused.

"Oh. I'm still sorry."

"Yeah." He turns away from me, heading to his seat, and I find a place in the circle. Nodding, shaking hands.

"Looks like Leon's in the throes." The man next to me leans close, familiar.

"Yeah, what's going on?"

"Oh, you know. Life sucks. His sugar is probably out of whack." He nods. "That's how I get when my sugar gets too low. I got the diabetes."

"Is he diabetic?" I ask, and the man shakes his head. "Oh." Then that doesn't seem to apply. Am I missing stuff today? Nothing makes sense. Not John, who was leaving his office before nine. Not Leon, who is cold and distant. Not the words this man is saying. Usually coming to the meetings makes me feel like part of something, but today I feel like I'm walking on a ledge. Maybe it is finally time to call the therapists on my list, see who can see me. Maybe it is time for some real help, before Sophie looks at me with those cold, wary eyes again.

The atmosphere is oppressive; the stories are depressing and pathetic. I don't want to be here, but the doors are closed and leaving would disrupt the meeting. It would be disrespectful. I stay seated, sipping the coffee, listening and trying not to hear.

"He moved out," a petite girl, somewhere in her twenties, is saying, sounding weepy, sounding drunk. She showed up for the first time in August; she'd been in a car accident, and her boyfriend had died. A month or so ago, she met somebody new and came in telling us how in love they were. "It's time to move on," she had said.

"Give yourself a year to grieve before you start building a new relationship," everybody had cautioned.

"But we are in love. He's the one," she had insisted, and the next week he was moving in, and they were making plans to get a dog.

Now he's moving out, and she is again talking about her first boyfriend, the one who died, and how he was her true love. Stupid girl. She's so self-absorbed she can't even grieve properly. I sit, running my finger over the rim of Styrofoam feeling uncharitable.

When the meeting is over, I wait, trying to catch Leon's eye, but he doesn't look at me, and I finally head up the steps into the sunshine. I open my phone while I'm sitting in the car and view John's last text. A simple Have a good day.

Do I send him a text and ask him where he is? Who he is with, what he is doing? I let my fingers hang over the screen, then I type: What is the new associate's name? I forgot. I send the message and wait, while the air conditioner slowly mitigates the heat in the car.

I don't expect an answer. I know her name. Of course, I know Janine's name. He talks about her often enough. I drop my phone into my purse.

I drive to the rescue on autopilot, not even thinking that I am going. What do married men say to their lovers? What kind of woman has an affair with another woman's husband, the father of children? Does he tell her how cold I am? How disconnected, how crazy? Does he say that I'm unstable and fragile and that's why he can't leave me right now? "Her mother just died. She's going through a hard time."

Shame burns in my veins, knowing that I have written his seduction script, given him plenty of reasons to sleep around. The thought of them lying naked together, talking about my failures, my inability to be affectionate, makes me ill. Do they laugh about my cold-fish hugs? Do they laugh about how I don't like to be naked? Does he tell her that we are getting a divorce, the way Dee's man has told her, but that it takes time?

I park my car in the lot next to the rescue and watch, unable to force myself out of the vehicle without the buffer of my children.

I watch for her, playing out the confrontation in my mind. The question, "Are you my mother?" rebounding through my head, like the words from one of Shelby's books, about the baby duck who searches all over the farm, looking for its mother. If I could solve this puzzle, would everything else begin to make sense? If I could understand my beginnings, could I heal all my broken pieces?

After half an hour, an old van pulls in and parks in the front lot. A man and a woman gather at the passenger door; another man stands with his phone held out, filming the moment. The couple lifts a box from the side sliding door of the van, and angle toward the door, followed by the man with his phone on record. The shelter door opens, and I see her—her face set in harsh lines, her mouth forming words that I cannot hear. A snake slithers down my back, recognizing something in the set of her mouth, feeling fear in the most distant way, an echo.

The couple and their box disappear into the rescue, and the man turns his phone to himself and says something toward the screen, then he follows the couple, the rescue animal, and Kristine Yaw into the shelter.

I wait longer still, watching the parking lot, seeing the vet clinic next to the Rescue. She had said her husband was the vet. Or was he just involved in rescues? I don't remember, but I am watching the man from the photograph that I found on the Internet—older, grayer, but tall and lean, as he strides across the parking lot from the vet clinic. I slip down in my seat, recognizing Sylvester Yaw. He glances at my car, stops his forward motion—just a pause, a hiccup. I swear he is looking straight at me. I am tempted to lift my hand and wave. I could get out of the car and offer to help. She would know me now, after the donation.

He lifts his finger and points, like a gun, then enters the shelter without looking back.

44

Stacy

My nerves fray as I drive back toward home. What did that mean? I check my mirror, expecting to be followed, paranoid. What did that mean—when he looked straight at me and pointed with two fingers, simulating a gun? The sudden pop upward of the tips of his fingers, the firing, a trigger pulled. That's what he did. Does he know who I am? Has he seen me watching the shelter? Surely, he wouldn't do that to someone who just donated money to his cause. Who does he think I am? Does he know about her?

The memory of the shadowy figure in the trees at our Labor Day party filters across my mind. That man had done the same thing, his fingers emulating a gun. Was that Sylvester Yaw? I had convinced myself it was a hallucination, that it didn't really happen. There had been no man standing at the edge of the crowd, sheltered by the trees. Now, though, I think there was, and that maybe it was Sylvester Yaw.

No, he had been bearded, and Sylvester Yaw is clean shaven. Was he younger? But now, when I stretch back through my mind, it is Sylvester Yaw standing in the trees, and I am no longer certain if he was bearded or not.

Twice, when I look in my mirrors, I think I see the BMW that followed me out of the cul-de-sac this morning, but then both times, it is gone when I look again. Why would Dee's boyfriend be following me? He wouldn't, but I don't know what vehicle Sylvester Yaw might drive, so any repetition of cars seems dangerous.

When I get home, I pull out the laptop, and I open the Bing browser, pull up Yaw's Paws Rescue. I look all through the site but can't find any link to a video, but I know that guy was recording. Where do people post videos? Facebook? YouTube?

I switch to Facebook and type in "Yaw's Paws Rescue" and scroll through their feed until I find one of the videos, put up by an organization called Fur Friends. I watch the video of a matted shih-tzu hiding under a car, unable to see his rescuers because its hair had grown over its eyes in dirty clumps. The dog is terrified. I am transfixed, listening to the voices on the recording, watching as they corner the dog and then get a leash lassoed over its mangy head.

My phone vibrates, and I look down to see Darren's face. "Hello?"

The video continues to run; they are in the van.

"Hey." There is a pause, and I hear him drawing breath, and I turn away from the video, suddenly alert. "Dad fell this morning."

"Is he okay?"

"No. He broke his hip."

"Shit, Darren." I hear John's judgment coming through my voice, the accusation.

The van has arrived at the rescue, and I pause the video just as she is opening the door to the shelter.

"Don't take that tone with me." I can almost see his hand flattening on his hip, the jut of his leg, the exaggerated stance.

"I'm not taking a tone," I say, taking a tone. "How did it happen?"

"He fell getting out of the shower. I think he has a concussion, too."

I hear the sounds in the background, the voices over an intercom, and understand he is at the hospital.

"Oh shit." I press my hand over my face, closing out the image from the screen, focusing on the more immediate reality. "I mean, that's bad."

"Yeah, it's bad. This just isn't working out."

"What do you mean?"

"He's gotten a lot worse since Mom died. Half the time, he thinks I'm his brother. We had to disconnect the stove downstairs because he left it on last week. He needs more care than we can handle. Someone has to be with him all the time. We've been taking turns sleeping downstairs because he sleepwalks, and we're afraid he'll walk out and fall into the lake." His words are pouring from his mouth in a torrent, the frazzled edges clipped and disjointed. "He thinks I'm Uncle Jimmy most the time."

"He can come here; we'll make it work." He took me in when I needed a place to be.

"No, Stacy, you don't understand. You can't leave him alone. Period. You can't leave him alone to run to the store; you can't leave him alone to go to the bathroom. You can't leave him alone to take your kids to school. Do you understand what I'm saying? He needs to be in a home."

"That doesn't feel right."

"Well, we don't have to decide today. He's going to have to be someplace until the hip heals anyway."

"Can we afford that?"

"Yeah, well, that's the other thing. I think we need to sell their house."

"No."

"He is never going to be able to live there again. The family that's renting it wants to buy it. It can pay for his care."

"I don't want to sell the house."

"Okay, you want to fund his convalescence? If you do, that's great, because we can't afford it. We need to sell the house. If you and John want to buy it, that's fine, but if you don't, we're selling it. I have power of attorney; I can do whatever I need to do. I'm telling you as a courtesy."

"Sometimes you are such an ass."

"I can't help it that you don't live in the real world, Stacy. But I do, and this is what needs to happen." He disconnects, and I stand there for a long minute, seething, my eyes rolling from one corner of the room to the next until they land on the clock on the microwave. I am late to get Shelby. Again.

45

Stacy

I am at the stop sign at the end of Afton Lane, getting ready to turn onto Durbin Creek, and the car rocks. It's not much of an impact, but I am instantly jolted out of my thoughts. My nerves are frayed, and my vision tunnels. It's just one more reason for John to try to get rid of my car. It's just one more thing I don't need right now. It's just one more thing to make me late for Shelby. I climb out of the car and walk around to the back. Two men are in the car behind me. I face them, waiting with impatience for them to come out.

"I need your insurance information," I call, and the man on the passenger side gets out. He is short and stocky. A scar presses against his top lip causing a perpetual sneer. I skirt toward my driver's door, feeling unnerved by the intensity of his look. The driver door opens, and the trunk lifts as if the two hinges are connected.

"Damn. Sorry, Stacy. Sure didn't mean to do that," the driver says. His voice is calm and subtle. My face is reflected in the aviator sunglasses, sepia-toned. "It is Stacy, right?"

"Do I know you?" Of course. It's Matt, who followed me out of neighborhood this morning. "You're Dee's boyfriend?" I glanced down at the car. It's not the BMW. I don't even know what it is—ancient, for one. The rust-colored primer paint gives it a dull finish.

"That's right."

The stomach churns and recoils. I try to relax.

"This is my cousin. Markus. He's a fine mechanic. He'll fix that little scrape right up, Won't ya, Markus?"

"Certainly" Markus agrees, a strong southern lilt in his voice.

"I'm really quite sorry, Stacy. We're still working out a few kinks on the old car. I think it's possessed," He chuckles, confident, oily. "She's gonna be a beauty when we're done, though."

I can see what she likes about him, the lines of his face are handsome in a clean-cut, self-assured way. The man from the passenger side has come around the front side of my car and is now between me and my door, which is still hanging open. He pushes it closed. It feels ominous to have him between me and my car.

"You should come and see me, Stacy," Matt says. "I could probably help you."

"What?" I ask, almost under my breath, feeling blood rising in my cheeks, remembering that Dee told him my story.

"We have a lot in common, you and I."

"I don't think so."

Markus is still behind me, and I can suddenly hear him breathing, as if he has moved closer. My eyes fall on the upraised trunk, and I step away into the street so I can see them both.

"I was adopted, too," Matt says, "I understand the complex emotions finding out can cause. How caged you can feel."

"I gotta go," I say, my teeth gritting. I am furious with Dee! "I have to go," I say again, indicating that Markus needs to move away from my door. Great divots pockmark his skin, either from teen acne or scars from a fire. His slick gray eyes slide down the length of my body, and I feel like he can see through my running clothes, which already don't leave much to the imagination.

Markus smiles at me, showing a gap where he is missing a tooth in the back. Every hair on my body is standing to attention, and I am legitimately uncomfortable.

"Don't worry about the car." I stammer, making a pretense of glancing down for damage.

Matt smiles, his beard shifting with the motion of his mouth.

"What? No, of course, we'll take care of it." He pouts, his bottom lip jutting forward, flipping his hand forward, extending his card, exaggerated, reminding me of Leon Freak and his magician's flourish. I take the card, because it is the thing to do, but I do not look at it. "I'm insulted that you think I wouldn't. What kind of man do you think I am?" Matt says, drawing my attention away from Markus, who is by far the more intimidating of the two.

In my mind, I hear a voice, younger, but with the same speech patterns. "I'm the man of the house."

My knees buckle, and I stumble, but Markus reaches out, catching my arm. I right myself, jerking to free my arm, but he holds fast, his fingers tight and immovable.

A car pulls slowly toward us, watching, seeing, and I glance around to see Gina with Tommy and the other one, the little girl—what is her name?—driving toward us.

"Hey, Stacy, everything okay?"

"I have to get my daughter." My voice is a whisper. I shake free. Markus is stepping away. I make eye contact with Gina through her open window and give the most imperceptible nod.

"I can help you, Stacy. I know what it's like," Matt calls out, seemingly sincere, his smile calm and soothing, the way Felicia Martin smiled, controlled, practiced. His eyes flick down toward the card still in my hand, an invitation.

I say to him, "I'm fine. I have to go. Don't worry about the bumper."

Markus, with his oily eyes, is now back at their car, sliding into the passenger seat. Gina is at a stop, watching me as I reach for my door.

"You sure do have beautiful children," Matt says, like a neighbor, like a friend. I fling open the door and slide into the car, pressing the lock, and I watch, in my rearview mirror, as Matt walks to the trunk, casual, relaxed, and closes it with a clang. Gina is still waiting, and he smiles and waves at her as she watches me. I crank the engine and push the shifter into drive, jerking forward, running through the stop sign onto Durbin Creek. Tires squeal behind me, and a horn honks.

My muscles are moving in jerks and spasms, and I push my hand against my ear to stop hearing his voice, to stop listening to the words my brother said in my half-remembered childhood the day he put a knife into my dad's chest. It was just the speech pattern—that's all. It was only the speech pattern that was similar. Markus meant no harm; he was checking to see if there was damage to my car. I was already keyed up from the morning, and now I'm incredibly late. My brother's name is Slim, not Matt, not Markus. But of course his name isn't Slim—nobody would name a child that. No, not Markus. He is entirely the wrong build, thick-jawed and stocky. Matt, though... Matt could be my brother Slim. He had said he was adopted, too!

Oh God! It can't be him. It can't be true.

I hear again the inflection, the similarities of speech, "I'm the man of the house," and "What kind of man do you think I am?" fall in the same rhythms, the same cadence.

I swing the door of the academy open and see Shelby sitting on one of the benches, looking through a book. "She's here," the woman behind the counter says, into the phone. "Yes, sir. Thank you."

"I'm so sorry." I scoop Shelby into my arms, dropping the book onto the floor.

"Where were you?" Shelby whispers in my ear.

"Mrs. Linde, really, if you need her to stay longer, you have to arrange for that."

"I know, I know." I glance up at her. "I just had a minor accident on the way."

"Are you all right?"

"Yes, I'm fine, just a little shook up." A tear springs from my eye, and I fold into Shelby. I squeeze her, drawing on her strength, and pull myself back together. "It was nothing. Just rear-ended coming out of the neighborhood. It was nothing." I can't keep the small quiver out of my voice.

"I'm glad you're okay. But this is the second time Shelby's had to wait here with me." The patronizing tone of her voice puts steel in my frame, and I turn back to face her, knowing there is ice in my eyes where before there was water.

"Yes. I understand. It will never happen again." I turn on my heel and exit the building, leaving the book we dropped lying on the floor.

46

Shiloh

I scour the web for the name "Markus" associated with an auto shop in the area and come up with a hit in White Springs. Bells chime through my head, and I remember the name of the town where they found those kids. Threaten me, huh? That's bullshit, and I ain't having it. Who does he think he is, jacking up the car, making me late to get the kid?

My vision is narrow and tight as I type the address into the phone.

"Mama?" Shelby is walking into the kitchen, and I look at her, waiting for her to tell me what she needs. "The bus should be here."

"What do you mean?"

"Sophie's bus. It's time to go get her."

"Oh." I close the laptop and follow her to the door. Outside, the woman next door is just stepping off the edge of her drive.

"Hey," I call out to her, a thought settling in my mind. "I've got something I need to take care of. Could you watch the kids for a little while?"

"Sure. I guess. Are you okay?"

"Yeah. I'm fine. Just some shit, you know." I slow my pace, antsy, now that I have a plan, to put it in motion. "Can she, like, you know… walk down with you?"

"Of course." The frown deepens on her face, drawing a crease between her eyes. "Stacy, are you okay?"

"Shiloh. It's Shiloh." She should know that by now, shouldn't she? I see her all the time. Shouldn't she know my damn name?

She stops in her tracks. The kid reaches up and takes her hand, drawing her forward. "It's okay, Miss Dee. It's okay. Come on." The kid doesn't look at me, just pulls Dee's hand and starts walking, straight-backed down the road. I turn back to the house and get the keys to the car. I pass them, still walking as I drive out of the cul-de-sac and turn toward Racetrack Road to get to the 295 ramp.

I am rocketing past other cars, angry when I get jammed in traffic. Fire is burning through my veins, and I keep replaying the threat, the implication that they could put me in the trunk and take me away. Does he think I wouldn't know him? Does he think a beard and sunglasses is gonna keep me from knowing him? I've seen his face enough in my dreams. I've seen him often enough watching me from some dark corner, thinking I wouldn't recognize him. I almost didn't see, because she didn't know, but now that we all know, we all see, and things are going to be different from here on out.

Threaten me? He did, the night of the Labor Day party. It was him, standing in the shadows. I know now... it was him! Rage is building, and a car in front of me turns into my lane. "Come on!" I yell through my open window and give the driver the finger.

Once I am past Jacksonville traffic, I am flying. The car is vibrating. I almost miss the exit toward White Springs but cut over and slip past another driver, braking hard into the turn of the ramp. Monty's Paint and Auto Body is a veritable junkyard, sitting on the outskirts of Lake City on the way to White Springs.

The card says Matthew S. Montelbaum. The body shop I found on the internet is Moon's, but in the right city, and Moon is almost Mooney, what does that mean? It should have flagged something, shouldn't it? Markus Montelbaum works at Moon's Paint and Auto Body. It feels thin, a stretch to think that there are links here, but I am convinced, and all I have to find is the ratty old car that hit me, and I will know.

My head hurts deep behind my eyes as I park the car on the side of the road, the keys still in the ignition, ready to turn and escape. I pop the trunk, disengaging the crowbar, placing the ball cap she keeps on my head.

Stacy is screaming, and she better shut up, because I can't hear myself think.

I walk the gravel drive, past the chain-link fence that protects all the junk, feeling the heft of the crowbar in my hand.

I am almost beside the car that had rear-ended me before I recognize it, being one of many in the lot, in various stages of preparation for paint. I stop, reaching up to pull my ball cap lower over my face, glancing toward the shop, where music blares from one of the bays. I shift my stance, holding the crowbar in both hands and smashing it down on windshield, which explodes inward, spraying the front seat in crystalline shards. I bring the crowbar down again, rending the metal of the fender, and again, busting the taillights… until my anger is a low simmer.

I stand, breathing heavy, small pops resounding inside my head, like doors locking, click, click, click.

The music from the bay doesn't pause, and I don't look over my shoulder as I walk back to Stacy's car. I replace the crowbar in the trunk and drop the ball cap in the seat. I start the engine and drive away, and nobody is the wiser.

It is dark when I pull back into the cul-de-sac. Stacy is pushing hard as I pull into the driveway and park the car in the garage.

Stacy

My hands hurt on the steering wheel and when I look at them, there are two popped blisters and one rising at the base of my fingers. They are dirty, rust-colored, and when I reach for the handle of the door, my muscles protest.

I glance into back of the car, expecting to see the girls, but I'm alone, and panic wells. It happened again, one of the horrible black holes, and

I'm terrified that I've left them somewhere. What have I done? What have I done? Did I kill my kids, like the woman who drove her kids into a lake and left them to die? Horror blanches my skin, and a sheen of perspiration dots my hairline. I am gasping for air.

I step around the car and out into the driveway, turning in a slow circle, trying to remember. Where did I go? Where are the girls? What have I done? It's the blackest of holes, and I am terrified at what might be there.

Dee's door opens, and she steps out onto the porch. "You're home," she says, sounding distant, aloof.

"Have you seen the girls?" I rush toward her, ready to beg for her help, to admit that I don't know where I've been or what I did.

"Are you okay? You're acting really weird."

"Where are my kids?" Tears spring and flow. Dee's face transforms from hostile to worried in a flash.

"They're here. Stacy. Don't you remember? I have your kids, remember? They're fine."

My knees give, and I nearly fall on her steps as I start to mount them, but I catch myself with the railing and pull myself up.

Sophie is at the door, behind Dee, looking out at me as if she isn't quite sure what she's seeing.

"You're bleeding," Dee says, pointing toward my face. I lift my hand, touch my cheek, and come away with a smear of blood.

"Oh my God," I whisper, and the world goes black for a split second before my vision spreads to normal. "I don't know how that happened."

"Are you okay?"

"Yeah, it's just a scratch."

"Where did you go?" Dee whispers.

"I don't know." My admission is as quiet as her question, and she must see the truth of it because she reaches out and draws me forward into a hug. For once, my body yields, and I am soft, like pudding.

47

Stacy

The house is locked. The dogs are loose; Bonnie is lying on the floor next to Sophie, and Brick is in his kennel, the door open. We are secure. I have checked every door and window. The sun is dropping low. I've done the dishes. I've swept the floor. I've showered, them then me. I've paced, pushing dog hair with the dust mop. I've wiped the table. I've put away clothes... and everything I have done, I have done with Shelby and Sophie in sight. The house is locked. Locked.

My nerves are raw, and I keep pulling the curtains back to look out at the empty cul-de-sac. I check the door. They knew my children. I check the windows. The house is locked.

My phone vibrates. "Hey," I say, pausing in the kitchen, scanning the room, my anxiety rolling off of me in waves.

"Hey, babe. You okay?" John has called four times this afternoon. The first call was to berate me for not being there for Shelby; the second, to make sure I was okay after I melted into a blubbering mess at the end of the first call. The third I missed while I was somewhere else. This is the fourth.

"Why aren't you home?" I ask, letting my irritation ring.

"Oh, Stace. I have a lot of work to get done."

My teeth close on my lower lip.

"John, I think you need to hire another associate. Your workload is too heavy."

"We can't afford to hire anybody right now. It's just a lot coming up on the calendar."

"You haven't been home for dinner in two weeks. Once. Sorry, you've been home once for dinner in the last two weeks."

"I know. It will get better."

"Will it?" My voice rises, and the hysteria rebounds against the walls. "You need help; your life is not your job." I see my reflection in the dark television, my hair still wet from the shower, stringing over my shoulders, the small cut below my eyes where I must have scraped against something. I look hollowed out, like a ghost.

"What's going on with you? Where is this coming from?"

"You are never here. Even when you're here, you're not." I drop my voice and step down the hall, having drawn Sophie's attention away from her book, and look in at Shelby, asleep with her arms spread wide.

"One of us has to work."

"What is that supposed to mean?" I hiss, keeping my voice low. There is silence on the line; he doesn't need to answer. "Look. I want a gun, and I want to learn how to use it."

"What, you gonna kill me because I missed dinner?" The laughter in his voice is low and muted, and I see him in my mind's eye and know that he is not alone in his office. His jocular tone is for someone else.

"No. But you're never here, and I don't feel safe."

"In Durbin Creek? What is going on with you?"

"Nothing. If you're not going to be here to take care of us, I want a gun."

He laughs, and I drop the phone away from my ear, not hearing his words.

"I want a gun or want you to hire an associate who doesn't work on her back." I hear his breath drawing in and can see the expression on his face. He stifles the phone against something, and mumbles something to someone else, shuffling, and I imagine Miss Thing turning out of his office with a backward glance and a blown kiss.

"What are you suggesting?"

"You heard me." I disconnect the phone and recheck the doors.

~ ~ ~

The garage ratchets up as I am tucking Sophie into bed, giving kisses and hugs. I go to the window after I turn her light off and see the back end of John's Mercedes as it pulls into the garage.

I don't wait. I go down the hall, into the kitchen, wiping the counter, yet again. I dare him to find something sticky on it. I hear him opening the door; the garage door ratchets back down. He walks on quiet feet down the hall. I am waiting for him when he hits the kitchen.

"So, you got your work done."

He shrugs, leaning in to kiss me. I turn my face, and his lips brush against my cheek, my unmarred cheek.

"House looks nice."

I nod, irritated. Of all the things we have to say between us, he chooses now to say something I've done well, finally. "Do you have an appetite, or did you already eat?" It's a challenge, and he hears the accusation. I see it in the narrowing of his eyes, the sudden shift away from mine. This is an admission as much as words.

"You think I'm having an affair?"

"Are you?"

"No. I can't keep up with you. I don't need another woman." The tone is one of defeat. Does he feel overwhelmed by this life we live?

"What's that supposed to mean?" I glare at him.

"What happened here?" he asks, his fingers touching lightly along my cheek.

I jerk away. "Nothing."

"You've got a cut. What happened?" His hands are reaching for my shoulders, but I step out of reach and go to the table, putting it between us. "How did you get that?"

"It's just a scratch. I walked into something."

"What happened today?" He steps closer to the table, his eyes never leaving me.

"Nothing." I look down at my fingers, tracing a knot in the wood grain. "So, you're not having an affair?"

"No, Stacy. I'm not having an affair."

"Promise?" My voice is small and sounds just like Shelby when she offers a pinkie.

"I promise." He reaches across the table, and I let him draw me around it, toward him. He kisses my forehead, pushing wet strands away from my face before folding his arms around me. "Are you okay?"

I nod, because I don't even know how I would tell him how not okay I am.

"Are you still going to the support group?"

I nod again.

He kisses the top of my head. "Do you think you should maybe talk to somebody, a professional?"

I shake my head. "No. I'm okay." I push away from him, trying to rebalance, and he lets me, stepping away himself, giving me space, reading all my signs. "There were just... I don't know. These guys in the neighborhood. They looked dangerous." I shake my head, turning, wiping a counter. It's not a lie.

Did they look dangerous? They were polite, apologetic even. They didn't say anything except that he thought he might be able to help me. If he meant me harm, would he have given me his card? The trunk—that's what made me so uncomfortable, that's what made me feel threatened, like they were going to take me. He admitted they were still working out bugs in the car, so wouldn't it be more likely that the trunk latch failed with the impact? Of course. It's just me. Uncomfortable, awkward me. Paranoid me.

"Did something happen?"

"No."

"Okay." Silence envelops us, the freezer drops ice, and the moment passes.

"Why were you late getting Shelby?" he asks, and I hear the hesitation in his voice, the kid-gloves quality of his voice.

I throw my fist down on the counter and turn to face him, looking for his criticism, his condemnation, ready to explode. There is no criticism, no judgment. He is not even looking at me. He is leaning into the refrigerator, looking for something to eat.

"I was on the phone with Darren. Dad fell. Broke his hip in the shower." Of course, that's why I was late getting Shelby.

"Oh. That's not good." John's grandmother broke her hip and died three weeks later. A broken hip bone is a death knell.

"Yeah. Darren is going to put him in a nursing home." It isn't a lie, what I am telling him, the excuse for my distress, but it isn't the truth either.

"Oh, babe." He reaches for me, and I let him hug me. "Do you need to go up there?"

"Darren said he was just letting me know. There's nothing for me to do."

"Should you go up?"

I shake my head, feeling selfish, because every time I go up there, my life implodes a little more.

I am stiff-backed, every inch a cold fish, and I finally push away from him. "I just feel like such a shit, you know? I should probably go."

"Well, we could get you up for the weekend."

I shake my head. "There's nothing I can do." He turns away from me, his back to me, dissatisfied with the choices for food. "Darren doesn't need me there. He has Scott."

"Okay. If you change your mind, we'll handle it."

"Thanks." I slide my hand down his back, thinking I am so lucky to have him. If he knew everything, he'd leave me. He's a man who doesn't do drama, and apparently I am nothing but drama.

"Anything to eat?" John asks.

"What do you want?" I am annoyed instantly, again, where I had just been feeling gracious toward him. His implication that there wouldn't be anything to eat jangles through me like a judgment, like one of his never-ending criticisms. There is a pantry full of food. A refrigerator full of food, a freezer, and another in the garage.

"Meh. Nothing. Maybe just a drink?" he suggests.

The idea spins in my head then slows. I imagine telling him to make one for me, imagining the magic numbness of alcohol in my blood. I watch him, taking out the liquor, getting ice for his glass. I let the moment pass. I can't afford the luxury of being numb. I have to be alert. I've put my children in danger with my immature, selfish search for a history better left unknown.

You have beautiful children. The words echo.

I let out a long sigh, and all the irritation ebbs from my body. I'm not angry at John. I'm mad at myself. I've created this, and now I have to fix it.

"Sophie had a chicken salad; there's some left. Sandwich?"

"That sounds good." He smiles at me. "I'm worried about your dad, though. You sure you don't think you should go up?"

"I'll think about it. I could drive so that I can take the girls." How hard is it to become somebody else? Where could I take my girls to keep them safe from all the evils of the world? Could I steal them from their father? But am I not one of the evils of the world? I should leave them, all of them, and disappear in a life where nobody depends on me.

I need to tell John the truth, about everything. I need him to understand why I've been so distant, why I've been so cold. I need him to know why we are in danger now, what I have done. I make him a sandwich and sit down at the table across from him.

"You okay?"

How do I start? How do I tell him about stalking Kristine Yaw? How do I tell him I've put our kids in danger? How do I tell him I lost almost three hours of the afternoon, and when I found myself, I didn't know where the kids were? I'm a coward of the worst kind, and I let the opportunity slide past. I'll have to fix this on my own.

48

Stacy

In dreams, I see his eyes. At parties when I was in high school, wasn't it his hand that gave me the pills that had put me in the hospital, the second time, intubated? I see his mustached face standing on the edge of a crowd at the Atlanta Zoo. I don't know that the dreams are born of memory or fear, but the effect is the same. It doesn't make sense for Dee's boyfriend to suddenly play a role in my dreams, my nightmares, but since the day he and his cousin rear-ended me, he has transplanted the faceless man that is my brother. I am almost positive that it was Matt that I saw in September, hovering at the edge of the party, watching me from the shadow of a tree. Maybe he was looking for Dee—did he already know her then? It wasn't Sylvester Yaw standing in the shadows, but Matt. My mind spins. I am certain of nothing.

I search the name "Matthew Moony," thinking that there may be some reference to his adoption. I find several—Moony is not an uncommon name—but none of them are Matthew Montelbaum. I search that, and come up with his thriving practice, and article in The Floridian about him joining his father's practice. "Dr. Curtis Montelbaum welcomes his son, Matthew S. Montelbaum to Montelbaum Mental Health in Jacksonville, Florida." It's not a story, per se; it's more of an advertisement posing as an article, in the Lifestyles section, showing smiling father and son in front of their signage.

My stomach churns staring at the picture. Dr. Curtis Montelbaum. What is familiar about that name? What is familiar about his face? My vision narrows and spins.

I feel paranoid. Kristine Moony. Slim Moony. Shiloh Moony. Moony, Moony, Moony. Montelbaum, Montelbaum, Montelbaum. Dr. Curtis.

"Shh... Don't let Dr. Curtis hear," Slim's voice is a thin whisper.

"Oh." I stare down at his face and feel the tug on one of the doors in my mind. If I push, I will know. Did Slim not end up back with Kristine but with the doctor who tried to help her, the doctor who made house calls and checked on her? The doctor who let us live in his trailer, next to his house? I try to hold on to Slim's whispered words. They feel important, but they evaporate, and where they were, I have only a strange, uneasy feeling, like I am being watched.

All my life I have seen him, occasionally with her, but mostly alone, in shadows nearby, and now I can only see Dee's boyfriend overlaying the memory of the boy. It isn't random. I know enough to know that if he is my brother, he used Dee to get close to me. Did he see his opportunity to get close and took it with some supposed chance meeting at the grocery store? Has he been watching us all this time? Has he been getting information from her, questioning her about her neighbors and friends?

It seems impossible, too narcissistic to believe. All the world revolves around me. I think again about contacting one of the doctors that Dr. Martin recommended but I don't make the call. I don't need a doctor to know I'm paranoid. Everybody is a threat in my fevered mind, and I know there is no logic to it. I keep thinking about the list that Dr. Martin gave me, something poking at my mind, until I finally grab my notebook from its hiding place and flip through until I find the list.

There it is. M. Montelbaum.

The world quivers around me, as if I am in a bubble and a finger just touched the film of it. He got to Dr. Martin, too! Panic swells until I am literally spinning in the living room, the book fluttering in my hand.

"Maybe he's just a good doctor," the only reasonable voice in my head says, and I hesitate, slowing to a stop as the room continues rolling around me.

Breathe. Breathe. Breathe. I do, and pull myself back from the brink of hysteria, tucking all my worries and fears into their respective doors and closing them firmly. I cannot think about that right now or I will melt on the floor, a heaving, bubbling mess. I focus on the floor, seeing a spray of hair at my feet.

~ ~ ~

I lose time three times the next week, and each time when I came around, I am tucked in the back of the closet, the garments hanging down in front of my face. Three times I had to write in my notebook the missing time. Twice I made a note that I was sucking my thumb when I woke.

I am alert and wary and prepared to do anything I have to do to protect my children. I wasn't the only one watching. They have watched me all my life. No, he has watched me. I am in real danger here. The vision of that open trunk haunts me through the days. They could have killed me, and nobody would have ever understood why. My girls would have grown up without me, and Shelby wouldn't even remember me. They could have erased me from my children's memories the way Kristine Moony evaporated from mine. I am not smart enough to be a sleuth, not smart enough to get involved with devious people. I may be a liar, of sorts, but I am not cunning. All of this is beyond me.

I try to remember if it was before or after that first time Dee's boyfriend followed me out of the cul-de-sac that I started remembering him in places, because I suddenly remember him everywhere. He was at the grocery store. He was at the gas station. He was walking a dog while I was out running. He was standing outside the church the day we got married, watching from the park across the road. I have to tell John about what is happening, starting with what I learned when Mom died. I have to tell him. He'll know what to do. But every day, I go to bed silent, fretful.

The nightmares and daydreams happen in slow motion. The two of them closing on me, and my frantic kicks in, my shouts subdued by the pressure of the stocky man's hand on my mouth. I can smell him, the rank odor of nicotine, rotting teeth, and dirty man. He is rancid in my dreams, transformed from a man to a monster. It's a single movement that lifts me off my feet and deposits me with a solid thunk into the trunk. My head bangs against the metal, and before I can gain my balance to climb out, the lid is slammed shut.

They were going to take me; I know it like I know I have ten fingers. There is no other reason for the trunk to be open. Had Gina not driven past us, had she not slowed down and asked if everything was okay, would I be dead and dumped in the ocean by now?

I will never be a victim again. I will never be numb, no matter how much it hurts. I will never be weak. That moment, of being off my feet and powerless, even if it was just in my dreams, sets steel in my bones.

This morning, after the nightmare, the girls ask for waffles. "Of course!" I oblige, happy to be able to supply them with some semblance of contentment. I can protect them. I can keep them safe. I can fix them waffles while they are home for Thanksgiving break, every day if they want it.

The phone vibrates on the counter, and I lick a smear of syrup from my finger before touching the screen. "Hey, Darren." My finger still leaves a smudge.

"Hey, Stace. Can you talk?" He sounds exhausted, and I turn away from the girls to focus, to listen.

My heart skips a beat. Is he ready to talk about what happened when we were kids, the night Dad was stabbed? "Of course, Darren, we can always talk." Another lie—we've never been able to talk.

"I think you need to come up, if you can."

I close my eyes, letting the smells of syrup and powdered sugar—the witch's cottage—take away my dread.

"Of course I can. What's going on?" It's been a struggle, I know, since Dad broke his hip. I should have just gone up when it first happened. I see that now.

"He's developed pneumonia."

"Oh, poor Dad. I'll come. I'll get a hotel." The logistics of where the girls and I will stay feel like a weight on my shoulders, but I'll figure it out. We need to go. It's overdue. I should have gone before now.

"No. Don't do that. Stay with us. The basement is ready for you. I just need to air it out."

"Are you sure?" I feel badly. I've left him to handle everything since Mom died. I skipped out like I always did when we were kids. I was the one who would cram the trash down to add something but not take it out, and Darren was the one called to take it out. But it's not the same, right? I'm not shirking my responsibility. I have kids; we live in a different state. I can't just pop over for an hour. It's not like I haven't had my stuff to deal with, that all-about-me-stuff, like always. There has been tension between Darren and me, and I think most of it is my fault.

"Of course. Scott will be thrilled to have the girls around."

I smile at this, and my heart reaches out. Scott, who is so much like mom. The child she should have had, instead of me. "I appreciate it."

"Yeah, of course. There's no sense in getting a room. We have all that space."

"All right. I'll be there." Relief washes down my shoulders, and I don't understand how I can feel relief that my father is ill. Then the dream flashes again, and I know I just need to be away from the threat of seeing Slim, or Matt, whatever his name is.

"Hey." I catch him before he can hang up the phone. "Do you think maybe we could talk about some stuff?"

"About when we were kids?"

"Yeah, maybe."

"I don't know much. But, yeah, we can talk." He sounds defeated, and I regret asking. None of it matters. My dad is sick, and nothing else matters.

"I'm sorry, Darren. We don't have to. That was very selfish. I'm sorry." Have I always been so self-absorbed? I shake my head, ashamed. Even now, when my dad has pneumonia and may be knocking on death's door, it is all about me.

49

Stacy

John is outside, cleaning the gutters, standing on the dangerous top rung of the ladder, and I look up at him. The morning is cold for Florida, and heavy, gray clouds are hanging low in the sky. It stormed last night and flooded the entryway because the gutters are crammed full of debris and palmetto bugs. John scrapes a load into his gloved hand and lets it fall. The thriving mass lands with a wet thwoop on the sidewalk. Half a dozen of the thumb-sized bugs skitter from the debris and into the grass. "I hate those things," John says, seeing me.

"Me, too." I watch as he drags out another soggy mess. "I need to go to Georgia," I explain that Dad is sick. "He's developed pneumonia."

"Do you want me to come?" Dread drips like water from his lips, and I'm not sure if it is dread that he may have to come or dread that my father may be dying.

"No. I'll take the girls. I know you have a lot happening at work."

"All right." He swipes another wad from the gutter, and I step back, watching the bugs skitter. "I do have that big closing on Wednesday, the land deal."

I nod, remembering. "I hate this house." The words escape before I know they are coming.

"I thought you loved this house."

"No. I love my neighbors. I hate the house. I hate the bugs."

"The bugs are Florida."

"Maybe I hate Florida, then."

I step out of the way of the next avalanche of debris. "How's the flip going?"

"It's a money pit." We've had the house for seven months, and sometimes John talks about the work happening, but it's slow-going. The goal with a flip is to turn it over as fast as you can to recoup your costs before you have to start paying for it. We've done it a several times successfully, but this one we've been paying on for months, and it still doesn't look any closer to being finished. We should have destroyed it and rebuilt. The foundation slab was cracked, and he had to bring in a team to fill and repair it. The cracked foundation caused damage to the sheetrock and stucco. He couldn't have looked at the house before he bought it. "It's in a good neighborhood, good schools. I'm thinking about keeping it for rental property."

"Does it have bugs?"

"It's in Florida."

"Hmm." I turn and go inside as he comes down to move the ladder another foot over. It's a half-serious thought, the idea of moving to a different house. I need to slip off the radar. I need to get my kids as far away from here as possible. The flip house is not far enough. I was stupid, using a personal check for our donation at Yaw's Paws Rescue, handing her a check with our address on it. Our address! Who does that? It's almost like I wanted the danger. It was just a game to me, not real until Matt rear-ended my car. Then it became real. I try to remember the event exactly as it happened, and I know I'm projecting. Matt wasn't threatening. He didn't say anything to suggest he was going to harm me or that he even knew me. I can't count on my memory; I'm an unreliable witness.

But he had said, "You have beautiful children." He was so familiar.

Was that a threat or just an observation?

I see Slim Moony, everywhere; I've even projected him onto Dee's boyfriend. It's too much coincidence, it can't be real. I'm making links because I am crazy, delusional. I've stopped walking; I'm just standing in the hall, lost in my thoughts, lost in the whirling chaos of my mind.

I don't know how long I stand there, how many time I hear the debris dropping from John's hand, how many times I hear the girls laugh before my vision clears and I start walking again.

The girls have finished breakfast and cleared the table. They're sitting on the floor with Sophie's iPad. "What are you watching?"

"Shadowgirl," Sophie says, not looking up, and I hear the British accent and the high enthusiasm coming from the screen.

"Hm. Well, do you think you could help me get packed?" They heard the conversation—they know.

"Come on, Shelby," Sophie says, and they rise, neither of them taking their eyes off the screen and shuffle together toward their rooms. I load the dishwasher and wipe down the counters before heading to my room to pack as well.

I reach beneath the mattress, and my hand closes on the pearl inlay grips of my gun. John had refused, of course; so, I went and bought one on my own. I registered for concealed carry—I'm legal. It was empowering, standing at the range, testing out the various guns in my hand until I picked up the Sig Sauer P238, and it felt like it belonged. I'd forgotten how it felt to decide something besides the menu for dinner.

The scrollwork along the barrel catches the light, and I check the safety before I tuck it into its paddle holster and down into the front of my jeans. It is loaded; the weight of the bullets make it feel more substantial than when it is empty. My shirt is long and loose, and the sweater over the top creates a complete concealment.

I bought the gun and negotiated ten hours of range time into the price. I've not had time to use any of the range time, but I've stood in the house and practiced with the unloaded weapon, pulling the trigger, getting used to the feel of it in my hands. I'm anxious for time in the range. It was good that I hadn't contacted the new psychiatrist, because had I been under care, I would not have been able to get the gun. I was nervous about the background check, but it came back clean, all my history washed away with the magic age of eighteen.

I'd like to show John, I'm so proud of it. When he is gone, I wear it slipped down in the front of my jeans, and I never leave the house without it. It rides low between the blades of my hips.

~ ~ ~

John has worked his way around to the back while we've been loading the car. "Is Grandpa bad sick?" Sophie asks in her mature, serious way when Shelby runs back into the house to get her stuffed bunny.

"He is," I pause, giving her my attention. Sophie worries, she stresses, and I'm afraid there is too much of the serious, dark, melancholy side of myself in her for it to be healthy. "He has pneumonia."

"Is he going to die?" she whispers.

"No" is on my tongue, and I bite down on it. I want my girls to understand life. "He might. He's very sick. Everybody dies at some point."

Tears spring to her eyes, but she nods and blinks them back.

"We just have to believe that he's lived a good, long life and that he'll be back with Grandma." I take her bag and lean down over her head, whispering, "Life is hard."

Sophie nods, rigid.

"You okay?" I pull her to me in a small side-armed hug, folding around her like a cocoon. She nods again.

"I wish you would take my car," John says, startling us, and Sophie pulls free.

"Nope. Can't trust you not to trade mine." He walks around the tires, kicking them. When he gets to the back of the car, he stops and stares, his brow wrinkling.

"What happened here?" he asks, kneeling down to inspect the bumper.

"What do you mean?" I step around to join him, and we look together at the slight fold in the bumper, the way it is out of line with the rest of the car. "Hm. I don't know."

"What did you back into?"

I shrug. "I don't know. It's been like that for years."

Her lips are moving, her lips are moving, and she lies, lies, lies. The lyrics roll in my head, and I turn away from John and the bumper, calling out to Shelby. He is unconvinced; he is looking at me with what might be doubt but could be an accusation. I pretend not to notice.

"Still want me to take your car?"

John puffs out a small breath, shaking his head. His expression is a mix of annoyance and concern. I hug him, but from a distance, not wanting him to feel the gun in my waistband. He lifts each of the girls in turn, and my heart tugs toward him. He's a good father when he is around. He's just so seldom around.

We load up, after last goodbyes, John runs through the litany of insurance card and driver's license and finally, "Do you have cash?" I nod and nod and nod.

Both the girls wave from the back seat.

The gun sits low, in the fleshy part of my stomach, between my pelvic bones, pressed in, hidden, just where I carried my children before they were born, as we drive out of the neighborhood.

50

Stacy

My mind rolls as we make the drive toward Georgia. The girls are settled, watching movies on their iPads. When I glance behind me, I can see that Shelby is watching Tiana, and although I cannot see Sophie's screen I am pretty sure she is watching the Book of Life. I had worried when she wanted to buy it, shortly after Mom died. I was afraid Sophie was grieving and that the movie would be unhealthy entertainment. She has my willingness to obsess in dangerous places. Both girls have headphones, and Sophie occasionally sings along, and I hope it is the music that draws rather than the storyline. Shelby gasps then giggles, and a quick look shows the two frogs tangled in each other's tongues. I relax. My girls are fine. They are normal and healthy. They are resilient.

I let my mind slide and look at the many demons that create my face. Anger is first out of the box, at Darren, because Dad is sick again. I try to let my fury rise and build an armor for me to go into battle and bring my life back to where it was before. The anger sputters in my chest and leaves me hollow. I have no right to be mad. He and Scott stepped up and took care of Dad. I didn't do that. Scott rearranged his whole schedule to work from home so he could stay with Dad while Darren was showing houses. An emotion presses against my chest wall, and I try to identify it. Appreciation? Respect? Love? Gratitude? All of those and more expand in my chest, and I wonder at the newness of them. They feel foreign. It doesn't matter how much I want to make Darren out to be an ass; it doesn't matter how angry I am that they sold the house or that Dad isn't better. What did I think was happening? What did I think the endgame would be? Did I think Dad would get his mind back and be able to return to his home? The fact is I haven't thought about the endgame for anybody but myself. I let Scott and Darren pick up all the pieces of our shattered family without so much as looking back.

What have I done since my mother died? I've acted like a child, playing with my old self-destructive behaviors. Stalking the family that I was taken from, pretending they would have answers for me. Shame replaces the fullness in my chest, and I feel a betrayer. My mother was the kindest, sweetest woman I ever knew, and I disrespected her all of my life.

A gasp escapes my mouth, and a tear leaks from my eye. I wipe it away and know that I have done nothing right. I have been a horrible daughter, a terrible wife. I can't blame John if he has found another woman. What man wants to be with a woman who can't even enjoy a hug? Should I leave and let him have his happiness? I have only been a good mother.

Haven't I?

All the sharp edges of my soul are exposed and glowing, and I dig through my purse until my fingers bring out my phone. I scan the contacts, in quick, furtive glances, keeping my eyes mostly on the road before me. My impulse is to call John, to tell him everything, to ask for his forgiveness for my failures. But I can't have that conversation like this. He deserves better than a phone call. He deserves to see my face when I come clean.

Leon. I press his contact info, and his face blooms across the screen. The phone rings on his end. I haven't talked to him in weeks.

"Leon Freak here."

"Hey." It is more of a sob than a spoken word.

"Hey, Stacy?" His genuine concern pitches his voice low and taut.

"Hey," I whisper and take the next exit off the interstate. How many times have I called him through the months, making him listen to me breathe? I park on the outer edge of a gas station lot, holding the phone away from my face, I lean back to the girls, who have looked up at the change in our direction. "Stay here. I need to talk to somebody. I'll be right here." They nod, and I step out of the car, and when I glance back through the window, they are watching me. I smile and wave, leaning my back against the driver's door, so they can both see me, so they know I am here. My head is above the line of the car, so they cannot see my face, so they can't watch me cry.

"Are you okay?" Leon asks, and I can tell by the changed quality of his voice that he has also stepped to a more private location. Does Leon have a life outside of meetings, outside of my random phone calls?

I let my words fall, all the bundled secrets that have been twisting and churning inside of me. He listens, and as I talk, I feel the weight lifting out of my body and all the sharp edges of my soul refolding inward, knitting together. It's not the whole truth, but it is the closest I have come to it. He listens, asking questions, making small comments along the way, but he is mostly quiet with intense focus. I underestimated Leon; of course he would understand. He has a dark ledge of his own.

"Did you report it to the police?" Leon asks when I tell him about the incident on the road.

"No." I look back in at the girls, watching their movies, my eyes wiped dry. Why didn't I do this before? I feel like the unresolved anger of my whole life has been scrubbed clean.

"You should have. You should also get a restraining order."

"He said I have beautiful children." The words come slow, their implied threat clear at last.

"And you think this might be the same guy? Your brother?"

"I don't know. I think I'm projecting. I don't know, but he said he was adopted."

"Lots of people are, but seriously, if you're uncomfortable, you need to go to the cops with everything, what you found out, what you've done. These could be dangerous people."

"You're right." I glance back toward the window and see Sophie watching me. I smile and wave. She tilts her head against the glass, observant and bored. "I will. I promise. When we get back from Georgia."

"I don't think I would wait."

"Okay. I know you're right. Thanks, Leon. You've been a good friend."

"I'll pray for you."

Pray for me? Pray to who? For what? Does he think there is some supreme being watching over us? I went to church every Sunday with my mom, and every Sunday, I listened to a sermon that talked about hope and the power of a loving God, but when I went to the Bible myself, what I found was building lists and genealogy records, and rules, commandments, and condemnation. I could never reconcile the duplicity of God, who commanded a child be torn in two, or who smote an entire people for not worshipping him enough. All those Old Testament horror stories are too much for me, and I never got past that, to the time when Jesus was a man and died for us, so I don't even know what to think of him. But for me, God was so much narcissism, and I had too much of that myself. The killing stroke for me and God was when the preacher talked about the abomination of homosexuality, and I had seen Darren's face blanch, then flush red. Darren is no abomination. Darren is a kind, generous, loving person who has done more good in the world than I ever will. That was the last sermon I heard preached, although Darren continued going along with my parents to church, to be judged and insulted and tormented. If Darren is damned because he is gay, then I don't want to believe in that kind of god.

"Thanks," I mumble. "I don't know that God cares so much about me."

"I'm convinced He does."

"Hmm?"

"He rescued you from an abusive woman and brought you to a family that would give you an opportunity to live a better life. You have a good husband, great children. You have everything you need."

"You're right. When you look at it like that," I concede, still not convinced that God is on my side.

"It's all about how you look at things. There's a plan. Just because we don't understand the plan doesn't mean it isn't there."

"I'll have to think about that," I say, as if I will. How can Leon talk about a plan? An accident destroyed his life, ended his career, wiped out a whole family, left him unreconciled with his father. There is darkness growing in my soul, where a moment ago it had felt scrubbed clean. The weight of the question of God is too much. What kind of plan is that? What kind of God allows such things?

I disconnect and climb back into the car, moving it to one of the pumps for gas, and then take the girls in to go to the restroom and get snacks.

As we pay at the register, the woman behind the counter offers a warm smile and says, "Have a blessed day."

A small bubble of laughter bursts from my throat. "Yeah. You, too."

I turn back at the door and see her smiling, watching us go. It's like I've stepped into the Twilight Zone.

There are choices in life that cause pivots, moments where everything that comes after is because of that choice—getting married, having children, denouncing God. I stopped being part of the Sunday-morning ritual when I was twelve. By thirteen, I was smoking pot and having sex with the seventeen-year-old boy who grew dope in the woods behind his house. Was there a correlation between the two? Was that the second pivot point?

Pivot one, being taken from Kristine Moony and adopted by Doris Alexander. The second pivot, pulling away from her, hating her for all the good she did.

The blackness spreads, and I see the unfolding of my life, the one destructive choice that led to the next, the self-hatred, the loathing. It was a great sucking downward spin that stopped, or slowed, with that first, forced meeting with Dr. Martin. I had sobbed, admitting that I didn't remember the three days I had been missing.

My mind is firing on all cylinders for the first time in months. I've been looking up through the surface of a lake since my mother died, and I've finally breached. My thoughts swirl and collide as I buckle Shelby into her seat and double-check Sophie's buckle.

"Wait, wait!" Shelby calls, looking out across the parking lot. "Don't forget Willy!"

"Willy came?" I ask. Willy is Shelby's imaginary friend.

She nods, pointing. I turn and look into the lot, half-expecting to see what Shelby sees.

"Of course he did. He likes Grandpa." I step back, and when Shelby assures me that Willy is in his seat, I close the door.

"I didn't know Willy was still with us."

She shrugs. "He likes the violin." My daughter sees people who are not there. Is that like hearing voices? Kristine Moony "suffered from mental illness." Is this some tail of that, some broken genetic coding that has passed through my tainted blood?

Is that how my split started, with an imaginary friend? Chills skitter down my arms, and my synapses jump from one nerve to the next. Was it voices that told Kristine Moony to lock her children in a dog crate to keep them safe? The kind of voices that tell you to drive into the lake or drown your children in the tub? I shudder. I would never put my children in harm's way. Never.

Haven't you?

"It's okay, Mama. He's just my 'maginary friend. You can't see him. You're too grown up."

I reach for her hand. "I remember Willy; you haven't talked about him in a long time."

"He was gone for a while, but Grandma found him and sent him back." She shrugs.

I've been prayed for and been blessed and had my daughter's imaginary friend returned, sent by my dead mother, in less than ten minutes. "That was nice of Grandma to send him. I wish she could have sent herself."

"Willy said she couldn't. She had some work to do. Do you think God had a house to sell?"

I laugh and tell her "maybe." I can't hold on to the unease, the discomfort of the last hour. Shelby is just an imaginative girl. But haven't I heard her practicing the violin in her room, her voice going as fast as the notes? My nerves stop misfiring, and I turn the key.

"He's here to watch over you, too."

I glance up, catching her eyes in the rearview mirror. A lump closes my throat. I nod but can't speak. My littlest daughter knows I need looking out for, and it makes me worry what they have seen.

She reaches forward, putting her hand on my shoulder. "It's okay, Mama. We're gonna be okay."

I want to believe her, but I feel numb, overwhelmed by emotion.

51

Stacy

Scott is waiting for us at the entrance to the hospital. We are road-weary and worn. Darren called me shortly before we got off the interstate to say, "Just come straight to the hospital, okay?" He sounded almost broken on the phone, and a cold knot sits high in my throat when I see Scott waiting for us. Darren did not feel like he could leave Dad.

A shudder rolls through my body as the girls and I walk across the lot. Sophie leaves me in the last few steps to the hospital, running straight to Scott, leaning in for a hug. Shelby follows, leaping into his arms. He lifts her with one arm and settles her on his hip, accepting her "squeezy hug" without ever letting his other arm drop from Sophie's shoulder. I smile at him, leaning in to kiss him on the cheek.

"Hey, Uncle Scott," I say, mimicking the girls.

"How was the drive?"

"Long. How is Dad?"

He holds my eyes but doesn't speak. A small compression of his lips is word enough. I swallow, running the heel of my hand over my eyebrow, feeling the low throb of emotions rising in an exhausted haze.

"Darren is up with him. You should go."

I nod, reaching for the girls.

"Let me take them to get a bite to eat," Scott says. "They have ice cream here."

"Oh." I understand. He doesn't want the girls to see him. So, he's really bad. "Okay. Girls, is that okay with you?"

"Ice cream," Shelby says with a wet grin, and Sophie nods, her eyes serious and dark, watching me.

"Okay?" I ask Sophie, looking hard into her eyes, her too-mature, too-knowledgeable eyes. She nods again and suddenly reaches out to hug me.

"I love you," she says, and I almost gasp at the shock of it. Sophie is so contained, so pulled in and closed doors that I can't even remember the last time she said it spontaneously. Of course, she tells me every night when I kiss her hands and tuck her into bed, but she doesn't come to it first. I fold around her, melting.

"I love you, too." I kiss the top of her head, and she turns to look at Scott.

"Do they have strawberry?"

"Chocolate and vanilla, I think."

"Bummer."

I kiss Shelby's cheek, and Scott and Sophie start off walking, Shelby snuggled into Scott's neck.

~ ~ ~

The door is cracked, and I push it inward, unable to see past the drape that hangs down from the ceiling, pale and blue. I move around the curtain until I find the opening, facing the window where gray clouds hang low over the earth.

I gasp at first sight of him, thin, with only his belly rising against the sheets and blankets. His hair hangs in strings and threads from his mottled scalp. His jaw is slack, his cheeks sunken, and for a moment, I think I am too late, that he is already gone. The ventilator pumps, and his chest rises and falls, and I can now hear all the sounds of the room, the faint rasp of his breath, labored and aided. Darren breathing where he sits. He looks up, and a quiet whisper of a smile spreads his lips, and in that instant, I see Dad as he was when he was young, in Darren.

I slide into the chair and reach to take Dad's other hand, knowing no words to say. Darren lets his head drop. The heart monitor beeps, a sharp mountain cutting up the screen, then falling, completing the pattern of a beat. A single heartbeat. A single moment of life. A single pulse.

We don't speak. We sit, and the beats march across the screen. The ventilator pushes and pulls. Breathe. Breathe. Breathe.

I slow my breathing to match his, to be in unison with him. The way I do when I practice yoga. The way I do with the girls when they are upset and need comfort.

"It was all over the news," Darren says, not looking up, his voice so low I am unsure that he spoke. "About these two kids, locked up in some sort of crack house."

"Oh." My breathing stutters and falters.

"Just listen. Okay?"

I nod, but I'm not sure he sees me. His head is still bowed over Dad's hand.

"Mom always wanted more kids, and they'd been on the fostering lists for a couple of years by then. We'd had six come and go before you. Kids who needed a safe place while their parents finished rehab or jail time. Whatever. It was just something they did. Mom always wanted more kids, but—you know?"

I shake my head; I hadn't known.

"She had some problems after I was born, and they said she shouldn't have any more. I don't know if they tried after that or just decided to foster. When she saw your story on the news, she was determined to take care of you and your brother. We were the same age, he and I, so she thought we'd be friends or something."

"How did they get us?"

"I don't know. The same way they got other kids, I guess. I doubt there was a big list of people wanting you. I mean, not you, but it was a pretty messed-up situation. Most people don't want to take in older kids from abuse; they're too messed up. You wouldn't let anybody touch you for... I don't know, maybe a month. It took even longer than that for you to speak. He'd gone away by then, and I always believed that's why you didn't talk... because he was there."

I swallow and close my eyes. "I'm the man of this house."

"He was only with us for three months or so."

I nod. Darren has already told me why he went away. I remember that part.

"Do you know the name Montelbaum?" I ask and look up to watch Darren.

He puckers his lower lip, thinking, remembering, before shaking his head. "Why?"

"Nothing. I'm just crazy." I say it lightly, the way people say such deprecating things all the time, so he won't know that I really am. "You don't have to tell me anything else."

"I don't remember anything else, except that once he was gone, you seemed to get better, even if you were quiet."

I smile. The ventilator pulls. The heart machine beeps. The rhythm stretches across the screen, steady and mechanical.

"I'm sorry," I whisper, sad that I've made him go through a history that has painful associations for him as well.

His lower lip flattens out, and he looks at me for the first time, shaking his head. "No need. They should have told you. I think they always meant to, but you were like a different person after he left. I think they were scared to mention him. They were afraid you'd slide backward if they brought it up. They didn't mean to hurt you. You'd already been through hell."

I nod. I understand. "I would have done the same thing."

Breathe... Beep... Breathe.

We sit.

Silent.

The heart monitor shrills an alarm, and we turn to see the ranges of peaks and valleys staggering, losing their height, becoming erratic and faltering. Darren stays seated, but I leap to my feet when the nursing staff rushes in with paddles to bring him back from the brink. Darren's eyes close on mine, and he shakes his head, slow, like a man trapped in Jell-O.

I shake my head, too. They are pumping his chest, the ventilator still pushing and pulling air in and out of my father's emaciated body.

"Stop," Darren says, and the nurse doesn't hear, continues the compressions.

"Stop," I say, my voice rising higher than his, over the din. Darren puts his hand up, and the nurse pauses, confusion etched on her face.

"Let him go."

"I can't do that." She continues her compressions, the monitor flutters but with each pass, the line draws flat. "There is no DNR."

I glance at Darren, surely he signed a "Do Not Resuccitate" order when they set him up as power of attorney. I raise my brows in question.

Darren gives a minute shake of his head, standing up, stepping away, coming to join me where I stand in the corner, out of the way. They work on and around him, and when the paddles are charged, they place them against his bare chest. "Clear!" His body arcs with the jolt and settles again.

Tears are dropping from Darren's chin, and he squeezes my hand. I put my arm around his shoulder and draw him close, the way I hold the girls when they have broken hearts. His cheek rests on my shoulder, and I turn my body so he doesn't have to watch anymore, as our father arcs again into the air, before settling, unresponsive, on the bed.

"Call it."

"Three twelve. Time of Death."

"Three twelve." Another voice confirms.

The ventilator is switched off and sits silent, and the tubes that linked fluids and medicine to his veins are disconnected. The foul scent of excrement fills the air.

There is no dignity in death.

52

Stacy

The afternoon passes quickly toward evening, and the girls and I follow in my car behind Darren and Scott into the neighborhood. We pause for a long moment at my parents' old house. In the back yard, there is a new playhouse and three swings.

I just want to look at it, the house, to look at the window that was my room. To remember my mother trying to encourage me to play the violin, or explaining why I couldn't hide food in my bedroom. To remember my father, so quiet in the way he spoke that when he had something to say, we usually wanted to hear it. It was a house filled with love. Even when I was terrible, there were moments of laughter, moments when we would all end up at the kitchen table together.

The tears slide slowly down my cheeks, and the front porch light comes on. They've noticed me parked here. A man steps out onto the front porch, putting his hand above his eyes to narrow his vision.

"I'm sorry," I call out. "I used to live here."

He nods and turns to step back inside. I wipe my face and drive on down to meet Darren and Scott at their house.

We are all exhausted. Darren shows us to the basement, and even the girls feel the emptiness like a wound. Darren and I are orphans. We are alone in the world. Not alone—we have our families—but we are nobody's children. We are the parent generation.

"You girls want to help me fix dinner?" Scott says from the top of the stairs, and the girls race each other to reach him first. I walk out the back door and stand looking out over the lake, familiar but altered by my changed perspective.

My phone vibrates, and I click to answer. "Hey."

"How is your dad?" John asks. I had called him from the hospital, and he hadn't picked up, and I hadn't known how to say it on his voicemail.

"He's gone."

A long breath whispers across the line, a door squeaks open, and I hear him moving from one room to another. "I'm sorry, babe."

"Where are you?"

"What do you mean?"

"Where are you?" Steel ratchets the length of my spine, and I listen to his environment.

"I'm at the house."

The steel in my spine melts, and I slide down to sit on the patio. My head drops low over my lap, too weary and pathetic to even care. There is no squeaky door in our house. They're all pocket doors. Why do I look for confirmation of what I already know? Of course he would deny it. What does it matter if I'm not willing to do anything about it?

We sit, neither of us speaking.

"Are you okay?" His voice pitches low, soft.

"No." I sob.

"I'm sorry, babe. I can head up now."

"No. Not tonight. We're just going to eat and go to bed. We're fried."

"Okay. Tell me what you need me to do."

"Darren wants the funeral to be Wednesday." That's what matters right now. What day are we going to put my father's body in the ground?

"Okay," he says. "I'll head up tomorrow."

"No. You've got that big closing on Wednesday."

"Somebody else will close it. I'm not going to miss your dad's funeral." There is a pause.

"Whatever." Does he know that I know he lied about where he is? I don't even care. "Don't feel like you have to."

"Oh my God, Stace. What is wrong with you? Of course I'm coming."

"Okay."

We sit again in silence, the black ledge of depression growing thin and narrow.

"I love you."

"I love you, too," I say but I am not at all sure that I do. I am not at all sure that I am capable of such an emotion. In my mind, I am thinking of the dark hole we will place my father's casket in and how peaceful and quiet it would be, there beneath the surface of the earth.

"I'm sorry about your dad," he says.

"Thanks. I gotta go. I need to feed the girls."

"How are they?"

"They're okay. Resilient."

"Children are." We disconnect, after we tell each other again the lie that we still love each other. I sit in the grass; the cold chill seeps through my jeans and into my skin before I rise, stiff-jointed, and go back into the house.

~ ~ ~

I'm almost at the top of the steps when the doorbell rings, and I see Scott walking from the kitchen toward the front door. Sophie is at the island breaking lettuce into a bowl, and Shelby is on a stepstool beside her, with her own small bunch of lettuce to tear and break.

I stop at the island and finish slicing the tomato that Scott left, the bright juice melting from the uncut half.

"Where's Uncle Darren?" I ask.

"He went to lie down. Uncle Scott says he didn't sleep last night."

I nod. "You guys okay?" They give stoic nods, focusing on their work. "Okay. What's for dinner? Besides salad?"

"Looks like lasagna," Scott says as he enters the kitchen carrying a casserole dish with flowered potholders.

"It's like magic," I whisper to the girls, feigning awe.

"Word travels fast."

"Yes, it does. Who is it from?"

"Sue Miller. Said she had it in the oven when Darren called and felt like we'd need it more than they did." I knew her as Sue Bellefonte, and even after I knew she had married, I still thought of her with her flowery last name, like her shop.

I have the strangest urge to rush after her, to tell her how much it meant to me after Mom died when she brought her little boy, Jack, over to play. How much it meant that she spent a couple of hours with me when I needed it so badly. I want to tell her what a great job she did on the flowers; I want to tell her that she is beautiful. We were never friends in school, but we've grown into different people, and I think Sue is maybe a woman who understands something about loss.

~ ~ ~

We eat, in the way people eat who cannot taste anything. The dishes are washed and put away. The girls have had showers, and I tuck them into Dad's old bed. I'll crawl in between them when I go to bed, rather than pull out the sleeper. Darren comes back from his room, looking less worn but not a lot less weary.

"How are you doing?" Scott asks, seeing him on the landing.

Darren shrugs, wrinkling his nose. The same way Mom used to, the way I do.

"Sue brought lasagna. It was good." I offer to warm him a slice, but he shakes his head. He sits down at the table beside Scott and leans into him. Scott rests his chin on the top of Darren's head.

I sit at the table across from them, my fingers stretched, splayed on the wood surface.

"I can't believe he is gone," Darren says, and we nod. Then we sit in silence until night has fallen, and we head off to bed, lost and forlorn, alone in our grief yet not alone.

53

Stacy

I wake to giggles, and when I open my eyes, the light from the living area of the apartment floods into the bedroom. The girls are gone, but Shelby's stuffed bunny snuggles close to my cheek. I don't move, feeling the pilled fluff of the toy, the warmth it has retained from my head. I stare up at the ceiling, slowly remembering where we are and why we are here.

Another peel of laughter comes from the living room, and my curiosity draws me from the bed. I find Sophie splayed flat, rolling from one side to the other in giddy hilarity. Shelby reaches into a box and comes out with another photograph and squeals with delight.

I laugh as I drop down next to them. "What are you crazy people doing?"

"Look!" Shelby hands me a picture of Darren and me when he was well past the age of dressing up for Halloween. We are dressed in clown costumes that my mother made. I giggle, taking in the narrow squint of Darren's eyes, the compressed lips, and remember that mom insisted he dress up to take me out to trick-or-treat. He had, against his will, donned the clown costume, because it didn't matter that it was too short. I flatten the picture to my chest. He was such a good kid, such a good big brother.

Sophie hands me the one that she is rolling with, still snorting, and there is Baby Darren, bare butted and powdered, grinning up at the camera, proud as a peacock of his plump posterior.

"Oh, heavens." I giggle some more, and we continue trolling through the box, laughing at the funny ones, me telling them small snippets of memory, me cringing at my seventh-grade picture. Acne explodes across the planes of my cheeks. My hair limp and flat, falling as far over my face as possible, shielding me from view as if I were a leper.

Scott and Darren hear the giggles and peek from the top of the stairs, then, when we don't offer an explanation, they come down the steps to see for themselves.

"What do we have here?" Scott asks, kneeling between the girls. Shelby hands him her latest treasure, giggling still, stammering something incoherent.

I hand Scott the naked-butt picture of Darren, and he cocks an eyebrow, looking mischievous and rakish, sending us all into new peals of laughter.

Soon we are all digging through the box, our laughter quieting as we find a picture of the Family Alexander as we once were. When I discover one from their wedding, I press it to my chest and bite hard on my lip to keep tears from falling. How can they be gone?

"Look at this!" Darren says and hands me a picture of the four of us on a camping trip, and I am all legs and arms sitting in Mom's lap, leaning into her, my head resting on the curve of her shoulder. A wide, lazy smile spreads my lips, and Mom's face is turned toward me, her mouth close to my ear. "I love my good girl." Her voice comes to me on memory, words I heard her say a million times, almost always in a whisper, almost always a small secret between us, an affirmation offered. Darren is rising from a chair with a flaming marshmallow, just lit. His mouth is a shocked O shape, and Dad is blowing on the flames, which shudder sideways.

I trade him my wedding picture for his campfire picture and I remember the moment, clear and distinct, then the memory stretches and unfurls like a sheet lifted over a bed. I was seven. The second year of my remembered life. We had spent the day swimming in the lake, jumping from a pontoon boat that friends owned. We'd hiked trails and come back to our campsite sunburned and famished. We ate hot dogs and roasted marshmallows until we were full and sticky. If I look closely at the picture, I can see the smear of my own last eaten marshmallow. In the far background is the son of the family we were camping with, a boy I remember vaguely, and only because he would never pee inside, even when not camping. I think he may be caught, here, peeing on a tree.

"That was a great day," Darren says.

"That was a great life."

"It still is," he says, and I nod.

We continue pawing through memories, remembering Christmases and Sunday lunches and my one miserable failed violin recital. "Where did you guys find these?"

"They were sitting over by the couch," Sophie says, and I glance over and imagine my father, with his waning memory, looking through this box. Did he remember any of these moments? In the end, did he remember what a wonderful life he lived, what kind of father he was, how much he was loved?

I should have come sooner, I know, but there is no room for regret. If I'm going to leave behind a box of happy memories for my children someday, then I have to let go of all the regret. I have to figure out how to grow up, how to stitch all my pieces together, how to incorporate all the different people that work together to make me one. I know I'm going to need help to do it and have already determined that when the holidays are over, I will call the therapists on my list and see which one feels most comfortable. Except for M. Montelbaum. I won't be calling him.

My phone vibrates across the room, and I rush to catch it.

"Hey?" I say.

"Hey, babe. I'm on the way." His voice is terse, aloof, waiting to see how I respond to him today.

"Good. What time do you think you'll be here?"

"I just passed Valdosta. Three hours or so."

"Great. I'm glad you're coming," I say, surprised at how much I mean it. Yes, I still love John. How could I ever not love John?

"Of course I'm coming." There is a small pause, then he says, "I finished the house last night."

"What do you mean?"

"The flip," he says. There is a smile on his face, I can tell. It's been a long, exhausting project, that damn house.

"Oh, really? Wow! That's exciting, I didn't know you were working on it last night."

"I told you I was at the house."

I'm such an idiot. I'd heard the squeak of a door across the phone line and assumed he was lying to me, that he was with some woman because he had the opportunity. He was working. I feel small and mean. I'm ashamed. I've been so ugly to be around since Mom died, so difficult, so quick to think the worst of everybody.

"I misunderstood. I thought you just meant you were home."

"I can't wait for you to see it. It's great. You may want to live in it yourself."

I laugh. "I can't wait to see it." The flip projects are John's surprises. He likes me to see them at the beginning and not again until they are done. "I'm so glad you're coming. We're sitting here looking through old photos. You should see some of them."

"I bet. I can't wait to get there. Are you holding up?"

"Yeah. I'm okay." I close my eyes, trying to block out everything but John, needing to connect to him. "When you get here, I have some things I need to tell you." I push the words out before I can change my mind and sit down on the edge of the rumpled bed.

"Okay. Should I be worried?"

"No, but I am." I let out an uncomfortable chuckle.

"Something bad?" His voice is soft, the way he talks to me at night when he comes in late from the office, crawling into bed, not wanting to pull me entirely from my sleep.

"Uh—complex, maybe? It's not about you."

"Okay. I love you."

"John?" I so seldom call him by his name that it sounds like a foreign word hanging in the air.

"Yes?"

"Nothing. Just... I love you." At that moment, I mean it more honestly than I have in years.

"I love you, too," he says, a smile in his voice.

"Okay. We'll talk when you get here."

"All right." There is an edge in his voice, discomfort, a guard. Is he trying to prepare himself for a confrontation about the affair? Does he think I'm going to ask for a divorce?

"Hey, it's not about you. I just have to explain some things about me, you know? So you'll understand where I've been lately." I shouldn't have mentioned it; I should have just got him here and spilled it all.

"All right. I'm on my way."

~ ~ ~

When John arrives, I let the girls have him for a time before I steal him and lead him down the back steps from the deck above the patio and walk with him down to the edge of the lake. We walk out to the end of the dock and sit, holding hands like teenagers, our shoulders leaning toward each other, touching. It's cool, but the sun is high and bright.

"I love this lake," I say, looking out across the shimmering water, hearing the push of the water under the dock.

"Mm-huh."

I draw a deep breath and start where I should have started when I met him. "I think I have some problems, like mental." I tap the side of my head with my index finger.

"What?" The disbelief in his voice is quiet, not his usual judgment.

"I should start at the beginning."

"Okay?"

"I should have told you when I started figuring things out, but I was afraid of how you would respond. I had to process some of it first."

He nods, and I see from the corner of my eyes as he turns away from me to look out over the lake. The muscles of his jaw are clenching and releasing.

"After my mom died I, umm, I found a box of old clothes from when I was little, and I washed them up for Shelby. You know that purple skirt? Shelby's favorite?" I tell him about the paperwork I'd found, about being adopted.

He shrugs, not understanding why that matters, his bottom lip pushing out, the same way Sophie does when she's preparing an argument—like father, like daughter.

"It's been quite a shock."

"It doesn't matter. You're still you."

"I don't know about that." I push my hands up through my hair, not knowing how to tell him what I need to tell him. "I think I always knew something was wrong, with me."

"There's nothing wrong with you. You're perfect."

He's trying to make it easy—I know he is—but it's just harder.

When I can't find words, I open my phone and scroll through my pictures until I come to the one with Slim and me, all bones and stretched skin. I hold it, face down, not ready to show him, and draw a deep breath. Breathe.

"Yeah?" There is hesitation in his voice, a deep dread of what may come next, a fear of what is not known.

"Well, along with the adoption paperwork were some pictures and a couple of newspaper clipping. It was pretty tough to process." My voice cracks.

"Being adopted is no big deal, Boyd has three adopted kids. It doesn't matter. Your parents love you."

I hand him the phone, truncating his argument, and I watch him as he takes in the picture. He uses his thumb and index to tighten on the girl's face. He swallows and turns to face me.

"I don't remember anything before I was six, you know. I'm serious that I have some real problems. When we get home I want find a professional."

He nods, he has been recommending it for a while. "That's you? And Darren?"

"No. Just me. Another boy." I clear my throat, and he reaches his arm over my shoulder, drawing me close, finally understanding that this is something big.

"Why didn't you tell me?" His voice is quiet, almost the echo of a whisper.

I shrug, letting myself be drawn in, letting him hold me even though every fiber of my body wants to pull free. Breathe. Breathe. Breathe. And I do.

My body relaxes against him, folding where I don't often fold, pressing where I am not usually comfortable being pressed.

"There's more." I reach for the phone and slide to the next image, the photograph of the newspaper clipping. I pass the phone back, and he reads, scrolling with one hand, his other arm still wrapped around me, holding me tightly. I bring my knees up and drop my forehead down onto them. When he finishes reading, he sets the phone down on the dock and wraps his whole body around me.

"You should have told me. We're a team. You don't have to go through anything alone." One finger slides over the top of my hand and up my arm.

"I found the mother, Kristine Moony," I say, jumping in with both feet. There is no turning back now. I have to come clean. "And I thought I found the son, but I'm not sure. I don't think it was him. The mother runs an animal rescue over in St. Augustine."

"Where you donated Shelby's birthday money?" he asks, and I hear the judgment, finally, in his voice. I nod, my head still on my hands. "Why would you do that?"

"I don't know. I just wanted to understand; I was trying to figure it out. I don't think she knew who I was, or maybe she did, but she doesn't seem like that same person anymore."

"Are you crazy? Did you take our kids to see this woman? Why would you do that?"

"I don't know." Tears fall over my lashes, and I press my lips tight together.

"And the son... where is he now?"

"I don't think it was him. He was all wrong—too young."

"Don't tell me you took our girls to meet him as well."

I shake my head, rolling in on myself, ashamed that I have been so careless. I'm not a good mother. "I know," I wail. "I was so stupid."

"That's why you wanted the gun?"

I nod, pulling myself together.

"Why did you make contact with them? Why didn't you just leave it alone?"

"I couldn't. I'm sorry." My voice is so small, slipping like drops of mist from my lips that I don't know if he hears.

"They could be dangerous people, and you pretty much invited them into our home."

"I know." He should be disappointed. He has every right to be angry. "But she seemed really nice."

"Are you kidding me? You have the pictures on your phone. She's not nice." There is no way I'm mentioning Matthew Montelbaum. That's too much after what I've already said. He'll think I'm insane, for sure, projecting the image of Slim onto a mechanic and then my friend's boyfriend. I feel ridiculous, pathetic.

The tension deflates out of his body, and he leans into me. "Okay. So what do we need to do?"

"There's nothing to do."

"We'll put out a restraining order. We can move. We can't have her coming into our life, risking our family."

"She hasn't done anything."

"We'll move, change our address, go unlisted."

"Okay."

"Will she look for you?"

"I don't know. I don't think so. I felt like they always watched me, you know? But now that just feels crazy."

"What do you mean?" His voice rises just past incredulous toward annoyance again.

"Do you remember our wedding, that man standing in the park across the street when we came out of the church?" I'm asking for confirmation; I'm not certain that I saw him. I'm not sure if it's just something I've created in my mind.

He shakes his head, pushing his bottom lip out.

"We talked about it; I know we did."

"I don't remember."

"It was him," I say, sounding more convinced than I actually am. "I think I saw him a couple of times during high school; I think they were both at my graduation."

"That's creepy."

"Yeah, it is."

"You should have told me. We could have worked through this together." I nod and rock against him. Does that mean it's too late for us to work through it together? Has he given up on me?

I listen to the rhythm of his heart; I imagine that I can hear his mind reforming around this new knowledge, trying to reconcile this new version of me with the woman he married.

"I wish you had told me."

"I'm telling you now." I keep my voice flat; this is a lot for him to take all at once.

"We'll figure it out."

Relief is like a blanket, that I am not alone, that John is going to take care of it the way he does.

54

Stacy

It rains all day Wednesday as we travel from the church to the cemetery. The rain beats a cadence before running in sheets from the edges of our raised umbrellas. I lean into John, holding the girls close in front of me, keeping them sheltered, as we move quickly through the burial. Just the family has come to the cemetery, and we have all cried our tears, and now only the sky is left weeping.

He no longer suffers; we should find comfort in that. He has left his failing body. The funeral seems almost a rebirth, and I feel it intensely. I'm ready to move forward, to go home and begin sorting the mess I've made over this last year. John knows almost everything; we talked through the nights, him asking questions as they arose, me answering in the darkness. I was more comfortable admitting some things in the dark.

I didn't tell him everything. He doesn't know about Shiloh and Baby. How do you tell someone that you not only have poor judgment but there are more than one of you with poor judgment? In the end, I admitted to him that I was prone to depression in high school, that I had seen a therapist. "I think I'd like to talk to somebody again," I told him.

"It might help with the depression, the coping," he agreed. "It's been a hard year."

Darren and I had spent several hours on Monday scanning the box of photographs into his computer so he could keep a copy and send the box home with me. "I want your girls to have them," he'd said, and it felt like the biggest gift I'd ever been given.

We depart after the burial and drive south toward Florida, leaving Darren and Scott to get back to their home, and life, without guests. The rain lets up the farther we go, and within an hour, the pavement beneath our wheels is dry. Dark clouds still scud across the sky, and the day remains dusk-like. We're all ready to be in our own spaces. I follow behind John, with the girls in my car, and even this is space I need. The days together, the nights of questions and answers, while comforting in a way, have also been a strain. My face can relax into whatever expression it needs for the first time in days.

As we pass through Valdosta, we follow John off the interstate for dinner. There is a break in the clouds, and Shelby and Sophie splash through the puddles heading into the Brickyard Diner, a mom-and-pop restaurant we've eaten at before when we're on the road.

"We should buy an RV and travel the country finding these diners and do a v-log," Sophie says.

"Like Triple D!" Shelby shouts, excited, ready for the adventure.

"I think that one's been done, kids," John says.

"Yeah, but it would be different, because we're kids and don't like all that stuff that he eats."

I laugh. "Great. A show about you two eating chicken tenders and grilled cheese sandwiches."

"We like fruit," Sophie says, affronted.

"And broccoli, but only if it's raw. And carrots... they're okay," Shelby says, skipping a few paces ahead of Sophie. John opens the door for her.

"We should just do breakfast places," he offers.

Sophie responds with, "Like Metro Diner?"

I pass under John's upraised arm, and we stand inside waiting for the hostess to seat us. I turn and look out to the parking lot, watching a shiny BMW pull in and park. Sweat breaks out on my upper lip and along my hair line.

I wish I'd seen the plates. I didn't. I've seen his car often enough parked in the driveway next door. Could it be him, so far from home? No. I've got to stop letting myself go. I've got to stop letting my mind run away with me.

"Hey." John nudges me, and I snap around.

"Sorry," I say, but I glance back to the parking lot, waiting to see somebody get out. Nobody does. The hostess seats us, and I keep an eye on the door, no longer able to see the car.

The metal of my gun presses low into my abdomen. It comforts me, although I couldn't use it here, in front of my children.

"You okay?"

"Yeah. I think I'm just tired." The weight of the lie, though subtle, feels like a wedge pressed between us. I place my hands on the table and turn to face him, leaning in. "I thought I saw someone. I'm just paranoid."

"What did you see?"

"Just a familiar car. I'm just tired, I'm sure." This time it is not a lie, and I am surprised at how calming it is to share my fears. I did not tell him about the incident in the cul-de-sac with Dee's boyfriend. I wanted to, but when I formed the words in my head, it sounded paranoid, overdramatized. It was just a simple accident, which I blew out of proportion because I was already stressed. Not every man is my lost brother. Dee's boyfriend may be a scumbag for cheating on his wife, but that doesn't make him Slim Moony.

"I'll go check it out." He starts to stand, but I catch his arm, drawing him back.

"No. Nothing to check out. It's just a car."

"You sure?"

I nod, and we focus on the menus, and when I glance over, I see that John is keeping half an eye on the door.

I put my hand on his leg and squeeze, mouthing the words, "It's okay."

Sophie and Shelby have been eyeing the menu and now they both say, "Pancakes, pancakes, pancakes."

"Breakfast for dinner?" I ask, my attention drawing from the door to my girls.

"It's Daddy's fault!" Shelby says, her finger pointing and accusatory. "He mentioned Metro Diner."

"Actually, darling, Sophie mentioned Metro Diner." John says, a stickler for the details.

"You brought up breakfast, though," Sophie says, transferring blame back to her daddy.

"Fair enough," I agree, letting John shoulder the responsibility for our poor food choices, along with everything else.

~ ~ ~

The car is still there when we leave, and without walking up to it, we cannot tell, through the tinted windows, if it is empty. John pauses, trying to catch a glimpse of somebody, but we walk straight to our cars. While I buckle Shelby in her seat, John leans down, inspecting my tires. I close the door and John speaks quietly to me.

"Listen, there's a GPS tracker under your car. Shhh."

"What? Are you sure?"

"Pretty sure." He wrinkles his nose. He may have thought I was a little crazy before, a little paranoid, but now I know he doesn't.

"Well, get it off."

He shakes his head. "We need to leave it. It looks like it's ancient; it probably isn't even functioning. But if it is, we don't want whoever placed it there to know we've found it. I really think we should consider going to the police."

The ramifications of the GPS tracking device on my car are too complex for me to even begin to process, so I just nod.

"Okay. I'll get in touch with Franklin. We can start with a restraining order." Franklin is the managing partner at John's firm. "Text me their names and the newspaper clipping, okay?"

"Okay."

"You'll have to tell them your story, you understand... everything you found out, everything you've done. Just what you've told me."

"I caused this." My voice quivers, and shame colors my face mottled shades of red and white, blood in cream.

"Well, I wouldn't say that, but I do wish you'd left it alone."

"Me, too," I admit, and John kisses my forehead, holding my door until I am inside. He leads us out of the lot, and we drive south. I watch my rearview mirror and don't catch sight of the car again. The girl's sleep, their iPad's finally dormant. By the time we are back on the interstate, the rain catches us, and the wipers slash, spraying water from the glass. I follow John, sitting straight up, squinting through the water to keep his car in view. I stop watching my rearview mirror, unable to divide my concentration in the rain. There are only lights in the gloom behind me, no individual car discernible. I let John find our path, let him lead us back home.

55

Stacy

The world is gray on Thursday, Thanksgiving, and we let it pass, thankful for our own quiet family and that we are all back home and safe. The girls help me clean the bunny cage by putting their rabbits in their outdoor hutch.

Sophie and Willow are walking in circles around the cul-de-sac, and Shelby is riding her bike, the training wheel clacking against the pavement with every shift.

"Hey, girl," Dee calls, opening her front door and coming to meet me on the drive. She looks beautiful in heels, pumpkin-colored slacks, and a cream-colored top.

"Don't you look nice? Where are you going?"

"I was so sorry to hear about your dad." She leans in, giving me the breeziest of hugs, not wanting any of my current activity to deposit on her finery.

"Thanks. He's not suffering anymore." We turn to watch the girls.

"We're having Thanksgiving with Lonnie's parents?"

"Who's Lonnie?"

"The fella I'm dating."

"I thought you were dating Matt?"

"I was, but you know how it goes. He was a little too strange, you know?"

"No. You never introduced him to anybody." I don't dare mention my encounter with him.

"Well, he was just real secretive. Nice enough. I don't think he liked kids, either. You know? He was too intense for me."

Relief washes through my body.

"When did you break up?" I try to keep my voice calm, feigning moderate interest.

"Right before Halloween." She wrinkles her nose. "He got a little weird, if you know what I mean. Kinda rough, too, and you know, I may have been willing to take some of that when I was younger, but I don't play that way."

My synapses are misfiring. Was it in October that he'd hit me? No, it was this month. I know it. I need to look at my notebooks to be sure. I know I've seen his car parked in her drive after Halloween. I know I have.

"You okay? You look like you saw a ghost."

"I think I've seen him in the neighborhood since then."

"Wouldn't doubt it. He liked what I had to offer," she says with a coquettish compression of her lips and a kick-out of her hip.

"I bet he did." I laugh, rebalancing. If I've seen Matt in the neighborhood since they broke up, it has surely been more about Dee than about me. "So do I get to meet Lonnie?"

"Sure, you can meet him now. He's picking us up."

Shelby, who always loves a pretty outfit, climbs off her bike and comes over to us. I glance at her as she looks up at Dee's glamorous personage. Her mouth is a pretty little O shape.

"So, Lonnie is pretty serious, then?"

"Yes, girl, indeed." She chuckles, unaware of Shelby's adulation. "Who would have thought I would like him the way I do? He's not really my type, but he's gotten all wrapped around my insides."

"Really?" I laugh, watching her cheeks flush.

"I don't know what it is about him."

"Well, that's wonderful. I'm so happy for you."

Down the street, we see a black Tahoe coming toward us, and Dee squeals. "There he is! I'm so nervous."

"Like a sinner in church!" I say in my best southern accent, a line from Tiana.

"Wish me luck. Willow. Lonnie is here. Come on." The girls make their way back, and we watch as the massive SUV pulls up. A short, square-built, red-haired man climbs out, his beard full and flaming. I glance down at Shelby, who is watching him with an even bigger O on her face. She tugs my hand, drawing me down.

"What, honey?"

"It's Merida's dad!" she whispers, and I laugh. I was thinking leprechaun, but Merida's dad is close enough.

He is a full head shorter than Dee, with her heels tilting her forward. He steps up, offering his hand. "I'm Lonnie."

"Yes, I'm Stacy, and these are my girls, Shelby and Sophie. Nice to meet you. We're all so glad Dee has met someone special."

"Special?" He grins, cocking an eyebrow. Dee blushes, sweeping her hair back from her face. "I think she's pretty special, too."

"See what I mean?" Dee hisses.

Maybe if Dee finds a man for keeps, she'll stop teasing all of ours. We spend a few more moments in the social graces before Spruce, Willow's twin brother, comes out to join them and they set off.

~ ~ ~

We are in bed on Friday morning; the world beyond the window is still dark. I've been awake for hours thinking about the restraining order Franklin is supposed to file today. We'll file it under stalking, and that's where I keep getting stuck. John has told me that I will have to tell Franklin everything. I'll have to put into record everything I did when I was seeking them, from using the Internet to find her, to sitting in the parking lot outside of Yaw's Paws. I am a stalker, too. She should put a restraining order out on me.

"So, if we do this, what happens?"

"They'll be served. If you see any of them within a hundred yards of your person or home, you call the police. If you think you see them, call the police."

"Okay." I feel small, young.

"You okay?" I feel him shifting his head to look at me.

"I don't know if this is the right thing to do."

"What do you mean?"

"I think I may have blown things out of proportion." I was up most of the night replaying the events over the last few months, thinking about how Kristine Yaw is going to feel being served with a restraining order when she is doing nothing wrong. I sought her. I tracked her. I stalked her.

Sylvester pointing toward my car could have been a simple wave. Kristine Yaw has done nothing to me, and I'm getting ready to accuse her of a crime.

"What about the tracking device?" he reminds me.

"I don't know. It probably doesn't even work. Who knows when that was put there? You said it looked old. It could have been there when I bought the car." I feel ridiculous. I'm embarrassed to think I'm going to have to admit to all the stuff I did that started this whole mess. Shane Moony… what will he think, being served with a restraining order because he's got a name that may be close to someone who may have once been my brother?

The only person I really feel threatened by is Dee's former boyfriend, but I can't segue a fender bender into a threat, even in my warped mind. What will Franklin think of me?

"You said you felt threatened. If you feel threatened, we need to do this."

"I think I just needed to talk to you. I don't feel threatened anymore. It just seems like I overreacted. Let's find out about the GPS, and then, if that links back to anybody, then we'll do something."

"You said you felt like you had seen them at different times in the past. What about that?"

"I think so. Can I guarantee it was them? Could I sign a sworn statement saying as much? Probably not."

I wish my mother had burned all the contents of the envelope I found; I wish I could just go back to believing that I am who I thought I was.

"I think I need to talk to somebody, straighten my head out. I just don't think I should do this to her. I keep thinking about how she's going to feel."

"If you feel threatened by her, I don't think you should care how she feels."

"I think I imagined most of it," I admit.

"All right. I'll call the police and have them check into the tracking device. If it links back to her, we're filing. Agreed?"

I nod, and Shelby crosses the threshold into our room and clambers onto bed in front of me. She is still heavy with sleep, and I fold around her, relieved.

56

Stacy

I've tucked the girls into bed; I've checked the locks. I've kenneled the dogs because they are both prancing around the house, acting nervous, whining. Neither of them like storms, and tonight we've had one crash of thunder after another. They are calmer now that they are safe in their kennels, but occasionally Bonnie still whimpers, looking toward the front of the house.

The dogs' restlessness infects me. I send a text to John: Soon?

I recheck the girls. A flash of lightning illuminates Shelby's room, and in that split second, the shadow of a man spreads across the floor. Thunder rolls, and the flash follows, lighting the room again. No dark figure falls across the floor, only the sharp-edged shadow of the bush at the windows edge. Spots flash in front of my eyes, and I lean in, touching my hand to Shelby's sleeping face. Her covers have shifted off, and I pull them back around her, tucking her again.

"Nothing is there," I whisper to myself. I know it's just a trick of light, a trick of my mind. Still, I shift and angle over to the window, lifting the edge of the blind, peering out into the rainy night, praying for a flash to illuminate, even as I pray to stay in darkness, unseen. Finally, when only the bush sways and moves beyond the glass, I am satisfied that it was just my imagination. I touch Shelby again, assuring myself that she is still sleeping, peaceful in her dead-man sleep.

Bonnie is barking, an alarm, punctuated by guttural growling. "Shhh," I call as I come into the living room, heralded by another crash of thunder.

My foot skids in a puddle, and the second before the lights go out I see a trail of water leading from the back door. Did I not check it? The sliding door... did I leave it unlocked? Panic rolls under my skin. My hand slaps against my stomach, feeling for my gun. I only feel my pajamas, and I remember that I had left if under the mattress after dressing for bed.

Stupid, stupid. I turn to go back to my children, to protect them with my body as best I can, but I am unable to move. A glitch. Do I go for my gun? Do I go for my children? Without the gun, I can do little to protect them.

It's probably nothing. The dogs probably tracked the water in, and I'd just missed it. Of course that's all it is. My eyes begin to adjust to the darkness in the house, sliding over the familiar shapes. I can move with my eyes closed from my bed to the girls' rooms and have done so many nights when they woke from fitful dreams. I want to light my phone, but if somebody is here, they aren't familiar with the layout the way I am. The dark is my only advantage.

Nobody is here.

I'm trying so hard not to overreact, to keep things in perspective, to be grounded. The dogs are whining, not barking now, but unsettled by the storm, unsettled by the nervous energy rolling off of me in waves.

But somebody might be here.

My heart thuds, resounding against the walls of my chest, and I feel hollow with the beat of it. I lower myself to the floor, to be as small a target as I can and crawl toward my room. I've decided to go for the gun. I am at the edge of the bed when I hear a movement behind me.

I make a mad reach toward the mattress, but large hands wrap in my hair in a sweep, pulling me back and away from my goal. I bite the scream in my throat. If I scream, the girls will come to me, and I am terrified that they will be in more danger then. Are they awake, with all the barking and chaos? Is that Shelby calling for me?

I am off my feet but kicking and bucking. Long-fingered hands are on my arms, lifting me off the floor. My vision narrows, light flashing in the dark. I strike out, feeble attempts, my hand clawed to scratch. His face is in shadow, his dark eyes sunk deep into the blackness of the house. He turns me toward him, pressing me against his body. I continue my pathetic attempts to strike him, flailing and childlike.

"You stupid little girl." Water from his beard splatters my face, and I can smell the whiskey on his breath. The voice is familiar.

"Matt!" I scrabble at his chest, trying to push back and away.

He laughs, then spits, throwing me like a ragdoll onto the bed.

"Why are you here?" I remember, from some long ago safety class, that you should use your attacker's name, to remind them of their humanity.

"Why are you doing this, Matt?"

"Matt!" he bellows, landing on the bed on top of me. I turn away, trying to roll out from under him. Thunder growls, and in the flash that follows, I see the black of his eyes, the wild white around the iris. "Don't you know me? Say my name."

"Matt."

"Say my name." He bounces the bed with each punctuated word.

I am three years old, and we are in my mother's room, and he has me pinned beneath him, bouncing me, laughing the way he did. His knuckle, in my memory, is thumping on the bones of my chest, bounce, thump, bounce, thump.

"Slim!" The word echoes in my head and out my lips, and he is cheering.

"Ding, ding, ding! She gets a prize. Little Miss Princess gets a prize."

He rises, his torso stretching up, his hands beating his chest like a gorilla. My mind unlocks, and suddenly the lost childhood flashes in rapid succession, flooding my mind. When he comes back down, his hands are around my neck. Flinging my body back and forth the way Bonnie shakes a rope. My shoulder and back crash against the bedside table and the lamp clatters to the floor.

"You shouldn't have followed me," he growls. "You shouldn't have followed me."

"I'm sorry!" The words are scratching past my vocal chords, a whisper of sound in an erupted world.

"I'll kill you if you get me caught." It's the sound of his voice, coming from a long way in the past, and I know him. I remember him, hollow-eyed and hungry, always with some bruise or wound healing. He was always picking at a scab, or his fingernails, worrying at himself. It was worse for him, I think. She was meaner to him, less patient.

"You have no idea what my life has been because of you. You got me caught."

"You were adopted, though. You didn't go back." My voice catches where his hands close around my throat. He had said it, hadn't he? That he was adopted?

"Out of the frying pan and into the fire," he whispers close in my ear, but I don't understand. Horror rips at my heart as I see him taken by one of the men. I wasn't supposed to see, but the door hadn't latched, and I could see down the hall and into the living room. Behind the tableau, man and boy, I see now the face of Dr. Curtis. Confusion at the scene folds my mind in on itself. It's an illusion. It can't be real—such things don't happen in real life.

"I'm sorry!" My words, my apology—is that all he needs?—breaks the loop of his words, and he leans close, his face inches above mine. My vision rushes back with the lessened pressure around my windpipe. His face contorts in anguish; all the anger washed out.

"I would have caught the other car. I would have been gone. You slowed me down." His anger renews, and he shoves me onto the bed, and I bounce, hitting my head on the corner of the nightstand, and he drops down, hovering just above me, his arms holding him up. Water drains from his coat onto the comforter.

"I'll kill you if you get me caught." I have no doubt that he meant it when he said it, and even if we are many years away from that day, I know that he has thought of me every day. I was the reason he was caught, why he ended up living whatever life he has lived.

"But you're successful," I whisper, because somehow that should count for something, somehow he should be okay because he has built a solid practice. "You're helping people."

"Who is going to help me?" His face contorts, and I see how wrecked he is, how tormented. Is he like me, suffering with a broken mind, delusional?

"We can help each other?" I offer.

"No," he whispers, so close that his trimmed beard brushes my face when he speaks. "I keep my promises."

The threat in his voice is steel-clad, hardened by years and frustration. I turn my face away and feel him extending his arms, rising up.

I lift my knee with as much force as I can, taking advantage of his moment of instability, and I nail him. He jerks up and off, and I roll, falling to the floor while he roars. I land awkwardly on my hip and reach for the crease between my mattresses, drawing short, ragged breaths.

"You tried to kill my father!" I hiss, not an accusation, but trying to understand, to figure it out.

He is snarling, a rabid dog, or maybe that's Bonnie and Brick trying to call a warning. He's on the floor, on top of me again, spittle and water drips on my face, like tears. His knee is pressing into my ribs until I think they will crack. I stretch, and he flattens across me. His hands press against my shoulder, pushing me down, and I flail, reaching toward the gun under my mattress. His hands close around my neck, and I groan against the pain of his touch. My flesh is already raw from his first assault. He is going to kill me.

I stretch and feel the cold grip of my gun. My finger pushes it, and I shift, trying to move closer as purple lights begin to spark against my eyes.

Is that the girls? Are they screaming? I try to call out, to tell them to go away, to go get Dee, to call the police.

I arch my back, pushing myself up and him with me, with strength I didn't know I possessed. The grip finally fits into my hand. He is pressing hard against my body. I can feel his erection, his power pressing against me.

I release the safety as I pull the gun free of the mattress and bring the weapon to touch his side. His thumbs are pressing into my neck, and the purple light is growing and getting brighter. We have been in this struggle for a lifetime.

"Mama!" I hear Sophie, loud and clear, terror wrapping the vowels of her word in crystal with sharp edges cutting outward. My hand is thick and cumbersome. I almost lose my hold on the gun, but I tighten my grasp and shove it against his stomach.

I squeeze the trigger, and for a split second, a long moment when time stops, I'm afraid I won't have the strength to engage. I've mostly fired the gun without ammunition, and the firing mechanism is much stiffer when loaded. I continue squeezing.

The gun erupts, and my hand jerks back against the bed. I nearly lose my hold again. He is still on top of me, roaring. Did I miss him? How could I have missed? I pull the gun up to his chest, into his armpit and pull the trigger again, more prepared for the pressure of the trigger pull this time. One long second more, and he slips, folding over me, his weight falling and crushing the cage of my ribs. I push him off, sliding in his blood. I don't think he is dead, but I'm not going to check. I want as far away from him as I can get. I push myself up, holding the gun, my hand clenched, unwilling to set it aside and rush from the room, drawing air into my lungs, tears streaming down my face. The girls' rooms are empty.

"Sophie!" I scream. "Shelby!" Thunder crashes, echoing in the chamber of my chest, and in the light of the lightning flash, I see the front door is open. I rush through, screaming for my children, and hear nothing but the ringing in my ears.

Dee's door opens, and she peers at me through the rain. "They're here," she shouts to me. Her eyes are wide, flashing with terror, horror, excitement. Before I can run to them, Dee puts up a hand, shaking her head. She closes the door, and lights behind me flash blue and red. A siren echoes down the cul-de-sac before the police arrive. A car stops at the base of the drive, a pool of white light radiating from the headlights. I glance back at Dee's house. She has my kids; they are safe. She doesn't want them to see what is happening. What did they already see? They are safe with her. The siren has stopped, but it only makes the ringing in my ears seem louder.

A blinding light hits my eyes. I can make out the silhouette of a person behind it and can hear muffled commands yelled at me, words that I cannot make out.

"What?" I scream, not understanding, not comprehending, not remembering that I am still holding my pretty little Sig Sauer P238, with its pearl handle smeared in my brother's blood.

"Drop your weapon!" My comprehension comes back, and I lean forward, setting the gun in the driveway and rising back to stand with my arms raised. "Come to me," the shadowy figure yells. I move toward the light and, as I reach it, hands stretch out like tentacles from behind the glaring light. They grab me and pull me past the officer, pushing my hands behind my back, and cuffs close around my wrists.

"Are you shot?" an officer asks. I shake my head, and he looks almost shocked by my response. I glance down the length of my body and see that I am covered in blood, which is being washed out by the rain and running into the drain at the base of the driveway.

"What is your name?"

"Stacy Linde." Stacy Alexander, Shiloh Moony, Baby. Bile rises in the back of my throat, and I lean forward, vomiting onto the street—little bits of lettuce and a bite of tomato to be washed away with the blood. I raise my head to clean my face in the rain, trying to breathe, trying to find a balance, a center, a core.

"Is this your residence?"

I look at him, unable to make those words into something coherent.

"Do you live here?" he says.

I understand the question this time and nod. He engages the cuffs and reaches his arm above his head, waving to somebody new who has arrived. I flinch away from his upraised arm, and another officer reaches for me.

"Is there anybody else inside the house?" the woman, the new officer, asks.

I shake my head. "I shot him." I can talk to her; she will understand. I yell, trying to shout over the ringing in my ears, "He's in there." I try to point, but my arms are dead weight, cuffed at my back, and I'm unable to lift them. I'm afraid they won't understand.

Shadowy figures of other officers approach us like phantoms in the night, hugging against the houses alongside mine. They speak with each other, shadows merging and parting, using arms and voices pitched low, before they walk again, a breaker rushing toward the beach. The officer walks me several houses down in the dark, her hand moving me forward with the slightest pressure on my elbow. Faces peer from the windows, friends I have known for years, turning their eyes away as mine catch theirs. Only Dee's blinds remain drawn and closed. God bless Dee, and I mean it in the sincerest of prayers.

We come to a side street, the officer and I, blocked by a parade of empty squad cars. The officer disengages the cuffs and reaches her arm above her head, waving to somebody new. I flinch away from the waving, and a woman comes up beside me, her blue scrubs spotted by the rain where her raincoat flaps open.

"I'm Keisha," the medic says, "and I'm going to take care of you." I nod and let her guide me to the back of the ambulance, where she checks me over, looking at the contusions around my neck, asking me about the welts and coming bruises on my back and shoulder. "How about your neck... can you tell me about that?"

"I don't remember." I remember nothing, the bane of my existence.

She leans close to me, in my face, speaking slowly, watching my eyes. "Were you raped?"

I shake my head. Not today, he didn't rape me. Not today.

Then John is in front of me, pulling me up and into his arms, his hand splayed protectively over my skull. He is shuddering, and I stand, in my cold fish-way, against him.

"What happened?" I hear him say.

I look at him, past him, my eyes unable to focus.

"Are you her husband?" Keisha asks.

John nods. "Yes. What happened?"

But I am missing whole conversations. Where are my children? That is what matters: where are my girls?

"We need to transport her. She'll have to be processed."

"The girls," I say, but they are talking around me. I am invisible, unseen. "The girls!"

"What?" John asks me, breaking away from the details about what happens next.

"Get the girls. Don't leave them here. Dee. They are with Dee."

"I know. Dee called me. They're okay. They're safe."

The dogs are screaming, in a frenzy at the chaos inside the house, and it finally penetrates my mind, and the poor rabbits... they must be terrified. I tell him, and he promises to take care of it, and I let Keisha and her partner Tim, help me up into the back of the ambulance for the ride to the hospital. Everything hurts. My legs and arms, my ribs, my head, my heart.

57

"Can you tilt your head?" Her finger presses on my temple, and I shift my head until the pressure abates. The lights overhead are glaring, intense, causing my closed eyelids to glow red against them.

"Now, can you tilt your head back?" The small touch of a finger on the center of my forehead, tilting my face upward, a click and a flash. Why would she need a flash when it is already so bright?

"And to the other side?" A fingertip is on my temple, tilting me. It's like doing neck rolls, like practicing yoga, with my stiff, unwieldy body. It was the same thing, wasn't it?

Breathe. Breathe. Breathe.

"Can you drop the gown down your back?" The fingertip catches the collar, and I clench the front, tight across my chest. "Mrs. Linde, are you all right?"

I squeeze my eyes more tightly shut, and the inside of my skull grows dark.

"Mrs. Linde, we need to get photographs of all of your injuries for evidence. Do you understand?"

I sit on the cold metal slab, my gown bunched in my hands. I can feel the small creases in the fabric under my legs and imagine red lines pressing into my skin, the way Shelby gets creases from sleeping in one position for so many hours.

A sob rebounds through the room, and for a moment, I do not realize it is mine. I close my lips, rolling them in on each other.

"Mrs. Linde?"

I nod and loosen my hand. The fabric slides down my back, and the cold air of the room assaults my flesh. Click, flash.

The gown slides up.

"Mrs. Linde. I need to see your arms."

I oblige, without requiring her to touch me, for both of my upper arms.

What happened to my arms? I remembered then. "Stupid little girl," he had said and lifted me, his hand wrapped around my upper arms like I was a doll. He had thrown me on the bed. Had he intended to rape me? Was that his plan? No. Maybe. He was going to kill me. Rape would have just been a pause on the journey, not the goal. His hatred, even now, is palpable. He'd told me, all those years ago, when we ran through the woods that he would kill me if I got him caught. If he hadn't come back for me, would he have caught a different car, would he have gotten away? I got him caught in his best-ever escape attempt, and he promised to kill me for it. Rape is just power, not desire. It's punishment—how can anybody not understand that? Is that why I don't enjoy sex the way I should? The visceral, bleeding, bruising, aching part of me knows that rape is domination. Rape is power. Rape is a weapon. He would have raped me, the way he was raped when he was a child, and then my girls, and then we would have all been dead.

I heave and vomit the bile in my stomach into a basin, already cleaned twice.

Somebody wipes a cloth across my mouth. "Mrs. Linde, we're almost finished. You're doing a good job."

When Keisha helped me into the ambulance, she had taped paper bags around my hands, explaining that she wanted to preserve the evidence. They swabbed my hands and scraped under my fingernails. I open my eyes, looking down to see what is left for them to preserve and see that the nail on my middle finger on my right hand has ripped from its bed and is missing.

The room shifts and I close my eyes again.

~ ~ ~

When I wake, I am no longer in the too-bright world of the ER. I'm my father, connected to tubes and wasting away in a hospital bed. My eyes are crusted closed, and it takes a few attempts to get them to open. Light leaks around the edges of the drawn blackout blinds.

My mouth is dry, and when I try to call out, my throat constricts, and no sound comes. My head feels thick, drugged, the morning after a terrific drunk.

I lick my lips with my dry tongue and hear the click of the door opening.

"John," I whisper, and he rushes to my side, setting his coffee on the table. "Where are the girls?" My voice creaks, and the volume is erratic.

"They're here, with Darren and Scott, in the visitor's lounge."

"Why are they here?"

John laughs and puts his hand on my face, cupping my cheek, shaking his head. "I knew we should have gotten the restraining order. Was it the guy from Lake City?"

I shake my head; the restraining order wouldn't have protected me. I never told him about the encounter with Matt, the uncomfortable feeling I had about him. I'd thought I was just crazy. I can't explain. I can't even formulate thoughts.

"Is he dead?" My voice is a croak.

"No. He's out of surgery, but it will take him some time to recover."

"Oh." I don't know how to feel about that, everybody deserves a second chance. Kristine Yaw's voice comes to me, and I am even more convinced than before that she had meant it as a message, a plea. She had to have known who I was. "What will happen to him?"

"Oh, he's under arrest."

Does that mean there will be trial? Does that mean I'll have to stand up in front of a judge and tell my story, my horrible broken story?

"That's your brother?"

I nod. "Dee's boyfriend," I croak.

I see the connections linking in his head, see him playing out the possibility that he had tracked me, that he had gotten involved with

Dee in order to get near me, I see the horror register on his face at how close I may have come to dying.

"Kristine Yaw, she's really your birth mother?"

I nod.

"She was here," he whispers, squeezing my hand, and terror washes through my veins, that she has come to finish the job that Slim didn't complete. "Shh," he says, seeing the fear on my face. "It's okay. She's not here now. It's okay."

I relax, letting my eyes close.

"Actually, I think you may have been right about her," he says.

I don't understand and shake my head.

"She admitted that he was her son, although he was taken from her when he was twelve, adopted by her therapist, if I understood correctly." I nod because that's the way I have it worked out inside my head. "I had a long conversation with her last night. She's the one who called the police. He called her from outside our house. He told her that he was going to—" His voice drops and he doesn't finish the sentence.

"Don't trust her."

"No. We won't trust her, but she was pretty open about what happened when you were a kid. She was a really sick woman. She's under care."

I don't know how I'm supposed to feel about any of the words he is saying, so I just stare at him, feeling numb. I glance around the room, as if she may be hidden somewhere and feel panic swelling. My eyes fall on his overnight bag and sitting on top of it is the notebook I've been writing in since I found the envelope containing my history. My crazy book. It is placed facedown, as if someone was reading it and got called away. I cannot make sense of it lying there.

He sees—my husband who I thought never looked at me at all—he sees my look and follows my eyes. He shifts until his face is between me and the notebook.

"Hey," he says and lets out long breath, looking so sad that I almost cry.

"You're reading that?" My face crumples, and I cry, horrified to think of what might be in there, what the picture it paints looks like.

His lips fall on my forehead, on my cheeks, his hands holding my face with the lightest touch, so I cannot turn away, "Hey, hey, hey," he says between kisses.

"I'm crazy." I tap my temple with my injured hand and cannot look at him.

He wipes a tear from my cheek. "No, you've been through a lot, Stace. I wish you had talked to me. We're a team. We can conquer anything, together."

"I need help."

"I know."

Relief. It washes through me and out the tips of my fingers and toes and leaves something clean in its wake.

"We'll do whatever we have to do, okay?"

While he holds me, and I have curved against him and breathed in all the scents that are John, my eyes finally fall to the open door, remembering suddenly that he said Kristine Yaw had been here. "You met her, then?"

He nods, not minding that he's already said this, giving me a pass, "She's not going to bother you. When you're better, there may be things the two of you should say to each other, but not now, not yet."

What did she say to him to make him see her as not a threat? How did she justify the past? Did she manipulate him, play him for a fool?

"Don't trust her," I whisper again. I was so stupid, searching for them, horrible people.

"Oh, no. We won't trust her, and if you don't ever want to talk to her, you don't have to, but if you do, I'll be there with you."

I nod and sit looking at the rim of light as it filters around the edge of the drawn shade for a long moment.

"How do you feel?"

My body feels numb. "Thirsty."

He continues gazing down at me, his eyes watery and fatigued.

"Water." I try again, and this time he understands, jerking up and pouring water from a pitcher into a plastic mug. He pushes a button on my bed, and the top rises until I am almost sitting. I take the mug in my left hand, which was uninjured in the struggle.

Swallowing is painful, but when I have let the water sit in my mouth, trickling slowly down my throat, I feel better. "What's wrong with my voice?"

"You damaged your vocal cords. They'll heal. Just try not to use them."

I nod and mouth the words, "Can I see the girls?"

"Yeah. Do you want to see Darren?" he asks.

I nod and smile.

John leaves, and I watch until the door opens again, and Sophie comes in, solemn and intense, followed by Shelby, who looks half scared to be here. John deposits Shelby on the bed, and she erupts into a hug.

"Gentle," John cautions, and Shelby relaxes, drawing her knees up, tucking under my arm.

I look at Sophie, still standing, her eyes cast downward. "Go see your mother. She's okay."

"Soph," I whisper, my heart breaking.

Her chin rumples, trembling, and her mouth spreads with the effort to contain her emotions, then tears are spilling down her cheeks, and she rushes to me, climbing onto the bed, finding her place beneath my right arm. I kiss her head. My brave, strong Sophie. John follows and sits on the edge of my bed, ready to draw her back if it is too much for me to handle. My heart swells toward him, understanding in a flash that all those moments when I felt criticized, he was loving me. All those times he showed concern, he was looking out for me.

"I was so scared, Mama," Sophie whispers. "I heard . . . And I just grabbed Shelby and ran to Dee's. We left you." She sobs, heartbroken, breath-stealing sobs, and I fold my face down onto her, kissing her, then Shelby, in some insane effort to capture all the kisses I could have lost.

"Hey," I say when Sophie has worn herself out and is finally quiet. "Hey, look at me." The ghost of a whisper. She does, and I tilt close, needing her to hear me. "You did good, Sophie Sunshine. You did good. You got your sister out; you called the police. You did right. Sophie, look at me. You saved me. You hear me? You saved me."

She nods and folds back in on me.

I have my children.

It's not really about the moment in the night when the police came, though. I realize I saved myself back there, or Shiloh did, with her insistence on the gun.

My family has always been there for me, their weakest link. John has given me structure, a foundation I lacked within myself. Sophie gave me purpose—from when she was born and until my mom died, I felt whole and well in a way I hadn't ever. Shelby, too. They gave me a life worth living. They connected me to the earth, to people, to society. They saved me.

This time, though, I saved myself. I didn't break apart. I didn't run away and leave Shiloh to fix it. All the shattered parts of me had come together, finally. When my lost childhood had come rushing back to me, I hadn't broken apart. Now I have the memories, horrible and confusing as they are, but they are memories and not a black hole in my mind. If I can learn to assimilate my past, can I assimilate all the parts of my personality? Can Shiloh, Baby, and I become one whole person? I have a long way to go, I know, but with my daughters, my husband, and Darren and Scott, the two best brothers a girl could ever have behind me, I know I can find a path.

Enjoy this Sneak Peek of the
first book in Alison's Journey

Alison Hayes Journey
Book One

INTOXIC
ALISON UNSEEN

Angie Gallion

Intoxic: Alison Unseen

PART ONE: SPRING

1

It is raining outside, and I am home alone. Mitch is working evenings at United this week and won't be home until midnight, which is good—I won't have to see him. I don't know where Mom is, just that the trailer was dark and empty when I came home. Milk and soggy Fruit Loops sit souring in a bowl on the table. I wonder which of them left it here. Probably Mitch, since Mom doesn't usually eat food. I tip the contents of the bowl into the sink. The window behind the table is up, and now everything is wet: the floor, the table, the windowsill. I push the window down, leaning over the table, rain splattering against the sill and onto my arm. My skin prickles to gooseflesh, and I use a rag from the counter to mop up all the water so the worn linoleum won't warp, a wasted effort considering the state of everything already. The metallic clang of the rain slapping against the tin roof of our trailer pings out a metallic chant. The lamp is turned over on its side, evidence of the morning battle. I set it right again. I believe Mitch is on his way out, which is good—it's past time.

The fridge is empty, except for some cheese, old cheese, left over from Christmas and wrapped in foil from one of those prepackaged sampler sets. The light in the fridge reflects off the foil and bounces a rectangle of white into the dark kitchen. I flip on the light switch and let the refrigerator door fall shut. I find chicken noodle soup in the cupboard and crackers in the cabinet. There is a pan in the sink, so I wash it and set it on the stove, adding water to noodles, turning the heat up to medium high. The flames lick out beneath the pan, blue fingers grasping at the scarred silver metal. Broth begins to bubble, and I eat a cracker, staving off my hunger while my mind hisses like gas from an unlit stove. I wonder where she is, where she has gone, and when she will return.

In my mind's eye, she is lying dead on the bed with an empty bottle of pills. I go to her room, turn on the light, and there she is, her head turned slightly to the side, her mouth open. Her chest is rising and falling in time with the shallow catching of breath that passes for snoring in the heavily sedated. I run my finger along the disintegrating edge of a bruise along her jawline. She said that she tripped coming up the steps, but I think it looks very fist shaped. I told Mitch that if I ever catch him hitting her, I will kill him. Maybe that's why he is working late this week, waiting until the evidence disappears.

On the bedside table is a glass, and peaking from beneath the bed, I can see the cap of her liquor bottle, her own self-prescribed tranquilizer. I bend down and lift the bottle, tilting it up to see the remains—a shallow pool of clear liquid in the bottom, all that was left to drain from the sides after the last drink was poured. I take her glass, too, and leave her sleeping. I rinse her glass in the sink and tuck the bottle into the trash can alongside another companion. Everything is getting worse and worse and worse. Something should happen to break the cycle, one way or the other, but what? Maybe Mitch leaving? She was a little better after Ed left, for a little while. I don't know.

I nudge her shoulder. "Mom." She groans and turns to face me, one eye opening to a slit. "Mom. Where's the car?" She groans, turning her face away from me, her hand drawing up to cover her head. "What are you doing here? You should be at work." She draws a deep breath and breathes out enough vodka vapor to stun a horse. "Where is the car?" Did she wreck it? How did she get home?

"S'at work." She groans yet again, her words mushed together like she is talking through mouth full of food.

"What? Your car is at work?" I pause. "Why aren't you at work?"

"Just leave me alone," she mumbles, trying to push me off the edge of her bed.

"Did you get fired?" I ask, my voice ringing in the room. "Mom, did you get fired?"

She tells me again to leave her alone and edges toward the other side of the bed to sit up, weaving when finally upright.

"What happened?" I ask. I demand.

"Leave me alone." There is a sheen of sweat erupting on her lip and forehead. "I'm gonna be sick."

I help her stand up, and she pushes my hand away, weaving toward the bathroom, banging solidly against the doorjamb as she enters. Maybe she did fall on the steps. I listen to her vomit splashing into the bowl and wait. The water in the sink comes on; she sluices the water around her mouth, spits. I am waiting for her when she comes back. Her eyes slide off of me like I am a shadow in the corner.

"Why did you get fired?"

She shrugs, her eyes touching the spot where her glass was, missing it, noticing that the bottle is gone from under the bed. Her eyes flash and flick to me, then the anger is gone as suddenly as it came.

"Were you drunk?" My voice whispers out of me, a sigh, a gasp.

"Lee me'lone." She flops back into her bed and closes her eyes.

I heave a huge sigh—disgust, anger, and frustration coming out with my breath. Crap. I make my way over her piled clothes and back into the hall, slamming her door behind me. Crap. Crap. Crap. "Goddammit!" I scream, slamming the side of my fist into the front door as I pass. My skin stings. Happy sucky birthday to me.

My soup is hot by the time I return to the kitchen, but my hunger is gone. I wonder what she did at work today. Did she go in drunk or get that way later? I turn back to my soup and dip a cupful out, leaving the rest to grow cold with the fire gone.

The noodles spin in my bowl, and I stare out the window, the water still sluicing in rivulets. Listening to the chant on the roof, I think about the woman lying at the end of the trailer, my mother. The word itself draws up images of something very different. Something that maybe she used to be but isn't now. I don't know. I just know I hate that drunk version.

The rain begins to slacken, and the rivulets running down the window break into drops, clinging to the glass, quivering with the force of gravity pulling them downward. The sun begins to break through the clouds, and I take the remains of my soup, which I haven't touched, and put it and what is left in the pan into a bowl covered with foil in the fridge. Another something to sit and wait for mold.

When I step outside the air is tinged in orange from the sun seeping through the still-roiling clouds. I grab my bike and peddle down our road, avoiding the potholes and puddles, weaving as the spray whistles off of my tires, heading toward Dylan's house, my mood hovering in dark corners until I see his barn break through the tree line.

We've always been friends, since I moved here. Friend by proximity I suppose. I don't know if I want Dylan to be there or if I just want the horses. I used to always want him to be there, but things have changed a bit since I stayed back in sixth grade and he moved into junior high. Even though we never really hung out at school because I am a year younger, that took him to a different school entirely, and we've never really gotten back to where we were. It made a difference, him moving on and me staying behind. Our worlds shifted a step further apart that year, and even though we are still friends, we are not the friends we were. It was stupid for me to have to repeat a grade, but it was the year my mom spent three months in the halfway house and I was left to shunt pretty much on my own. She was clean when she finally came home, and stayed that way for a bit, long enough to get Mitch to come home to her, but it was too late for me. I had already missed too many days of school to pass on, regardless of how my grades turned out. So I stayed behind, and the kids in my class figured I was stupid, even though I'm not, and that changed everything. The kids coming into sixth grade also figured I was stupid because they saw me as going backward. It was a really bad year. By the time I did make it to junior high, I almost didn't care that I was mostly alone in it.

I wheel my bike into the lane and swing off. The ground is soft under my feet, and the muck sucks up around my shoes and makes a low, thooping sound as I pull away. The clouds tumble just above the barn, and the soft, orange glow fades as the sun is forced back behind the shifting clouds. It could rain again at any second. Thunder growls around me, and the newly budded leaves on the trees turn their light sides up against the wind. In the distance, a flash of lightening slashes through the grey. The grass is bright, vivid with color after the long winter, shimmering when the errant sun sparkles across it. Not that there has been much sun over the last week, with one storm system rolling in after another. But the buds on the trees and bushes lining the lane are beginning to pop, just ready to open.

The barn stands to the left of the house. The gingerbread house, with its white siding, deep green shutters, and orange roof. It's a beautiful house. In the spring and fall, it blends with the colors of the trees around it, and in the winter, it's a splash of color against an otherwise desolate landscape. As I come through the paddock, I see the horses, nuzzling at the trough, waiting for their feed. There are three of them: Pride, the white Arabian; Adelaide, the chestnut; and Chessa, the red with a thick blaze on her face. Chessa and Adelaide are Morgans, with finely shaped heads but not as delicately boned as the Arabian. With the three of them nuzzling at each other and watching the front of the barn so intensely, I know Dylan must be there, portioning out oats and grains for the feeding. I hesitate and almost turn back, but then I slip inside. There he is, just as I thought, filling the pail with oats and cracked corn. The naked bulb overhead swings, throwing shadows across the walls. I lean against the jamb, just watching. He won't see me until he turns to come out.

He is dressed in blue jeans and a white T-shirt. His rubber boots come up to his knees. He leans into the feed bin and back out, pouring oats and corn into three separate buckets. He is liquid motion. He has very loose limbs that don't seem hindered by joints or bones. He is hanging the buckets for the horses when his dad, Jake, arrives in the doorway beside me. I jump, bringing my hand to my neck.

"Didn't mean to scare you." He says in his very calm, well-mannered voice. I like Dylan's dad okay, but he makes me nervous.

"You didn't." I smile and look away, feeling my face flood with color. I step closer to the wall, giving him more berth to pass through.

"Dyl, dinner's on," he calls from where he stands beside me. Dylan turns and grins when he sees me. I raise my hand and wave. "Have you eaten, Alison?"

"Yes sir, I ate at home."

"That's too bad, there's enough for thrashers." Jake smiles, displaying large, somewhat crooked teeth.

"She'll eat." Dylan closes the feed bin. "Won't ya, sneaky?" It's not so much a question and neither of them wait for a response. He really hasn't changed. It's just me. I'm the awkward creature in the corner of the room, the one drooling and farting and gnawing on the carpet.

"Great, I'll tell Vaude to set a plate." Then Jake turns on his heel and is gone, loping toward the back door as Dylan reaches up and pulls the beaded chain to make the light go out.

"Ya sneakin' up on me, Al?" He makes his way toward me.

"Not really." He drops his arm over my shoulder, and I duck under before he can catch me in a headlock. He never hurts me, he just doesn't let me get away. It's something he's done for years, a holdover from younger days when we'd wrestle across the living room floor, trying to pin each other. That was before he hit his growing spurt and gained about sixty pounds on me, and before we both hit puberty. I like it though, his arm resting across my shoulder, the fingers dangling, following the curve of his wrist. I like his closeness. But today I feel so prickly that I have to shrug my spines away so I don't poke him.

"How ya been?" We walk toward the back door, swaying slightly, squishing into the wet grass. I haven't been around much this spring.

"All right, I guess." I pause. "Mitch is working late this week." I don't mention that my stupid mother got herself fired today. I'm not ready to divulge that personal tragedy yet. "You know you don't have to feed me."

"Thought so. His truck wasn't there when I went by. I looked for you after school." He ignored my last comment, and my stomach turns over.

"I caught the bus." We've reached the back door, and he swings it open. "I thought you had your student council thing tonight."

"Got cancelled. John's got the flu, and Mindy had cheerleading." We step inside, and he bends to pull off his boots, removing his arm from my shoulder. I kick my shoes off, too, and leave them, covered in muck, outside the door beside the welcome mat. I can hear Jake and Vaude talking as Dylan pulls up his socks, and we pad our way to the dining room. I love Dylan's house. It's very clean, with cream-colored carpets and vaulted ceilings. The dining room opens out from the kitchen, where Vaude and Jake are putting the finishing touches into a salad.

Even though I love the house, I don't like being inside it. There should be signs that say "DO NOT TOUCH" across everything. I feel like I'm going to run into something or spill cranberry juice on the carpets. It used to be homier, but now it's pristine, like newly fallen snow. The carpets still smell new. It's overwhelming, all that white, and when I get overwhelmed or nervous, I get very quiet, like a hummingbird, hovering, but never quite touching down.

Jake and Vaude are smart and funny, and they seem to love each other too much to have been married forever like they have. What makes that work for some people and not for others? I can't imagine Mom ever making a salad with someone. Actually I can't honestly imagine Mom cutting up a salad—maybe an olive for her martini. She's not a fan of "rabbit food," and when it comes right down to it, mealtimes are certainly not events in my house. Maybe that's the problem, not enough roughage. But Dylan's family is nothing like mine, and I sometimes find myself wondering what my life would have been if Jake and Vaude had been my parents instead. Would they be talking about colleges for me and planning our summer trip to Alaska or something? What if I had won the family jackpot and Dylan had been dealt the snake eyes.

"How is your mother?" Vaude asks, as she always does, polite and mannerly.

"She is fine." I answer as I always do. "Thank you for asking." Vaude was my seventh-grade history and English teacher, which was odd but nice, since she already knew me so well.

We eat lasagna, garlic bread, and salad. I watch them and listen as they talk about their days. This is how it's supposed to be: a FAMILY, in great big capital letters. I wonder if they are different when they're alone. Do they fight and yell and throw whatever is handy? I glance at their flawless walls and know there is no throwing of anything in this house. Still, I wonder if they keep the peace until the house is empty and then let it rip, when nobody can hear. They seem almost too much like "family," the way families are supposed to be, like it just comes easy and natural. Unlike my family, where the basic form of talking is yelling and the general topic is complaint. I wonder if that is the difference, what makes them the "Haves" and us the "Have Nots."

About the Author

Angie Gallion grew up in East Central Illinois and now resides with her husband and their children outside of Atlanta, Georgia. Angie's writings often deal with personal growth through tragedy or trauma. She enjoys exploring complex relationships, often set against the backdrop of addiction or mental illness. Her debut novel, Intoxic, received the Bronze Medal from Readers' Favorite in the General Fiction category. Intoxic was well received by audiences, and reader response inspired Gallion to continue the Alison Hayes Journey, a coming-of-age series, which now include four novels: Intoxic: Alison Unseen, Purgus: Alison Lost, Icara: Alison Falling, and Emergent: Alison Rising.

Angie's first psychological thriller, Off the Dark Ledge, is about Stacy Linde, a wife and mother who discovers dark secrets about her origin story and must reconcile her past or risk losing everything. Two new projects are expected in 2021 and 2022.

Follow Angie at www.angiegallion.com and connect with her on social media.

Books by Angie Gallion

Intoxic: Alison Unseen, The Alison Hayes Journey, Book 1
Purgus: Alison Lost, The Alison Hayes Journey, Book 2
Icara: Alison Falling, The Alison Hayes Journey, Book 3
Emergent: Alison Rising, The Alison Hayes Journey, Book 4
Off the Dark Ledge, a Psychological Thriller